NIGHT DECEPTION
#2 TILDAS ISLAND SERIES

TAMSEN SCHULTZ

To Zoom happy hours and the friends and family that join them.

Acknowledgments

As always, I can't thank the following people enough—they are as invested in my writing as I am, and I will always be grateful: my PA, Stephanie Thurwather, my editors Woody and Rebecca Fridae, and my cover designer Valerie Leah (who managed to fit the same historical reference into this cover as she did on a Fiery Whisper! Let me know if you find it, there might even be a small prize for the first person who emails me with the correct reference).

I also just want to say how much I'm loving writing this series so far. The Virgin Islands is such a unique place that getting to "live there" while writing, has been a treat—even if Tildas is just a fictional island and I'm only there in my own mind.

And last but not least, thanks to my family and friends for continuing to support me…even if that means we talk nothing but murder at the dinner table.

PROLOGUE

Isiah Clarke stood behind the bar drying glasses as Marty, his second in command, mixed up a batch of Painkillers for the group of tourists sitting at table eleven. He slid a clean rag into a glass, wiping away the condensation left over from the dishwasher, as his gaze swept the room. As it always did, pride teased the corners of his mind when he took in the scene.

After more than a decade as a Navy SEAL, he'd needed something to do with his time—and his life—so he'd bought a piece of land perched high on a bluff on Tildas Island and started building a bar. Slowly, he'd transformed his little bit of paradise into a place everyone, but more particularly locals, felt comfortable.

His gaze slid over the patrons then to the long screened-in veranda. Now that night had settled over the Caribbean, he couldn't see the collection of islands that lay beyond the shores of Tildas. Nor could he see the deep, vibrant ravines that ran down the sides of the mountain to the shore, or the swirling blues of the Caribbean Sea. But they were there, and just knowing that soothed his soul a little bit.

As he set the glass down in one of the tidy rows that lined

the shelf, the hairs on his arms stood up and a prickle of energy whispered across the back of his neck. He looked up to see the source of his unease just as *she* stepped into the bar.

He hadn't seen her in months, not since the end of December and it was now the end of February, but she wasn't a woman he'd easily forget. She paused in the door and, as always, everything about her—from the cut of her clothes, to the simple gold chain that hung from her neck, to the perfect hair and nails—screamed *expensive*. But it was more than all that that drew his attention; it was the way she carried herself. Even when she'd walked into his bar that first time there hadn't been a lick of self-consciousness about her. No, she'd walked in like she fucking owned the place. And while he generally avoided tourists as much as possible, and she wasn't his type, he had to admire her confidence.

Out of the corner of his eye, he watched as she approached. Her deep blue dress crossed over her breasts then fell in waves to the floor. Her long dark hair was pulled into a high ponytail that fell straight between her shoulder blades, and as she stepped, he caught glimpses of her pale toenail polish. With her smooth skin, pale blue eyes, high cheekbones, and full lips, she was a stunning woman.

Even if she wasn't his type.

"Double Laphroaig," she said when Marty turned toward her. The same drink she'd ordered in each of her previous five visits.

Marty grinned. "Good to see you again. No Painkiller or Mojito today?" he asked. The same question he'd asked in each of her past visits.

"Get the woman her drink, Marty," Isiah said on an exhale. "If she'd wanted a Painkiller or Mojito, she would have ordered one," he added. As he spoke, she turned her head toward him, and the air left his lungs. Very carefully, he set down the glass he'd been holding.

"What happened?" he asked with a nod toward her cheek. Growing up, he'd seen the same kind of mark on his mother's face enough times to know what it meant. And though he had no right to ask, he wasn't going to ignore it.

"Walked into a door," she said with a shrug. His eyes lingered as she returned her attention to Marty who was adding a small piece of ice to her drink, the way she liked it. She didn't appear to be self-conscious about the bruising or cut that marred her right cheek, not like he would have expected if she'd been a victim of domestic violence, but still...

"Let me know if you need any help fixing that door." Somehow he managed to sound casual though his stomach churned with acid at the thought of some man hitting her.

She flicked a small smile in his direction, then took her drink from Marty and placed twenty-five dollars onto the counter. "I took care of it myself," she said, then she slid off the barstool and headed to the veranda.

Isiah picked up another glass and began drying it as he watched her walk away.

"What do you think her story is?" Marty asked, grabbing a lime wedge from the container and adding it to a gin and tonic. She'd taken her preferred seat in the corner with her back to the wall of the bar, and sat staring out into the darkness, as if she could actually see the view through the thick of night. She quietly sipped her drink, not once looking around her or pulling out her phone.

"I've got no clue," Isiah answered honestly. He'd been around the block enough to get a good read on most people and it wasn't often that people stumped him. But that woman most definitely stumped him.

Or she would have if he gave her much thought.

Which he didn't.

Because she wasn't his type.

3

* * *

*A*lexis rolled the tumbler between her fingers and let her head fall back against the wall. It had been a hell of a day—overall, a good one, but still, getting kidnapped, tied up, and yes, even hit a couple of times, earned her a drink. Or two.

Even if it was—more or less—part of her job.

As an FBI agent, and part of a special task force based on Tildas Island, not once had she doubted that her teammates had had her back. But even so, the memory of the rope cutting into her wrists, and the forced immobility that came with being tied to a chair, had driven her to visit The Shack and to the distraction that was Isiah Clarke.

Yes, she knew his name. She knew a lot about Isiah Clarke, thanks to her family's security team. She knew the kind of things that should be shared between friends, or lovers, as a relationship develops, and as trust grows. But that wasn't how her family rolled. Not anymore.

And so she knew all about Isiah Clarke. Product of a broken home and an abusive father, he'd enlisted in the Navy at eighteen and worked his way to becoming a distinguished SEAL. He'd sent home all of his paychecks so that his younger sister could go to college and his mother could get her own coffee shop and inn up and running (once she'd kicked her now ex-husband to the curb for the last time). After retiring eight years ago, he'd bought the land for The Shack and from what her security had told her, Isiah was a good man, running a solid business and keeping his nose clean.

Awareness shimmered across her skin, and Alexis knew Isiah was looking over at her. From his position behind the bar, most of her face was hidden from his view. But that didn't stop him from looking. Or her from noticing.

Which was exactly why she'd come tonight. Isiah was a man her friends would definitely refer to as eye candy. He had eyes so dark they were almost black, sharp features, and thick hair that he wore in a clean, short cut. He hadn't let his build slip from his SEAL days—at least not enough to notice—and his six foot two frame all but begged to be touched. That she'd noticed him the first time she'd set foot in The Shack wasn't a surprise. But tonight, it wasn't his looks that pulled her back to the bar.

No, tonight, the uncomfortable awareness she felt around him was just what she needed to take her mind off the events of the day. So, sitting in her corner, sipping her drink, she welcomed the way her pulse accelerated in his presence. She lingered over the question of whether or not he was watching her. And yes, she even craved the way every nerve in her body came painfully alive when she looked at him.

It was the distraction she needed, even if she never acted on it. Not that she hadn't thought about it, because she had. Frequently. But as they say, it takes two to tango and every indication Isiah had given her told her he wasn't up for the dance.

She took a sip of her drink and thought back to the night he'd had made it very clear that while she might not mind the prickling awareness between them, he wasn't comfortable with it. From the moment she'd arrived, he'd avoided looking at her or speaking to her—not even sharing any of the standard island pleasantries. But it was when Isiah had called Marty over to take her drink order when she'd been standing across the bar from him that she'd grasped just how strongly he felt about putting distance between them. And being an adult, Alexis acknowledged that since it was his bar, and he couldn't leave, it was up to her to withdraw. Which she had. Until tonight.

But tonight, she needed his nearness to take her mind from the ropes and the guns and violence. Maybe it was selfish of her, but if it was, so be it. After all, it was just one night and Isiah Clarke struck her as a big boy, able to handle whatever he thought of her.

Closing her eyes for a moment, she savored the peace that

the whiskey, and the comforts—and discomforts—The Shack brought. In her mind's eye, she conjured the view of distant islands dotting the seascape, rising up from the bright blue of the Caribbean. She saw the lush, green mountains interrupted by brilliant orange and red Flamboyant trees. And she felt the sweet sting of the sun touching her skin as its heat cut through the humid air.

"Need another?"

Alexis's eyes jerked open to find Isiah standing in front of her. Not once in her prior visits had he ever come to check on her. The Shack didn't have tableside service. It was one of the things she liked about it.

Her gaze held his, then dropped to her glass. Her empty glass. She didn't remember finishing it, but the proof was before her. She debated for a moment—she'd had a beer with her teammates before coming here, and then the double Laphroaig. She didn't need another drink, but then again, she wasn't even close to tipsy and she was walking home, anyway.

"A single this time, please."

Isiah nodded and reached for her glass. Their fingers brushed when she handed it to him and a jolt of energy flooded her nerves. She fought the urge to jerk her hand back from the simple touch that was somehow so intimate. It was only her years of training that made it possible for her to pretend there was nothing out of the ordinary. She released the glass into his keeping and murmured a quiet thank you.

Yes, this distraction was exactly what she needed to take her mind off the day she'd had.

And all the memories it had dredged up.

CHAPTER ONE

Isiah glanced at the open door—and the woman framed within it—then at the calendar that hung on the wall behind the bar. A bright tropical bird marked the month of June. Four months to the day since she'd last been in. And why he knew that so quickly was something he wasn't going to explore.

He was the only one behind the bar and he watched as she walked toward him. Her long legs, clad in a pair of cut-offs, quickly covered the ground between the door and the bar. Other than her shorts, she wore a loose, black tank top, a pair of strappy, black sandals, and her long hair had been braided in hundreds of box braids then pulled up into a bun. Her mixed ethnicity had always been evident in the rich color of her skin and her pale blue eyes, but before today, he'd only ever seen her with sleek, straightened hair. He'd be damned if he admitted that seeing her in braids—a nod to a heritage they shared—did a little something to him.

"Double Laphroaig?" he asked when she reached the bar.

She smiled. A real smile this time. Not just a hint of one. And no, he would not admit to the way his heartrate suddenly leapt.

"It's a little early for that, but I'll take an ice tea if you have it?"

He nodded and reached for a glass. As he filled it with ice, the door opened again and two more women walked in. One was tall and thin with long black hair. The other was a little shorter, a lot curvier, and had curly shoulder-length, sun-streaked brown hair.

"Alexis," the woman with the long hair said with a smile as she rushed forward to engulf his mystery woman in a hug. So, "Alexis" was her name.

"So good to see you, Charlotte," Alexis responded. "How long are you on island this time?"

He set the ice tea on the bar and cast a questioning look at the two women, both of whom asked for the same. Seeing her now, he had a sinking feeling that he might have been wrong all those month ago. If she hadn't come in today, he would have gone on thinking she was just another snowbird. But June wasn't exactly high season for tourists.

"A month this time," Charlotte answered. "Then I need to be in Europe for a month. But I'll be back in September for at least four months. I may need to take a few trips, but I'll be staying here."

"Damian must be happy," Alexis said.

Charlotte laughed and reached for the tea Isiah had set on the bar top. After thanking him, she turned back to Alexis. "We're both happy. Believe me."

The three women wandered over to Alexis's favorite table and their conversation became indistinct. He glanced over a time or two, and this time, he could see Alexis's face as she'd given her friend, Charlotte, her usual seat.

It was a slow Saturday afternoon and he spent his time tidying up behind the bar and stopping by to refill Alexis and her friends' ice tea. He didn't catch much more of their conversation but if the vibe was anything to go by, the women were enjoying their time together.

It was a side of Alexis he hadn't seen before—no surprise there. And even as she relaxed on his veranda and laughed with her friends, he considered that maybe it would have been better if he hadn't. She'd already figured in his thoughts more than she should have. And that was even after he'd tried to give her the brush off in December.

Yes, he'd admit to being kind of a dick that night six months ago. But the chemistry between them was too strong to temper and instinctively he'd known—he *knew*—that no vacation fling would ever be enough.

And so he'd done what he'd thought best for the both of them and he'd pushed her away. With every slight he'd dealt that night, he'd told himself it was the right thing to do—after all, she lived off island and she'd be gone by March. But now, well, now that it appeared she lived on island, he could no longer deny what he'd always known that night was about. Acknowledging the intensity that vibrated between them had seemed...big. And messy. And so, he'd never even given her, or them, a chance.

Her laughter floated in from the veranda, drawing his attention. What would it be like to hear that every day? He wouldn't blame Alexis if she wanted nothing to do with him. His actions in December had been those of a coward and they weren't something he was proud of. Certainly not something likely to draw the interest of a woman like Alexis.

Turning back to his chores, Isiah forced himself to get lost in the mundane activities. An hour later, three men strode into the bar. It didn't take more than a second for Isiah to peg two of them as former military. The third looked like he'd stepped out of an ad for O'Neil surfboards.

"We'll be back," one of the military guys said to him as the three passed by the bar and headed toward the women. Isiah had a fleeting thought that they might all be couples, but when only the one named Charlotte stood, he reassessed his stance.

Out of the corner of his eye, he watched her hug the one who'd spoken to him and the one who looked like a surfer—calling then Dominic and Jake, respectively—then she stepped into the arms of the third, the other military guy. Now *they* were a couple.

"Thanks for picking her up at the airport, Beni," the man said, not taking his eyes off Charlotte.

"Anytime," the woman with the curly hair replied.

He must be the "Damian" the women had been referring to when they'd first arrived. From where Isiah stood, he could see Charlotte's smile before Damian dipped his head and placed a lingering kiss on her lips.

Isiah looked away from the intimacy and, instead, allowed himself to ponder questions he'd previously refused to consider. Did Alexis live on the island? If so, what did she do and was it something that would keep her on Tildas more permanently? Seeing her with her friends made him think that she might work at one of the luxury hotels—there were quite a few that hired former military as security. But still, that didn't feel quite right.

"Can I get four beers and two gin and tonics?" Dominic asked, as he approached the bar.

Isiah pushed the lingering questions aside as he refocused on his job. "Draft or can?" he asked as he started to gather the ingredients for the GnTs.

"Draft, please. And I hear you have food, too?" Dominic asked.

Isiah inclined his head. "We serve until six pm. After that, it's just the bar."

"Good enough. Dominic Burel," the man said, surprising Isiah.

"Isiah Clarke." He held out a hand.

"Nice place you have here."

"Thanks."

"When'd you get out?"

Isiah looked up sharply.

Dominic grinned back. "Takes one to know one. Former PJ," he said, rightly assuming that Isiah would recognize the nickname for the elite Airforce Pararescue teams. "And that one," Dominic said, pointing to Damian, "Is a former Ranger, but I don't hold it against him. Much."

Isiah's lips twitched at that. "Been out eight years. SEALs." He very rarely talked about his military career, but something about the easy comradery within the group reminded him of his own team.

"What are you all doing down here?' Isiah asked as he set the gin and tonics on a tray.

Dominic shrugged. "Right now? Drinking and welcoming our friend, Charlotte, back to the island. She's Damian's fiancé but lives off island, although I think that's going to change pretty soon."

"And when you're not drinking?" Isiah knew the former PJ might not answer—old habits died hard when you'd been trained as part of an elite team and the need for discretion and secrecy was something drilled into each of them.

"FBI," Dominic answered. Surprise shot through Isiah. Not at Dominic being FBI, it wasn't unusual for former military to go into the Bureau, or even the fact that he'd admitted to it, since working for the FBI wasn't exactly a secret. But his answer encompassed Alexis too, and *that* he hadn't seen coming.

His eyes swept over the table as he poured the last beer. "All of you?"

"Except Charlotte."

Chagrinned at the assumptions and judgments he'd made about Alexis—judgments that didn't reflect well on him—he told Dominic the first round was on the house. After sliding the tray over and setting a menu on top, he watched the PJ return to his friends. Isiah's eyes lingered on the group for a moment, straying to Alexis more than once.

FBI.

He hadn't expected that.

* * *

*J*siah glanced up from the tap filling the pint glass in his hand when Alexis's voice carried from the veranda.

"Go," she urged. "Seriously, I'll have one more than head home."

Of her colleagues, all but Dominic were standing, clearly getting ready to leave.

"I'll stay and have one more with you," Dominic said. Isiah's eyes darted between the table that held his attention and the nearly full glass in his hand. By now he was certain the five agents were all just friends, but it was still nice that Dominic seemed to be looking out for Alexis.

Not that she needed looking out for, he reminded himself. Not only was she trained in self-defense, but she'd been in his bar enough times for him to know she was perfectly capable of getting herself home.

"I've had enough of you for the night, Dom."

"No one ever gets enough of me, Lex," he interjected which gave rise to a chorus of snorts and sarcasm from his colleagues.

"Go," Alexis repeated. "If you leave now you won't wear out your welcome and I might still like you tomorrow."

Isiah lost track of the conversation as he took another order, though he did give a nod to the crew, including Dominic, as they filed past him toward the door.

Not bothering to ask, he poured a double shot of Laphroaig and took it to Alexis. She was typing something into her phone when he arrived and she glanced up in surprise.

"I'll take it if you don't want it," he offered.

She peered around the corner, looking inside the bar. The afternoon had started slow, but now all the tables were taken as were all the spots at the bar. Marty, who'd arrived a few hours earlier, was taking orders for a group of eight and there were even a few people dancing.

"Now I feel kind of bad for wanting it, it looks like you might need it more than me," she said, reaching out for the glass.

"Good thing I know where to find more of that once this place clears out."

She held his gaze for a moment and then gave him a lopsided smile. "It's always good to have a job with benefits."

He lingered for another second not wanting to leave but seeing the line already backing up at the bar. "It's on me." Damn, he wasn't sure why he'd done that. He'd already given the table a free round—they'd bought another, and some food, and had tipped well. But still, this felt like unfairly crossing the line he'd not so subtly drawn in December.

She shook her head. "I'll pay on my way out. You better get back." She nodded to the bar. "Marty is good, but tonight looks like a two person job. At least," she added.

He nodded. He couldn't blame her for insisting on paying, not after the message he'd sent six months ago—one she'd obviously received loud and clear. But even so that didn't mean he had to like it. The urge to sit down, have a drink with her, and explain everything was strong. But what would he say? "Sorry I was an asshole, but I thought you were a tourist?" Somehow, he didn't think she'd be impressed by that apology.

No, he needed to be more strategic. He also probably needed a little more time than just the past few hours to consider what he actually wanted. He'd apologize either way, but he should give some thought as to what he wanted, or hoped, might come after.

And besides, Alexis didn't seem to want company. Or at least not his. She'd gone back to looking at her phone as she rolled the tumbler between her thumb and forefinger. Again, he couldn't blame her for all but dismissing him.

With a small shake of his head, he returned to the bar and the next hour flew by. It wasn't until he was outside, dropping a bag of trash in the bin, that he heard Alexis's voice again.

"Don't do this, gentlemen. Why don't you head inside and we'll all go on our merry ways."

He closed the lid of the bin and stepped around the building, his heart stopping at what he saw. Two men had Alexis backed up against a car. They weren't touching her, but they were definitely in her personal space and leaning in even more with every passing second.

"I don't know," one of them said. "I think you should come back inside and party with us."

"You might be this big of an asshole in your real life, but even then, I'm guessing you don't do this at home," Alexis replied. Her voice sounded more curious than concerned, and that was the only thing that kept him from charging out there. Oh, he wasn't about to let anything happen, but not only was she trained for this kind of situation, but *his* training was based on the premise of using the least amount of force necessary in the circumstance. Now sometimes that meant a shit ton of force, but was now one of those times? As much as his muscles bunched and tensed to pounce, and as much as his instinct hollered at him to protect Alexis, he recognized that it wasn't. At least not yet. He needed to give Alexis the space to deescalate the situation, because if he stepped in at the wrong time, it could get infinitely worse.

Taking deep, measured breaths, he melted into the shadows as he moved closer, craning his head to listen. One of the men said something and the other laughed. The muscles in Alexis's legs went taut. Isiah hadn't a clue what she had planned, but while she kept her voice calm, her body was ready for the storm.

"Now I'm going to give the benefit of a doubt to whoever raised you both and assume they taught you right from wrong. Obviously, you've chosen not to listen to them, so I'm going to give you another chance to make a better choice," she said.

The man closest reached for her and Isiah's entire body flooded with adrenaline. But before he had a chance to move, Alexis had the man up against the car. With her body behind his, she forced him forward against the door, his right hand held in a grip against his waist, and his left bent up behind him. He jerked against her restraint, but she held him immobile.

"If you don't want this to escalate any further, I suggest you back off." For a moment, he thought Alexis was talking to him, but when the second man stepped back, Isiah realized she was in complete control of the situation.

"Now you are going to listen to me, gentlemen. And yes, I use that term loosely." When neither man responded, she continued. "You're both going to make better choices from now on. Just because you're on vacation does not mean you get to be assholes. Obviously, that's your default personality, but like I said, I'm going to wager that you know better." She lowered the man's left hand enough that she could grip it with the same hand she held his other wrist in, then she spoke again. "Now, what you're going to do is walk inside, have a drink or two, be polite to everyone, then head on back to your hotel and never visit here again. In fact, I'll even help you out."

Isiah thought his eyes were deceiving him when Alexis dug into her pocket and pulled out what looked like some money. But when she spoke next, he had to look away to keep himself from stepping into the situation and telling her she was crazy.

"The drinks are excellent here. Marty makes a mean Painkiller. Try a couple on me." She shoved some cash into the man's pocket. "But when you leave here today, don't ever come back. Do you understand?"

Isiah forced his attention back to the scene to see the man behind her nodding. But the man against the car hesitated.

"Now, now now," Alexis admonished. "Now's not the time to hesitate. Just give me a nod and you and your little friend can go on your way."

Isiah tensed as the seconds ticked by. But then the man finally gave a terse nod. Alexis moved back, one step at a time, until she released the man's wrists enough that he could shift away from her.

Isiah's heart thudded against his ribs, and the preternatural calm he'd always felt when on a mission swept through his body. His attention remained focused solely on the man Alexis had released. If the situation was going to go to hell in a hand-basket, now was when it would happen.

The man spun around but kept his back to the car.

"Make a good choice," Alexis said. Her arms hung down, relaxed, but her hands were still and ready should she need to use them.

A beat passed. Then another. Finally, the two men stepped away then scuttled into the bar. Alexis stood still, watching them. But once the bar door closed behind them, she took a deep breath, let it out, then started walking up the road. Alone.

He couldn't—wouldn't—let her go on her own. Not after what had just gone down. But even with the little bit he'd learned about her, he knew she wouldn't want his company. Asking her to wait for him was out of the question, but so was letting her go—as much for her sake as for his. Okay, maybe more for his. She may not be interested in having anything to do with him after what had happened in December, but he wouldn't be able to sleep unless he knew for certain that she'd made it home safely.

Decision made, he quickly slipped back into the bar through

the rear exit and stepped up next to Marty. The two men who'd cornered Alexis were in line for drinks.

"I need to step out for a minute," Isiah said.

Marty's head swiveled in his direction and his mouth opened to say something. Then it promptly snapped shut. "Everything okay?" Marty asked.

"Those two." Isiah subtly jerked his head in the direction of the men and Marty glanced over. "I wouldn't be opposed if their drinks were sub-par. And if they so much as look at someone sideways, kick them out."

Marty eyed him for a moment as he poured a beer from the tap. "Got it. Anything else?" he asked, turning back to the drink.

"Sorry to leave you—"

"Go," Marty insisted, "Whatever you need to do, go do it. I got this."

Isiah hesitated, it was a busy night. But then Marty jerked his head toward the exit and Isiah took the hint. Not wasting any time, he left through the back door and, pausing under the emergency light, he scanned the street for Alexis. His heart stuttered when he didn't immediately see her—the road stretched in either direction and there were only two ways she could have gone—but then he caught a glimpse of her form as she picked her way along the side of the road, heading south.

Letting out a deep exhale, he allowed all his training and experience to come to the surface, and silently, he made his way toward the cover of the foliage and began to follow her.

* * *

*A*lexis turned and walked up a short driveway to the entrance of a luxury apartment building. Tapping in the code, she walked through the first door, then used a key to get through the second.

Smiling to herself as she stepped into the elevator, she hit a button and the door slid closed. As the lift rose to the fifth floor, she wondered if Isiah would breathe a sigh of relief thinking she was home.

It was kind of cute how he thought he'd be able to follow her without her knowing. And no, she wouldn't admit that she kind of liked that he'd tried. Okay fine, she'd admit it. But that didn't mean she'd gloss over how unexpected it was.

Not that seeing her safely home after being accosted in his parking lot was unexpected—that was something Alexis chalked up to basic human decency and the fact that, despite his previous behavior, Isiah wasn't immune to her. But what was unexpected was what he hadn't done. He hadn't interfered with her handling of the two drunks and he hadn't rushed to her side and treated her like a helpless victim. No, he'd hung back, assessed the situation, determined that she could handle it, and stayed out of her way. He'd respected her skills while ensuring her safety, and all without pulling the alpha-male/he-man card.

Not that she doubted he was one—a man didn't become a SEAL without being an alpha—but it was one thing to be one and another thing to know when you didn't need to *act* like one. And damn if it wasn't sexy as hell that he knew the difference.

The door opened on the top floor and, pushing thoughts of Isiah to the side for the moment, she stepped out. There were two doors in the hallway, both of which led to apartments owned by her parents. The one to the left housed Yael and Eric Goodman, her head of security and her cook/dog trainer, respectively. To her right was Rachel Goodman's flat. Rachel was Eric's mother, but she was also Alexis's house manager— she'd been with the family since before Alexis was born and was like a second mother to her.

To the right she went.

She didn't have to wait long for Rachel to answer, and the door swung open before she'd even had a chance to rap a second time.

"What's wrong?" Rachel asked, stepping aside so Alexis could enter the apartment.

"Hey, Yael. Eric." Alexis ignored Rachel's question for the moment and greeted Rachel's son and daughter-in-law instead.

"What's wrong?" Yael repeated from where she sat on the couch with her feet in Eric's lap.

Alexis rolled her eyes. "Nothing is wrong. There were a couple of troublemakers at the bar and Isiah followed me home. No doubt to make sure I made it safely after the encounter."

"Encounter?" Rachel asked, handing her a glass of wine without asking.

"Followed you home?" Yael asked, at the same time.

"Two assholes, who were already one too many drinks in, took a safari taxi up to The Shack. I was on my way out when they decided I needed to party with them," Alexis answered Rachel first. "I disagreed. One got a little handsy but it took less than fifteen seconds for them to realize they'd made a bad decision. Frankly, if you ask me, my guess is that most of their lives are made up of one bad decision after the other, but that's my armchair psychology for you," she added.

"You're not hurt?" Rachel asked.

Alexis shook her head. "Didn't even get my heart rate up." Not entirely true, but close enough.

"I want to get back to the part where you said Isiah Clarke followed you home. You mean he walked you home? Why are you here?" Yael asked, confused.

Again, Alexis shook her head. But this time it was in equal parts to answer the question as well as to shake the image of Isiah in her home out of her mind. "We barely know each other but he saw the whole thing go down—"

"And he didn't step in?" Eric said.

"He wouldn't have wanted the scene to escalate," Yael interjected, prodding her husband with her toe. Dutifully, he started kneading her foot again.

"I give him props for recognizing you could handle the situation," Yael continued. "Most men, particularly military men, wouldn't have been so, what's the word…"

"Equal opportunity?" Alexis said.

"Level headed," Rachel offered.

"Those are not the words I'd use," Eric muttered.

Yael shot her husband a quelling look and shook her head. "So then what?"

Alexis took a sip of her wine as she shrugged. "Not much. I started walking home. I assume he went in to tell Marty he wanted to keep an eye on me because it was a few minutes before I caught his shadow moving along the side of the road following me."

"And you came here, why?" Yael asked. "Is there something you think we should know about him? A feeling you get or something?"

Yes, there was a feeling she got from Isiah Clark, but not the kind Yael was referring to. Again she shrugged, hoping to play off her discomfort. "My teammates don't even know where I live. I wasn't going to lead Isiah Clarke straight to my doorstep," she answered. The words sounded even lamer than the real reason she hadn't gone home. Isiah now knew she was an FBI agent, but only because Dominic had set him straight earlier. Given Isiah's earlier actions, that knowledge had to have influenced his opinion of her because before today, there was no way she could have missed the judgment in his eyes when he looked at her. She'd had enough experience with the press and media to know exactly what kind of story he'd concocted in his head about her and it wasn't flattering.

And she didn't want him to see where she lived because, as pathetic as it was, that modicum of respect she saw on his face when he looked at her now—and the respect he showed her outside his bar—was something she wanted to savor. If he saw where she lived, he might still think of her as an FBI agent, but, if history was anything to go by, he also wouldn't be the first person to wonder if she'd bought her way into her position. And the idea of him thinking of her that way wasn't something she wanted. No, the nine-thousand square foot island mansion she lived in—a home her family had owned for more than twenty years—was something she liked to keep to herself. And, as she pointed out to Yael, not even her teammates had seen it.

Of course, that second little bit of truth spoke to a whole different set of issues that she liked to push under the rug. After more than six months together, she'd grown closer to her team on Tildas Island than any other group of people she'd worked with—or known—in her life. She trusted them almost as much as she trusted her family and the Goodmans, and more than that, she *liked* them. And even more than that, they trusted her. There was not a doubt in her mind that her teammates wouldn't be fazed by the grandeur of where she lived, and not for a second did she think it would change their perception of her. Dominic and Jake might rib her endlessly like a pair of giddy jackals, but it would be done with their special brand of affection.

And yet, she still hadn't ever invited any of them over. Ever.

Alexis sighed and took another sip of her wine, surprised to find it almost gone. "Anyway, on to more interesting topics. Where's Satan?"

"Hanging from my curtains, no doubt," Rachel sniffed. "If she's not there, she's probably clawed her way into my laundry basket and is shredding my undergarments."

Alexis laughed. The two pound, all black kitten she'd talked Rachel into fostering had grown into a six pound ball of terror. An adorable ball of terror, but a destructive one.

"You know I'll cover the cost of anything you need to replace," she said.

Rachel shot her a repressive look and Alexis took that to mean she should drop the subject of reimbursements.

"And how did Howdy do today?" she asked, turning to Eric. Howdy was a little brown and white nine-month-old female island dog she fostered. The island shelter and animal rescue community didn't have a fostering program, but she'd started her own. She had a huge house, an even bigger yard, and a cook who both adored dogs and training them. He was damn good at it, too. Currently, she had four dogs living with her, but since she'd moved down to Tildas the previous November, she'd fostered a total of eleven. All were mixed breeds, none more than forty pounds, and each of which, when the time was right, she'd had flown to various animal shelters who'd helped place them in their forever home.

They were all special, but Howdy was just a little something more. Alexis wasn't ready to admit it yet, but she had an inkling that Howdy might be her first foster-fail.

Eric smiled as he rubbed his wife's feet. "She's great. I got her to pick up a wooden spoon I dropped today while I was cooking. She looked so proud of herself that I think her tail wagged her body."

Alexis smiled, it wasn't a hard image to conjure. Howdy was the most perpetually cheerful dog Alexis had ever met.

"How many treats did she get?" she asked.

"Just one," Eric answered. Alexis arched an eyebrow. Eric cleared his throat. "One for the task then maybe a couple more because she kept smiling at me."

Alexis, Yael, and Rachel all laughed. Eric was definitely the most soft-hearted out of all of them.

"And Red, George, and Allie?" she asked referring to the other three dogs living with her.

"I think Allie and George will be ready to head north in a month or so. I took them both shopping today and they did great. Met lots of people, other dogs, kids. I think Allie would be most comfortable being a city dog, but George could go either way."

"So maybe Miami or Dallas for them?" she asked. She had networks all over the US, but the trick was always finding the right family.

"Dallas might get a little cold in the winter for our Princess Allie, but she'd love Miami and the beach. George would do well there, too. Especially if we found him a nice family in the suburbs with a pool, so long as they don't mind him sharing it. I swear that dog would live in your pool if we let him."

Alexis smiled at that and set her wine glass down. Eric wasn't exaggerating. There'd been a time or two when one or the both of them had had to jump into her pool and herd George out.

"And Red?" Red was their newest addition. A shy, thirty pound four-year-old. She wouldn't hurt a fly, but life had taught her that there were a lot of things out there that could hurt her. It would take a while for her settle in and it broke Alexis's heart every time she saw Red flinch at something so simple as the ice machine coming on.

"She's coping, but not much more," Eric replied. "I try to give her a lot of quiet time every day, and when I can, I'll sit with her and just pet her. I have to believe she'll come around, but it's going to take a while. I honestly think that in a year or so, she'll be an excellent candidate to be a service dog in a retirement community."

"She does like old people," Rachel said, patting her grey hair.

Alexis let out a deep breath and glanced at the clock on the bookshelf. Thirty minutes had passed since she'd stepped through the door. She loved her teammates, but there was something to be said for spending time with people who both knew and accepted her completely. Feeling more relaxed than she had all day, and knowing Isiah would have likely left to go home, she rose from her seat, snagging her wine glass along the way.

"Thanks for the wine, Rachel, and the chat. I'll head home

now that my shadow has probably abandoned his post for the night." As she spoke, she walked into the kitchen and deposited her empty glass. When she returned, Yael was slipping on her flip flops.

"You don't need to come with me," Alexis said.

"I know. But I want the real story about Isiah Clarke. You know, the one you won't tell your second mother or faux brother." She jerked her thumb in the direction of her family. "The one you probably won't even tell yourself," she added.

Alexis snorted. "And what makes you think you'll get it?"

Yael shot her a flat look and shook her head as she opened the door. "Former Israeli intelligence agent, remember? You don't have a chance."

CHAPTER TWO

ISIAH STOOD AT THE BAR, as he did almost every day, and dried freshly washed glasses. The endless task of keeping the bar clean was made easier by his military-everything-in-its-place-and-a-place-for-everything training. It didn't hurt that when he'd first opened The Shack, the mundane tasks had given him a purpose, occupying his body while his mind slowly filtered through and processed his years in the Navy.

But he wasn't processing his career or his missions now. No, he was definitely thinking about Alexis. Or more precisely, the unsettled thoughts—and maybe even feelings—he had when it came to her. He didn't like that he'd so misjudged her, but he still wasn't sure if his new found knowledge of her changed anything. Scratch that, it definitely changed things—knowing that she both lived on the island and lived close by had fueled his imagination the night before. But other than his body being on board with a "get to know Alexis" plan, what was different?

He knew she worked for the FBI, but there was also something else about her that he couldn't quite get a handle on. He'd seen evidence of her professional skills, but he couldn't ignore the part of her that, until yesterday, he'd seen the most often.

The part of her that had led him to believe she was just one more rich tourist.

The door swung open and the object of his thoughts walked in. Being Sunday afternoon, the bar was pretty quiet. A family of six was finishing brunch on the porch, but once again, he was the only one behind the bar. Taking a seat, she uncharacteristically rested her elbows on the bar top.

"I'll take an iced tea. It's a little early for whiskey," she added with a smile. Today, her hair was pulled into one long braid that hung down her back and she wore a tank top, shorts, and sandals. No jewelry.

"You got it." Isiah poured the tea from a pitcher and slid the glass over. When he started to release the glass, she wrapped her fingers around his. It was just the slightest touch, but it was enough to hold him.

"Don't follow me home again, Clarke. It's creepy as fuck."

He studied her for a moment. She didn't shy away from his scrutiny but she also didn't look particularly creeped out. He gave a short nod and slid his fingers out from under hers.

"Noted. Next time I'll walk *with* you." Rather than wait for a reaction, he went back to drying his glasses. But he didn't miss her quiet, under-the-breath laugh.

"Got your mail." Marty's voice carried down the hall from the back entrance of the bar. The man soon followed, dumping a padded envelope on the counter. "I left most of it on your desk, but thought you might want to see what that is." He pointed to the yellow piece of mail. "I also dropped by the bank, placed the new order with the fish guy, and arranged to have the produce delivered a little earlier than usual on Tuesday so it doesn't cut into our prep time. But I didn't get a chance to place the order for the chicken, since Ms. Mary was at church with her family so not at home. But I can stop by later today."

"Tomorrow's fine," Isiah said, picking up the envelope. "We have enough for Tuesday if she delivers on Wednesday." Even as he spoke, his attention was drawn to what he held in his hand. It was addressed to him and had a return address that he didn't recognize—or part of one, anyway, since it was just a street name and zip code. Judging by what he could feel, something rectangular and slim was inside.

Frowning, he gently tore the top and out slid a phone. He stared down at the device, looking sleek and shiny on his scarred worktop.

"That's an odd way to deliver a new phone," Alexis said.

He glanced up. Despite her casual demeanor, she was watching him with the intensity of a trained investigator.

"You got the bar, Marty?" he asked, ignoring Alexis for the moment. His little package gave him a bad feeling and he wanted to be alone when he tried to figure out why.

Marty waved him away and he slipped down the hall to his office, closing the door behind him. Taking a seat at his desk, he eyed the device before bringing it to life.

In an instant, he knew whose phone it was, Kevin Karington's—or Huck as they called him in the SEALs. A picture of the two of them, in some desert somewhere, filled the screen.

Isiah turned the device over, looking for any evidence of tampering, but found none. Flipping back to their two smiling faces, he slid his finger over the bottom of the screen and the number pad popped up. Of course it was locked. He stared at it, letting his mind wander a bit. If Huck had gone to the trouble of sending him the phone, he would have made sure Isiah could open it.

Reaching for the envelope, he tilted it up. When nothing came out, he looked inside. Still nothing.

Setting it down, the return address caught his attention— 1917 High Street with a zip code he recognized as coming from somewhere on the east coast.

Knowing he'd have more than one chance, he pulled up the key pad on the phone again and keyed in 1917. Instantly, the screen changed and he was faced with more icons and apps than anyone could humanly use.

Opting to take a precautionary step before culling through the files and apps, Isiah plugged the phone into his desktop with a USB cord and started a download of the content onto his hard drive. As that ticked by, he familiarized himself with everything Huck had on the device.

He opened the notes app first and found what appeared to be a couple of shopping lists, some going back years. He smiled at that glimpse into Huck's day-to-day life. His friend had a thing for Chunky Monkey ice cream. Then again, after more than ten years traveling in and out of the desert, Isiah could hardly fault the man. There might even be a quart or two of Phish Food in his own freezer.

Closing the notes app, his finger hovered over the recorded messages app. Something deep inside him held him back— without any confirmation, he knew the reason Huck had sent him the phone would be found in that app. It was the only thing that made sense. He could have kept the phone and sent an email, or made a call. But Huck had either made a point to send the device for its own sake—which was weird—or he'd been in such a hurry that sending the entire phone was the surest way to get Isiah whatever message he needed to convey.

Neither option boded well for Huck, but Isiah chose not to think about that at the moment. Instead, he took a deep breath and hit "play" on the most recent message.

"Boongy," Huck started, referring to Isiah by his SEAL nickname. *"I can see you sitting there in your beach bar, living the life. I should have joined you when I had the chance. But now's not the time for whining like a baby. So here's the thing. Angela Rosen, my boss, asked me to track down an asset we refer to as* The Gentleman. *She said we needed to bring him in because there was a chance he'd been compromised. I fucking believed her, of course, and started digging. I tracked him to a region in Honduras, you'll see that in my notes. At*

least that's where he was as of today. Anyway, I went to report this to her and overheard some crazy-ass shit. I mean, seriously, not to sound dramatic, but there's a good chance I'll be dead by the time you receive this. The short story is, the asset was never compromised. Angela was talking to some dude about the price they'd get for his identity. I didn't see who she was talking to, just some guy, tucked into the corner of her fucking office out of my line of sight when I went to talk to her."

Huck paused and Isiah could hear the sounds of traffic in the background and his friend huffing into the phone, no doubt as he retreated quickly away from where he worked in the DC offices of the CIA.

"Boongy, Angela Rosen is up to something, including selling the identity of at least one key CIA asset. I have no idea if she had other analysts finding other agents so there might be others, too. The conversation I overheard didn't identify a buyer, but they did mention Tildas Island and the Summit next year which is why you're the lucky SOB to get my message. That, and out of the team, your address is the only one I can remember without having to look that shit up which I don't have time for. In fact, I'm dropping this little bomb in your lap and ghosting. It's too hot for me right now and I was only sort of joking about being dead when you get this. But you know me, if I can get to you in a way that won't compromise you or your loved ones, I'll get to you. It may take me a while, but I'll get there. And if I don't, well, let's say it's a good thing I don't have much family to mourn me.

"I couldn't take all the time to write this shit down, but I was able to move all my research to my private drive." Huck rattled off the URL to his private cloud drive, then continued. *"I don't know what it will tell you other than where I tracked* The Gentleman *to, but fuck it. Take what you can and do what you can or pass it on to someone else if you have to. It's been too long since we talked and maybe you've got people in your life and you don't want to get involved and that's okay, too, but just pass this shit on to someone from the team. I don't want to trust it to anyone else."* And then the recording ended.

Well, hell.

Isiah sat back in his chair while the rest of the content of the phone finished uploading. His first instinct was to visit Huck's cloud drive, but he no longer had access to a secure internet connection. Huck would have hidden the data transfer from his work computer to his drive, but if someone went looking, they'd know a transfer took place and could start digging into where the data had gone. If Huck hadn't hidden his tracks well enough and if Isiah then accessed the data from a non-secure site, they'd know exactly who Huck had gone to with his information. Which would mean he'd have these people—Angela Rosen and whoever else might be involved—knocking on his door.

"We got a crowd coming in, Boss," Marty called down the hall as Isiah became aware of the rumbling of diesel mini-bus in his parking lot. Great, just what he needed, a bus full of tourists from the never ending stream of cruise ships that stopped at the island. Mostly, the cruise companies didn't offer a trip to his bar, but sometimes families or large groups looking for a place off the beaten path organized an outing.

Unplugging the now-backed-up phone, he unlocked his safe and placed it inside. He was locking it back up again when Marty appeared in the doorway.

"Party of thirty," Marty said. "Family outing with kids and all. At least it's not a bachelor party."

Isiah wasn't so sure. He found it way easier to deal with a drunken thirty-old man than a screaming toddler, but to each their own.

"They gonna want food?" Isiah asked as he ushered Marty back toward the bar, shutting his office door behind him.

"Of course they are."

Isiah sighed. "I'll get the food orders then hit the kitchen. You good handling the house?"

Marty gave him the side-eye and handed Isiah a stack of menus as the party started ambling in. "Yeah, I'm good."

Isiah took in the tourists with their sunburned faces, shorts, and smiles. A stab of disappointment lanced through him when he saw Alexis's chair empty, but the chatter and laughter of the large family filled The Shack and it was hard not to absorb a little bit of their happiness.

Forcing a smile he didn't entirely feel, he stepped from behind the bar and started greeting his guests.

* * *

*T*hree hours and thirty very satisfied customers later, Isiah locked the door to The Shack. He typically closed early on Sundays, but today, he was earlier than usual. He needed to figure out what the hell to do with the information Huck had dropped in his lap.

"Hey, Marty," he called. Marty emerged from the kitchen, wiping his hands on a dishtowel.

"Yeah?"

"Why don't you head home for the day? I can get the rest here."

Marty eyed the room. Most of the dishes were already done, but the tables needed to be cleaned, the seats put up, and the floor swept and mopped.

"I can make my way through everything. I don't have anything else to do this afternoon, but I seem to recall there might be a lady from your church you were thinking of inviting out to coffee and cake?"

"I can invite Ms. Alice out tomorrow night when we're closed. You should leave all this to me and go do something fun. You don't do enough fun," Marty said.

Isiah couldn't argue with that last statement, but it wasn't like he didn't *ever* have fun. He did, just not as much as the average thirty-eight-year-old bachelor. He'd had enough fun in his early twenties and valued the stability these last few years on Tildas Island had given him—very little had been stable in his life until settling on Tildas and it wasn't something he took for granted.

Isiah shrugged. "You can stay, but I have to stay anyway. I have the books and bills to go through and then a few other things to take care of. At least if you go, one of us will be having fun."

Marty narrowed his eyes. "That's a piss poor argument."

"Ms. Alice going to like language like that?" Isiah teased.

"Ms. Alice has raised four boys who show nothing but respect for their mama. I suspect Ms. Alice could swear you *and* me under the table in a match."

Isiah laughed. He'd seen Alice Fasher, she was five foot nothing and looked like she'd blow over in a good wind, but Marty was right, she was tough as nails and would have no compunction about putting either of the men in their place.

"Go," Isiah said, still chuckling even as he waved his friend toward the back door. "And don't let me see your face until Tuesday afternoon. I got some shit to do and don't want to be disturbed by your constant chatter."

Marty sniffed, but started toward the door as Isiah followed. "You like my chatter. If it weren't for my chatter, The Shack would be silent as a tomb. You know, you should try it more often, that talking thing. They say it's good for your heart and mind. Better than locking everything inside..."

Isiah shut the backdoor behind Marty and his voice faded away. For a moment, he stood in the hallway, drawing strength —and calm—from the silence. The family that had descended on The Shack had tipped well, been polite and fun. But even so, he'd found it hard to focus and remain *the host* while Huck's phone sat in the safe in his office and questions kept bouncing into his mind.

Taking a breath and girding himself for whatever came next, he reached for the handle of his office door. Just as a shadow moved across the bar.

His heart kicked up and his blood vessels expanded as adrenaline shot through his system. Was it possible that Angela Rosen, and whoever Huck had overheard in the office with her, already knew that Isiah had the information?

"Don't fucking move," he barked out the command as his body tensed for confrontation. A second ticked by then another. He assessed his options and was considering slipping into his office, where he kept his one and only firearm, when the figure appeared in the doorway.

Alexis leaned against the frame, crossing her arms over her chest. "You've been jumpy as a cat in a dog pound since you opened that envelope today. Care to tell me what it's all about?"

"What the hell are you doing here?" he snapped, striding toward her. Truth be told, he was more annoyed at being taken by surprise than at her still being at the bar, but she didn't need to know that.

She smiled at him as he approached. He stalked toward her but drew to a halt two feet away. She didn't bother to move or back away. Her fucking confidence was going to drive him crazy. He'd seen it that very first time she'd set foot in his bar and not a thing had changed since then, only now he was well aware that she had the physical ability to back it up.

"Someone's a little cranky at being taken by surprise."

"You're trespassing," he replied.

She lifted a shoulder. "Not really. I've been here the whole time, just out on the veranda and mostly out of sight. You locked up the bar with me in it. Arguably, I'm being held hostage here by you."

He glared down at her, though not that much *down* since she was only four inches shorter than he. She stared back. His gaze dropped from her light blue eyes to the freckles that dotted her nose and cheeks. He'd noticed them before, of course, but he'd never been this close to her and though she was all woman now, he could almost see the little girl she'd once been.

She smiled again as his attention drifted to her lips and the perfect rows of perfect white teeth. Who was this woman? Other than a woman standing before him, smiling and not the least bit intimidated.

His mind stumbled over that thought. Why the hell would he *want* her to be intimidated by him? It was a good thing she wasn't, right? But then what was his problem?

"Fuck, I'm a mess." Taking a step away, he leaned his back against the wall. "Sorry about that. You're right, I'm a little on edge."

She studied him before speaking. "Let's pour ourselves a drink and you can tell me all about it."

He rolled his head to look at her. "Tell you?" She might be FBI, but that didn't mean he trusted her.

He studied her. She met his scrutiny with an unflinching stare of her own. He didn't trust her like he'd trusted his team, but there was a lot of wiggle room between having no trust at all and the kind of relationship he'd had with his team. He couldn't expect to feel the latter with someone he barely knew, but his instinct—and yes, maybe even something more primal than that—was telling him that on the spectrum of trustworthiness, she landed closer to his team than to the other side. A lot closer.

"Who better than your friendly, neighborhood FBI agent?" she asked, flashing him another smile as she pushed away from the door frame and made her way into the bar area. "What can I get you?" she asked as she spun back toward him and held her arms akimbo, taking in all his bar had to offer.

He didn't bother to suppress the chuckle that emerged from his chest. It was a little rusty and grumbly, but it was definitely a chuckle. "So what's the deal? You pour me a beer and I spill my secrets?"

"Beer it is." Then with a wink, she grabbed a pint glass and made her way to the taps. She poured the draft like a professional, even wiping the nozzle clean before handing him his drink.

After she'd helped herself to a gin and tonic, they made their way to the porch. Choosing a chair opposite her, he sank into the seat. For a few minutes, they said nothing, each sipping their drink and enjoying the view. The blue sky stretched as far as the eye could see, boats dotted the Caribbean ocean, and not-so-distant islands beckoned his imagination.

"It's been a long time since I've sat out here in the daylight." In fact, he couldn't remember the last time he'd taken the time to enjoy his own place. Maybe the last time his sister had visited?

"It is pretty special, isn't it?"

The wistfulness in her voice caught his attention. No doubt she sensed he'd now shifted his attention to her, but she kept her face turned toward the view.

"You seem different," he said.

Her eyes flickered to him. "Than last night? I would hope so."

He shook his head. "No, different from when you first started coming in here last fall." If he hadn't been watching so closely, he would have missed the way her shoulders tensed a hair, before they relaxed again. He hated that she might be remembering that night in December and his behavior toward her, but before he could open his mouth to apologize, she spoke.

"It takes me a while to warm up to people and new situations. I'd just moved here and recently met my new colleagues that first time I stopped by. I know my team—and the job—better now, and it's become easier to let my guard down a little bit. I suppose it's that comfort level you're seeing."

Interesting that her words hinted at the thoughts he'd had

35

earlier about trust. But her answer hadn't answered what he'd wanted to know. "That explains your more frequent smiles and the laughter I overheard yesterday when you were here with your team, but it doesn't explain why you're suddenly different with me. Especially, after the way I treated you."

He didn't need to elaborate and the corners of her mouth tipped down. For a moment, he thought she was going to reach for her drink and down the whole thing. But after a beat, she let out a long breath and gave him a rueful smile.

"I have an idea of why you did what you did in December and while I'm not excusing the behavior, I can respect that you needed distance. But then you followed me home last night. And more to the point, you had my back out in the parking lot. How you went about it gave me some insight into who you are as a person and, regardless of what happened in December, I liked what I saw."

"You saw me?" he asked, "I mean actually saw me, not metaphorically 'saw me,'" he clarified. She nodded. He might be a little out of practice, but he wasn't *that* out of practice. That she'd seen him gave him another glimpse into her skills—not only was she confident, but she was competent, too and damn if that wasn't sexy as hell.

He shifted in his seat. The need to reach for her, to feel her body against his, hit him with the subtlety of a sledgehammer. The craving was so intense that it threw him mentally off balance. Unsure what to do or say, he forced himself to turn away from her and he fixed his gaze on the horizon. His fingers twitched on his glass, itching to touch her, and he forced a few breaths in and out.

"And it didn't bother you that I didn't step in?" he managed to say.

"I actually appreciated that." She graced him with a wry smile. "I had the situation under control and you knew that. I don't really know you at all, but even so, I could see you ready to intervene. You had my back if I needed it but didn't force your way in and that's what's important."

He pulled his gaze from the Caribbean to her. "So now I'm on team Alexis?"

She laughed at that and he smiled. "You're hardly that, Clarke. But you're proving yourself worthy of consideration. Now, why don't you tell me about that phone? I already know it's not good," she added.

He took a sip of his beer and stared off into the distance. Did he have a choice but to tell her? She'd have access to a secure internet connection, and more to the point, she—and her team —might be the *only* people he knew with such access. Unless he traveled back stateside and looked up a couple of his former teammates. But he wasn't in a position to be gone that long, not with the bar and his other responsibilities.

So, no, he didn't really have a choice if he wanted help. But that logic wasn't what drove him to do what he did next.

"I'll be right back," he said, rising from his seat. Grabbing her empty glass, he dropped it behind the bar on the way to his office. Two minutes later, he was back, Huck's phone and a headset in hand. Setting both on the bar, he made Alexis a quick refill, then picked up all three items and rejoined her on the porch. What he was going to do might not be his best idea, but his instinct told him it was the right thing, even if his judgment of Alexis was mired in his attraction to her.

He set her gin and tonic on the table, unlocked the phone, and handed it to her along with the headset. "Listen to the first recording in the app."

Without a word, she plugged the headset in and did as she was told. Her gaze flickered to him a few times during the message, but for the most part, she kept her attention fixed on nothing in particular as she listened. When the message ended, she removed the headset and handed it, and the phone, back to him.

"Is your friend who sent you that reliable?" she asked.

His loyalty to Huck had Isiah opening his mouth to say "yes" before she'd even finished the question, but he forced himself to take a step back. Yes, Huck was reliable. Damn reliable. But it had been three years since Isiah had seen him, was it possible he could have changed? Was it possible this was some elaborate hoax? But if so, to what end?

"He was my teammate for seven years," Isiah answered. "One of the best there was. He left the year after I did and went to work for the CIA. I don't know exactly what he does for them. His message seems to indicate he's an analyst, but I'm pretty sure that's what they call people who do things the CIA doesn't want to have to explain."

"How long has it been since you've seen him?"

"He got out seven years ago. Traveled around for a couple of months. Stopped by here for a few weeks. Helped me build this porch, actually. Three years ago, he came to visit for a week, but I haven't seen him since."

"And you can't exactly call him now, can you." She nodded to the phone.

"Even if I could, I'm not sure I'd want to. I know I have to consider the possibility that the message might not be legit, but if it is, and I believe it is, I don't want to do anything that would call attention to him. Or to the fact that I now have the information that made him fear for his life," he said.

Alexis picked up her drink and took a sip, returning her gaze to the ocean. The silence stretched and though he'd been itching to do something all day, he found he didn't mind the quiet contemplation now.

His beer was nearly gone when he spoke again. "I have a friend in a security company in DC. I can have him discreetly look into Huck."

"And you need a secure internet connection that's protected

to the nines to check out what he might have left you on that cloud drive," she said.

He downed the rest of his drink and set his glass on the table. "I know. But I don't live in that world anymore and the only person I know who might have access to such a connection is sitting next to me."

Alexis shifted her gaze and stared at him. A beat passed, then she blinked and looked away. "The FBI office?"

He nodded.

"No," she said. "Not a good idea."

"I know it's not a good idea, but it's the only one I have unless you have one?"

She stared out toward the ocean for so long that Isiah wondered if she'd even heard him. But then she closed her eyes for a second, as if girding herself for something. When she opened them, she focused those baby blues on him.

"As a matter of fact, I do have another idea."

CHAPTER THREE

ALEXIS LED the way as she and Isiah left The Shack. The sun was on its downward slide toward the horizon and shadows had already consumed the lower parts of the dense foliage that lined the road.

Her feet didn't falter but her mind definitely did. She was about to bring a man she barely knew, one whom she wasn't even sure liked her, into a deeply private part of her life. With each step closer to where she was taking Isiah, the voice in her head telling that this was a bad idea—maybe not the worst idea she'd ever had, but a bad one nonetheless—got louder and louder. There was no way she'd be able to silence it—it was too demanding and too logical—and so halfway to their destination, she gave up trying to reason with herself and just accepted that she was acting so out of character that there was no making any sense of it. It just was.

"We headed to your house?" Isiah asked.

She shook her head. She wasn't *that* far gone so as to invite him to her home. "A friend's."

His steps slowed behind her. "Friend?"

She stopped and faced him. "Look, I know you don't trust

me like you trusted your team back when you had one and I wouldn't expect that from you. But I don't want to take you to my office because, while there is a secure connection there, the Bureau also has the ability to track traffic into and out of the network."

"But where you're taking me doesn't?"

"It doesn't, but it will require that you trust me—and my friends. At least in this."

He eyed her. "Who are these people?"

"I could tell you or you could form your own opinions when you meet them."

"I'll form my own opinions whether you tell me about them or not, but there is no way I'm walking into something blind. Who are they?"

Alexis sighed and looked toward the shadows as she thought about how to describe Eric and Yael. She could sugar coat things, but if Isiah found out later that she hadn't told him the complete truth, it might rattle the little trust he had in her, and protecting that kernel of trust between them felt important. But there was more at stake, of course. Yes, she wanted his trust on a personal level, but professionally, she *needed* it. She needed to find out what, if anything, Rosen's activities had to do with the Summit. Not to mention, if Rosen intended to compromise the identity of a CIA spy, that wasn't something Alexis or her team could overlook.

"Eric and Yael Goodman," she said. "I've known Eric my entire life and Yael is his wife."

"And they just happen to live here on Tildas Island?"

She almost smiled at the doubt that colored his tone. "No, they moved here because I'm here. Eric is my cook and my dog trainer—"

"Dog trainer? What the hell?"

That he'd been more surprised that she had a dog trainer than had cook did make her smile. "It's a long story, but I'm pretty involved in dog fostering and rescuing. I have four dogs living with me now and Eric trains them so that they have a better chance at finding forever homes when they go up for adoption."

Isiah crossed his arms over his chest. "Okay, that makes sense—the training part anyway. What doesn't make sense is why you have *staff* to do that."

"Because I don't have time but I do have the money, and Eric is the best," she answered, knowing full well it wasn't a complete answer.

"I worked for the government, I can pretty much guarantee you don't make enough to hire a fulltime dog trainer and cook."

And there it was, the question—buried in a statement—that she'd both expected and dreaded. Oh, her teammates knew who she was—or rather, who her parents were—but almost no one else knew. There were very good reasons for that. But Isiah did not look like a man who would let the issue go. Not entirely anyway.

"My family has money," she said quickly. "Like, a lot of money. I'd rather not talk about it, if you don't mind. But Eric's mom has worked for us since before I was born. Eric and I grew up together. After he graduated from college, he did a brief stint as a cybersecurity engineer at a private firm in DC before deciding that cooking was his real love. The dog training was something he picked up along the way."

Again, Isiah searched her face, giving nothing away. Then he nodded. "And Yael?"

"She's Eric's wife. She's former Mossad—Israeli intelligence —and she's both my personal trainer and, when needed, personal security." She turned away at that last admission. Admitting that she sometimes needed personal security made her a little nauseated. Partly, it pricked her pride that she couldn't always protect herself. But the admission also reminded her of the one time she'd needed personal security.

She hadn't had it then, and that day had changed everything. Ever since, no one in the family traveled without it.

"Personal security?"

To his credit, Isiah sounded more curious than judgmental.

Alexis nodded but said nothing more.

"You need personal security because of your family's money or because of your job?"

"I've had personal security since I was twelve. But I imagine my job hasn't made it easier. Yael has been with me since she and Eric got married fifteen years ago."

Isiah looked off into the foliage, much as she'd done moments ago. Finally, he let out a long breath, and with it, the tension eased from her own body.

"And you trust them?" he asked.

She nodded. "Literally with my life."

"And you think they can help?"

"I know Eric has a secure connection, and mad computer skills. I know he can *try* to help. But I can't guarantee he'll find anything. But then again, no one can guarantee that."

She saw him weighing her statement. Even if they found a quiet way into Huck's cloud drive, there was no guaranteeing that what they'd find there would help Huck or the spy in question.

Evening birds started to sing to each other in the trees and thunder rumbled in the distance. From the sound, Alexis knew the storm would bypass the island, but the air had grown heavy with moisture and the mosquitos were starting to make an appearance.

As Isiah raised his face to the skies his shoulders dropped an inch. "I don't love the idea of bringing other people into this when I don't know what *this* is, but at this point, I don't think I have a choice. Not unless I want to risk putting a big target on me by accessing the drive myself through unsecured channels."

Alexis hadn't expected him to concede any more than he had

—in his position, she would feel the same reluctance. With a nod of acknowledgment at his well-founded hesitancy, they continued on to Yael and Eric's.

In silence, they walked the remaining ten minutes to the apartment building. They were standing in the lobby waiting for the elevator when Isiah spoke again.

"You don't live here, do you?"

She ignored the twinge of guilt and shook her head.

"So, last night?"

"I wasn't going to let you follow me home, but I knew you wouldn't go back to The Shack until I was somewhere safe." The elevator doors opened and they stepped inside. "Yael and Eric, and Eric's mom, Rachel, all live here on the fifth floor."

"The top floor." It wasn't a question, he could see the buttons for the floor numbers. But again there was a question buried in the statement. She didn't have to answer, but she did.

"My parents own both of the penthouse apartments. They bought them for the Goodman's when I took the position on the task force and moved to Tildas Island. My parents treat all of our employees very well. Especially those with whom they entrust their only child's life."

"I think I might like your parents," he muttered as the doors opened and they stepped into the hallway.

"They might go a little overboard," she acknowledged. "But they do try to let me have a relatively normal life. This is our compromise," she said, gesturing to the two doors.

"Fair enough. Although one day, you're going to have to tell me who your parents are," he said as he followed her to Yael and Eric's door.

"Look it up. You wouldn't be the first," she said as she knocked on the door.

"I'd rather hear it from you. And I'm a patient man."

As he spoke, Eric opened the door, giving her an excuse not to dissect Isiah's statement. She had texted both Eric and Yael to let them know they were coming over, but not why, so while he wasn't surprised to see them on his doorstep, she could see the question in his eyes.

"It's a weird story, Eric. Isiah will tell you all about it," she said as she walked past him and into the open living room where she saw Yael.

When Eric closed the door, she faced the three people watching her expectantly. "Yael, Eric, this is Isiah Clarke. Isiah, this is Yael and Eric. Eric, we need your computer skills because it's highly likely that someone in the CIA is selling out our assets."

* * *

*W*ell, hell, Alexis didn't pull any punches. Isiah watched both Yael and Eric's reactions. Not surprising, as a former intelligence agent, Yael displayed none whatsoever. Eric raised a single eyebrow.

"Well, that was dramatic," Yael said.

Alexis smiled at her. "I'm capable of drama. I just don't indulge in it very often."

Yael rolled her eyes. "Isiah, can I get you something to eat or drink? Beer?"

He started to shake his head, then changed his mind. "A beer would be great. This has been an interesting afternoon. In more ways than one," he said, shooting a glance at Alexis.

Eric chuckled. "I bet. Now, you want to tell us what's going on?" he asked, gesturing for him and Alexis to take a seat.

Isiah studied the man as they arranged themselves on the two couches in the living room. Eric Goodman looked to be in his mid-forties and was the same height as Alexis. He was definitely a little softer around the middle than his wife, who was whipcord lean, but he still looked relatively fit. Wire-rimmed glasses perched over a pair of brown eyes that looked to take in more than most people probably gave him credit for.

"Here," Yael said, re-entering the room with three bottles of beer and a glass of whiskey for Alexis. Yael Goodman was probably close to five foot four, but her petite bone structure and lean muscles made her seem even smaller. He imagined that was an advantage back when she'd been an agent—with her build, coupled with her wildly curly dark hair and wide eyes that were an even darker shade of brown than her husband's, she'd probably been easy to underestimate.

"So what can we do for you?" Yael asked once she'd settled herself at her husband's side on the love seat. The love seat was on the other side of the coffee table from the couch where he and Alexis sat—on opposite ends.

Rather than answer, he took the phone out and set it on the table. Unlocking the device, he played the message. It did not get any clearer or less alarming hearing it for the second time.

When Huck's voice ended, he shut the device down, slipped it into his pocket, and looked up at his hosts.

"You want to get into the cloud drive?" Eric asked.

"Stealthily," Yael added.

Isiah nodded.

"That a problem, babe?" Yael asked her husband.

Rather than answer right away, Eric leaned forward, picked up a pencil and a piece of paper, and, from memory, wrote the address of the drive down. He eyed it for a moment, frowning, then shook his head.

"It won't be a problem, but I'm not sure how long it will take," he said. "Even though my connection here is secure and easy to obscure, I'll want to bounce the signal around a fair bit to be on the safe side. I think the best thing to do, depending on how much information is there, is to copy it quickly to another drive that we control and then we can go through it without having to worry about being discovered. We could even print it, if need be. A little old fashioned, I know, but sometimes that's the most effective way to view data, especially data that we don't know what we're looking at or for."

"Can you start tonight?" Alexis asked.

Eric rose from his seat. "I can start now."

At his comment, some of the tension eased from Isiah's chest. Intellectually, it was foolish to trust these people so quickly, but he'd passed the point of turning back when he'd handed Alexis the headset back at his bar. Besides, Alexis clearly had some significant trust issues and yet she trusted these people. He wouldn't bet his life on them—not yet—but he was willing to bet they could help him with this.

"My computer is in the office which means I have to release the kraken," Eric said, gesturing for Isiah to follow him.

"The kraken?" Isiah asked, rising. Both Alexis and Yael did the same. Apparently, this would be a group adventure.

"He's not that bad," Alexis said.

"At least he's not Satan," Yael muttered, utterly confusing him.

"Satan?" Isiah asked.

"Satan is a kitten Rachel is fostering," Alexis answered as they walked down the hallway.

"And that adorable little shit definitely lives up to her name," Yael said.

"And the kraken?" Isiah asked as Eric opened the door and a brown dust mop went flying by him. No, not a dust mop, a dog. A very small, long haired dog that stopped at Alexis's feet and started bouncing up and down. And peeing on the floor.

Yael let out a loud sigh. "Isiah, meet Puddles. Aptly named as you can see. We call her the kraken because she attacks everyone—lovingly, of course. You won't find a sweeter dog, though she's a bit much for some people. I'll get the paper towels," she said then disappeared back toward the kitchen.

"You're the best tiny brown dog in the world aren't you,

Puddles," Alexis crooned to the dog, whom she'd picked up and was now cuddling. "It would be better if you learned not to pee every time someone walked into the house, but you're working on that aren't you?"

Puddles wiggled in her arms, then went completely limp, draping herself over Alexis's shoulder.

Alexis laughed. "She's almost like a ragdoll cat. If we could only get her to stop peeing then I have no doubt dozens of families would vie to adopt her." As she spoke, she rubbed her cheek along the dog's long brown coat. In the past twenty-four hours, he'd seen Alexis in a lot of different lights and this was yet another. He didn't know her well, but how she looked now, cuddling the tiny dog, was the most relaxed he'd ever seen her and it was hard not to want to wrap an arm around her and join in the snuggles. Although, as he thought about it, he realized that even though he'd learned a lot about her, he still had no idea what her last name was.

"What's your last name?" he asked.

"We'll bounce it through the university in Alabama first," Eric said, cutting off any reply Alexis might have made, which was, no doubt, the intent.

"Why Alabama?" Isiah asked, allowing the man to distract him. What Alexis's last name was, was neither here nor there at the moment, but eventually he'd get her to share.

Eric shrugged. "Why not? From there we'll pop through a couple of places in Europe and Africa, then back to the States, then maybe through the Middle East. I'll have to see how I feel at that point."

"Anything I can do while you're doing that?" he asked as Yael appeared in the doorway.

"The floor is clean," she announced. "And no, there's nothing you can do. You're welcome to stay here and watch, but Alexis, can you come to Rachel's with me for a moment? She called earlier and needs some help setting up that new accounting software."

Alexis shared a look with Yael then gave a little shake of her head. "Rachel doesn't need help with her software," she said to Isiah as she handed Puddles into his arms. The dog lifted its head, scrambled its little paws against his chest, then relaxed in his arms. "This is Yael's way of getting me on my own so she can interrogate me about you."

Yael lifted her gaze upward and let out a small sigh. "I was trying not to embarrass you, but I'll know better next time." Then turning to him, she added. "We already know nearly everything about you just as we do about everyone who comes into Alexis's life on a regular basis. But what I don't know is what *she* thinks of you. So if you'll excuse us, I'm going to steal her away for some good old fashioned gossip. I'll return her when I'm satisfied with the answers she gives."

"Anything I should know or be worried about?" he asked Alexis.

"Not a thing," Alexis answered. "It will probably be her easiest and fastest interrogation ever."

"No, that interrogation was when I met Eric," Yael said with a grin.

"Yeah, yeah, yeah," Eric said. "We've all heard that story a million times. Now would you please go away so I can concentrate?"

"Yes, dear." Yael dropped a kiss on her husband's head before gesturing Alexis out of the room. Following Alexis out, she paused in the doorway and turned back to Isiah. "He accidentally hacked into a Mossad network. They sent me to figure out who he was. Took less than five minutes to get his entire life story."

"That's because you're terrifying," Eric said, his attention never leaving his computer screen.

"You're so sweet, Babe. Love you and we'll see you in a

little bit." Yael gave a little wave then Alexis dragged her from the room, muttering something about getting things over with.

"I've known Alexis her entire life," Eric said as he rapidly keyed in something. "She won't talk unless she wants to, no matter how much Yael prods her."

Isiah lifted a shoulder. "Alexis has made it pretty clear what she thinks of me. She trusts me a little but not too much. She cares enough about what was on that message to want to help me. But as for the rest, I think she's withholding judgment."

Eric snorted a little laugh. "Yeah, that sounds exactly like Alexis. Now let's talk about something a little more interesting. Do you want to see what intel your friend left you?"

"Holy shit, you're in that fast?" he asked, moving across the room to stand behind Eric.

"Not quite, but the relays are working well tonight and I've bounced it off of more than enough locales to cause some serious confusion, but I have one...more...stop...here."

Isiah looked at the screen and saw nothing but code scrolling. Eric keyed in something, waited a few minutes, then keyed in something else.

"What are you doing?" Isiah asked.

"I'm making it look like the connection to Huck's files came from the company's data center. That way, if anyone else finds the file and tries to discover if there has been any other access, it will look like the service provider made a mistake and pinged one of its accounts rather than someone gaining any actual access."

"So the first level of defense is misdirection?"

Eric nodded. "And the second is complete confusion, which is why I have it pinging all over the world."

"I knew enough about computers to be efficient when I was in the service, but not much more than was necessary. That said, your plan sounds like a good one to me."

"Good, I'm glad, 'cause we're in. Now, where should I save it?"

"You have a drive?"

Eric's attention left the computer and landed on him. "You'd trust me? Trust us?"

Isiah studied him. "Is there a reason I shouldn't?"

"No," Eric drew the word out. "I guess I've been around Alexis and my wife a little too much. Neither one of them trusts easily."

"Whether or how much I trust you all is a little moot since you're already in the file and can access it again whenever you want. Just save it to your drive and let's print everything. I want a hard copy that I can review without having to worry about anyone looking over my shoulder."

"You got it." Eric turned back to his computer. "Alexis's family has a private data center. I'll copy the data there, obscure it, secure it, and then block all access except from me. It will also limit *your* ability to access it. I can't give you rights to that data center, but I can't think of a better place to keep it."

"As long as I have a copy, I'm good," Isiah said, but the man was so focused on what he was doing that Isiah was pretty sure Eric hadn't heard him.

Within seconds, the printer kicked in and sheets of paper started feeding through. They were still feeding through ten minutes later when Alexis and Yael walked in.

"That's the info?" Alexis asked, joining Isiah at the printer.

"Yes, almost all of it. How many files are left, Eric?"

"Two," he answered. "That was a short interrogation," he added. Isiah assumed he was talking to Yael, as both he and Alexis had their backs to the couple.

"When there's nothing to hide, it's a short conversation," Alexis shot back. "Sorry," she said, speaking to him. "She's this weird cross between a bodyguard, personal trainer, and mother hen."

"No worries," he said, taking the last of the papers from the feed. "I figure if there's something I should know you'll tell me. In the meantime, I just want to figure this shit out." He held up the papers. "I don't mean to be a downer, but there's a real possibility that someone who I consider a brother is dead because of something in these files."

Alexis's expression softened even as her lips pressed together. "I know, and I hope that's not the case. I'd like to help, if you'll let me. I know Eric has access and could make more copies without you ever even knowing, but I'd rather not go behind your back."

He shot her a grateful look. "I'd appreciate your help. It's been a while since I was in the game, and though some training never fades, there are always new players coming in and I'm nowhere near as knowledgeable as I once was about the underbelly of the intelligence world."

"If you'll allow, I'd like to help, too," Yael offered. Both he and Alexis turned at the comment to find the couple standing side-by-side. "Like Alexis, I hope we can find your friend and that he is well. But as a former member of the intelligence community, I find the fact that this spy might have been, or is being, betrayed by one of his own, unconscionable."

One by one, Isiah looked at the three people waiting for his verdict. His gaze lingered on Yael who, with her connections to a foreign intelligence agency, was the biggest risk.

"You have no reason to believe me, but if we find this man, the one you call The Gentleman, I will keep it to myself. My former countrymen will never know. At least not from me."

"Tell him, Yael." Eric took his wife's hand in his as he spoke. She looked at her husband and the two communicated silently before Eric nodded.

"Huck, he is like a brother to you, no?" she asked.

Isiah nodded. "Serving in the special branches is, well, special. It's different than the lone wolf work intelligence officers—spies—do and it's an even tighter bond than those in the regular ranks. We knew everything about each other. We knew each other so well, we almost became extensions of one another. So yes, he's like a brother to me, and yes, I want to do everything I can to find him—alive or dead—because we don't leave anyone behind."

Yael considered this, then nodded. "Mossad killed my brother when his identity was compromised. We were both with the agency at the time and someone on the inside leaked his name. It was a petty reason, not even motivated by money but by the fact my brother would not marry the man's daughter. And because of this slight, Jacob died."

Yael spoke calmly, but her grip on her husband's hand was tight.

"And it was your brother who paid the price—not the man who sold him out—because he was the one with the most secrets," Isiah said.

Yael gave a sharp nod. "I had been considering leaving the agency when that happened. I'd already met Eric and knew my future was with him. But the day my brother was killed was the day I walked away from that life completely. I'll not do anything to actively harm them, but I'll not do anything to help them either."

"I'm sorry about your brother," he said.

Yael's jaw tightened and she blinked a few times before looking away. "Thank you. I still miss him. It's been fifteen years, and I still miss him every day."

Eric tugged her close and, releasing her hand, he wrapped an arm around her waist as she leaned into him.

"If you're willing, I'd like your help, too," Isiah said.

Yael nodded, her head resting on Eric's shoulder. "Then let's make some copies and see if we can bring your brother home."

CHAPTER FOUR

"WE NEED to focus primarily on two things," Alexis said as she looked around the table at her three cohorts. "First and foremost, we need to find out where the spy Huck referred to as *The Gentleman* is—or where he was three days ago. We know he was in Honduras when Huck recorded the message, but nothing more specific than that. It would be great if we could figure out his real identity, too, but I'm guessing Huck would have mentioned that if he'd discovered it, so I'm not counting on it being anywhere in his files. The second thing I want us to look for is if there is anything in these documents that relates to the Summit being held at Hemmeleigh next year. There's no indication that Huck knew any more about it other than what he overheard, but if it wasn't part of his primary investigation, he might have gathered intel about the event that he didn't know he had."

"Huck mentioned the Summit, but it seems like his comment means something more to you than just an offhand remark?" Isiah asked.

Alexis glanced at him and realized that despite the fact that, as a member of the FBI team responsible for ensuring the safety of the event, *she'd* been living and breathing the upcoming Summit of World Leaders being held at Hemmeleigh Resort on Tildas Island the following May, Isiah had no idea what she and her teammates had been tasked with. It took two minutes for her to update him and when she'd finished, his expression was grim.

"So that's why—or at least part of the reason why—you wanted to go through this information?" he asked, indicating the printed files on the table.

Alexis considered taking offense at the implication of his statement—that she'd had ulterior motives to helping him. But after a beat, she decided it wasn't worth it. "As you said, it's *a* reason I want to know more about what Huck found. It's my job to ensure the security of the Summit, and that's something I take very seriously. But the Summit is eleven months away and I suspect that whatever Rosen wants with the asset is much more imminent. First priority is The Gentleman and stopping Rosen, *then* we will deal with how the Summit comes into play."

She didn't shy away from Isiah's probing attention. She didn't blame him for questioning her motives, but she'd have to let him come to his own decision about her integrity.

Finally, he nodded. Alexis ignored the exhales of Eric and Yael who had, apparently, been holding their breaths during the exchange, but she did shoot them a wry look.

"Isiah, none of us here knows Huck." Alexis eyed the four copies of the files that were stacked on the table. "Based on what you know, do you think we'd be better off dividing the documents and each taking a fourth or do you think he'd arrange his files in such a way that we'll each need to review all the documents to get a clearer picture?"

Sitting across from her, Isiah considered his answer. "I hate to say it, but I think we all need to go through all of the docs. I don't think it will be too convoluted, but between being a SEAL and then working for the CIA, I seriously doubt that he'd store information in a way that was completely linear or organized, in a traditional sense of the word."

"Good, then we all have our marching orders," Yael said, picking up the first page of her stack.

"And let's hop to," Eric added, raising his beer in a mock salute.

There was a round of "here, here's" then for the next four hours, silence reigned with only a background soundtrack of the sound of pens moving across notepads, the rustling of paper, and the clink of glasses against the wooden table.

When Alexis's mind started to wander off task, she rose and murmured to the group that she'd make a pot of coffee. As it brewed, she stepped outside and onto the balcony that wrapped around three sides of the apartment. Several hours earlier, she would have had views toward the west and the magnificent Caribbean sunset. But as it was, she could only see the twinkling of lights from a few houses and the general glow of Havensted, the main city on Tildas Island, emanating from the other side of a small range of hills.

She breathed in deeply, and the air, heavy with scents of the trees and flowers, filled her lungs. At close to midnight, it was still eighty degrees and she was more than comfortable in her shorts and tank top. Over the winter, she'd had a few days where she'd longed to be able to throw on a coat or a cute pair of boots, but all in all, the warmth of the tropics suited her.

Glancing back inside, it was a little disconcerting to see Isiah sitting with two of the people who knew her best in the world. He had his head down and a red pen in his hand, a yellow note pad beside his stack of printouts. He'd had a lot dumped on him in the past several hours, but judging by the looks of it, he seemed to be taking everything in stride.

Everything including what she'd shared about her life. She had to give him credit for not prying. Not much anyway—yes, he'd asked a few questions, but he hadn't pursued those she hadn't answered. And she appreciated his forbearance.

Didn't she?

What if it wasn't forbearance on his part, though, and was just a general lack of interest? Alexis frowned at that thought. The chemistry between them hadn't dulled in the months since they'd seen each other, but that didn't necessarily mean he had any interest in acting on it. He certainly hadn't in December.

But she wasn't the only one who'd changed in the past few months. The night before, he'd been remarkably in tune with her—in tune with her in a way that wouldn't have been possible if he hadn't felt connected to her to some extent. Was it possible that they both might be open to seeing what was between them now?

Her eyes lingered on the man who occupied her thoughts as she considered the question. As she watched him sitting with Yael and Eric, an eager awareness prickled over her skin. Like climbing the uphill of a roller coaster. Half the fun was in the anticipation of reaching the top and the other half was the thrill that came with the freefall and the remainder of the ride. Intentionally or not, last night, they'd both buckled in for the ride. She might not know when they'd tip over the top, but it was inevitable they would.

With that thought, an edgy kind of energy gripped her. She wanted to hit that tipping point *now* and embrace everything that came after. She wanted to feel his skin under her fingertips and his lips against hers. She wanted his smile and to hear his laugh. She wanted it all.

But that wasn't how the real world worked and while she may want all of that, that didn't mean she—or Isiah—was ready for it yet. It also wasn't something she could decide on her own nor was the time right to raise the possibility. After all, they did have a spy to find.

Alexis looked away from the window and back into the

darkness. Telling herself to let things unfold as they should, she pushed all thoughts of Isiah aside and turned her mind to what she'd found so far in her review of Huck's files.

It was clear that, as of a few days ago, the person Huck had been tasked to find had been in the area of Trujillo, Honduras—a small town on the Caribbean coast—and was operating under the name of Sebastian Petrillo, one of the four aliases she'd found for the spy. But what he was doing there she hadn't a clue. Nor did she know if he'd still be there three days later, or what, if anything, he had to do with the Summit.

She was pondering the potential connections to the Summit when the sliding door from the kitchen opened and Isiah stood outlined against the lights pouring from the room.

"The coffee is ready if you want some." His face was in shadows and she couldn't see his expression. He'd been doing a remarkable job hiding the anxiety he felt about his friend. But she'd seen it. It had been in the jerkiness of how he poured a drink, the intentionally casual way he'd spoken with his customers, and the steely calm he projected when talking with Yael and Eric.

"We'll find him," she said quietly, knowing she shouldn't be making that promise, but making it anyway.

"We'll do our best," he corrected. He was right, of course. Huck might already be dead and they'd never find him. But her heart sank a little at his comment, and she ached to reach out and comfort him. And even though what she should be most concerned with protecting the spy and figuring out what, if anything, this business had to do with the Summit, finding Huck felt almost more important. It was something she needed —wanted—to do because it was important to Isiah.

"We'll do our best," she repeated as she moved past him and back into the kitchen. "But I think I'm going to need a little of this," she said, raising the pot of coffee, "If we're going to do that."

* * *

*A*lexis looked up as Isiah sat back in his chair and frowned. "Find something?" she asked.

"When did you say the Summit is?"

"May ninth through the fourteenth, with an arrival reception on the eighth," she answered.

"You found it, too?" Eric said, sliding a sheet of paper into the center of the table. Isiah picked it up, studied it, then nodded.

Two more hours in and they'd nearly finished their individual reviews. They each sat with a pad of paper, filled with notes, beside them.

"Care to tell me what it is?" Alexis reached for the paper.

"It's just a date, May tenth, and a name, Nathalie Rose," Isiah answered, reaching over the sheet to point it out to her. "But some of Huck's research goes back a few years, so I don't know if that date is supposed to be during the Summit, or if it was something from the past," he added.

"I wonder who Nathalie Rose is and if that's her real name," Yael said.

"Or her full name," Alexis said—"Rose" could easily be either a last or a middle name. "I didn't find anything that could potentially relate to the Summit, but it looks like you two got a little farther ahead than I did?" Alexis looked between Eric and Isiah.

"Not much," Eric answered, "But we're all pretty close to the bottom of our stacks so is it time to share, kids?"

"Yes, it's time to share," Yael said, taking the lead. "Your 'Gentleman' has definitely led an interesting life. Based on what I got from Huck's files, this Gentleman seems to work primarily in South America and Africa."

"Africa and South America seem like a big territory," Isiah said. "Then again, I know very little about how the CIA operates. We had our fair share of them coming into the camps or stationed in the towns nearby when I was deployed, but it wasn't like we ever sat down and talked career paths."

Yael smiled at that before continuing. "From a language perspective alone, it would be unusual for an agent to cover more than one major region. That assumes, of course, that he's fluent in not just the dominant languages but some of the dialects as well."

"How long do you think he's been in the business?" Alexis asked Yael.

She frowned and wagged her head. "I'd say roughly anywhere from fifteen to twenty years. Why?"

"It's just a thought, but the identity of a top spy might be a closely guarded secret now," Alexis said. "But fifteen or twenty years ago when he was a fresh recruit, attending training? His records might be buried, but there would have been some evidence of him somewhere."

"It's a good idea," Isiah said. "I don't know how we'd track that information down, but I have to believe that figuring out who he *was* might be easier than finding out who he *is*."

"I can work on that," Eric offered. "I still have those connections at my former company."

Yael nodded in agreement. "And I can ask some of my former colleagues. I still have a few I consider, if not friends, at least trustworthy—those who were nearly as upset as I was at my brother's death."

"Thank you," Isiah said. "I appreciate all you're doing to help me, but I want to be clear on one thing—nothing we do can put this spy at risk. I might not know who he is or who he was, but I have no interest in outing an intelligence asset, even inadvertently," he added.

Alexis sat back in her chair and Puddles took that as an invitation to jump onto her lap. But athleticism was not her forte and she landed with her front paws halfway around Alexis's thighs and her back paws dangling off the floor. Quickly moving to adjust the dog and bring Puddles fully onto her lap, Alexis knocked the small stack of papers that contained the last few pages she hadn't looked at. Two went sailing across the table, leaving the final one in her line of sight.

Her attention landed on a line of text and four rows of numbers. Shifting Puddles, she picked up the paper.

"Oh shit," she said.

"What," everyone at the table responded at the same time.

"Do these look like tide times?" she asked, handing the paper to Isiah.

He frowned and nodded. "They do look like a tidal table, but we'd have to look it up on the internet to find which day."

Alexis took the paper back. "I'm guessing it's the tides for the date you found, May tenth. But what's even more concerning is that." She pointed the name written below the timetable. "Nik Balraj is an explosives expert who likes to hire himself out to the highest bidder. He very nearly killed Damian and Charlotte, twice."

CHAPTER FIVE

"I know this isn't the point, but if he tried to kill your friends twice and didn't succeed, then maybe, if he's being hired to do something on the tenth of May during the Summit, he won't be very good at it?" Eric suggested.

Isiah looked at Eric and wasn't sure whether to shake his head or laugh. On one hand, Eric had a point—how good was an assassin who'd failed twice? On the other hand, he didn't know the whole story behind the bombs and maybe Balraj's objective hadn't been to kill.

"Regardless of how good he may or may not be," Isiah said. "Between the comment Huck overhead and the intel he collected, even if Balraj is terrible at his job, I think it's safe to say that someone wants something bad to go down in May."

Yael nodded. "And we don't know if The Gentleman is trying to stop it or trying to instigate it. Or, for that matter, if he's involved at all. Clearly, they are connected somehow or Huck wouldn't have filed everything together." She gestured to the papers as she spoke. "But we don't know to what extent."

Alexis let out a deep exhale. "Which means we need to find

him. Aside from warning him, we need to find out if he knows anything about this." She pointed to the papers with the tide table and Balraj's name.

"And like Yael said," Isiah continued, "if he does know something, is he trying to start it or stop it? And if he's trying to start it, whose orders is he following?"

"Big questions," Eric said then leaned back in his chair and stretched, reminding Isiah it was well past two in the morning.

"They are," Isiah agreed. "And maybe we should think about them tomorrow?"

Across from him, Alexis shook her head. "You can think about them tomorrow, but tomorrow *I'm* going to talk to my boss. There's enough here that raises questions about the Summit that I think Director Shah will agree to sanction an investigation. If she does that, a trip to Honduras might be in order."

"Trip?" Isiah asked, ignoring her use of "I" rather than "we." Then it hit him what she was saying. "You don't seriously think we can just take off for Trujillo tomorrow, do you?"

Alexis shrugged. "We all know The Gentleman was there three days ago. It's our best lead. It's possible he's gone. Maybe even likely. But do you have any other ideas?"

That was the problem, he didn't. If he had the same access to intel that Huck had, he'd suggest trying to pick up—or confirm —the last sighting of The Gentleman using some other resource. But he didn't. Alexis did, though, which was another reason why her suggestion sounded a little on the crazy side.

"Wouldn't it be easier to try to track him the same way Huck did? Surely you have access to solid intel and good tech people who can electronically pick up this search?" he asked.

Alexis inclined her head. "We do and we will. But it will take them some time to catch up. If we fly out tomorrow we can start looking for him while the computer people do their thing.

If they get any good intel, we'll already be there to act on it. If we wait for them to find him *before* heading to Honduras, there's a greater chance he'll slip away in the time it takes us to get there."

"Or he could be gone already and we'll have wasted a trip," Isiah countered. But at least she was using "we."

"Then he's gone and we're no worse off than we would be if we stayed here. We'll still be waiting for the computer folks to feed us intel. We'll just be waiting there rather than here," she pointed out. And damn if she wasn't right. If the spy was in Honduras, they were better off being there looking for him. If it turned out he'd moved on, whether he and Alexis were in Honduras or on Tildas Island wouldn't matter—they'd still have to jump on a plane and track him.

And when did he start agreeing with her use of "we"? Sure, the "I" had bothered him, but he'd been out of the Navy for eight years, he had no authority and no jurisdiction. Just what did he think he could do? Well, scratch that, he could *do* a whole lot, but should he? Based on what Alexis had said, she made it sound like a forgone conclusion that her team would get involved—but could they even do that in a foreign country?

"I think we should sleep on it and figure it out tomorrow." He didn't know what they'd figure out, but there were too many questions floating around his head and he wanted some time to himself to weigh the pros and cons. He also wanted a little time to sort through the niggling panic that had his chest feeling tight. It hadn't kicked in until Alexis had suggested they fly to Honduras together to track an elusive CIA asset, but now that he was aware of the feeling, he didn't like it at all.

He'd been nervous before—hell, a person didn't have the kind of job he'd had with the Navy without ever being nervous —but this was different. This was Alexis.

The unreasonable fear that gripped him was new, and

frankly, confusing as hell. He might have *known* Alexis for six months, but for all intents and purposes, he'd really just met her the day before. He shouldn't be experiencing this near panic clawing at him, especially not now that he knew she was a capable agent.

But while his mind tried to apply logic to the situation, his body—as evidenced by the tension in his shoulders and the churning of his stomach—had already made its decision. Alexis —and her safety—mattered to him. A lot.

And if that reality was unavoidable, he needed to sort through his shit before he agreed to anything. He sure as hell wasn't going to go on an op with her if he couldn't trust himself to stay focused on the mission and not get distracted by thinking he needed to protect her—especially because, as he kept reminding himself, she could damn well protect herself.

Alexis didn't quite raise an eyebrow at him as his mind performed its mental gymnastics, but it did twitch up. He was pretty sure she was questioning whether or not *she* wanted to be on an op with such an indecisive partner. He could hardly blame her, but he also wasn't going to be pushed into a decision. He'd only agree to go if he thought he could operate at a hundred percent. If not, she'd be better off with someone else. Probably.

"Tomorrow," he reiterated.

She muttered a muffled "Fine," then placed Puddles on the floor and rose from her seat. "I'm going to talk to Shah tomorrow at ten. If you're in, give me a call," she said. *And if you don't, you're out*, remained unsaid.

He understood she needed to bring what they'd found to her boss, but he'd be lying if he said her proclamation, and quasi-ultimatum, didn't bother him. Which was yet another reason he needed to take a few hours to figure out if he could separate what needed to be done from the things Alexis made him feel.

He forced himself to nod, then gathered his set of papers as he rose. "Thank you," he said to Yael and Eric. The couple remained seated, but nodded. "Do you live nearby?" he asked, turning to Alexis who was standing with her hands on her lower back stretching. A thin strip of skin peeked out between the bottom of her tank top and the top of her shorts. He looked away, tapping the papers to align them in a tidy stack.

"I'm good," she said, not answering his question. "I'll stay and help Yael and Eric tidy up."

It was a lie, he thought. Other than putting a couple of glasses in the dishwasher, there was nothing else to do—well, maybe wash the coffee pot. But he wasn't up for arguing with her, so he just nodded.

"Thanks again," he said to the Goodmans. "I'll let myself out."

"You need my number," Alexis said. He turned from where he stood with his hand on the door. "If you decide to go with me in the morning, you need to be able to let me know," she added. He supposed it was her way of extending an olive branch for the abruptness—and finality—of her earlier pronouncement. And though it might seem petty, he wasn't ready to pick that branch up quite yet. The weight of the situation was pressing down on him and he wanted to get away, to be out in the night, in the fresh air and on his own to think.

"Stop by the bar in the morning. I'll let you know then." Then he walked out the door before she—or he—said any more.

Taking the elevator down to the ground floor, he let himself out into the night. Cursing the new moon, he pulled out his phone to use the flashlight. The darkness suited his mood, but between the lack of any ambient light and the looming jungle-foliage on both sides of the streets, he needed the light to navigate the road to The Shack and his apartment that sat above it on the second floor. If he decided to go with Alexis tomorrow, he didn't want to show up at the FBI office with a big-ass bruise on his face because he'd stepped into a pothole and fallen.

He inhaled a deep breath of the tropical air. Ha, who was he kidding? Of course, he was going with Alexis tomorrow. There had never been any question in his mind that he'd see this through, not with Huck's life on the line. But he did need some time to figure out how he'd manage the feelings Alexis elicited from him with the seriousness of what they'd need to do when they reached Honduras.

In the last thirty-six hours every reason he'd given himself to stay away from her had been stripped away. And in that wake, a primal and visceral attraction had taken hold of him, electrifying his senses and bringing his body to high alert. And those sensations only grew stronger the more she let him see into her life. There was something almost unspeakably evocative watching her defend herself against those two men then turn around and snuggle up with a little brown dust mop with a weak bladder. And he wanted to experience more of everything that Alexis was.

But a trip to Honduras wouldn't be a fun-filled vacation where they could spend time getting to know each other, though. He'd need to get his head in the game and figure out how to both tap back into his SEAL training and not let his feelings for Alexis influence his actions. It wouldn't be the hardest thing he'd ever done, not even close. But the situation was both sudden and unexpected, and as the safety lights of The Shack came into view, he admitted it made him uneasy. There was a lot at stake—not just Huck, The Gentleman, and Alexis, but maybe even this fledging *thing* between them, too.

A few minutes later, he let himself in then locked the door behind him. Turning to his left, he unlocked and opened another door then started up a flight of stairs to his studio apartment.

The familiarity of the space calmed him and using only the light he'd left on above the stove, he prepared for bed. Climbing between the sheets a few minutes later, he stared up at the ceiling. After he'd left the Navy, he'd never thought he'd step back into the game, let alone step back in willingly.

But come ten o'clock tomorrow morning that was exactly what he planned to do.

* * *

*H*e was in the parking lot, leaning against the door of The Shack when Alexis drove up in her jeep. He climbed into the passenger seat and couldn't help but notice the way her skirt draped across her thighs, falling into a little vee where they met.

"Sleep well?" he asked, forcing himself to look out the window as she started down the road.

"Well enough. You?" she asked.

"Fine," he answered. Which was the last word spoken for the next fifteen minutes. He didn't know where the FBI office was, but figured, based on the route Alexis was taking, that it was somewhere near the main town of Havensted.

"You okay?" Alexis finally asked.

"What are you going to tell your boss?" he replied, rather than answer her question. He still hadn't quite come to terms with everything that had happened in the last two days—especially the changing nature of whatever was going on between Alexis and him —and talking about it at this moment didn't seem like a good idea.

She paused, as if debating whether to call him on his evasion, but then answered. "I'll tell her what we found last night. After you left, we confirmed the table is a tidal table. Without the year specified, there were a couple of dates it lined up with. One of which is—"

"Let me guess, May tenth," he interjected.

She nodded.

"I know you just learned about Rosen last night, but tell me more about Balraj." When she hesitated, he pressed. "If I'm going to be involved in this, there can't be any secrets. Not ones that relate to Huck or what we learned last night," he clarified. By now, he was well aware that Alexis preferred to keep most things pertaining to *herself* a secret.

After a beat, she bobbed her head. "Fair enough. Do you remember reading about the boat that blew up in the marina last February? And then the one that blew up over by Norman Island not long after."

"Let me guess, those explosions weren't due to mechanical failure as reported in the news?"

She shook her head. "They definitely weren't, but you know, we can't let the tourists think there's a mad bomber on the loose."

"Is that sarcasm I hear, Agent whatever-your-last-name-is?"

She let out a soft laugh at that. "Wright," she said.

Hearing a sarcastic "right," he raised an eyebrow at her. Was she still not going to tell him her name?

She looked at him and shook her head, still smiling. "No, my name is Alexis Wright. With a 'W'."

A wave of relief washed through him that was dispropor-tionate to the minor fact she'd shared. He shook his head at his folly, but the small movement didn't stop him from noticing the slight tightening of her hands on the steering wheel. He didn't recognize her name, but clearly she was waiting for a reaction.

"You catch Balraj?" he asked. Her hands relaxed.

"Unfortunately, no. The Coast Guard wasn't far behind him, but he's from the region and has a network here. You've been here long enough that I'm sure you can imagine how easy it is to slip on and off islands."

They took a hairpin turn and the town of Havensted came into view. He always had mixed emotions about appreciating the beauty of the town—with its well-preserved colonial build-ings and stringent building codes, it was objectively beautiful.

But the wealth of the colonies had been built on the back of the slave trade and the Virgin Islands had hosted some of the biggest slave markets in the western hemisphere in the eighteen-hundreds.

Rather than dwelling on the origins of the island's population, he shifted his attention to its modern-day source of income and commented on the obvious. "There are two cruise ships in town today," he said. No one could miss the two behemoths docked on the western edge of the wide bay.

"Our office is on the north side of town so we'll avoid the worst of the traffic," Alexis responded as she whipped around a corner, startling a rooster who squawked at her as he hustled into the bushes alongside the road. "It's just a few more blocks."

As she navigated the narrow roads, he considered what she'd told him about Balraj. With more of the story than he'd heard the night before, he now had a better appreciation for why she'd been so uncompromising about the need to speak to her boss. Yes, Rosen's activities were important, but Balraj had intentionally tried to kill one of their team—not once, but twice—and still lived to tell the tale. He'd made it personal.

"You said those bombings were four months ago?" he asked as she pulled into a covered parking area on the northern edge of the town.

She nodded.

"Was anyone hurt?"

She hesitated. "Not badly." She'd pulled into a parking spot and was avoiding his gaze as she shuffled around for her purse.

"It was that night, wasn't it?" he demanded, the timeline suddenly clicking in his mind. "That night you came into the bar—the night you had the shiner. *You* got hurt, didn't you?"

She gave him a half shrug as she opened her door. "Like I said, no one got hurt badly. Charlotte was stabbed and I got a little banged up. But we're all fine, now."

She slid from her seat and shut the door behind her, leaving him staring at the empty space beside him. When he didn't immediately move, she gestured for him to get rolling.

He closed his eyes and, taking a moment to let his new reality sink in, he accepted the fact that Alexis Wright—the badass FBI agent who had more secrets than a bank vault, and was hands down the sexiest woman he'd ever met—was probably going to be the death of him.

CHAPTER SIX

ALEXIS SNEAKED a glance at Isiah as they rode the elevator to the fourth floor. The local FBI office was in a newer building in Havensted, and though it looked like a charming colonial-era mansion from the outside, the inside was tricked out with all the bells and whistles of a twenty-first-century office. In fact, it was easily the nicest FBI office she'd ever been in and she'd be lying if she said she didn't feel a special affinity for it—despite it being nothing more than a temporary post.

The elevator door opened and she and Isiah stepped into the lobby. Steven, their receptionist, greeted them with a smile.

"Agent Wright, nice to see you. I thought it was your day off," he said. At five foot ten, clean-shaven, and with baby soft skin, Steven looked ten years younger than his actual thirty-six. Dressed in a lime green button-down, deep purple slacks, and a burnt orange vest, he also looked as harmless as a high school drama student. But in his case, it wasn't just that looks *could be* deceiving, they actually were. Steven spoke seven languages and had been an agent with MI6 before falling in love with a woman who'd come to the Caribbean to study medicine and never left. Alexis had never asked how it came about, but she did know that three years ago, he'd walked away from his career, moved to Tildas Island, proposed to his love, and gotten married. And he'd worked for the Bureau since the week he'd landed on the island.

"It's nice to see you, too. I do have the day off, but I was hoping to speak to Director Shah. Is she in?"

Steven's gaze darted to Isiah before he answered. "I'll buzz you through." He nodded toward the door. "She has an appointment at eleven, but she's free until then. Someone did just stop by to see her, but I don't think that will take very long."

Acknowledging that they might need to wait to see Shah, Alexis nodded then, when Steven unlocked the first of two secure doors, she led Isiah into a hallway. Using her badge to unlock a second door, they proceeded into what some would call the bullpen, but was just a room with five desks scattered around the open space. One wall had a huge picture window that let in beautiful natural light, but the others were lined with offices and a couple of conference rooms.

When the task force had gathered in the building on their first full day on the job, each had been offered an office of their own—a rarity at the Bureau. But collectively—their first group decision—they'd agreed that they'd all rather sit in the open bullpen and use the offices for calls, conference space, or, when working cases, war rooms. The one exception was, of course, Director Shah, who had taken an unassuming office tucked into the corner to the right from where they'd entered.

It was in that direction that Alexis looked first when they entered the space. But seeing the blinds up and the office empty, she looked back to the bullpen to see which, if any, of her teammates might be present.

Jake was leaning against the front of his desk, talking to a woman who had her back to Alexis. The expression on his face hovered somewhere between polite and confused as he said something Alexis couldn't hear. The way the woman stood, her head cocked to the side with one foot curled around the heel of her other, seemed familiar but Alexis couldn't quite place her.

Until she turned around.

Agent Sarah Webster.

"Alexis!" Sarah said, smiling brightly. "I was hoping to see you and say 'hi.'"

With Sarah's back to him, Jake made a face at Alexis and his hands came up in the universal what-the-hell gesture.

Alexis almost laughed at her teammate, though judging by the way Sarah was coming toward her, as if she expected a hug from her colleague, Alexis suspected Sarah thought the smile was for her. Instead of embracing her colleague, she stepped back to stand beside Isiah.

"Sarah," Alexis said. "This is a surprise."

Sarah stopped a few feet away, still smiling, and shrugged. "I'm down here on vacation. I thought I'd stop by and say 'hi' to you and Director Shah. Jake said she stepped out for a minute though."

Behind her, Jake mimicked a baseball base coach, pointing to the exit with one hand and wildly circling the other. Shah hadn't just stepped out, she'd run.

Which didn't sound like Shah, but then again, it was entirely possible that Shah already knew why Agent Webster was in town and just wanted to leave the agent to cool her heels. Because one thing Alexis knew for certain was that there was no way in hell Sarah Webster just happened to be on Tildas Island for a vacation.

"And who's this?" Sarah asked, her eyes drifting over Isiah appreciatively.

Jake cocked his head and silently asked her the same question. He already knew *who* Isiah was, but no doubt Jake wanted to know why he was there with her.

"This is my boyfriend, Clarke." Alexis slipped her arm through Isiah's. As she leaned closer to him, she caught a faint scent of aftershave. Had he smelled this good in the car? She lifted her face toward the collar of his shirt and the bare skin above it, but Isiah gave her arm a little squeeze. "It's my day off," she continued as she put an inch of space between her and Isiah. "I needed to drop off a file and pick up my waterproof earbuds before we head to the beach."

Jake snorted then covered it with a cough. Alexis wasn't the least worried about the way Sarah was eying Isiah, but she'd never trusted Agent Webster and she wasn't going to start now.

"Speaking of which, Babe," Isiah said. "Tony is waiting at the boat, we should get going." He added that last bit as he tapped on his watch. Jake, the thirty-seven-year-old pre-pubescent boy, was now making exaggerated hip-thrusting motions, pointing to Isiah, and mouthing "You the man."

Then suddenly Jake straightened and Director Shah walked into the room.

"Director Shah," he said, his voice as serious as an undertaker's. Shah shot him a look of amusement then, without missing a beat, she came forward. "Clarke, it's nice to see you again." She held out her hand to Isiah. Alexis had no idea where Shah could have been standing to overhear the subterfuge, but she was damn glad both Isiah and Shah were quick on their feet. Not that she would have expected any different, but still, it was nice not to be disappointed.

"Director Shah, good to see you again. You ever get a chance to try that restaurant I recommended?"

"The one over on the point? I did and it was perfect. Thank you," she answered. Then turning to Alexis, she added, "It's your day off. Not that I don't like seeing you around the office, but you know how I feel about taking the time when you can."

Alexis nodded. "I came to grab my earbuds and drop this to you. It's that file you asked me to look at." As she spoke, Alexis handed the manila envelope filled with the papers from Huck's file to her boss.

"And what did you think?" Shah asked.

"I think it's likely the defense will claim diminished mental state, but I think the prosecutors will be able to counter it pretty efficiently. My notes are inside," she said, bullshitting her way through the situation. That Shah also felt it important to keep things hidden from Sarah Webster was something Alexis would ponder later.

"Great, thanks. I'll take a look. Now, weren't you headed out to some beach on St. John or something today?" Shah asked.

Alexis nodded. "We need to swing by Beni's and pick her up then we'll head out." She hoped Shah would pick up on what Alexis was telling her.

"That sounds like a good plan. You three have a good time today. We'll catch up when you're back. I hear the fish tacos at the Island Time bar are amazing," she responded.

"They are and we'll have some for you." Isiah reached for Alexis's hand. "You ready?"

"Let me grab my earbuds," she said, taking two steps toward her desk. Her desk that held no earbuds.

"Here they are." Jake walked toward her carrying a pair. "I used them this morning when I went for a run, but don't worry, I wiped them down after," he added with a grin.

Alexis had no intention of using Jake's earbuds, but still the thought grossed her out. "You better have more than wiped them down," she said. "You better have cleaned the channels and taken off the tips to disinfect them."

"You are by far the pickiest person on the planet," Jake groused. "Can you just take her away for her day off and maybe, you know, *relax her*," Jake gave Isiah a loaded look.

"Thin ice, McMullen," Shah warned.

"For the good of the order, I'm willing to take the risk, Director," he shot back.

Shah shook her head. "You two, get out of here, before McMullen does anything that will land us with a sexual harassment lawsuit." She gestured Alexis and Isiah toward the exit. "Agent Webster, Steven said you're in town for a visit. Why don't we go into my office and you can tell me what I can do for you."

Alexis and Isiah were out the door before Shah and Webster set foot in Shah's office. Five minutes later, they were climbing back into Alexis's car. But before she started it, she pulled out her phone and started typing a quick text to her teammates. She hesitated to add Damian, who'd taken a few days off to spend time with Charlotte, but ended up adding him, knowing he'd be pissed if she left him out of the loop.

"Any interest in telling me what that was about?" Isiah asked as she hit the send button.

"Hell if I know," she answered. And she really didn't have any idea why Sarah Webster was showing up on Tildas Island. She only knew she didn't like it.

"Whoever that agent was, you don't like her," he pressed.

Alexis considered brushing him off, but he'd stepped up to the plate and gone along with her impromptu story and she owed him for that.

"You're right. I don't. I worked with her in the New York office the year before I transferred down here. She'd been in the DC office for a while, but I think she had a mentor or something that decided she needed to get some experience outside of the beltway. Anyway, she never did anything I could specifically take issue with, but she always struck me as one of those agents more interested in whose ass she could kiss rather than what crimes she could solve."

As she answered Isiah's question, she pulled out of the parking lot and headed toward town. "It was weird to see her here. Don't get me wrong, Director Shah's ass is one she'd definitely want to kiss, but I can tell you that she isn't down here on vacation. First, she can't afford it. She has a brother with a gambling problem and more than once she's talked about all her money either going to paying off his bookies or going to his rehab costs."

"And second?"

She refrained from answering as she navigated a particularly tricky intersection that, for some reason, had both a stop sign and a stoplight. "Island charm" is what tourists called it. Most of the locals called it a nightmare. Especially when the cruise ships were in port and none of the visitors knew how to cross the street.

"Second," she said, picking up their conversation once she was on the road she needed to be on. "Second, even if she is here on vacation, I can't imagine why she'd want to stop by the office. Sure, Director Shah is there, but it was just as likely as not that Shah would have refused to see her."

"Would she have come in order to visit you or any of your teammates?" he asked.

"Damian is the only other member of the task force she *might* know because they were in DC at the same time. But Jake was based out of LA, Beni out of Boston, and Dominic joined the Bureau after she'd been transferred up to New York, though he was based in DC. There's no one for her to see except me, and believe me, we weren't enemies, but we certainly weren't friends."

Isiah remained silent as she made a few more turns and inched her way through the cruise ship crowds that swarmed the shopping area of Havensted. She was two blocks from their destination when he spoke again.

"So the sudden arrival of Agent Webster aside, what are we going to do about the apparent reappearance of Nik Balraj and Rosen's plan to compromise an asset?"

She graced him with a quick smile. "Dominic is going to follow our friend Webster to see if we can figure out why she's really here. But in the meantime, we're going to Beni's and as soon as they are able, Jake and Director Shah will meet us there."

"We're doing cloak and dagger shit already and we haven't even left Tildas Island?"

Alexis laughed. "We don't know where Webster is going or where she's staying—not yet anyway—and I don't want her to see us out and about when she thinks we're heading out on some boat. I don't trust her one teensy, tiny bit and so we need to go somewhere we can have the conversation with Shah that we need to, and not worry whether Webster will see us—or worse, overhear us."

"And Beni's is the place to do that?"

Alexis tossed a smile over her shoulder. "To be honest, I'm not entirely sure Beni will welcome having us all invade her apartment. I mean we—the team—have been there, but I don't think Shah has. But to be even more honest, I could use a little bit of fun today and it will definitely be fun to watch Beni get all worked up as we descend on her space."

She sensed Isiah's attention on her and though he didn't know the exact dynamics of her team, he'd been part of an elite team like hers. She trusted that he'd recognize how important the teasing and taunting among teammates was to forming strong bonds—bonds that would serve them well in the field.

After a beat, he shook his head. "You all are weird, you know that? Kind of cool, but weird as shit."

She laughed and he let out a low chuckle, too.

"All the good teams are, Isiah. All the good teams are."

* * *

Isiah followed Alexis into Beni's apartment, a third floor walk-up in a building that had seen better days but more than made up for it with its location in the heart of Havensted. The owners of the six-unit complex hadn't bothered to put much into upkeep but still, Isiah was pretty sure that Beni had lucked out finding the place, given that it was walking distance to both the beach and nightlife spots.

"What's going on, Alexis?" Beni asked as she shut the door and herded them into a small living room with an eat-in kitchen off to one side. A sofa, two upholstered chairs, and a coffee table filled the living area and a bistro-style table and four chairs graced the kitchen area. It was a nondescript room that the agent hadn't bothered to personalize, but it did have a large sliding door that opened to a narrow balcony. If Isiah stood on his tiptoes, he could probably get a glimpse of the ocean.

"A couple of things," Alexis said. "But one can wait until Director Shah gets here."

Beni stilled and Isiah seriously considered whether lasers were going to shoot out of her eyes with the glare she directed at Alexis. "Director Shah is coming here?"

Alexis nodded.

"Bullshit. She doesn't even know where I live."

"Did you really just say that?" Alexis asked. "She knew you were six when you lost your first tooth, of course she knows where you live."

Beni's eyes narrowed to tiny slits, but then abruptly, she swung around and stalked to the kitchen.

"I got home at eight this morning after spending eight hours training the security night shift at Hemmeleigh," she said, referencing the resort where the Summit would be held the following year.

"How'd they do this time?" Alexis asked as she flopped down on the couch. Kicking off her flats, she curled a leg underneath her, obviously comfortable in her prickly teammate's home.

"Better, but that's not the point. Why are you here? Why's *he* here." She gestured to him. Alexis shot him a grin. She was definitely enjoying this.

"Need some coffee, Beni?"

"Fuck off. I need some sleep." At Beni's reaction, Alexis laughed.

"You can sleep once we're all gone. You're going to want to hear all this anyway and would have been pissed off if we hadn't looped you in," Alexis said, rising from the couch. "Isiah, since Beni is incapable of playing the host, please have a seat. Beni, come sit down. I'll make the coffee."

"It's the least you can do. Besides, it's mostly made already, anyway," Beni grumbled as she passed Alexis on her way back to the living room. Beni sank into a chair then tugged a throw pillow out from behind her. Hugging it against her chest, she scrutinized him. "You going to take a seat?" she asked.

He eyed her for a moment, then sat on the opposite side of the same couch Alexis had just abandoned.

"Wait, you said 'once we're all gone.' Who else is coming over?" Beni asked Alexis, glaring in the general direction of the kitchen where Alexis was sliding the coffee pot from the machine.

"Jake will be here, too."

"Dominic?"

Alexis shook her head. "We had a visit from Agent Sarah Webster. You ever meet her?"

Beni considered the question then shook her head. "No, what's she doing on island?"

"Said she's on vacation, but I don't believe her. Neither does Shah, which is why we're meeting here and not at the office. Dominic is going to follow her."

"You all seem awfully blasé about following one of your own," he said.

Both women looked at him, then Beni looked at Alexis as if to ask if she wanted to field the question.

Alexis poured two cups of coffee, then rummaged in Beni's fridge for something. Pulling out what looked like a jar of juice, she proceeded to pour a glass of that as well. After putting the jar away, she brought all three drinks over, setting the two coffees down on the table. "No cream or sugar, Beni doesn't believe in them," she said to Isiah.

"I believe in them," Beni said, picking up her mug and cradling it between her hands. "I just can't be bothered to shop so I'm usually out."

"Anyway, about following Agent Webster," Alexis said, holding her glass of juice and retaking the seat she'd vacated earlier. "You know how in any group there's always that one person or a few people who clearly have their own agenda?"

He nodded.

"It's less of an issue in a corporate setting, but you should know how detrimental it is to teams that need to operate the way ours does—the way yours presumably did."

"By the time anyone got to the teams, those people were usually weeded out. But yeah, I know what you're saying."

"The Bureau is bigger than the SEAL teams. We're elite, but not as elite as the SEALs, and so sometimes agents slip through. Sarah Webster is one of them. I don't like that we have to keep a watch out for people like her, but we'd be crazy not to," Alexis said.

Alexis had a point there, the Bureau was much bigger than the SEALs and with size came more room for error. "Fair enough. But what do you think you'll find by following her?" Isiah asked.

"And you said that I'd want to be looped into whatever it was you wanted to talk to Shah about and I can't imagine Sarah Webster—as interesting as her presence is—rises to that level," Beni interjected.

"You're right, she doesn't. And as for what we'll find by following her?" Alexis shrugged. "Who knows? Maybe nothing. But like I said, I'm not the only one who thinks her visit is weird. Shah does, too."

"And the reason we're meeting?" Beni pressed.

"We'll wait for Shah and Jake to get here so we don't have to repeat ourselves," she said. But she'd no sooner finished her sentence when there was a knock at Beni's door.

Rising from her seat, Beni left the room then came back with Shah and Jake trailing behind her.

"Coffee anyone? Juice?" Beni asked, gesturing Shah to the second chair in the room. Jake looked around then rather than sit between Isiah and Alexis, he grabbed a chair from the dining table.

Shah declined the coffee as she sat.

"Is that Alexis's juice?" Jake asked, eyeing the glass in Alexis's hand. When Beni nodded, Jake accepted the offer and less than a minute later, Isiah was surrounded by three FBI agents and one of the most renowned—and elusive—FBI leaders he'd heard plenty about but never met. Yes, that was a little something he hadn't shared with Alexis.

Alexis had spoken with respect about her boss when they'd been at the Goodman's. But that hadn't been the first time he'd heard Shah's name. Over his more than a decade as a SEAL, he'd heard her name at least a dozen times during his deployments. But it wasn't just the quantity of times her name had been mentioned that had him recalling her, it was also the people who'd spoken about her. Leaders he respected, those at the highest levels, whispered about her—usually with gratitude, but always with respect and maybe even a little awe.

"So, Alexis," Shah began. "Why don't you tell us all about this little bombshell you stumbled across? Pun intended," she added as she placed the file of papers on the coffee table. "By the way, Lieutenant Clarke, it's nice to actually meet you." Shah leaned over and offered her hand.

"Thank you for your help, December fourteen years ago," he said.

She didn't acknowledge the comment, but he thought he saw a little twinkle in her eye.

"You two know each other?" Jake asked.

"No," Isiah answered.

Shah responded at the same time, "We just met today."

Alexis shot him a look that told him he'd need to explain later. He wouldn't, of course—he *couldn't*—but he could tell her it was classified. Technically, he shouldn't have said anything at all, but for two reasons he had. First, the intel he and his team had received that had come from her had helped save lives. He owed her his thanks now that he had the opportunity. And his second reason was because he *liked* this quirky team of FBI agents Shah had put together. As meaningless as it may be, he wanted them to know he had some history with their boss and that he respected her as much as they did. Would it make him one of them? No. But it might make them think of him as something other than an outsider.

"Alexis?" Shah gestured to the folder sitting on the table, prompting her.

Alexis threw him one last look then briefed everyone on what they'd found the night before. It didn't take long, but her delivery of the succinct summary definitely packed a punch and by the time she'd finished, both Jake and Beni were sitting up straight and looking ready to batter her with questions.

"She's told you everything," Isiah cut in before Jake and Beni could begin. "But have a look yourself." He gestured to the file and Beni quickly snatched it up, leaving Jake grumbling beside her.

"So what are you thinking, Alexis?" Shah asked.

"I think we need to go to Honduras. We need to warn the asset—whoever he is—that his identity is at risk and we need to find out what he knows about any plans being made that involve the Summit."

"I agree, but I can't get you clearance to go into the country for at least a few days," Shah said.

"But do you even want to get that clearance? I don't know

how much of this Huck shared before sending it to me." Isiah gestured to the papers Beni was now poring over. "His superiors may already know, or suspect, that The Gentleman is in Honduras and suddenly having a team of FBI agents request extra-jurisdictional authority might raise some red flags."

"That is an issue," Shah conceded. "I can get around it but it might add a day or two."

"Or we could just go," Alexis said. "It potentially has to do with the Summit, which is our jurisdiction. I say we go and ask forgiveness later."

"Or we could go as regular people," Jake suggested. Everyone turned to stare at him. "What?" he demanded at the sudden scrutiny. "All I'm saying is that with the exception of Damian, who took that vacation in February before Charlotte came to the island, none of us has taken a vacation since we moved here last November. What if we take a vacation? To Honduras," he added, no doubt for the dramatic effect.

"Even if we did do that, we can't all go and leave the island without any of us," Beni countered.

"No, but Alexis and Jake could go. And I assume you'd want to go as well, Lieutenant?" Shah asked. "If you did, it would lend credence to the vacation story…a couple of friends taking a few days off."

"Call me Isiah, please, and yes, I'd like to go. I understand that your priority is the Summit, and I support that, but mine is finishing what Huck asked me to do."

"We can take my plane," Alexis offered.

Isiah swung his head to look at her. "Your plane? You have a plane?"

She arched a brow at him. "I *told* you my family has money. We have a couple of planes. One of which is at my disposal and parked at the airport. Mostly because my parents think if it's here, I'll visit them more often. But I hardly ever use it," she added, apropos of nothing.

Isiah scanned the room to see if anyone else thought it a little surreal to have an FBI agent casually talking about using her private plane. But Beni's attention was still on the papers, Shah was staring into the middle space—no doubt calculating their next twelve moves—and Jake looked ready to hop up, head home, and start packing.

"Okay," he drew out the word. "So, as weird as all that sounded, is it a go?" he asked, directing his question to Shah.

"Alexis and Jake, are you both okay with that plan? You won't be completely on your own if something goes sideways, but it will take us longer to coordinate any extractions or assistance, if needed." Shah looked from one agent to the other as she spoke.

To their credit, neither answered immediately. Instead, they looked to each other and did something Isiah had seen—and experienced—a hundred times before. They held an entire conversation without saying a word. After a minute, Jake nodded.

Alexis turned to Shah. "Yes, we're okay with that plan. We understand the risks and if I call my pilot now, we can be wheels up as soon as we can get a runway time."

An hour after setting the plan in motion, he and Alexis were back in her jeep headed toward The Shack. They'd spent some time at Beni's looking at maps and comparing them to the information from Huck's files. They had a pretty good idea of the general location The Gentleman was last in but, as everyone was quick to point out, the information they had was now four days old. They *might* be able to locate the elusive spy, but it was just as likely that he'd already moved on.

"You going to be able to find someone to cover the bar for you?" Alexis asked as they climbed their way to Center Road, the road that ran down the center of the island.

"I already texted Marty and he's fine to cover the front of the house and bar. He has a lady friend who sometimes comes in to help cook. He's going to stop by her place this afternoon and see if she can cover the kitchen for a few days. She's a damn good cook, but she won't cook everything on the menu, so we'll have to make some adjustments."

"Why won't she cook everything?"

Isiah gave a rueful chuckle. "If it's not specific to *these* Caribbean islands, she says it shouldn't be served in a Caribbean food restaurant on *this* island."

"But you're from the Bahamas, surely that means you can legitimately serve Bahamian food?"

"How did you know I was from the Bahamas?"

Her pinky twitched on the steering wheel. She remained silent through a hairpin turn. Then finally, she let out a quiet breath. "Personal security, remember?"

"I remember, but what does that have to do with me?"

She glanced out her side window, more to avoid looking at him than for any other reasons, he'd wager. "When I first moved here, I visited The Shack a few times."

"Five times," he interjected. That got her attention and she cast him a look of surprise before quickly shifting her attention back to the road.

She nodded. "Anywhere that I go regularly, Yael runs a security check on the place, including background checks of the owners and employees."

He had so many questions—"Why" being the most obvious—but he opted to not go with the obvious.

"How the hell does that even work with your job? I can't imagine the FBI would be happy with your personal security inserting themselves everywhere."

He saw the edge of a smile. "They don't know. Shah knows, of course. She pretty much knows everything, but not the rest of them. I made a deal with my parents that when I'm at work, there is to be no interference. But when it's personal, like going to The Shack, or the spa where I get my hair and nails done, or where I shop for groceries, then Yael has free rein. And speaking of Yael, can I ask you a favor?"

"Seriously?"

She shot a worried look at him. "I can't tell if that's a 'seriously, you have to ask if you can ask a favor?' or a 'seriously, you have no right to ask a favor'?"

He chuckled at that. Still a little fascinated by how her personal security intertwined with the professional life she'd chosen to lead, he opted to let her drop the subject for now and go with the flow. "The former. I know your priorities, but as I said, you're also helping me help Huck. That means something to me."

"Is it possible Huck would have gone after The Gentleman, himself?" Alexis asked.

It was a question Isiah had pondered as he'd stared at the ceiling in his bed the night before. "Yes, it is. If he realized that the intel he'd gathered was being used for the reasons we think it was being used, then yeah, I wouldn't put it past Huck to try and right those wrongs and warn him."

"So it's possible we might find him in Honduras."

Isiah looked out the window to the verdant hillsides. "It's possible, but I'm not counting on it. Now what's this favor?" he asked, not wanting to talk more about Huck.

Alexis paused as if she wasn't quite ready to drop the topic, but then she answered. "My teammates don't know about Yael. She'll have to travel with us if we're on the pretense of being on vacation and she'll co-pilot the plane, as well. But I would appreciate it if you would pretend you've never met. Otherwise, it will raise questions with Jake, and then he will needle us both until we want to throw him out of the plane without a parachute."

Isiah couldn't help but smile at that. He'd only caught a glimpse of the agent's personality but, yeah, he could see Jake McMullen doing exactly what Alexis didn't want him to do.

"Will there be anyone else on the plane that I should pretend I don't know?"

She shook her head. "No, Teddy will fly us, Yael will co-pilot, and Oscar will be the cabin attendant."

"How many people does your family employ?" he asked, staring at her.

She lifted a shoulder. "A lot. But several do more than one thing. Teddy is also part of the security team. He lives onsite in the guesthouse and works for Yael. Oscar is the assistant house manager. Rachel manages all the bills, schedules, that sort of thing, but Oscar does all the running around and getting things done."

"You really are loaded, aren't you?" he said more than asked. Of course, he'd known she was, but the way she casually spoke of having staff spoke volumes.

"My parents are," she corrected. "And yes, I know I have massive privilege because of the wealth they've built, but at the end of the day, it's their money." As she spoke, they pulled into the parking lot of The Shack. "Is that going to be a problem for you?" she asked.

He nearly threw out an automatic "no," when something in her eye caught his. She wasn't issuing a challenge in the guise of a question, she looked to be genuinely curious if the fact that she had money—or her family did—was going to be an issue for him.

He'd met a lot of wealthy people on the island, some he even considered friends, but in her question, there was a little something more—something that maybe hinted at the attraction that simmered between them. Almost as if she was trying to sort out whether or not she should squash the fledgling interest.

Biting back his initial response, he shifted in his seat to face her. "I'm not going to lie and pretend it's commonplace for me to be hanging out with someone who has private planes and staff. But those things are only a part of who you are. I already know you must be one hell of an agent to be working with Director Shah, and I also know you have the loyalty of Yael and Eric—yes, they work for you, but they also *care* about you. Those things tell me more about you than the plane your parents gave you. So no, it's not going to be an *issue*. It might be a little awkward for me at first, but it's not going to be an issue."

She studied him for a moment, then gave him a soft smile. "I'm glad."

And suddenly, he was, too. More than her simple statement warranted. But he sensed he'd passed some sort of test—no, not a test, she hadn't asked him the question to *test* him, but maybe he'd—they'd—passed some sort of hurdle?

"I didn't even ask if you wanted to be dropped at home." Alexis leaned forward to look at the bar through the windshield as she spoke. "I just assumed I would drop you here, but do you need a ride home so you can pack? We'll be wheels-up in just over two hours."

Their scheduled take-off time was later than they'd originally planned, but apparently, commercial air traffic took precedence over private planes—a fact he hadn't known before a few hours ago. In the scheme of things, it had been for the best, though, as it gave him and the team more time to plan.

"I live here," he said, answering her question. He wasn't at all ashamed of where he lived, but he did wonder what Alexis would think of it.

"Here?" She leaned forward even more. "Don't get me wrong, the view must be amazing. But where?"

He chuckled. He loved the ingenious design. The angle of the roof and strategically placed eaves all but hid his private quarters from prying eyes. "There's a room on the second floor that runs the entire length of the bar. My closet and the bathroom are the only closed off spaces, and the rest is all open. There is a long balcony that runs most of the length of the building, and there is a massive plantation glass door that opens onto it."

Alexis continued to stare at the building, and he could see her trying to imagine it. He'd take her up there one day, but not today.

"You'd never know there was anything like that over the building," she said.

"I did that intentionally. From the sides of the building, you can't see the balcony. You could if you were down the hill looking up, but it's pretty private."

"And you must have the same view from your home as you do from the verandah of the bar, don't you?"

"I do. Maybe even better since it's not screened in."

"God, I bet that's gorgeous," she all but whispered. A little something inside him shifted at the sound of awe in her voice. His home wasn't luxurious, as he assumed hers was, but that she seemed so taken with the idea of the beauty he woke up to every day told him a lot about her, it told him much more than the fact that she had a plane and staff.

As if realizing he'd seen something in her that she hadn't intended to show, she cleared her throat and sat back. "Pick you up in an hour? Or do you need more time than that? We don't need to show up any more than twenty minutes before our runway time."

But he didn't want her to shy away from being herself—at least not with him. Picking up her hand, he brushed his thumb over her palm. "It is gorgeous," he said. "And maybe, when we're back from Honduras, I can show you."

Her blue eyes held his and slowly, a smile teased her lips. "I'd like that."

He held her hand for a moment longer, absorbing the softness of her skin against his. Then allowing reality to intrude, he released her and reached for the door. "An hour's fine," he said, opening it and sliding out. "And I haven't said it before, but thank you. I know this is all wrapped up in your task force and the Summit and the whole reason you're down here to begin with. But it didn't start out that way. You didn't know what you'd find when offered to help me, and so thank you."

She didn't look away from him and, after a beat, she answered. "You're welcome. See you in an hour?"

He nodded, shut the door, and took three steps back. Then standing in the parking lot of his business, he watched her drive away.

CHAPTER SEVEN

ALEXIS SAT BACK and contemplated the cards on the table.

"You can't win. Admit it," Jake said.

They were airborne, flying at twenty-four thousand feet somewhere over the Caribbean. Yael, Oscar, and Teddy had introduced themselves to Jake and Isiah then promptly set about doing their jobs. Of course, Yael knew the real reason for the trip and Alexis was pretty sure the woman was secretly relishing being part of an op, but for the others, it was business as usual when working for the Wrights.

"Look!" Dramatically, Alexis pointed out the window. "A cloud shaped like a penis,"

Out of the corner of her eye, she saw Isiah look up from where he sat on a couch on the other side of the plane. But to her dismay, Jake didn't take the bait.

"Are you trying to cheat, Alexis Alexandra Wright?" he asked.

She might have thought she could snag a glimpse of his cards while he looked out the window. "Alexandra isn't my middle name."

Jake smirked. "I know. I just like the idea of calling you Alex Alex Wright."

Alexis rolled her eyes and folded her hand.

"Her middle name is Emelia, with an 'E,'" Jake said to Isiah. "I figured if you're going to be her boyfriend, you should know that."

"He's not my boyfriend. I only said that because Sarah Webster is a parasite and I didn't want her to start wondering why I was bringing a retired Navy SEAL into the office." As soon as the words were out of her mouth, she wondered why she'd bothered. Jake knew full well her comment had been nothing but a ruse, but that wouldn't stop him from tormenting her.

"Right," Jake drawled. "It's all because of Sarah Webster." He winked at Isiah.

"For the love of god, Jake," Alexis muttered, then reached for the cards and started shuffling.

"What do you think Shah is going to do about her?" Isiah asked. Alexis glanced up as she bridged the deck. Shah had been suspiciously silent on the topic of Sarah Webster.

"Dominic is still following her. But I know nothing more than that," Jake said.

"Did you ever meet her?" Isiah asked. "I know you worked in LA, and Alexis said Webster was based on DC then New York, but did your paths ever cross?"

Jake shook his head. "Not once, but that's not surprising. So what's the story when we get there?" he asked.

Alexis was used to Jake's abrupt changes of topic, but she saw the momentary blank look on Isiah's face as his mind shifted to the same train.

"I guess I'll be Alexis's boyfriend," Isiah said.

She glanced at him, then dealt the cards. "No, because then that's weird that Jake is there. Jake can be my boyfriend, you can be my brother."

She looked at her cards, not bad, a ten and an eight. When

no one spoke, she raised her head. Both men stared at her. "What?"

"You have a thing for imaginary boyfriends?" Jake asked.

She shrugged. "They're easier to get rid of than real ones. You going to look at your cards, Jake?"

She held Jake's gaze waiting for him to make his play. But instead, he looked over to Isiah. Alexis glanced in the same direction to find Isiah watching her.

"Oh my god, you guys. Get over this. We're on an op," she said, lowering her voice though it was doubtful Oscar, who was in the galley, would be able to hear her over the engines. "Would you two prefer to be a couple and me tag along as the friend?"

The two men looked at each other, then Jake shrugged. "Sure, I'm in if he is."

She had to admit, that surprised her. Not because Jake had any hang-ups, he was the most open—in every way—person she knew, but...why did it surprise her?

She looked at Isiah. "Sure, works for me. Actually makes more sense, since if we run into anyone you know, they'll know you don't have a brother. I mean, at least I assume they will."

He had a point. She'd stayed out of the media for the past twenty-plus years, but if someone recognized her or they ran into someone she knew, they would definitely know she didn't have a brother.

Slowly, she nodded. "Okay, that does make sense. I'll let Yael know. We do have a house to ourselves so no one actually has to share a room or a bed." Oscar had found and rented them a luxury compound. The main house had six bedrooms and the gatehouse had three. She, Isiah, Jake, and Yael would stay in the main house, and Oscar and Teddy would occupy the gatehouse.

"I've slept in worse conditions than sharing a bed with two other people," Isiah said.

"Those early years on the surfing tour were kind of grubby —fun, but grubby," Jake said. "I've shared more beds than I can remember—and not in the fun way—but it will be nice to live in the lap of luxury on an op. That will be a first for me."

"Okay, so I guess that's our story. Three friends, two of whom are a couple, are off for a week of fun and sun in Trujillo. Now, are you going to look at your cards?" she asked.

Jake shot her a look then raised his two cards. Slowly, a smile spread across his face. It was amazing the man was an FBI agent. He had zero game face.

"You're going down, Alexis Julia Wright."

"You're a moron, McMullen."

* * *

An hour later, they landed, and as Alexis stepped out of the door and onto the stairs to the tarmac, she would swear it was ten degrees hotter than on Tildas Island. They were roughly the same latitude, but maybe it was something about being in Central America versus on an island?

"Holy fuck, I'm gonna melt," Jake said, coming to stand behind her.

"Don't be a big baby," Isiah spoke, bringing up the rear. "This is nothing compared to the desert."

"That's *dry* heat," Jake said as they started down the stairs. "Everyone knows dry heat isn't the same as humidity."

"You ever been somewhere where it's 130 degrees?"

Both she and Jake paused and looked at the man.

"You're fucking with us," Jake said. "Nowhere outside the Sahara is it that hot."

Isiah lifted a shoulder. "Sure."

Alexis eyed him then continued to the tarmac. He wouldn't be able to tell them where he'd been, but damn, 130 degrees?

"You're a badass son of a bitch, Clarke," Jake said. "I'm glad you're my man," he added as he looped his arm through Isiah's and smiled at him.

Isiah chuckled. "You *are* a lucky son of a bitch. Now, do we have a car or something?"

On cue, two cars pulled up. One for her, Isiah, and Jake, and another for Yael and Oscar. Teddy would stay with the plane until it was serviced and fueled, and then he'd join them at the villa.

Yael had hired the drivers, but still, it didn't hurt to play it safe. And once seated in the blessedly air-conditioned SUV and through customs, they chatted away, discussing little more than their evening plans.

They debated which beach bars and clubs they wanted to visit—there weren't many in the area, but there were a few—and they may have let drop the fact that they were federal agents. That last piece was a bit of a gamble. Political unrest was a growing occurrence in the country, and letting people know that government agents from the US were in the region could backfire on them. But it could help them, too.

If the man they sought was nearby and heard the news, he might be curious.

And it wouldn't take someone like The Gentleman long to figure out their ruse, which might make him even more curious. And contrary to the saying about curiosity and the cat, sometimes it was a good thing.

Alexis kept her attention focused out the window as they made their way from the airport to the villa. The streets were clean and well organized. It wasn't a wealthy town, but it was pretty. Although, based on the maps they'd pulled up, not far outside the town borders, it transitioned into untamed jungle pretty quickly. Which meant there were probably lots of villages —both mapped and not. Villages they'd need to get some feelers into, somehow.

Thinking it might be a good way to start getting a feel for the outlying villages, she turned toward Isiah. "Should we go on a hike tomorrow?" she asked as they navigated onto a dirt road.

"I'd like to get to know the town," he said, his attention on the scenery. "Why don't we head to town tomorrow, then hiking the day after?" He flicked a glance at her then Jake before switching it back to the roads.

Alexis looked at Jake to gauge his thoughts. They might be FBI agents, but Isiah was the only one among them with experience in gathering intel in a foreign country.

Jake nodded, "Sounds like a plan." He then leaned against the door and caught her eye. Subtly he inclined his head toward the driver. She switched her attention to the man behind the wheel as Jake continued. "I've heard that sometimes the villages around here don't like visitors so it's worth getting the lay of the land before we go traipsing off into the jungle."

The driver glanced at them through the rearview mirror as Jake spoke, but Alexis couldn't tell if that was because Jake's assertion was ridiculous—which was possible, given that she'd heard nothing but good stories about Honduran hospitality—or because he was wondering what Jake was alluding to.

The man's eyes lingered on the mirror for a moment too long and something dawned on Alexis. Pulling out her phone, she jotted off a quick text to Yael.

"You hand-picked the drivers, right?"

Little bubbles appeared, then a response. *"Yes, I thought they might be helpful."*

Alexis smiled at her sneaky-as-shit personal security detail. *"I suspect you're right,"* she wrote back.

"Who are you texting over there?" Jake asked, craning his head to see.

"No one," she answered, slipping her phone back into her purse.

"With a smile like that, that wasn't no one," Isiah countered.

"My boyfriend, of course. He was sorry he couldn't make it," she added.

Isiah's lips twitched, and Jake let out a huff. "You go through men faster than anyone I know. What's he? Like the *third one today*? It's a good thing he didn't come because you probably would have broken up with him on the flight."

Isiah covered his laugh with a cough.

Alexis smiled at her goofy teammate. "What can I say? I'm a woman with a short attention span. Maybe I'll meet someone interesting tonight, though. You never know."

"All I can say is that you need some consistency in your life, so thank god you have me because I'll always love you," Jake said. "And don't you dare hint again that I only love you because you have a private plane. That was *very* unfair of you last time. All I wanted was to go to Miami to see the Justin Timberlake show. You could have just said no."

Alexis snorted and refrained from responding. What could she say? If she started something, there was no way Jake wouldn't finish it, and there were no limits to how outrageous he'd be. She kind of admired him for that—he had zero filter and zero fucks to give. He could be annoying as shit sometimes, but sometimes a little part of her envied the way he moved through life.

Ten minutes later, they pulled through a gate and up to a sprawling villa. From where they parked, and with jungle encroaching on either side of the property, Alexis could see very little other than the multi-story home that spanned the property. But she knew the Caribbean stretched as far as the eye could see on the other side.

Walking through the double doors into the house, they were met by the cook, Maricela, who greeted them with a tray of drinks. The three each grabbed one as the property manager welcomed them, explaining that Maricela had left them several prepared meals in the kitchen that they could heat up, but that she'd be happy to come back and prepare something fresh for them at any time during their stay. He also offered a guided tour, but Jake was the only one interested. The house was gorgeous with no luxury spared, but Alexis had been in a thousand ones just like it. Not that she didn't appreciate it, but she did not need the property manager explaining to her how to work the electronic Toto toilet/bidet.

Instead, she slid the glass doors to the back patio open, kicked off her sandals, and stepped out on to the warm tile. A beautiful pool glistened in the sun before her and beyond that was the beach and the ocean. The only little surprise was that the ancillary building they'd called the gatehouse wasn't actually by the gate, but rather it was tucked into the jungle on the north side of the main house. The entire property—all three acres of it —was walled in, but the walls didn't extend to the sea, so she supposed it made sense to have the gatehouse closer to the beach and its easy access to the main house.

The energy around her shifted and she didn't have to turn around to know Isiah had joined her. A beat later, the heat from his body radiated across her back. He was standing close enough that she could lean back into him. And in her mind's eye, she felt it—felt herself leaning back, felt his arms come around her, felt him pull her against him.

But they had a cover to keep and imagining such things would only make it harder.

"Do you think we'll find him?" she asked instead. No need to identify who they were talking about.

"The driver was certainly interested in our presence," he answered. The low rumble of his voice traveled across her skin and though she couldn't go as far as she wanted, she did lean her head back and rest it against his shoulder. Like a friend might.

"Caught that did you?" she asked on a quiet chuckle. "I texted Yael, she picked him for that reason. Who knows what, if anything, he knows, but he's definitely not on the up and up." Isiah's fingers danced lightly along her lower back as she spoke. Like hers, his touch would look nothing more than friendly if anyone was watching, but her body's reaction definitely didn't fall on the "friendly" end of the spectrum.

"We'll keep our *friends on vacation* cover up tonight since we wouldn't want to be too obvious, but maybe tomorrow night we can start to let it slip." His lips brushed against her ear as his voice washed over her and chills raced across her skin. Alexis took a deep breath and her back pressed into Isiah's chest. Strategically, that might not have been her best move. It didn't help that Isiah's breath hitched at the contact.

Forcing herself to take a step away, she smiled as a bird, bedecked in brilliant green plumage, sailed by. "Jake will be so disappointed."

Isiah took a step back as well and chuckled as the man himself leaned over a railing above them from one of the many terraces that were sprinkled around the house. "Isiah, Babe," Jake called down. "You *have* to come see this shower. It's big enough to fit *all* of us. It will even hold all of Alexis's hair products *and* all your body washes."

Isiah's chuckle turned into a laugh that he tried to hide by ducking his head. "Where the hell did Shah find that guy?"

CHAPTER EIGHT

Isiah leaned back and took a sip of his beer. After a short amble around town, the three of them now sat at a beachside bar sipping on drinks after a monster meal of some of the best fish tacos he'd had in a long time.

In the ambient light cast by the restaurants and bars, kids and adults walked on the beach and danced in the waves. There was an alluring calmness to the town that would have made it easy to let his cares drift away if his "care" hadn't been as important as fulfilling Huck's request and helping Jake and Alexis with this spy business.

As they'd meandered around earlier, they'd made themselves known—subtly, of course, but a few comments here and there about the Bureau had served the purpose of linking them to the FBI. And now they relaxed, just three friends out for a casual night, while they waited to see if anyone interesting would appear.

He had no idea if The Gentleman would try to check them out or, for that matter, if he was even still in the area. But hunting one man in a jungle, with very little intel, wasn't exactly the same as hunting groups of insurgents and terrorists in the desert. And so he had to trust Jake and Alexis on this—and Shah, as it had ultimately been her plan.

He chanced a glance at Alexis, who was staring out toward the ocean. Trying to stay in role, he'd avoided looking at her too much, afraid he'd get sucked in and end up ogling her most of the night. She sat across from him, leaning back in her chair, her long legs crossed. She had on simple black sandals, a pair of cut-offs, and a deep orange sleeveless top. On her wrists hung four gold bangles and around her neck, two gold chains at different lengths.

His eyes tracked the longer of the strands until it came to rest at the small butterfly pendant hanging from the end between her breasts. Her top was made of silk and the thin material cupped and curved with every part of her body that it touched.

He wanted to see her in that shirt and nothing else. No, he *needed* to see her in that shirt and nothing else. Preferably on his balcony, leaning over the railing, with him buried deep inside her from behind.

With that heated image taking root in his mind, and the primal strength of his desire for her, the muscles in his stomach jerked and other parts of his body perked up, too. Right then, he made a promise to himself that when—not if—sex became a part of their relationship, he was going to make sure that little fantasy came true.

Beside him, Jake cleared his throat, and Isiah pulled his eyes away to look at his "partner."

"Another round, folks?" Jake asked.

Isiah nodded, but Alexis shook her head and stood. "I'm going to go for a little walk on the beach."

He didn't bother to hide the scowl on his face as she made her way toward the beach. Though he couldn't help but admire the view.

"If you keep looking at her like that, I'm going to think you don't love me anymore," Jake said with a grin.

Isiah laughed. "Go get me a drink. I'll pine for you while you're gone. Promise."

Alexis kicked off her shoes and stepped into the edges of the water. A couple of kids splashed around her, but her attention was focused somewhere down the beach. He tried to follow her gaze, but the patrons—and the sporadic palm trees dotting the beach—blocked his view.

Not sensing any danger, Isiah returned his attention to the bar. Two older men were conversing, but several others were nursing drinks on their own. There was a table of six in their early twenties who had that "diver" look to them, and what looked like a family celebration of some sort happening at a table for twelve. He didn't speak any Spanish, but whatever it was they were celebrating looked to be a happy affair, and the table had erupted with laughter more than once in the last few minutes.

He let his attention return to the bar as Jake made his way back to the table carrying two bottles of beer. In the few seconds it took the agent to cross the space, Isiah idly wondered who those six people drinking alone at the bar were. Two of the men looked to be in their late sixties, as did one of the women—perhaps this was their local watering hole? The third man appeared to be in his twenties, and the remaining two—a man and a woman—Isiah would place in their forties. Maybe getting some quiet time away from their homes?

"Anyone raising the hairs on the back of your neck?" Jake asked quietly as he set the drinks down.

"Not a one, but then again, a spy wouldn't be a very good spy if he set off people's Spidey senses."

Jake raised his beer in acknowledgment. "That, and it's not like this isn't a little bit of a goose chase. A nice one." He nodded toward the ocean, "But still a goose chase."

"You do what you have to do when you don't have many leads to follow," Isiah countered.

"So, you and Alexis?" Jake asked with a wag of his eyebrows.

"Not going there."

"But you like her?"

"Not going there," he repeated.

"She's fucking hot. I mean, look at her. Her legs are like a mile long, can you imagine—"

"That's your teammate. Show some respect," Isiah cut him off with a sharp glare only to find Jake grinning. "You are such an asshole, McMullen. Anyone ever tell you that?"

Jake took a sip of his drink. "All of my teammates, just about every day."

* * *

The next day they wandered back into town for lunch. After a satisfying—but way too big—meal, they hit the streets of Trujillo.

As they poked in and out of shops, Isiah recognized three men and one woman that he'd seen at the bar the night before. He also saw one of the men from the celebratory table. But they all looked to be doing things that regular people would be doing —chatting on a street corner, grocery shopping, and likely going to and from work.

Around five, they decided to call it a day and head back to the villa to plan their "hike". Shah had picked up some additional intel and there was a small encampment that had shown up on satellite, but not on any map, and she wanted them to check it out.

Before dismissing the driver for the night, Alexis had told him what time they wanted to leave the next morning. She'd also given him the general direction of where they wanted to go —just enough information that if he were at all sketchy, as they all thought him to be, he'd know they were heading close to the encampment. But she imparted nothing so specific as to hint that they were doing anything other than exploring the area and local villages.

Much later that night, and unable to sleep, Isiah slipped out onto the terrace off his room. Clouds were scattered across the sky and they moved over the slim moon casting him, and the villa, into random shadows. But he didn't mind the dark, never had. Many people believed that bad things happened at night, but daylight could be—*was*—as dangerous. And at night, there was something in the lack of light that calmed him. Oh, he'd been through his fair share of hellish nights, but in general, there was nothing quite like the blanket of darkness to soothe his frayed edges.

Unless, of course, Alexis Wright was standing ten feet away on her own terrace wearing nothing but a silk tank top and sleep shorts.

The moon emerged from the clouds and the pale pink of her pajamas lit up in the night. He was glad he'd thrown on a pair of athletic shorts before stepping out.

"Can't sleep?" he asked quietly. She'd come out onto her terrace after him and judging by the slight jerk of her body, she hadn't seen him.

Like him, she took a place at the rail and leaned her forearms on it. "I haven't even tried yet. I was talking to my parents, then Beni called. I don't feel like taking another shower tonight so I thought I'd step out to see if the still of the night would be enough to calm me."

"Feeling anxious?"

She hesitated, then shook her head. "Not anxious. Just all the thoughts running around in my head. I don't sleep well in general, but when I'm in the middle of something, it's sometimes hard to get my head to quiet down."

He smiled at that. His first few years in the service he'd been the same way. But then he'd learned to sleep any chance he got. In some cases, it was a matter of survival. But Alexis's life as an FBI agent was different than his as a soldier, and given the potential machinations of what was going on—a spy, a missing CIA analyst, something with the Summit—he could see why she might have a hard time stopping her wheels from spinning.

"Do you like what you do?" he asked.

She turned her head to look at him, perhaps surprised by the question. Then she nodded.

"I do. I know it probably seems weird that someone like me would want to do a job like this, but I love it."

"Someone like you?"

The clouds moved again, and he saw the hint of a smile. "Yes, someone like me. Someone who owns a plane, can drop ten grand a night on a villa without blinking, and has personal staff."

"Is that why you hide it? Or, I guess 'hide it' isn't the right phrase, but you certainly keep it to yourself."

She looked back to the water. "That's part of it. My teammates do know some of it, though. It was part of the dossiers that Shah gave us on each other when we joined the team. We actually have few secrets from each other. Shah wanted it that way, insisting that the team is only as strong as its weakest point—"

"She's right."

Alexis chuckled, the sound rolling through him. "I think she's pretty much right about everything."

He let out a quiet laugh, too. "Yeah, I think she probably is. But even though your team knows your background, you still keep mostly to yourself. Jake didn't know about Yael until this trip and I'd wager I'm not the only one who you've kept your house a secret from. Why? Do you not trust them?"

She was shaking her head before he'd even finished his sentence. "No, the team is solid. The issue is with me," she said bluntly. "There are reasons I've kept my life private, and I think at this point, it's become more of a habit than anything else. At the risk of sounding like a cliché, it's me, not them."

She cast him a rueful smile, then faced him. The silk of her top hid very little and the sight was spectacular. But as he stared at her, what coursed through his body wasn't just a physical pull. He wanted to be the one that she let in, to be the one that she let see *her*. He wanted to laugh with her, joke with her, love with her, and argue over what to have for dinner or who was going to take the trash out—not that the latter was likely given her staff, but it was more the thought than the reality. He wanted to be someone with whom she could just be *her*.

"What are you thinking?" she asked.

He smiled. "That I'd like to take you on a date when we get done with all this."

She blinked at him. "We've been attracted to each other since the first night I set foot in The Shack. With the tensions and emotions that run hot during an investigation, don't you think that by the time this is all over, we'll be beyond the 'date' stage?"

"Maybe," he said, relieved that she hadn't shied away from the heat between them. "But that doesn't mean I won't still want to do it."

"Why?" She cocked her head and her long hair fell over her bare shoulder. He judged the distance between the terraces. If he jumped, he'd make it. Probably.

He wouldn't do it, though. Now was not the time or the place. But that didn't stop him from letting his mind fill with thoughts of her as he answered. "I have every hope of taking you to bed, or against a wall, or in the water, or wherever. In fact, in the last few days, you wouldn't believe the number of fantasies I've created in my head about us being together. But that doesn't change the fact that a good relationship starts with communication and going on a date is a good opportunity to communicate."

"A relationship?" Her tone told him he'd gone from zero to sixty too fast, but he knew better.

He smiled. "You've already exhausted your cliché quota for the night, Alexis. Don't bother telling me you're not looking for a relationship. I see the way you look at me—I feel it—and it's more than physical attraction that's piquing your curiosity."

She studied him for a long moment, the silence interrupted only by the gentle breaking of the waves. Then finally, she gave him a wry smile.

"Fine, maybe I am curious. About you and what might be between us. We both know there's something there, but neither of us knows if it means anything more."

He inclined his head. "Hence, the date. I have no doubt we'll be more than compatible, physically. But it's up to us to see if it's more than that."

She stepped up to the side of her terrace that was closest to his, and her gaze swept his body, lingering on his shirtless chest before tracing with her eyes the lines of his shoulders, down his arms, to his hands. He could see speculation written on her face —what could his hands do to her, how would they feel *on* her? His stomach tightened and her gaze jerked to his. Her blue eyes held his for an unwavering moment, then she licked her lower lip as she stepped back.

"I suspect you're right about that." Her gaze lingered a little longer. "I think I may need that shower after all." And with that, she walked back into her room, closing the door on his laughter.

CHAPTER NINE

ALEXIS GRABBED THE 'OH SHIT' bar above her seat as they hit a particularly big pothole. Or could it even be called a pothole when the road was dirt? She bounced against Isiah, who sat in between her and Jake, and though he didn't reach out to steady her, he stiffened his body, giving her something to brace against.

Luis, their driver, sat casually behind the steering wheel, looking for all the world like he was driving on a highway. Behind them, Yael and Oscar rode with their driver, Tomas.

Glancing at the map on her phone, they were twenty minutes out from the village closest to the encampment. They planned to grab some lunch there then head out on a hike along the river to a waterfall Tomas had mentioned to them. In reality, once they ate, they'd start in the direction of the waterfall, then switch back and make their way to the encampment.

Closing her app down, she slipped the phone into her pocket rather than her backpack, and looked out the window. There wasn't much to see other than jungle. It was green and vibrant, but so thick she couldn't see beyond four or five feet from the road.

"Is there a lot of subsistence farming here, Luis?" she asked, curious to know if the soil was as good for food as it was for jungle flora.

"Si," he answered, looking over his shoulder. "The land is very—"

But he never had a chance to finish his sentence.

A precise hole appeared in the windshield. The glass cracked in a small spider-web pattern, and Luis was thrown back against the driver's seat. Instinctively, Alexis knew what had happened, even if her mind hadn't fully processed it, and she, Isiah, and Jake all ducked to take cover from any more shots.

The SUV lurched forward, no doubt as Luis's foot jerked against the gas pedal, and veered to the left. There was nothing to do but hope no more shots were fired and wait for the inevitable impact of the car with the jungle. If they were lucky, they'd hit the thick brush which would slow them down, rather than a tree.

As luck would have it, their collision was a little bit of both. The dense foliage slowed them down, but they all pitched forward as the SUV crumpled against a tree.

"Is everyone okay?" Alexis asked, when the car came to a halt. Her face was inches from Isiah's who'd slid from his seat and was now squeezed between the back bench and the console.

"I'm good, just a little wedged in at the moment. You guys?" Jake asked.

Alexis looked up to see a spattering of blood on Isiah's face. "You're bleeding, Isiah."

"It's not my blood and I'm not the only one covered with it," he answered. He managed to get a hand free and brushed it over Alexis's shirt. It came away red. "Luis."

She looked up to see Luis's head canted toward them, blood dripping from an impressive exit wound. "That's a hell of a bullet," she whispered.

"Definitely not some farmer mad at trespassers," Isiah concurred. "Jake, can you open the door? You're closest to cover and I think we all need to make a break for it into the woods. What about Yael and Oscar?" he asked Alexis. As he spoke, Jake managed to get the door open and humid air rolled into the vehicle.

"I heard an engine roar as we started to drift. Alexis, are you sure she's on the up and up?" Jake asked.

It was weird that the other car had taken off, but there were a hundred reasons that might have happened that didn't have anything to do with Yael. Unfortunately, none of them boded well for her.

"First things first," Isiah said. "Jake, how do you feel about being the guinea pig and climbing out? I'd offer to do it, but it would be a hell of lot easier if you did."

Jake let out a dramatic sigh as he twisted from his position and started to inch his way out. "Always taking the easy way out. I don't know Clarke, if this is how it's gonna be, I'm not sure there's much hope for us. After all, I need a partner who isn't afraid to face the hard stuff."

No one did gallows humor—or inappropriate jokes—quite the way Jake did. And despite the fact that their driver had just been shot, they were going to have to hoof it into the jungle, and Yael was nowhere to be seen, Alexis laughed. A tense, uncomfortable laugh, but a laugh nonetheless.

Isiah shook his head. "Get the hell out of here. And be careful."

The lighthearted moment ended as she watched Jake wiggle his way out of the car. Facing her, Isiah couldn't see Jake well, but he had his head tilted and an intense look on his face, as he listened. Jake slid out, grabbed his backpack, then stepped into the shadows of the jungle. Knowing time was of the essence—they had no idea if the shooter was still out there—Isiah quickly followed, pausing only to grab his pack and her hand as she crawled from the floor of the car and stepped out. Slinging her own pack over her shoulder, they joined Jake.

Together, they made quick tracks into the woods. If the shooter was watching, he—or she—would have seen them leave and so, in those first few minutes, they erred on the side of speed rather than stealth. But as they trekked deeper into the jungle, the softer they walked and the more careful they were not to leave too many obvious tracks.

There was generally no cell signal in the jungle, but being the smart agents they were, they'd packed compasses and had saved images of the area on their phones. With his compass in hand, Jake led the way, and because Alexis trusted him—despite his sometimes dubious sense of humor—she followed without question.

Thirty minutes later, they came to a river and Jake drew them to a stop while they were still in the cover of the trees, avoiding the small, but open, riverbank.

"This is the river that flows into the village we were originally headed toward," he said. "If my bearings are right, the encampment is a mile that way." He pointed in the direction of a ridge on the other side of the river.

"Are we going to talk about what the hell that was all about?" Isiah asked. At his sharp tone, Alexis looked over. He was facing the swiftly flowing water, his arms crossed, and his jaw tight. He was angry, but she wasn't sure at what.

"Hard to talk about something when we have no idea what to talk about," Jake shot back.

Alexis stepped into the conversation before Jake said something to *really* piss Isiah off. "We can surmise a few things. Luis was likely the target. It was a hell of a shot which makes me think that if the shooter had wanted to hit one of us, he—or she—would have hit us."

Isiah inclined his head in agreement. "It was a military-grade weapon, too. Any chance it was The Gentleman?"

Alexis glanced at Jake who was looking at the ground. "At this point, anything is possible," she said.

"And Yael?" Jake asked.

Isiah's eyes flickered to her. Jake had no idea how long Yael had been working for her and he had a right to be suspicious. She took a deep breath and responded.

"It's not Yael. She's worked for my family for fifteen years. There was an incident when I was younger. I've had security travel with me ever since." She glanced at Isiah to see his attention zeroed in on her. Unable to take the scrutiny, she switched her focus to Jake who wore an almost exact same look on his face.

"You're going to have to do better than that, Lex." Jake crossed his arms over his chest.

"There's a reason," Alexis said. "But now is not the time or place to get into it. I will say, though, that she goes everywhere with me and has for fifteen years. She's married to my cook, who is also my dog trainer, and her mother-in-law has worked for my family since before I was born. Whatever put Luis in the crosshairs, it didn't have anything to do with Yael other than the fact that she intentionally picked him because he was a little shady and she thought his loose lips might help get the word out about who we are."

She took a deep breath and met Jake's stare. For the first time since she'd met him, his expression was unreadable, and she had a sinking feeling that maybe she shouldn't have kept so much of her life private.

"You have a fucking dog trainer, Lex?" he demanded. "I didn't even know you had a dog, let alone a dedicated trainer. Do you have a little dog? Or is it a big one? I kind of hope it's a big one and I kind of hope it's poorly trained because if anyone needs to be dropped on their ass every now and then it's you. What's the big fucking deal about sharing this shit with us? And why wasn't it in your dossier?"

"It wasn't in her dossier because no one would take an agent seriously who had her own personal security," Yael answered, stepping from the shadows. She'd been so silent in her approach that her sudden appearance startled them all and all three reached for the weapons they carried.

Yael chuckled. "At ease, everyone. Sorry I'm late." She tucked her weapon into the holster at her side as she added, "Our driver heard the shot and panicked. It took me a little while to convince him he needed to stop and let me out."

"What kind of convincing?" Jake asked, his eyes narrowing on Yael.

"Nothing drastic," Yael snapped back. "You okay?" she asked, turning her attention to Alexis. Alexis appreciated how Yael didn't rush to her, but her eyes did do a full inventory. "Whose blood? Luis?"

Alexis nodded.

"How'd you find us?" Isiah asked.

"Alexis has a tracker on her phone that only her parents and I have access to."

Isiah looked at her and Alexis nodded. She also had one embedded in her skin that she could turn on if needed. She always thought that one was a bit of an overkill on the part of her parents, but it was an easy thing to concede in order to give them peace of mind.

"All of this is a lot to process," Jake said, holding up his hands. "So maybe we should try to focus on our original plan and head to the encampment? Granted, we might not have a ride back once we scout the area, but we all have our phones and Oscar and Tomas are still out there, so we can figure that out when the time comes."

Anxious to get the attention off her, Alexis nodded. "I think that's an excellent idea." Isiah stared at her then slowly nodded, too.

She turned to Yael. Yael studied her for a long moment, but Alexis didn't back down from the scrutiny. Finally, the former intelligence agent shook her head. "Your mother is going to kill me, Alexis, but what the hell. Any chance there's a bridge nearby, McMullen?"

They never found a bridge, but they did manage to find a crossing that wasn't too deep or swift—which had the added bonus of allowing her and Isiah to wash Luis's blood off them. Having been prepared for a hike, and having the wherewithal to remember to grab their backpacks, which held water bottles and snacks, the mile they traversed toward the encampment could have been much worse. Oh, it wasn't easy, by any stretch, walking through the jungle carving your own trail up and down hillsides never was, but it wasn't the worst thing she'd ever done.

Yael and Jake had come to some understanding and were jointly leading their little entourage. Alexis followed behind with Isiah bringing up the rear. She was watching where she placed her foot as she climbed a small hill littered with mossy boulders when the heels of Jake's feet came into view. Drawing to a quick stop to avoid colliding with her teammate, Isiah's hands landed on the small of her back, presumably coming to his own unplanned halt.

She looked up to see what had brought Jake to such a sudden stop. Yael was standing at the front, her hand up in the sign to remain still. Then taking a few steps back down from the crest where she'd been standing, she gestured them down. Without question, everyone dropped to their haunches.

"The encampment is there, but I think it might be more than we bargained for," she said in a hushed tone.

"We're not here to do anything other than look around...oh shit, we're going to need to do more than look around aren't we?" Isiah said.

Yael's gaze shifted left, then she took a breath and met Alexis's stare. "From what I saw, I think it's a staging ground for human trafficking. There are three tents, and I could only see inside one. There were four women, all locked in a single cage."

"A cage?' Jake repeated. Yael nodded but kept her attention on Alexis.

"Fuck," Isiah said.

Ignoring the rapid beating of her heart, Alexis spoke. "We have to get them out."

"We can't, Alexis. Not without risking a major international incident," Jake said.

"Fuck that. We are *not* leaving them here," Isiah interjected before she could say anything.

Jake and Isiah shared a look. Jake sighed. "Are you sure they're caged? Are you sure they're being trafficked?" he asked Yael.

Yael's eyes narrowed. "Yes, I'm sure they are caged, but no, I'm not sure they are being trafficked. It's possible they are being used as mules to move drugs."

Isiah let out an exasperated breath. "They're caged, McMullen. Nothing good can come of that." Before Jake could respond, Isiah slipped by him and crouch-walked to the crest. Dropping to his belly, he pulled the binoculars from his backpack and started surveilling. Not a minute later, all four of them were laid out along the ridge.

Sure enough, four women, none looking older than twenty, were huddled in a cage in the tent farthest from them. There were two other cages in the same structure, both of which were empty.

There were four men with guns wandering the camp and every few minutes, a fifth man would pop his head out of the tent closest to them and holler something. Each time, one of the four men walking the grounds would answer.

"Anyone speak Spanish?" Yael asked.

"French, Italian, Portuguese, Swedish, and a little Russian. But you knew that," Alexis answered.

"Pashto and Arabic," Isiah said.

"I feel like I brought a knife to a gunfight with you all. I guess

I'm going to have to be everyone's subtitles," Jake muttered then listened to a little back and forth before filling them in. "The four men keeping watch appear to be more than guards. I think they are each head of a region, and each is responsible for a certain number of women. They haven't said anything specific, but the man in the tent is either the leader or the accountant, and he keeps popping out to ask each man what his count is for the month and when his team will be bringing the goods."

"The women," Isiah corrected. "They're bringing women."

Jake shot him a look then went back to watching the camp through his binoculars. "I get it, Clarke, but those were his words, not mine."

Alexis's attention stayed trained on the women. Two were backed into a corner, hugging each other and the other two, though close by, weren't touching. Three looked terrified while the fourth had an infinitely worse expression—she looked resigned. Alexis could see it in her face, she'd already given up.

"What are they saying?" Alexis forced herself to focus on the situation and not the women. "When are the women that each man is responsible for bringing supposed to arrive?"

"You see the guy walking toward us now?" Jake asked. Alexis switched her focus to a man who looked to be in his early forties, but with his round, pock-marked face, it was possible he was much younger.

"Yes," she answered.

"The four women in the cage are his contribution," Jake said as the man in the tent popped out again, called out a question, then disappeared back into the tent once he'd received an answer. "The one who just answered said his will arrive later today. And the one who now has his back to us, said his will also arrive today. He said he's bringing one more than required."

"One more than required," Isiah repeated. "This is part of a bigger ring and someone is coordinating all this." No one responded to that comment. There was no need.

"And the man who just stepped into the third tent then back out?" Alexis asked.

"It's a woman," Yael said.

That possibility hadn't occurred to Alexis. All four were dressed in the same army green fatigues, all four carried the same weapon, and all four—with the exception of the pock-marked man who looked to be at least fifty pounds heavier than the other three—had roughly the same build. She trained her binoculars on the person in question and magnified the view. There was very little to give her away, but Yael was right—that fourth member of the team was a woman. It was in the shape of her hands and, oddly enough, her eyebrows.

"Then the woman," Alexis said. "What's her timetable?"

"Tomorrow morning," Jake answered.

Alexis shook her head. "If we wait until tomorrow morning when all the women are here to go get help, they might be gone by the time we get back. We can't risk that."

Yael and Isiah agreed.

Jake hesitated. "It's not that I don't want to go in and get those women out, get them to safety and back to their families —assuming they have them—but by tomorrow morning, there will be thirteen more women. If they aren't brought here— somewhere we *know*—then they'll be taken somewhere else. By saving these four today, are we sentencing the thirteen more we know are coming to a life none of us even wants to contemplate?"

"You have a valid point, but I'm not leaving this jungle without knowing those women are safe," Isiah said. "Any ideas?"

They were all silent, and Alexis had no doubt that her colleagues were doing the same thing she was, evaluating the options, considering plans, weighing the risks.

"Two of us could keep watch while the other two hoof it back to the villa and call Shah. She may be able to rustle up a tactical team quickly," Alexis suggested. "I know it's not the best plan because it splits us up *and* because we have no idea if Shah will be able to convince the right people to do the right thing, but it's the plan I've got."

Jake shook his head. "We can't commandeer a US team to come down here. Does anyone know if Shah knows someone high enough in the Honduran military or politics, let alone someone who would care enough about this, to do something?"

Beside her, Isiah huffed a quiet laugh. "The only person who could answer that with any authority is Shah herself. But if anyone were to know who to go to in Honduras, it would be your director. It's a chance, but I'm with Alexis, I don't know what other choice we have."

"Who goes and who stays?" Yael asked.

"No one else speaks Spanish," Jake said. "I think I need to stay. And since Shah is our director that means Alexis needs to go."

"I've been in situations like this before, I can stay with you," Yael offered.

"So have I," Isiah countered. Then looking to Yael, he added, "Don't you need to stay with Alexis?"

"I don't need a babysitter, Clarke," Alexis snapped. "This is work and Yael is officially off duty when I'm at work." Technically—legally—this wasn't work, but the glare she fixed on Isiah dared him to point that out. Instead of the argument she'd anticipated, he grinned.

"Fine, Yael can stay. If you wanted to spend time alone with me so much, all you needed to do was ask."

She opened her mouth to deliver a set down, then snapped it shut when she saw Jake's shoulders shaking with silent laughter.

"Seriously, Clarke," she said. "One jokester is about all I can take right now." Scooting back down the hill, she started digging into her backpack and removing everything that she could leave with Yael and Jake, including her portable phone charger and extra water bottles, protein bars, and clips. They all carried the

123

same weapons and she thought it wise to leave most of their ammunition—though not all—with Yael and Jake.

Isiah joined her and did the same. Then they consolidated the few items they were keeping into one bag and filled the other bag with the extras. By the time they were done, Yael had joined them.

"You'll be careful?" Yael took the bag Alexis held out.

"As careful as we can," she answered. "We'll head back to the road and follow it into the last village we passed through. I think it was five or so miles back. I'll call Shah as soon as I have a signal and fill her in. I know we came here to find The Gentleman, but if things go south with this." She jerked her head in the direction of the encampment, "Then I think it might be best for us to return to Tildas Island. This area will be hot and even if he was still here, he probably won't be for long."

Yael nodded, and Alexis glanced at Isiah. His attention was fixed on the crest where Jake still lay on his belly watching the camp. Isiah had been adamant about not leaving those women. She wondered if seeing them reminded him of his mother, of the myriad ways in which women could be used and abused. Or maybe that hadn't even crossed his mind. Either way, his sincerity and conviction reinforced what she was already starting to believe—that Isiah Clarke was a good man. Oh, she'd known he was, but knowing and truly believing were two different things. One required more trust than the other and that kind of trust didn't come easily to her.

Without another word, she and Isiah started down the hill, back toward the river. When they'd walked a good thirty minutes, Isiah drew to a stop.

She turned to face him. "Water break?"

He shook his head and looked toward the west. "I studied the maps before we left. If we go upstream for a couple of miles when we reach the river, it will put us closer to the village we passed just before Luis was shot."

"Okay," she said, sensing there was more.

"Do you think Shah will have a way of handling this?"

They were getting closer to the matter now. Judging by the way Isiah's gaze kept pulling toward the path they'd just taken, she'd wager he was having a hard time leaving those women's lives to chance.

"If she doesn't, we'll go back and handle it ourselves," Alexis replied.

He searched her face. "You'd do that?"

For many reasons she would, but she didn't want to get into that at the moment and so she nodded.

"I don't think we'll need to. Like you said earlier, if anyone can find a way to resolve the situation, it will be Shah. But we need to get her the information so she can act. The sooner we get her the intel, the sooner we can get back to Jake and Yael and be there if needed."

The look in his eyes softened and the corners of his mouth tipped up. "So you're saying we should get our asses moving?"

She smiled back. "It might be in our best interest."

They reached the river fifteen minutes later and started heading upstream. Alexis glanced at her watch. It was close to four o'clock. They'd make it to the village before dark, but wouldn't be able to make it back. Not without night vision goggles, which, thinking they were only out for a day hike, they hadn't bothered packing.

She looked over her shoulder to raise this with Isiah when he sucked in a quick, sharp breath. Spinning, she saw him clutching his right thigh. She barely had a second to notice the dart sticking out of his leg before a sharp stab pierced her own. And then the world slid into darkness.

CHAPTER TEN

ISIAH WOKE SLOWLY, his muscles protesting even the smallest of moves. Forcing his eyelids open, he stared up at the jungle canopy into the darkness. The sudden realization that he'd lost hours of his life sent a jolt of adrenaline through his system and he bolted upright.

Even as his mind recognized the familiar surroundings—he'd been left where he'd fallen—his first thought was for Alexis. In a near panic, he scanned the area looking for her. He didn't have to look far as she lay on the ground, not two feet away, still asleep.

Or tranquilized, he acknowledged, remembering the dart he'd seen in his thigh just before he'd passed out. Glancing down, he noted it was no longer there and he didn't know what disturbed him more, the fact he and Alexis had been attacked or the fact that whoever had done it had had their hands on his body, and presumably, Alexis's, without either of them knowing.

Forgoing any further thought on that question, he scrambled to Alexis's side and felt her pulse. He let out a breath when it beat steady and strong beneath his fingers. A quick look at his watch told him they'd been out for just under ten hours and it was close to two in the morning. With the difference in their body weights, if Alexis had been tranq'd with the same dose as he had, she'd likely be out for a bit longer. Knowing they couldn't go anywhere in the dark and that this attack had essentially disabled them until dawn, Isiah opted to let Alexis sleep it off while he regrouped.

Unslinging the backpack he still wore, he opened the main compartment. Nothing was missing. Not his phone, not the water bottle, not the extra charger they'd kept. Nothing.

Frowning, he looked around as he contemplated what had happened. If someone had meant them harm, it would have been easy enough to accomplish while they'd both been knocked out. But that hadn't happened. Not only were he and Alexis both essentially fine, all their stuff was still in his possession.

Pondering the situation, he rose from where he sat on the jungle floor and began to pace. Not even five minutes later, Alexis started stirring. Given the short amount of time from when he woke, he wondered if her dose *had* been adjusted to her weight. Which was yet one more unusual thing to consider in this situation.

Her eyes fluttered open and she stared at the sky, much as he had, then, again, much as he had, she bolted upright.

"It's okay," he said calmly, wanting to soothe the panic he saw on her face.

She whipped her head in his direction and stared. He counted to six before he saw recognition sink in and her expression morphed from fear to confusion.

"What the hell happened and what time is it?" she asked.

"We were both hit by tranquilizer darts and it's close to two in the morning."

Her brow dipped as she considered his words. "Did anything

get taken?" she asked nodding to the backpack that lay between them on the jungle floor.

He shook his head.

"And you're okay? We're both okay?"

He nodded.

"So somebody wanted to delay us, but not harm us. Or at least not harm us permanently." She voiced the conclusion he'd come to as well.

"Appears that way."

She glanced around, letting the reality of the situation sink in. "Fuck."

He couldn't agree more, but stayed silent. She pulled her phone from her shirt pocket, glanced at it and scowled.

"Any chance you have a signal?" she asked.

He shook his head. "I looked earlier when I checked the backpack. I think we have at least another mile or so before we're close enough to civilization to get a signal."

"We should have brought a satellite phone," she grumbled.

"Would have been nice, but since we didn't think we'd stumble upon a group of human traffickers or get put down by a tranq gun, I think we can skip feeling bad about that decision."

She slid him a wry look. "No way will we be able to move until dawn. I mean, I think we could pick our way along the riverbank, but the risk of injury is much higher and our rate of progress will be much slower. It will be better to wait."

"My thoughts, too. But here's the million-dollar question—now that the time Shah has to get shit done has been cut by a good fourteen or fifteen hours, will it be enough? Will she be able to do what needs to be done in time to save those women?" he asked.

"Or should we double back and rejoin Yael and Jake and see what we can do ourselves?" she finished his thought. And that *was* the million-dollar question—without a doubt, he and Alexis could make it back to the encampment as soon as it was light. Then they could formulate a plan for freeing the women. But it was risky. The other alternative was to continue as planned, call Shah as soon as they had a signal, and hope she had enough time to do something.

"Realistically, we're not in that different of a situation as before," Alexis said. He looked up and met her eyes, startlingly light in the darkness.

"How's that?"

"We never knew for certain whether Shah would be able to help anyway. She'll have less time to organize now if she can, but we don't know that she can. And we always intended to rejoin Yael and Jake. I vote that as soon as it's light, we head toward the village, but only as far as we need to to get a signal. We call Shah, then head back as planned. She can either get something in place, or she can't. Either way, we agreed that we weren't leaving the jungle until those women are safe."

It didn't take him long to see the truth in her words. Their plan now had a compressed timeline, but it was essentially the same plan.

He nodded. "Sounds good. We have about four and a half hours before it starts to get light. Any interest in a midnight snack?" he asked reaching for the backpack and the protein bars inside.

"If only we had candlelight and a checked table cloth," Alexis said with a smile as she rose. "Nature calls, but as soon as I return, I'll take you up on that generous offer."

* * *

Once the dawn light started filtering over the horizon, it didn't take them long to hike to a spot that had reception. Isiah stood close enough to Alexis so that he could hear her call with Shah without having to put the phone on speaker. When Shah answered, Alexis gave her boss a succinct summary of the situation, answering a few questions along the way and providing specific data—like GPS coordinates of the camp—when needed. When Alexis finished, Shah quickly assured them that she'd reach out to her contacts to see what they could put in motion.

But what Shah didn't do was issue a direct order for Alexis and Jake to stand down. And she hadn't said a word about him or Yael.

By eight that morning, they were on their way back to Yael and Jake. As they left the outskirts of the village, they detoured a half-mile to the west to meet up with the road they'd driven in on the day before. It was a little longer, but they'd agreed that the time they'd save walking on the road more than made up for the additional distance they'd add to the return trip.

They traveled quickly and it was not yet ten when they left the road for the final mile walk through the jungle that would take them to Yael and Jake. Neither spoke the words, but judging by the way they were hoofing it, both he and Alexis were anxious to get back.

Finally, they approached the encampment, slowing their progress and softening their footsteps. By his calculation, they were approximately a quarter of a mile away, or less than ten minutes.

He started to confirm his estimate with Alexis, when, in a heart-stopping moment, an explosion sent vibrations rocketing through the air, shaking the ground under their feet.

Alexis swung around in surprise and the questions he saw written in her expression were probably the same as the ones running through his mind. The explosion wasn't close enough to them to put them in danger, but it had come from the direction of the encampment—the direction of Yael and Jake.

"Shah worked fast," he said.

"I don't know if she worked *that* fast," Alexis countered, then they both started running, not bothering to stifle their footsteps. As they arrived, a second explosion ricocheted through the forest. In addition to the blasts, the sounds of men shouting, women screaming, and gunshots being fired also echoed between the mountains.

They rounded a boulder and started up the hill where they'd left Yael and Jake. And to his surprise, both were still where he and Alexis had left them, flat on the ground, binoculars fixed on the encampment. When they started up the hill, Jake waved them over with a small flick of his wrist.

They crouched to stay below the ridgeline as they jogged up. When they got close, they dropped to the ground and inched their way next to Yael and Jake. Isiah dug the binoculars out of their backpack and handed a pair over to Alexis before focusing his attention on just what the hell was going on below them.

"Whoever it is, doesn't look military," Yael said.

Isiah did a sweep of the area before zeroing in on the unfolding scene. About fifteen people dressed in black had descended on the camp, and the men—and the woman—who'd been patrolling it were fighting back. There were two more guards than the day before, but even so, the fight was now fifteen to seven and Isiah understood why Yael hadn't made a move. If the fighters in black—who appeared to be some sort of militia—were there to rescue the women and could do it on their own, then the four of them would be better off leaving them to it.

Another explosion rocked the hillside on the other side of the encampment and it distracted the man with the pock-marked face enough that someone fired a shot and brought him down. Isiah watched him fall, but then movement on the left side of the camp caught his attention. The accountant ducked into a tent then emerged with a semi-automatic.

"Damn, that might even out the fight," Jake muttered. Until the accountant had emerged, the fight had mostly involved handguns.

"Oh, hell no," Alexis said suddenly as she unholstered her weapon and started to rise. "He's not trying to even out the playing field."

Isiah moved to yank her back down but stopped when he saw what she'd obviously seen. The accountant wasn't going for the fighters, he was going for the women.

In an instant, Isiah was standing beside Alexis as she raised her weapon.

"I'm not disagreeing with your intent, but make sure it's what you need to do," he said. She nodded, understanding that it might be better to wait until the accountant was about to pull the trigger because between right now and that moment, one of the militia might do the job for her and the four of them could remain out of sight.

"I hear you. Be my eyes," she said, keeping her weapon trained on the man as he ducked and dodged the gunfire, skittering around the tents trying to keep cover.

Isiah didn't hesitate and he started scanning the area. It was an incredible show of trust on her part to ask him to keep an eye on the scene while she kept her focus on the accountant. If he saw someone moving in to do the job she was prepared to do, he'd call it and she'd drop her weapon. If not, he'd call that too, and she'd take the shot.

He kept his attention on the encampment. The fighters who'd invaded were doing a good job of holding off the traffickers, but they'd taken a few casualties. From where he stood, Isiah could see four down. Of the six encampment guards, three were down—leaving three still returning gunfire. Those three were doing it well enough that the militia was too occupied to notice the accountant.

Shit.

He'd given orders to kill before but only to his own men. Alexis was trained for this, of course, and taking a life was always a possibility as an FBI agent, but damn did he hate having to make the call. It didn't help that it had been more than a few years since he'd been in this position—a position he never thought he'd be in again. But the accountant was inching closer and the chances of a militia fighter taking him out were slipping with every second.

Isiah did another quick scan of the area as the man rounded the corner of the tent where the women were caged.

"Isiah," Alexis said.

Taking a breath, and focusing on the women, he made the only call he could.

"Take it."

Without hesitation, Alexis fired and the accountant went down. It was a head shot—a damn hard one to make—and the man wasn't going to get up. Without thinking, he placed a hand on Alexis's lower back as they surveyed the scene.

The one woman guard rounded the tent and nearly tripped on the accountant's body. She looked down, then her attention jerked up. And up. Until she spotted them.

She was exposed and knew it, not making any move to raise her weapon as she studied them. Then very slowly, she turned her head toward her left.

On instinct, Isiah followed her line of sight to an old jeep. Energy rippled over his skin and he looked at the woman again. She gave a small jerk of her head in the direction of the ancient vehicle, then ducked out of sight.

"What the hell?" Jake said.

"We need to get the women out. And in that jeep," Alexis said.

"It could be a trap," Isiah pointed out, but more because he felt it needed to be said and not because he believed it. He was as certain as Alexis obviously was that the woman had been trying to tell them something.

"Alexis?" Yael asked.

"I can manage the lock, can you guys cover me? Jake, I may need you to translate," she said.

Jake was coming to his feet, even as he spoke. "This is crazy."

Yael joined them. "Where will we take them?"

"To the villa and then we can see what Shah wants us to do from there," Isiah said.

"Did Shah do this?" Jake asked, gesturing to the encampment.

"We don't think so," Isiah answered. "Alexis talked to her, but she wouldn't have had enough time to organize something like this. And as to why she wouldn't have had time, we'll tell you that story once the women are safe."

"Okay, here's the plan," Alexis said, grabbing her backpack. "We'll make our way to the women's tent. Once there, you three stand watch and I'll get the women out. It will take all four of us to cover them between the tent and the jeep and it's not ideal, but we'll do the best we can. I'll drive the jeep, you three stand guard as we leave."

"And what if there's no key?" Jake asked.

Alexis snorted. "As if you don't know how to hotwire a car. I sure as hell do."

"And quickly, too," Yael confirmed.

Isiah's attention was drawn from the conversation back to the encampment as another round of gunfire filled the area. He didn't like the odds, but he wasn't going to leave the women's lives to chance.

"They're distracted right now, we should go," he said. Alexis caught his eye and she nodded. Without waiting for Jake or Yael to confirm, they started making their way down the hill, taking cover from what trees they could.

When they reached the bottom, no one hesitated and surprisingly, they fell into a natural formation, each of the four covering one direction. They made it to the tent that held the cage without drawing attention to themselves and Isiah gave a silent thanks to the militia for keeping the guards occupied.

A few of the women let out soft screams and whimpers as they entered, but he kept his focus on the surrounding area, trusting Alexis to do what needed to be done.

"Jake, tell them what we're going to do while I get the lock," she said.

Jake started speaking in Spanish and the clunk of metal hitting metal as Alexis managed the lock filtered through the chaos. Not thirty seconds later, the squeak of a rusty door echoed through the tent. He glanced back to see Alexis opening it and a few of the women approaching the tentative freedom.

"Jake, we need to switch positions," she said. "You need to give directions and I'll take the lead as we make our way to the jeep so that I can hotwire it, if needed, while you all load the women."

Isiah didn't think it would be that easy. Oh, the hotwiring would be, but convincing seventeen women—the original four plus the thirteen that had arrived while he and Alexis had been gone—who'd been kidnapped to go willing with four people they didn't know wasn't going to be easy. And sure enough, he didn't know what the women were saying, but he definitely recognized tones of protest emerging from a few.

"Jake?" Alexis said.

"I got this," he replied, then started speaking in rapid, but soothing tones. It took longer than Isiah would have liked, but finally Jake updated them.

"They are wary, but I've told them our plan—to bring them to the villa and then either return them home, if it's safe, or find them somewhere to go—and I've pointed out that they could overpower us, if needed."

"Ask if any of them know how to handle a weapon," Isiah said, sensing a continued caution on their part. He could understand it, but if they weren't committed to the plan, any hesitation could get them all killed.

"Isiah," Yael said.

"Do it," he snapped. As Jake asked the question, Isiah looked over to see Alexis regarding him, her expression filled with a mix of curiosity and respect.

"I do," a woman answered, stepping forward and speaking English.

Not wasting a moment, he motioned her forward. She took a tentative step and then another until she was beside him.

"Can you work this?" He handed her his Glock. She took it, turned it over in her hand, and when she checked the safety, he let out a deep breath. She'd do fine.

She nodded.

"Good," he said. "Will the rest of the women trust us, at least enough to get you all to safety now?"

The woman with long black hair and pale brown eyes said something in Spanish to the rest of the women. Another bit of weight lifted from his shoulders when he saw them nod.

"Yes, we will go with you," she answered him.

He swung his attention back to Alexis. "Ready?"

"You have your back-up?" she asked.

He grinned. "Even better. I'm going to take that semi-automatic from the accountant when we leave the tent."

A beat passed then she smiled. "Nice plan, Clarke. Now everyone, let's move out!"

He snagged the semi-automatic as he passed and then he, Jake, and Yael, surrounded the women as best they could as Alexis led everyone toward the jeep.

They didn't go unnoticed, but the militia managed to engage the remaining guards enough that they were able to get the women loaded into the jeep with only a couple of shots fired by Jake. It was a tight fit getting everyone aboard, but the women sat on laps, on the floor, and anywhere they could squeeze in.

Isiah and Yael took up position, standing sentry on the back corners of the jeep, each with one leg on the bumper and the other inside the back bed. The jeep rumbled to life, and Jake hopped in front. A second later, they were making their way down the pitted and barely-there dirt road that led out of the encampment.

The last twenty-four hours had been more intense than Isiah had anticipated and his body—which was no longer primed for the kind of action they'd seen—was starting to feel the post-adrenaline let down a lot sooner than it should have considering they weren't out of danger yet.

Which was the only explanation he could come up with as to why he missed the guard who stepped out from the trees behind Yael and took aim at the jeep. Isiah's weapon was down, but before he could even raise it, a shot rang out.

He flinched in surprise as the man at the trees dropped, then jerked his head toward the direction from where the shot had come—right beside him. The woman to whom he'd given his gun had her gaze fixed on the place where the man had stood. She was twisted in her seat, and her hands that held the Glock were resting on the back tail of the jeep.

After a beat, she raised her eyes to his. Slowly, he smiled. Tentatively, she smiled back.

"That was a hell of a shot. Thanks."

She blinked and handed the gun back to him. "You're welcome, but I don't think I need this anymore."

CHAPTER ELEVEN

ISIAH FOLLOWED Alexis and Jake into the FBI office exactly three days to the hour after they'd left. It was good to be back on Tildas Island. They hadn't been gone that long, but it had been a hell of a three days. He understood why Shah needed to see them, but he was definitely looking forward to some downtime on his balcony once the debrief was over.

"Alexis, Jake, Isiah," Shah greeted them as they entered the bullpen. Beni, Damian, and Dominic were all present as well, each looking grimmer than the next.

"I'm sorry you didn't have a chance to head home before coming in, but I thought it might be better to get this meeting over and then you can have the rest of the evening off. Tomorrow, too, barring any unforeseen events," she continued.

"Sounds like good news," Jake said, throwing himself into a chair. But he popped back up again. "I need a drink. Is there any of Alexis's juice left in the kitchen?"

Damian nodded and Jake bounded out of the room. That was the second time Jake had referred to Alexis's juice, Isiah filed that random piece of information away as something to ask her later.

They waited in silence while Jake made a run to the kitchen. And even though Isiah wanted to get home, he was hard-pressed to give Jake any grief.

It had taken less than twenty-four hours for an advocacy group to come to the villa in Honduras and take charge of getting the kidnapped women back home—if that was safe—or to wherever they felt they needed to be. It was a complicated process and for the few that didn't have a place to return, the foundation Alexis's parents ran had offered to pay for housing and, if desired, education for the next year. All of the women were offered therapy as well.

It was the best outcome they could have hoped for, but it was still beyond shitty that it had happened and the fact that all Jake wanted was two minutes to get some juice seemed a minor thing. Isiah would have gone for a double whiskey, himself, if he weren't sitting in the FBI offices.

Beside him, Alexis glanced around the bullpen then suggested they move to a conference room where they could all take a seat. She was cool; neither her voice nor her body betrayed any of the stress of the last day, but there was a tightness in her eyes that belied her composure. It was going to take a while for any of them to stop seeing those women in that cage.

A few minutes later, Jake returned with a tall glass and took a seat beside Dominic. "Whatever it is, it doesn't look good, so just lay it on us," he said, speaking to Shah.

A ghost of a smile appeared on Shah's face, then it quickly disappeared. She handed Alexis and Jake each a file. "Sorry, Isiah, I don't have one for you."

He waved her off. He was surprised he was even allowed in the room and he wasn't going to do anything to call attention to the breach of protocol.

Shah leaned back in her seat. "The summary is that while you were in Honduras, we were doing some digging into Angela

Rosen. The man who Huck overheard that day in her office, but didn't see, was Duncan Calloway."

That name obviously meant something as Jake swore under his breath and Alexis went still.

"Calloway?" Isiah asked.

"How sure are you?" Alexis asked.

"Sure enough," Damian answered Alexis first then turned to Isiah. "Calloway was the lead on a World Bank project here in the Caribbean that wrapped up recently. His name came to our notice in an investigation earlier this year. There appeared to be some potential financial misconduct with the project. We didn't find any *actual* misconduct, but there was enough evidence to raise some flags on our part."

"He's an international businessman, though what his precise business is, no one can pin down. He was an odd fit for the World Bank job," Alexis added.

"He was also a fraternity brother of the Vice President and, now we know, in business with Rosen, a traitor," Beni said.

"So, based on Huck's information, we know Calloway and Rosen are working together to orchestrate the sale of The Gentleman's identity. Calloway is connected enough that he could have been the one who found the buyer," Alexis suggested. "Or, I suppose, the buyer could have sought him," she added.

Isiah took in the information coming at him and as he sorted through it, a question arose. "Is it possible that he's the connection to Nik Balraj, too?"

Shah inclined her head. "It's possible, yes. Calloway was in the Caribbean for a little over a year. Long enough to develop contacts. And couple that with Balraj's role in the investigation that initially led us to Calloway, I think it's a safe bet, though we don't have any direct evidence, yet."

"Balraj's role in the initial investigation?" Isiah asked.

Damian nodded and answered. "Charlotte was down here

vacationing with some friends and to make a long story short, they accidentally uncovered something they shouldn't have. Balraj was hired to take care of them—"

"The explosions you mentioned a few days ago?" Isiah asked, turning to Alexis. She nodded. "And Calloway was involved in that?"

"We don't know for certain," Shah answered. "Like Damian said, there are a lot of things about Calloway that don't sit right. But we don't have any evidence of any actual wrongdoing."

"So what's the plan?" Alexis asked before Isiah could jump in with another question. He had several, but he supposed they could wait. It wasn't his job to unravel Rosen and Calloway's relationship and if he was ever going to make it home, letting Alexis and her team get down to brass tacks was the fastest way to ensure that. Besides, if he held his tongue now, it would give him an excuse to spend time with Alexis later. Not that he planned to talk much work once he finally did get time with her —real time with her, like that date she'd promised him.

"Oh, we're not done yet," Dominic jumped in, interrupting Isiah's train of thought.

"Agent Sarah Webster?" Damian asked, looking to him, Alexis, and Jake for confirmation that they remembered the visit. All dutifully nodded, and he continued. "Her mentor is Ronald Lawler. Ronald Lawler is married to Angela Rosen's sister."

Silence fell after that statement and though Isiah had seen the distrust the team had had toward Agent Webster, he was having a hard time following how those two things—Duncan Calloway helping Rosen sell CIA assets and Agent Webster showing up on Tildas Island—could be connected. Other than Rosen herself.

"I never liked Ronald," Shah said. "He's a toady and he's taught his mentees the same." Isiah had to believe that discretion had played a big role in Shah rising to the level she had and her blunt statement surprised him. And if the stares pointed in her direction were anything to go by, it surprised the team, too.

"He lobbied to have one of his mentees on this team," she continued. "I know you all know this, but I don't think you understand the full extent of how unusual this team is—it's an elite team, *you* are an elite team. It would have been a feather in his cap to have one of his mentees selected for this group."

After a beat, Alexis spoke. "But other than both Calloway and Webster—through Ronald Lawler—being connected to Rosen, are there any other links we know?"

Shah smiled. "We were a little busy yesterday smoothing over the incident in Honduras and fielding calls, so we didn't get much further than what we've covered here. But I hear your frustration regarding the gaps in our intel. Beni?" She gestured for the agent to take over.

Beni nodded. "We're going to start by digging into Rosen and the web she lives in. It includes both Calloway and Lawler, but we need to know who else. We also need to each tap into our own intelligence networks to see if there is any chatter about The Gentleman. If we can learn who wanted to buy his identity, we might be able to trace it back to Rosen."

Shah nodded. "I think we can all agree that Agent Webster's visit earlier this week wasn't a vacation. Especially considering that Rosen knows that Huck overheard her mention the island. She's involved in something and we need to figure out what."

"What about the spy?" Jake asked. "Are we going to keep looking for him?"

Shah glanced out the window as she spoke, her voice tinged with regret. "I think we all know that the likelihood of finding The Gentleman now is pretty low. If he was even in Honduras when you arrived, the events of the last few days would have driven him deeper undercover." Shah paused, tapping her fingers lightly on the table. Her team stilled, waiting for her final directives. Finally, she looked up. "We'll keep our eyes open for any signs of the asset—if we can protect him, we will. But I think we're going to have to put our faith in his ability survive. And for now, all roads lead to Angela Rosen. She's our number one priority."

CHAPTER TWELVE

ALEXIS PULLED her jeep to a stop outside The Shack and let out a long sigh.

"You look like you could use a drink," Isiah said from beside her in the passenger seat.

She almost smiled at his comment. The drive from the office had been silent and of all the things that could have been said in the twenty-minute ride, it seemed oddly fitting that those were the first.

"I have a nice bottle of Ardbeg in my office. We could go sit up on my deck, watch the sunset, and not talk," he added.

At that, she did laugh. She was used to being on her own, and talking things out or rehashing events didn't come naturally to her. That Isiah was either the same or recognized the trait in her and was okay with it, made her feel comforted in a slightly uncomfortable, but welcome, way.

Looking at the man beside her, she had to admit—if only to herself—that when he'd handed the woman his weapon as they'd left the encampment, her heart may have tumbled into a little bit of something with him. He'd given not just Julia—as that was her name—a sense of power and comfort, he'd given it to *all* the women. He'd known, or sensed, that's what they'd needed, and he hadn't hesitated. That kind of awareness, that kind of empathy, was rare—especially when packaged together with a man who had the training of an elite operative and the body to go with it—and it was distractingly sexy. And she could use a little distraction about now.

"That actually sounds great." She unlatched her seatbelt as she switched the car off. "Let me text Yael and let her know."

She followed him through the back door and into the building without comment as she texted Yael. She'd just slid her phone into her pocket when Isiah unlocked the door to his office and held it open for her.

Stepping into the room, two things struck her right away. The first was that Isiah was meticulously tidy. And the second was that they weren't alone.

She froze and Isiah nearly walked into her, putting his hands on her hips to steady himself.

"Everything—"

But he didn't finish his sentence because sitting in the chair at his desk was a woman. Not just any woman, but the one who'd been a guard—or trafficker—in Honduras. The one who Alexis would have sworn had tried to help them.

The door to Isiah's office clicked shut as he stepped in front of Alexis, putting himself between her and the guard. The three studied each other in silence. The woman's hands were visible, resting casually across her stomach, no weapon in sight. Her feet were propped up on the desk, and she wore a black tank top, pair of loose-fitting cargo pants, and boots. Her hair fell to her shoulders, framing features that were strong, almost masculine.

"I hear you've been looking for me."

Alexis understood the words but couldn't cipher the meaning. Until she did.

"*You're* The Gentleman?"

At her pronouncement, Isiah's back and shoulders tensed.

The woman smiled. "At your service. Now would you care to tell me why the FBI was traipsing around the jungles of Honduras?"

Isiah glanced over his shoulder at her. His message was clear —he'd follow her lead.

Alexis eyed their guest, weighing the pros and cons. It was possible she was lying about her identity and she was not the spy they sought, but too many pieces of the puzzle clicked into place for Alexis to give that doubt much consideration. She'd not only been in Honduras, as Huck had indicated, but had helped them rescue the kidnapped women—both facts weighed in her favor. And then there was her gender fluidity—such a skill would make her much harder to track than the average asset and it explained how she remained so elusive. And how she'd been so successful over the years.

"Why don't we all sit down and have a drink," Alexis said, her attention fixed on the woman.

"A beautiful woman of business, just my type," she replied with a smile.

"I'll need to get another glass from the bar. I only have two in here," Isiah said, turning his body to half face her.

Alexis switched her attention to him, still keeping the woman in her peripheral vision. "I'll be fine."

His jaw tightened and it didn't take a genius to figure out he didn't want to leave her with their uninvited guest. But after a beat, he nodded, then he shot the spy a warning look before leaving the office to retrieve one more glass. When Isiah returned, he poured three drinks, then he and Alexis took a seat on the couch on the opposite side of the office from his desk.

"So, why are you looking for me?" The Gentleman repeated.

"Because someone in the CIA is trying to compromise your identity and we wanted to warn you." Alexis maintained eye contact as she spoke, looking for any reaction. The only thing she got was a small frown.

"And how did you know I was in Honduras?"

"Who are you?" Alexis countered. "I don't care what your real name is, but I'd like *a* name, since we're getting all cozy and everything."

The woman smiled again. "You can call me Serena. And no, that's not my real name."

"Let me guess, it's safer if we don't know?" Isiah said. Alexis could all but hear the accompanying eye roll.

"Sure, let's go with that. Or maybe just I don't like my given name. Now, how'd you know about Honduras?"

Alexis swiftly sorted through her options before landing on the most efficient. "Isiah, do you have the phone?"

Slowly, he nodded. Then with the barest hint of a sigh, he rose and knelt before a safe. Keeping his back to Serena, he punched in a code and placed his finger on a scanner. When the door popped open, he withdrew both the phone and the files they'd printed from Huck's private drive.

"What's this?" Serena asked when Isiah placed the phone on the desk in front of her. Rather than answer, he played the recording.

Alexis had heard it enough times and so, rather than focus on Huck's words, she watched Serena. Not surprisingly, the spy's expression was so inscrutable that she could have just as easily been watching the trees sway in the breeze as hearing her countrywoman selling her out.

When the recording ended, Isiah slid the phone into his pocket and returned to sit beside Alexis on the couch. An owl hooted in the distance and other than Isiah glancing out the window, no one moved or said anything for a moment.

Finally, Serena let out a huff. "I always knew Angela Rosen was dodgy as shit. Granted—and I shouldn't admit this and blow the whole spy mystique thing—this surprises even me."

"Well, I'm glad I'm not the only one she fooled, but more to the point, I can't tell you how glad I am to find you alive."

The sudden new voice startled everyone. Alexis and she started to rise as she reached for her weapon, but Isiah yanked her down. Serena had no such barriers, though, and she was on her feet with a gun in one hand and a knife in the other.

A man, maybe a few years older than Isiah, stood in the doorway. His beard was scruffy—and not in a stylized way—and his brown t-shirt and tan shorts were loose and frayed at the edges. He held his hands, his empty hands, in front of him, palms out.

"As soon as Serena puts those weapons away, I'm going to beat the shit out of you, then give you a big ol' island hug," Isiah said. "It's good to see you, Huck."

The man grinned at Isiah before letting his attention drift to Alexis. His grin widened and he gave her a wink.

Alexis shot him a flat look. She could have done without the dramatic entrance. "Isiah, would you care to do the honors?" she asked.

"Kevin Karington, may I introduce Agent Alexis Wright and operative Serena Whatever, also known as The Gentleman. Serena, Alexis, this is Huck, the man who kicked this whole thing off." Isiah had leaned back against the couch as he'd performed the introductions and draped his hand along the back, letting his fingers brush her neck.

Serena and Huck eyed each other before Serena lowered her weapons and re-took her seat. The next instant, Isiah was off the couch and embracing his friend.

"What the hell?" he demanded, once they'd parted. "You okay? You need anything?"

Huck shook his head. "It's good to see you, too, man. It's been a hell of a journey down here. The only thing I could use right now is a big glass of water."

Isiah threw Alexis a questioning look. She nodded, and he slipped from the room.

"Not that I'm not pleased to see you alive, but I'm going to need a little more of an explanation from you than I think Isiah will require. I suspect Serena will have her own questions, as well," Alexis said.

Huck's attention darted from one woman to the other, then abruptly, he strode across the room and took a seat in an old wooden chair. Isiah returned with the water and handed it off before retaking his seat next to Alexis.

"Okay, here's the short version," Huck said. "The recording pretty much tells you most of the story that I know. I managed to ditch the SIM card on the phone then make my way to Tildas through a proverbial series of trains, automobiles, and boats. I knew my package would beat me here, but I had hoped to get here in time to pick up the search for Serena," he stumbled over the name a bit. "But it looks like, as usual, Boongy's been more efficient than I gave him credit for and you've already done the job I wanted to get done."

He paused and took a long drink. When he finished, his gaze lowered and rested on the glass in his hands. "When I overheard Rosen that day in her office talking about doing what she intended to do, I wanted to both throw-up and kill her. Not only was she going to sell out one of our assets, but she'd involved me in it, too." He paused, then looked up. "I'm done with the Company, Boongy," he announced. "Any chance you need an extra bartender?"

His words were light, but everyone in the room knew it wouldn't be that easy to leave the CIA. Still, Alexis could see the torment in Huck's eyes as the reality of how close he'd come to being a part of something that went against everything he'd trained for.

"What about Culpepper?" Serena asked.

Huck turned his attention to the woman behind the desk.

"Adrian Culpepper? Was he your handler?" he asked with a frown.

"Was?" Serena clarified, straightening in her chair.

"He died a little over two weeks ago in a car accident," Huck said. "We were told he had a heart attack and his car hit a tree. But if he was your handler, I'm thinking we may not have gotten the full story."

The corner of Serena's left eye twitched, but that was her only outward reaction to the news.

"There's more to it, though," Alexis said. "The man you overheard Rosen speaking to?" She directed her question to Huck, and he nodded. "He's a man we're already familiar with. Duncan Calloway is his name." Alexis knew she was taking a gamble revealing what her team had found. But then again, technically, both Huck and Serena were still federal agents, under oath.

Serena snorted in disgust. "He's a dodgy shit."

"Don't know him," was Huck's response.

Alexis took the next few minutes to fill Serena and Huck in on the Calloway-Rosen-Lawler triangle. When she finished, she looked to Serena, "As I'm sure you can imagine, Rosen is now our primary person of interest, but any chance you've heard of Nikhil Balraj? His name was in Huck's files, but we've encountered him before."

Serena frowned in thought then shook her head.

"He's a bomber-for-hire. He nearly killed a colleague of mine twice last year," Alexis said.

Serena laughed. "He's obviously not very good then, which would explain why I don't know him. I don't do business with second-rate people."

Not that Alexis had expected Serena to know Balraj, but it would have been nice. She also recognized the truth in the operative's statement. Serena hadn't lasted as long as she had by working with people who didn't do their jobs.

"So what's his story?" Serena asked.

"His name, and a date that happens to be during the World Summit the island is hosting next May, appeared in the files Huck had on you."

Serena's attention dropped to the file Isiah had set on the desk. "Hm, yes, I can see why you'd be concerned about both Balraj and Rosen. But maybe we should ask *him* why this information cropped up in his search for me?" She jerked her head in Huck's direction.

"I didn't know who Balraj was until just now," Huck said. "His name came up twice as I was culling through intelligence reports from the area. You're a very difficult person to find, Serena. I'd started looking for you in Africa, then finally tracked you to the Caribbean before narrowing in on Honduras. I culled through a lot of information, reached out to a few of my resources, and as part of that, Balraj's name came up. When it cropped up a second time, I jotted it down along with the date. I didn't know if he was related to anything you were involved in, but I didn't like that his name had popped onto my radar more than once. I figured that once I sorted out where to find you, I could go back and dig into *him*. Of course, then I overheard Rosen's plans and it kind of changed things. I never had the chance to look into him."

Alexis's mind spun with the possibilities. In some ways, it sounded like a bad joke—what do you get when you combine a traitor, a bomber, and a resort full of world leaders? Unfortunately, the possible punchlines were anything but funny.

"First things first," Alexis said. "We need to know everything there is to know about Angela Rosen. From both of you." She gave both Serena and Huck pointed looks. "But I want to call my director; she'll likely want to join this cozy little chat."

"I'm all for bringing Rosen down—along with any and all of her colleagues—but that's your game," Serena said.

Alexis stared at the woman. "For someone whose identity is being sold, you sound awfully chill."

Serena waved a hand. "Rosen is your investigation. She'll never be able to dig up my real identity, anyway, and I couldn't care less who is trying to buy it—there are dozens who would cough up the cash."

"But there is something you do want, isn't there?" Alexis asked cautiously.

Serena smiled. "There's always a trade, darling. I'll help you find out what we can about Rosen and her colleagues, and in exchange, you'll tell me everything you know—and everything you learn—about the trafficking ring in Honduras."

CHAPTER THIRTEEN

IT WAS WELL past midnight when Alexis pulled into her drive. After Serena's quid pro quo offer, she'd called Director Shah, who'd joined them at The Shack to hash out the details. The plan was relatively simple—as far as these things went—and starting tomorrow, Serena would begin an orchestrated dance of reaching out to Rosen, then pulling back, then reaching out again before pulling back. The back and forth would be designed to lull Rosen into believing that Serena was testing out whether or not to trust her. And as for Huck, they'd decided that he'd stay off the radar and essentially play "dead." There'd be no reason for Rosen not to move forward with her plan if she believed Huck hadn't run off and alerted someone about what he'd overheard.

Turning off the car, Alexis smiled, thinking of the four happy dogs who would greet them once they entered the house. But the smile faded when she took in the silent person in her passenger seat.

Isiah had given up his studio to Serena and Huck, and, not wanting him left without a bed to sleep in, Alexis had offered him one of her guestrooms. Glancing over at him as he took in the expansive house, she was pretty certain she'd made the wrong decision. It wasn't that she thought he was going to freak out—he already had a pretty good idea of the luxury she had at her fingertips—but it felt disloyal to her teammates. She'd known them for seven months and not once invited them over. And here she was, more or less days after her first real conversation with Isiah, inviting him to stay the night.

"What are you thinking over there?" he asked in the darkness of the car.

She hesitated. Telling him what was going through her mind would open her up in a way she hadn't been open with someone in, well, ever. In the grand scheme of things, what he was specifically asking, was a small thing. But to her, it was the equivalent of turning the knob and cracking open a door she hadn't ever considering opening.

"Alexis?"

His voice rumbled softly through the car and she contemplated how, even in such a short time, he'd shown her the kind of person he was—honest, empathetic, and confident without being arrogant. He was a *good* person. Not to mention she was ridiculously attracted to him. The strain of working with the kidnapped women had kept her focused on work these past few days, but now they were home...she *wanted* to open that door.

She took a deep breath and looked at him. His dark eyes met and held hers. "I don't invite people home with me," she said.

His brows came together. "I have two CIA spies staying at my house—both of whom I'm not sure are one hundred percent sane. You offered me a bed to stay in, not a one night stand."

At that, she smiled. "I appreciate you not making any assumptions about my offer to stay here. But that's not what I meant. What I meant was that I *literally* don't invite people over. In the seven months I've lived here, I've never asked any of my teammates over. I have friends at the shelter that I spend a lot of time with on my days off and I've never invited them over either. I mean, look at this place." She gestured out the window. "It's a prime spot for a high-end fundraiser, and while I'm not interested in loaning it out for that kind of thing willy nilly, I *know* the shelter and the work it does and the people who are committed to it. Offering to host something like that seems like something I should do, right?"

Isiah studied her for a long moment. It was interesting that other than a general sweeping glance of her home, he hadn't stared or gawked. With three stories, a three hundred and sixty degree view—not that they could see that at this time of night— and a flowing lawn and large pool, it was definitely gawk-worthy. With his SEAL training, he would have taken in more than a usual person, but still, he seemed more curious than awed.

"We'll talk about the fundraiser thing later because it seems like something you'd like to do but maybe haven't admitted to yourself yet, but tell me what's at the core of what's making you uncomfortable in this moment. Is it having *me* here? Or is it more fundamental than that? Like, regardless of whether it was me or Serena or Huck or anyone else, this would be a big thing for you?"

Her heart rate kicked up a little at the question that stripped everything down to the real issue. She took a steadying breath and answered. "The latter," she all but whispered.

Slowly, he nodded his understanding. "You're a rational, intelligent woman, Alexis. There has to be a reason you've never invited your teammates—who I know you also consider your friends—over."

In an instant, her mind flashed back to when she'd been eleven years old. Happy and carefree in the way that only a well-loved child could be. Summers with her grandparents in their summer house on the sea in Sweden, endless days of swimming and horseback riding, and countless sleepovers. But then that naïve carefreeness had vanished in minutes. And left behind the beginnings of the woman she was now.

She liked who she was now. She truly did. But sometimes she missed that carefree, laughing girl she'd once been.

She let out a quiet sigh. "There is. And it's kind of a long story."

"They usually are," Isiah said, his lips tipping into a knowing smile of acknowledgment.

A small chuckle escaped her. "It's not *that* long, but I think it might be time to share it with the team. And you, too."

Surprise flashed across his face when she included him, and his expression softened.

"Any time." He reached across the console and picked up her hand. Bringing her palm to his lips, he brushed a soft kiss in the center before setting it back down on her leg again.

His movements had been slow but deliberate and she wasn't sure if she was glad for that or not. Had he lingered with his mouth so close to her palm, she would have brushed her fingers across his cheek and cupped his strong jaw. From there, with her skin touching his, it would have been so easy to draw him into a kiss. She wanted to kiss him—she craved that connection to him—but she knew that if she and Isiah walked that path it would be more than a casual affair. And though she was drawn to that—to him—her years of keeping most people at a distance gave her pause. Not because she didn't want to open that door and travel that path, but because if she was going to, she wanted to do it right. And that meant she needed to lay, if not all, at least some of her cards on the table.

"I know this may sound weird, but I feel like I need to tell my team first. Or maybe not first, but at least at the same time. You're right in that I consider them friends and I think a few of them might feel a little put out if they aren't the first to hear it."

It was Isiah's turn to chuckle. "Jake?"

She returned his smile. "And probably Dominic, too. Beni would be a little pissed, but she'd get over it."

"And Damian?"

"He's the only one who I know for a fact would just nod, says 'thanks for telling me,' and move on."

"In the brief time I saw you all interacting, I can see that. So," he said, returning to the topic with a nod toward the large double-hung mahogany front door. "Are we ready to go in? You okay with it?"

Her eyes flitted to the door and she nodded. "I need to invite everyone over for a barbeque tomorrow or something. But yeah, I'm ready to go in now."

He didn't give her a chance to second guess herself, and before she was done speaking, he was swinging the car door open and stepping out. By the time he snagged his bag from the backseat and rounded to the driver side, she was standing on the flagstone drive.

"Barbeque sounds good. I'll even cook. In the meantime, why don't you tell me what exactly I'm stepping into," he said, gesturing in a circle to their surroundings.

His words could be taken in more than one way, but the smile on his face led to only one conclusion—he still couldn't quite take it all in, but he was game if she was.

* * *

*A*lexis answered his unasked question as they stepped through the door. "My parents bought this place a little over twenty years ago."

Isiah paused and took in the massive foyer. The ground floor of the home was built somewhat into a hill and it was obvious that this entry level, though grand, wasn't the main living area of the house. The floor was travertine tile, as it was with many of the houses in the Caribbean, and in front of him was a huge mahogany "Y" staircase. On either side of the staircase, against the back wall of the house, were two hallways, one running in each direction.

To his left was a wall with a huge black and white print of a city street scene—likely somewhere in Europe, judging by the architecture. On the wall to his right hung another scene, though this one looked to be somewhere in the rural south of the US, if the cotton field in the distance was anything to go by.

"That's Stockholm. Where my mom grew up." Alexis pointed to the cityscape. "And that's an area south of Savannah, Georgia, where my dad is from," she said, indicating the other picture. "There are two bedrooms that way," she added, pointing to the left. "And a media room, that way," she said, swinging her arm in the opposite direction. "The floor above us is the main social area. It has the kitchen, living room, my office, that kind of thing. And the third floor has four more bedrooms."

She'd barely finished her sentence when three dogs came barreling down the staircase in a cacophony of nails against bare wood. Isiah cringed at the thought of the damage being done to the floor, but Alexis didn't seem to notice as she dropped to her knees and welcomed all three dogs into a big group hug.

Isiah watched in awe—knowing he was seeing a side of Alexis very few had the privilege of witnessing—as she rubbed and petted and talked to each dog, telling them how much she missed them and what good boys and girls they were. The dogs danced around her, tails wagging, tongues licking, and noses nudging her for more love.

Glancing up, he noticed a fourth dog hanging back on the landing of the intersection of the staircase. Reddish in color and not particularly big, the dog stood still, watching the scene below, much as Isiah had.

"Alexis."

From her position kneeling on the floor, she looked over her shoulder at him even as the dogs continued to jockey for her attention. He nodded toward the staircase. She looked in that direction and smiled.

"Hello, Red," she said. The dog's tail waved once. "How's my pretty girl doing?" Again a single tail wag. In the meantime, a small brown and white dog that looked to be the youngest of the bunch, and one who Isiah would swear was smiling, wandered over to meet him. He knelt to pet the puppy as he watched the dog on the stairs.

"Eric said you had a good day yesterday," Alexis crooned to Red. "Did you have fun dipping your feet in the pool?" That question got her three wags of the tail. "Yes, he said you had a good time swimming with George here."

"George? Red?" Isiah asked as another dog made its way to him and joined the puppy in sniffing him out.

Alexis rose as she spoke. "That's Red, at the top of the stairs. She's painfully shy but incredibly sweet. We're trying to get her to come out of her shell, but her early years were hard and it's going to be tough. That's George." She pointed to the black and white dog. "And that's Allie and Howdy," she added, pointing first to the black and tan adult dog then to the puppy.

"All foster dogs?" he asked, giving Howdy one last pat before rising himself.

She nodded. "Allie and George will likely be heading to Miami in a month or so to be adopted up there. Red, we're still not sure about."

"And Howdy?"

She cocked her head as she looked at the little dog who was now sniffing his shoes. "Howdy is, well, we're not sure yet. There are a couple of options we're looking into."

Something in her voice caught his attention, but when he looked at her in question, her expression told him they'd discuss it later. He wasn't sure why, but it also wasn't a big deal and so he picked up his bag and gestured toward the staircase.

"Wait, you didn't turn off an alarm when we came in. I have a hard time believing that you don't have one."

She laughed. "Oh yes, there's an alarm. My security team would have turned it off when they opened the gates at the bottom of the driveway. Teddy shares security duties with Mac and both live in the gatehouse."

He had noticed the building when they'd come through the gates and remembered Alexis mentioning Teddy living onsite. "Makes sense, but do you need to turn it on now that we're inside?"

"There are alarms—both pressure-sensitive and motion-detecting around the entire perimeter of the property." They started up the stairs as she answered. "Once we get ready for bed, I'll turn the house alarm on. It's not motion-detecting inside, but all the doors and windows are wired. It can tell the difference between whether a door or window is opened from the inside or outside, though, so even if the alarm is on, if we open a door to, say, step out onto the balcony, the alarm won't go off."

As she finished, they stepped onto what he'd call the ground floor. Given the design of the house, this level, with its expansive kitchen and living area, flowed out onto outdoor patios on each side, and a balcony stretched along the front.

"What if we step outside, shut the door, then open it from outside when we need to get back in?"

Alexis chuckled. "I had the exact same question," she said as she bent down to give George a head rub. George, Allie, and Howdy were still circling their heels while Red hung back, watching them from the living room. "Do you want any water or anything before we head to bed?" she asked.

When he shook his head, she led him down a short hallway. A floating staircase lined a wall that ran parallel to the back wall of the house—a wall that was made entirely of windows. It was an unusual construction—to have so many windows that weren't viewable from any of the main living spaces. But he supposed that in the day, they let in a lot of light that was diffused and soft, rather than glaring.

"As to your question, yes, they will go off in that scenario if you don't re-open them correctly. I hope you don't mind, but Yael scanned your thumbprint into our system. There's a pad on each door. If you put your thumb on it when you open it, it will recognize you."

They reached the top floor and the wide, wood plank floors of the landing. He walked toward a glass and metal railing and looked over, down into the living room below. Turning his back to it, he noted that, similar to the entry level, there were hallways headed off in each direction along the back of the house.

"My thumbprint? Do I want to know how she got that?"

Alexis pursed her lips and for the first time, looked a little concerned. "I know we should have asked…"

Yes, they should have. Or at least told him it was a condition of staying here. But then again, he wouldn't have said no. And, more importantly, it meant that she trusted him to be here.

"It would have been good to know, but it's not a big deal," he said. She searched his face and for the first time, he glimpsed a hint of vulnerability there. Yes, in the car she'd voiced her doubts and her questions, but this was a different kind of vulnerability. One that told him that it mattered to her if she'd upset him.

Slowly, he walked toward her, his bag brushing his side with each step. When he was close enough, he cupped her cheek with one of his hands. "Like I told you earlier, this will take some getting used to, but it's not going to scare me off. *I* know you're safe with me and I hope you know it, too. But if your security team needs my fingerprints to confirm that, I'm not going to get all het up about it. There's a reason for your security, and hopefully you'll share that with me some day, but in the meantime, I wouldn't be worth your time if I put up a fuss about people who love you trying to keep you safe. And I want to be worth your time."

He could feel her rapid pulse under his fingertips, and her blue eyes never wavered from him. Slowly, he lowered his lips to hers and kissed her. She opened to him willingly, and he finally got a taste of the heat between them. But only just a taste. By unspoken agreement, they kept this moment gentle, a tentative exploration of their physical and emotional connection.

When he pulled back, she looked more confident and a small smile teased her lips. "Thank you."

"For?"

"Understanding. For not freaking out. For not letting this," she said, making the same circular gesture he'd made outside, "get to you. Then again, with your background, probably not a lot gets to you," she added, giving him a full—if somewhat rueful—smile.

He chuckled and stepped back. To some extent, she was right. As a SEAL he'd seen enough of humanity and inhumanity that the daily ups and downs of civilian life didn't warrant getting too worked up about. But in other ways, she was dead wrong. Because *she* got to him. Got to him in ways no one else had. Her intelligence, her competence, her moments of vulnerability, drew him in. And though he was careful not to show it, he was fighting some strong caveman instincts when it came to her. He didn't want to possess her or control her, but wanted *her* —in every way possible.

Taking another step back, he forced his desire to the sidelines. At least for the moment. "So, want to tell me which guestroom I'm sleeping in?"

CHAPTER FOURTEEN

ALEXIS WANDERED into the kitchen at a little after eight the next morning. As usual, Eric was already there prepping meals for the day. She glanced at the calendar on the wall—yes, she kept an old fashioned paper calendar—and noted that today was one of the days Eric delivered lunch to the shelter staff. The shelter's funding was below the national average, and because most people who worked there were volunteers, twice a week, Eric prepared big lunches and took them over as a gift of gratitude for the work they were all doing.

"Coffee?" he asked as he diced an onion.

"I'll get it," she mumbled as she walked by him. Then she backtracked. "Where's Red?" she asked. Howdy, George, and Allie were all lined up on the other side of the room, just outside the kitchen—all were eagerly watching Eric, hoping for treats no doubt, but still obeying the "no kitchen" rule.

Eric looked up, smiled, then gestured with his head toward the patio that was visible through the floor to ceiling windows and sliding door. With his back to the house, Isiah sat, gazing out at the view, a coffee cup in one hand and his other hand resting atop Red's head as she sat beside him.

"Holy shit," she whispered.

Eric let out a soft laugh. "I know. He was already out there when I came in for the day. I let the dogs out after feeding them and brought Isiah some coffee when I let these three back in. Red seemed curious, though, so I left her out. Took her about ten minutes to approach him, but they've been sitting that way for at least fifteen minutes."

Alexis stared at the man in the chair. As she watched, he lifted his hand ever so slightly, then replaced it and rubbed Red's head. Red gave the smallest of flinches when Isiah's hand reconnected with her head, but then, as he rubbed, her tail swished across the floor.

"That gives me hope that we might be able to get through to her," she said.

"Either that or Isiah is going to find himself with a dog," Eric countered.

"That might not be such a bad idea." Alexis smiled at the thought as she headed to the coffee maker. It wasn't hard to imagine Red hanging out with Isiah at The Shack. She might not ever make a good restaurant dog, but hanging out alone in Isiah's apartment above the bar while he worked wouldn't be a bad life for her. Alexis wanted to see her be more comfortable socially, but the reality was, Red might not ever be that kind of dog. And if spending time on her own, in a place she felt safe, and with a person she trusted was the right fit for her, then Alexis wanted to make that happen.

After brewing her coffee, Alexis made her way to her office and placed the first set of phone calls that she had on her schedule. Shah had directed her and Jake to take the day off, but there were still things she needed to get done, like invite all her teammates over to dinner. She hoped Isiah would be able to join them. He'd offered to cook, of course. But she wasn't sure if he'd been serious, and given that he also had a business to run and had already been gone for a few days, she couldn't blame him if he needed to attend to his own life.

By the time she was done making the calls to each of her teammates, she was laughing to herself. She loved them all, but they were so predictable.

"That sounds like a good way to start the day," Isiah said from the doorway.

"Come in." She waved him over with a smile. "It is. I invited everyone over for dinner tonight and their reactions made me laugh."

"In a good way?" he asked, taking a seat.

She nodded. "Dominic asked if I had a swim-up bar in my pool and if so, whether it was stocked or not. Keep in mind, he doesn't even know if I actually have a pool or not. Damian simply said 'Sure' then asked if he and Charlotte could bring anything. And Beni sounded suspicious as hell."

"And Jake?"

"I think I woke him up. God knows what he did last night to blow off steam after what happened in Honduras. But he grumbled something along the lines of 'It's about fucking time. I'll be there at six,' then hung up on me."

Isiah laughed. "That sounds like Jake. So what are your plans for the day?"

She sat back in her chair and tucked a leg underneath her. "Before we get to that, will you be able to make it tonight? You've been away for a few days and Marty's been running the place, so I don't want to assume. But if you can, I'd love for you to join us."

"You going to tell everyone why you haven't invited them before?" As he spoke, Red wandered by the door and Isiah gestured her in. The dog hesitated, her eyes studying Alexis, then she inched her way in just close enough for Isiah to rest his hand on her head again.

"I think you have a friend," she said with a soft smile. In reply, Isiah gently stroked Red's soft fur. "As to your question, yes, I'm going to tell them. But we can discuss it later if you have to work. It's not a secret." She paused, then rephrased that because in fact all the records around the events that had happened were sealed. "Actually, it is a secret. But it's one that I can share with you all."

"I'll be here. What time?" he asked without hesitation.

"You sure?"

He nodded. "Wouldn't have said I'd be here if I wasn't sure."

Fair enough. "I told everyone six. Knowing Dominic, he'll show up in swim shorts with a bottle of tequila at five."

Isiah laughed. "I'll come at five and help prep. I can cook."

She shook her head. "You don't have to do that. Believe it or not, I can cook, but Eric is here today, too. It is his job, and he'd be crushed if I didn't ask him to take care of the food for my first, well, I guess you could call it a party. Seriously, I'm not just saying that. He'd be really hurt if I didn't ask him," she added when the expression on Isiah's face told her he wasn't entirely sure he believed her.

"Fine, then. I'll come at five and we can sit outside and have a cocktail while Dominic makes a fool of himself in your pool. Do you think he's going to pretend he's in an episode of MTV Cribs or something?"

Alexis laughed. "That, or he'll be scripting out his run on The Bachelor. With Jake egging him on once he gets here."

"I can definitely see that," Isiah said, with a shake of his head. "So now that that's settled, are you actually going to take the day off?"

Alexis glanced away.

"Alexis?"

She met his gaze and made a face. "Sort of?"

"Sort of?" he repeated.

"Serena and I are meeting for lunch at Toto's and then going for a walk along the beach after."

Toto's was a beach bar thirty minutes from her house. It had amazing fish tacos and an even more awe-inspiring beach.

"A CIA operative and an FBI agent having lunch and a walk. Sounds positively casual. Like there will be no work talk going on," he teased.

Alexis offered him a cheeky grin. "Just girl talk. Assuming girl talk includes chatting about traitors who sell government secrets."

"If you go get your nails done together, maybe you'd even have time to cover the topic of human trafficking, too?"

Laughing, Alexis threw a pen at him. "Don't you have work to do or something?"

He caught the pen mid-air and rose from his seat. Red skittered backward but stopped her flight at the door. Rounding the desk, Isiah pulled Alexis up and slipped a hand around her waist, the other held her against his chest.

"You'll be careful?" he asked.

With her body flush against his, her pulse skittered into an erratic beat. She wasn't used to a lot of physical contact in general—yes, she'd had her fair share of sexual partners over the years, but this kind of physical contact was different. It wasn't a means to satisfy a physical urge or a step to finding some kind of release. No, this kind of contact was intimate, it *meant* something. She raised her hands and flattened them against Isiah's chest, feeling the definition of his muscles under her palms.

"Alexis?" His voice had dropped.

"Hmm?" she managed to say as she absorbed the feel of him against her—their hips pressed together, his fingertips brushing the skin above the waistband of her shorts.

"Are you ever going to kiss me?" he asked.

His fingers continued to brush the skin at the small of her back, and she became aware of every muscle in his body, how it tensed and adjusted with her every move, her slightest touch, as if he were poised and ready. The heat in his eyes stole her breath and Alexis suddenly realized that the man standing before her was keeping his desire—his need—for her on a very tight chain. He *wanted* her. Fiercely.

Without hesitation, she slipped a hand behind his neck and pulled him down into a kiss. This one wasn't sweet and gentle as the one before. No, this one was pure fire.

In an instant, his hand was splayed under her shirt across her back while his other cupped her backside and pulled her tight against him. Their tongues danced and battled and tasted and explored as she drew her fingers across his back, against his bare skin.

Then suddenly he was gone. It took her three breaths to realize he now stood two feet away. They were both breathing hard and her attention drifted lower as he adjusted himself in his shorts. As he did, all sorts of images flooded her mind. And as she let those images take root, so too did the knowledge that nothing was going to stop her from what she planned to do next.

"Alexis." His voice held a soft note of pleading. "We're in your office. The door is open. Stop looking at me like that."

Her eyes flitted up to meet his gaze. His words might be conveying one thing, but his eyes were telling her a whole different story.

A smile teased her lips. "Oh, I'll stop looking at you. At least at parts of you." And before he could stop her, she dropped to her knees and lowered his shorts.

"Holy shit." The words whooshed out of him as she took him in her mouth. But he didn't try to stop her. Instead, he leaned a hip against her desk, bracing himself with one hand while the other threaded through her hair. As she tasted every inch of him, he continued to mutter words to her—coherent words of encouragement mixed in with a fair bit of curses along with sounds she couldn't make out. Not in any language anyway— but the meaning was most definitely clear.

"Alexis," he hissed, tugging at her hair, letting her know he was close. Rather than pull back, she took him deeper. And he came hard, calling her name. Then kissing a spot to the side of the trail of hair down his belly, she pulled up his shorts and rose.

His hand had fallen from her hair and his arm now hung by his side. His eyes were closed and his chest was moving rapidly under his shirt.

"How was that for a kiss," she said with a smile as she brushed one more across his lips, then danced out of the way as his arm came up to encircle her. His eyes flew open and he straightened up from the desk.

"I'm going to head to the shelter today before meeting Serena at Toto's. I should go get ready. Don't you need to head back to The Shack? Check in with Huck and Marty?" She was taunting him. And enjoying it.

He stalked toward her. She could have bolted out the open door, but she was more than looking forward to seeing what he'd do when he caught her. And catch her he did, backing her against the floor-to-ceiling bookshelves that lined a side wall.

Bracing a hand on either side of her, he leaned in, forcing her to tip her head to meet his gaze.

"That *kiss* was far more than I had in mind, Alexis," he nearly growled.

She waggled her eyebrows at him. "I know. I also know you enjoyed it."

He let out a rueful laugh. "I guarantee that your mouth *anywhere* on my body is going to be something I enjoy, but yes, that was fan-fucking-tastic."

"Then why so growly?" She raised a hand as she spoke and trailed a finger along his jaw. The muscle twitched under her touch.

"Because you're right. I *do* need to check in on Marty and Huck and The Shack. But now I have to do it all with the image of you on your knees in front of me haunting me all day."

She laughed. "Surely, there are worse fates than that?"

The smile he gave her was feral. "Oh, there are. And turnabout is fair play." Then he leaned forward and whispered in her ear every little thing he planned to do to her later that night. When he finally finished and pulled back, her breathing was rapid and she was so turned on she was legitimately surprised she didn't orgasm on the spot.

He pushed away from the wall and started to walk away. Pausing at the door, he looked back. She was still leaning against the bookshelves, trying to get her breathing under control.

"And Alexis?"

She managed a nod.

"Don't take care of things yourself. And don't deny that you were thinking about it," he said with a knowing smile.

She stared at him. She *had* been considering it. Seriously, considering it. She had her fair share of adult devices and knew how to use them.

"Don't," he repeated.

"And if I do?"

She half expected some cliché to come out of his mouth—something along the lines of he'd punish her if she did. But what came out was even worse. "If you do—and I'll know—then I won't lay a finger on you. And everything I just said I'd do, every way I described how I would touch you, pleasure you…"

He seemed to want some sort of acknowledgment, and so she nodded.

"You'll have to wait. You'll have to wait until I decide we're good and ready," he said with a grin.

She blinked. "That's evil."

His grin widened to a smile. "I know. I also know you kind of like it," he said, throwing her words back at her.

And damn him if he wasn't right.

* * *

A gentle wave washed over Alexis's feet as she and Serena meandered down the beach after their lunch. A turtle breached the water twenty feet from shore then bobbed back down. "So you and Shah worked out the details of how you'll contact Rosen?" Alexis asked.

Serena nodded. "Already kicked it off. When I landed in Honduras last week, I sent a message to my handler, Culpepper, with an update. I never heard back—which is no surprise, since he was already dead—but while that wasn't unusual, in this case, I'm going to act like it was. So, I sent a follow-up message to him this morning. It should take less than twenty-four hours for that email to make it to Angela Rosen. I suspect I'll hear from her tomorrow. Once we do, I'll start the dance of making it seem like she's earning my trust. We'll have to play it a little by ear, but if she's greedy and unethical enough to want to sell me out, she won't be able to resist falling into our plan."

They walked in silence for a bit longer. Occasionally, the relative quiet was interrupted by the playful shouts of kids or a particularly loud seabird, but overall, the afternoon was deceptively calm.

"Speaking of Honduras, talk to me about the trafficking," Alexis asked.

For the first time since they'd met, Serena showed some emotion and let out a long sigh. "The group first came onto my radar two years ago. I was keeping an eye on a young man who was making an unusually fast rise in the political leadership of a country I'll not mention. Anyway, he was invited to a party at a villa along the Mediterranean. Some women were brought in, which wasn't unusual, but these women were clearly from Central America and not the usual ones we see brought in from

Southeast Asia or even the US. It piqued my interest and so I started to look into it. What I found was that it was a new and relatively small ring. But given that it was so highly connected, it raised flags."

"What kind of flags?" Alexis asked.

Serena lowered her head. "I wondered if maybe arms sales were the primary funding of the group and they were just diversifying and adding trafficking to their business model. Or maybe drugs rather than arms."

"By the tone of your voice, I'm thinking you didn't find evidence of either?"

They drew to a stop and faced toward the sea, letting the waves lap over their bare feet. "I didn't. That's why I decided to try and break the ring up. If it's just trafficking, it's a lot easier than if the trafficking is part of something bigger."

"Did that raid break it up, then?" Alexis asked.

Serena shrugged. "I hope so. We took down the leader, but if we didn't clean up all the trash, it's possible someone else will step in to take over. And by the way, sorry I had you and Clarke tranq'd. I already had my plan in place and I didn't want you guys getting in the middle of it."

Alexis waved off the apology. Once she'd known who Serena was, she'd assumed that had been the case. "Something's bothering you though, isn't it?"

"I don't know, is it?" Serena looked at her.

Alexis all but snorted. "You asked us for help, so yes, you think there *is* something else going on even if it's not arms or drugs. A small trafficking ring from Honduras doesn't get to the level of providing women to parties in North Africa without some connections. But you don't know what those connections might be. And if you don't know, then you also don't know if you've truly ended it."

A hint of a smile touched Serena's eyes, if not her mouth,

when Alexis finished. "Why do you think the party was in North Africa?"

"It could have been in Europe, but Huck said he started looking for you in Africa," Alexis answered.

"Huck is damn good at his job," Serena said, acknowledging the accuracy of the analysis without actually acknowledging it. "I'm not sure they'll let him leave the CIA and it would be a loss if they did. But after his career, I can hardly blame him for wanting to ditch it all and work somewhere where he doesn't have to question people's loyalties all the time."

"You ever get tired of it?" Alexis asked as they started back toward her car.

Another sigh. "Sometimes. I don't think I'd be human if I didn't. But sometimes it's easier to keep doing what you're doing than it is to try something else. I know that sounds defeatist and I don't mean it that way. I'm good at what I do and while some days are better than others, what else would I do? There isn't exactly a career path for an ex-operative unless I want to go into private security, and believe me, I do *not* want to go into private security."

"You have a high opinion of them, don't you?" Alexis teased.

Serena snorted. "Some of them are okay, but they all rely on teamwork and do I *strike* you as a woman who works well in a team?"

At that, Alexis laughed out loud. If one was going to be a life-long spy, then at least one could be self-aware about it.

CHAPTER FIFTEEN

THE DOGS WERE BESIDE THEMSELVES. There was no other way to put it. Well, all of them except Red, who hung back each time the doorbell rang, but still stayed close enough to keep an eye on things. And Isiah, who she'd clearly decided was her person. Not that Alexis could fault her taste.

Alexis glanced back at the staircase to where Red stood watching her and Isiah make their way to the door for the third time in ten minutes—a novelty not just for the four-legged residents of the house but for Alexis, too. Damian and Charlotte were already out on the patio, sipping wine and taking in the view and, as anticipated, Dominic had made himself at home in the pool.

Alexis swung the door open as Howdy, George, and Allie skidded to a stop beside her. Jake and Beni stood on the other side, Beni carrying a bottle of something and, surprisingly, Jake held a bouquet of flowers. A bouquet he promptly tossed at her before striding into the foyer and dropping to the ground.

"Dogs! You have dogs!" he exclaimed as he flopped onto his back, welcoming all the wet noses poking and prodding him as they clearly identified him as a person on their mental wavelength. Tails wagged, nails clattered on the tile, and Jake laughed as he rubbed and roughhoused with each.

Beni stepped in and handed Isiah the bottle she carried as she nodded toward Jake. "It's too bad your trainer can't do anything with *him*." They all looked at the agent who now had Howdy standing on his stomach as she bathed his face in kisses.

"He told you about my dog trainer?" Alexis asked, stepping around her colleague and leading Beni upstairs. Isiah followed behind them and she figured Jake would make his way up when he no longer had an audience.

"It's all he could talk about on the way over here. Apparently, he had the world's best dog growing up. One that used to surf with him all the time. He died just after Jake decided to retire from the pro tour. Don't get me wrong, he clearly loves dogs, but I think some of his love is wrapped up with the memories of being on the surfing circuit."

They hit the landing and made their way to the kitchen. Alexis continued to the pantry to grab a vase as she spoke. "You're starting to sound like me, Beni. You never know, maybe you'll even start analyzing your own issues soon."

Beni snorted. "Ha, don't count on it. That would imply I have issues. Which I don't."

"Right. And neither do I," Alexis said, rejoining them in the kitchen just as Isiah handed Beni a beer.

Beni took a sip then shrugged. "You seem pretty well adjusted to me. I mean, other than the fact that you never mentioned you have staff, or live in a mansion, or rescue dogs in your spare time. Other than that, you're almost as much a sharer as Damian."

Alexis laughed. "You're so full of shit." *No one* was as much of a sharer as Damian. And speaking of Damian, the three made their way to the patio and joined him and Charlotte on the couches and chairs scattered around a low-set table.

To Alexis's surprise, Jake didn't join them for a full ten

minutes—maybe he missed dogs more than she and Beni gave him credit for. And maybe she should introduce him to her friends at the shelter—he couldn't have a dog because of his schedule, but she'd bet he'd enjoy hanging out with them when his schedule allowed.

As the sun started to sink, they sipped their drinks, snacked on the food that Eric kept delivering, and caught up. Dominic joined them at some point during that time, but when Eric popped his head out to give them a twenty-minute heads-up for dinner, it didn't surprise Alexis that Beni was the one to call out the elephant in the room.

"So are you going to tell us why we're all here, Lex?" she asked. The rest of her teammates fell silent. Charlotte shot her a sympathetic look and Isiah's hand came to rest along the back of her neck.

"Actually, it's not why we're here that I want to know, it's why we've never been here before that I think is the more interesting of the two questions," Beni clarified. And she was more right than she knew.

"You don't have to tell us now," Charlotte said as Damian picked up her hand. Charlotte had lived a very different life from Alexis, but of all the people sitting around her patio, she might be the one most able to understand.

Alexis cleared her throat. "No, it's good timing. Mostly because dinner will be ready in twenty minutes and that will force an end to what is likely going to be an awkward conversation."

"Awkward for us or you?" Dominic asked.

"Me. Almost no one knows what I'm going to tell you except my parents, my therapist, and a few members of law enforcement. It's not something I talk about, so I'm probably going to be a little rusty," she said.

Jake put his feet up on the table and adjusted Howdy, who'd crawled into his lap ten minutes earlier. Howdy wasn't usually allowed up on furniture, but at this point, Alexis didn't feel like laying down the law.

"So just jump in," Jake said. "May not be the most graceful, but it is faster and less painful. Usually."

He had a point. And so, taking a deep breath, she proceeded to share with them a story she hadn't spoken out loud in years.

"When I was eleven, my parents bought an apartment in New York City," she started. "We spent a lot of time in Sweden where my mom is from, and a lot of time in Georgia where my dad is from, but that year they decided they wanted to spend a little time in New York. There was a music studio there that my dad was interested in working with and it was easy for my mom to pop over to Europe when she needed to, that kind of thing."

Out of the corner of her eye she noticed Isiah's brows draw together. She hesitated, wondering at the reaction, then realized that he had no idea who her parents were—he'd traveled with her and stayed in her home, but had never once asked. "My parents are Jasper and Vera Wright," she said to him. She studied his face as he processed the information. A beat passed then his eyes widened and his head drew back as he connected the dots.

"*The* Jasper Wright? The famous R&B singer?" he asked.

Her dad was a musician as well, but she nodded.

"And your mom is a supermodel," he said, more than asked.

Again she nodded. "Well, she's not doing much modeling now, but she still works in the industry. She has a clothing line and a small agency."

Isiah stared blankly at her for a moment, then swallowed and nodded. "Okay, that explains a few things. Why don't you finish your story, or keep starting it, or whatever…"

She almost smiled at his nonplussed response. But when she turned back to her teammates, the moment of lightness faded.

"Anyway," she continued. "I enrolled in school there for the year and became friends with a girl in our building. She was a year older, but we were the only kids our age in the co-op and so we ended up spending a lot of time together.

"Her mom wasn't in the picture and her dad wasn't around a lot. He was a banker of sorts, or so we thought..."

This was when the story got hard. As if sensing her wavering resolve, Isiah slipped his hand from her neck and, much like Damian had done with Charlotte, he twined his fingers with hers and gave her a good squeeze.

Focusing on the feel of his hand, she tamped down her emotions and continued. "The following spring, my friend and her father invited me to go on a vacation with them to Costa Rica. We'd known the family for seven months by then, and my parents felt pretty comfortable with them so they agreed. Turned out it wasn't such a good idea."

She stilled for a moment, welcoming the rapid beating of her heart and her shallow breathing. Her physical reaction to retelling the story wasn't comfortable, but in its discomfort, it reminded her that she was still alive—not only alive, but surrounded by people who cared about her.

Her hands shook with the memories, but Isiah wrapped his around hers, giving her his warmth and strength.

"Two days into the trip, I was kidnapped and held for ransom. My friend's father turned out not to be such a great banker and owed a lot of people—dodgy people—a lot of money. He'd encouraged his daughter to cultivate her friendship with me. I think originally, he thought maybe he could borrow money from my parents or get them to *invest* in something, but somewhere along the way, his plans changed."

She took another deep breath and let it out slowly. Keeping her gaze fixed on her hands entwined with Isiah's, she finished her story. "Of course my parents paid the ransom. But then there was a second demand. They paid that, too, and it wasn't until the third that the private security team my parents hired was able to find me." She paused as her teammates uttered various sentiments, but she was too lost in the memory to distinguish them.

Clearing her throat, she continued. "The man—my friend's father—was prosecuted and found guilty, but because I was a minor, almost none of this came out publicly. Which is why you've never read or heard about it. My parents also wanted it to remain as private as possible both for my sake and for the sake of other kids like me, kids who might be in a position to be used for ransom—or as the kidnap and ransom teams call us, *high-value targets*. The records were sealed and after that, we moved to Sweden to be closer to my grandparents and out of the public eye as much as possible. We stayed there for two years."

Everything around her felt suddenly very still. Unlike moments ago, none of her guests spoke or even moved, even the dogs seemed to sense the weight of her words. Forcing herself to find one more ounce of strength, she looked up and met her friends' eyes.

"After that, security became the top priority of the family. As you can imagine, I wasn't in a place to determine what was reasonable and what wasn't, and the level of security my parents instituted just became how we lived. And ever since then, it's been hard for me to invite people into my life and most especially into my home. I know I was only eleven when it happened, but the consequences of trusting someone were so extreme that even though I know I'm not that child anymore, it's still hard to overcome. And at this point, I think my way of life is more habit than logic. But that isn't how I want to live.

"And so here you are. I'm not going to make any excuses for why it took me so long to invite you over and I'm not going to pretend that now that I've told you the reason that suddenly everything is okay. But I do hope you'll see this evening for what it is and know that I'm trying. I'm trying to break the habit —not entirely, but at least with people I know I can trust."

With that, she let out another long exhale then did what she most needed at that moment. She grabbed her beer and took a nice long sip. When she set the bottle back down, the reality of the moment hit her and she looked first to Beni then to Damian.

"How long were you kept?" Damian asked softly.

Despite having just taken a drink, her throat dried. She cleared it before answering. "A little over a month."

Both Jake and Dominic uttered a few choice curses while Beni said something in Spanish that caused both Damian and Charlotte to raise their eyebrows.

"How much over a month?" Isiah asked.

She looked at him. There was curiosity in his expression... and something more. Then in a flash, she understood what he was truly asking of her. "I was kept in a cage. A ten-by-ten cage in someone's basement. In total, it was four weeks, three days, and eight and a half hours." There, she'd said it. She'd said the words, but she'd also told everyone surrounding her how much she remembered. How much the events of that spring still affected her.

Isiah rubbed his thumb along her hand, then raised it to his lips. "You'll be okay. We've all got you."

At his simple words, tears sprang to her eyes. He'd voiced what she'd needed to hear. In her heart, she'd known her team, and he, wouldn't let her down, but hearing it was something else altogether.

"He's right, Lex," Dominic said. "We've all got your back and I'm glad you know it."

Everyone murmured their agreement and Charlotte reached over to give her arm a little squeeze of solidarity. They'd both been victims of betrayals and violence—in much different ways, but it was a bond they shared.

Jake scratched Howdy's ears and reached for his beer as he spoke. "I get it and all. I mean, I see why it's taken you so long to have us over and I totally get why you don't trust a lot of people. But seriously, could you at least have told me about the dogs?"

"You're such an ass, McMullen," Beni said, throwing a pillow at him, careful to miss Howdy. But his comment had the impact Alexis knew he'd intended when suddenly, everyone was laughing.

* * *

*J*siah closed the door on the last of Alexis's guests to leave. He'd thought Jake or Dominic would be the stragglers, but as it turned out, Damian and Charlotte had stayed a good hour after the others—including Eric—had left. But there was a lightness to Alexis's expression now that he'd not seen on her before. And she wore it well.

"Did you and Charlotte have a good talk?" he asked, wrapping his arms around her. He knew nothing about Charlotte's background, but shortly after Beni, Jake, and Dominic had left, the two women had slipped off for a good long chat in a cozy little outdoor seating area tucked away in the trees on the other side of the pool. He and Damian had had another beer while they cleaned up the last of the dishes, and chatted about their respective times serving their country—not that Damian wasn't still serving his country, but the armed forces was a little different than the FBI.

"We did." Alexis leaned into him and rested her head on his shoulder. "I'm a little wiped out, but it was good."

He leaned back to look down at her. "I know this isn't much, but I'm sorry you went through all that."

She didn't look up but nodded against his shoulder. "Thank you. I was lucky to have the parents I did and the extended family I had. We spent those years in Sweden completely out of the limelight. I mean, I was never really in it—my parents were always pretty good about protecting me from their public lives

184

—but after that, they put everything but me on hold. And then, of course, there were my grandparents and cousins who helped, too."

Releasing her, he slipped his hand into hers and they started toward the staircase. "How many cousins do you have?" he asked. He caught a flash of a smile before she answered.

"My mom is one of four and my dad is one of five. I have nine cousins on my mom's side and eight on my dad's."

"And are you all close?"

Her smile lingered this time. "Yes. I don't know how my parents and aunts and uncles figured it out—we, the cousins— sometimes think they planned it, but on both sides, there's only a four year age gap between the oldest and the youngest. I'm the youngest on my mom's side and in the middle on my dad's. What about you?" she asked as they continued up to the third floor.

"Just me and my sister. My dad's been out of my life—out of *our* lives—since I was seventeen. I think he might have a brother somewhere, but I don't know. My mom had a younger sister who got caught up with the wrong crowd and died of a drug overdose when she was twenty-three." It felt weird, almost awkward, telling his brief family history after hearing Alexis's. She'd had everything as a kid—still had it if the way she talked about her family was any indication. A large, loving extended family, supportive parents, financial security. With the big exception of having been kidnapped, her life almost seemed a fairytale. It *was* a fairytale compared to his. But even though he wondered what Alexis might think of his upbringing—and he hadn't even told her the half of it—he wasn't *worried* about it. And that was the telling part. Because in truth, with the exception of his mom and sister, both of whom he loved dearly, he'd always felt a niggling sense of shame about his family.

More specifically, shame about his alcoholic abusive father who Isiah hadn't been able to protect his mom from for years.

But standing on the third-floor landing of Alexis's Tildas Island mansion—which was one of god knew how many homes her family owned—he, strangely enough, felt none of the embarrassment that had plagued him for years. She wouldn't judge him, of that he was certain. And so pulling up some of the same bravery she'd shown earlier, he told her.

"My home life wasn't great. In fact it was pretty shitty." He dropped her hand and walked to the railing to look down on the living area below them. After a beat, Alexis joined him, but stayed out of reach, giving him space.

"My dad drank. A lot. And when he did, he got violent. Mostly, he went after my mom, occasionally, me. Thankfully, never my sister who is eight years younger than I am. That kind of uncertainty and betrayal—because that's what it is when someone, like a parent, who is supposed to protect you, does the opposite—doesn't make for a healthy way to grow up."

He paused and looked through the windows and out into the night. "It made me angry, as you can imagine. I was a bit of a volatile kid. But the good news was that by the time I was sixteen, I was finally big enough to stop him. The first time I took him down, he thought it was a fluke. But then it happened again. He left the Bahamas and went back to the States a month after that. We never saw him again. Thankfully," he added.

"What happened after he left?" Alexis asked, her voice quiet in the night.

Isiah gave a rueful laugh. "We lived on pins and needles for a few months, wondering if he was going to come back. But then my mom was served with divorce papers—he'd met someone else and wanted to get married. I'd never seen her sign anything so fast." He smiled at the memory of his mother's joy and the celebration that followed that night. Isiah had been working at a local dive shop and had saved a little money. It was the first time he'd ever treated his mom and sister to dinner.

"After that, it was like the world opened up to us. Oh, it was hard. My mom worked in the kitchen of one of the big resorts and didn't make a lot. My sister was only ten, and I had just graduated. But we made it. I had my US citizenship through my dad and so I enlisted, figuring that if I lived on the Navy's dime, then everything I made, I could send home. Eventually, my mom was able to open a bakery—something she'd dreamed of as a girl. We also managed to get my sister through college."

"Resilience," Alexis said, running a hand down his arm until her fingers rested on his.

"Definitely."

"And now?"

"Now, my mom still runs her bakery, but it's attached to a small bed and breakfast she runs. My sister is a marketing exec at one of the luxury resorts on the island and is married to a good man who owns a boat charter company. They just had their first baby, a little girl, last year." Smiling, he pulled out his phone to show Alexis a picture.

"This is Amelia Grace." He held up the device that had a picture of his chubby-cheeked niece sitting on the beach in a sun hat and little red bathing suit all covered in sand. She was grinning, and two teeth peeked through.

"She's adorable," Alexis said, the genuine warmth in her voice filling his soul. "Do you get to see her often?"

He opened his mouth to answer, but his words were cut off when his phone rang and his private landline number showed up on the screen. There was only one person it could be.

He glanced at Alexis. Her brows were furrowed and she now wore a tiny frown.

"Huck?" he answered. He could hear the faint sounds of his friend moving around in the background, then suddenly Huck stilled and exhaled.

"You need to get home. Your spy has gone missing."

CHAPTER SIXTEEN

"WHAT EXACTLY DO you mean by 'missing'?" Isiah asked as he and Alexis walked into his apartment over The Shack. All thoughts of where the night *could* have led were now just distant memories.

"There aren't a lot of ways to misconstrue that," Huck said, pacing the width of the room.

"Actually, with a seasoned spy, there are," Alexis countered. "Why don't you tell us exactly what happened."

Huck paused, glanced at her, then at Isiah. "Don't look to me for direction," Isiah said. "I'm just a bartender now. Alexis is the federal agent."

Huck blinked, then gave a little shake of his head and turned toward her. "Sorry, Alexis. Kind of habit to look to Boongy, Isiah," he clarified. "I didn't mean any offense."

Alexis arched an eyebrow and looked not quite sure she believed him, but gestured for Huck to continue.

"She was sitting there, on Boongy's computer." He pointed toward the small desk on the far side of the room. "I don't know what she was doing, but then suddenly she freaked out, grabbed her bag, and left."

Isiah moved toward the computer as he absorbed the fact that it now felt weird to hear his nickname. "Boongy" and "Clarke" were the only names he'd answered to for years—formative years—but he was rarely called "Clarke" anymore and he hadn't heard "Boongy" since the last time Huck had visited, three years ago.

"Define 'freaked out'," Alexis said.

"What do you mean? She freaked out," Huck answered, then resumed his pacing.

"Again, I have a hard time picturing Serena freaking out, so I'd like to know *exactly* what you saw," she said.

Huck threw his hands up. "She cocked her head to the side, said 'huh,' then grabbed her bag and left."

"And that's 'freaking out'?" Alexis clarified.

"Huck's prone to hyperbole," Isiah said as he eyed the computer. Serena hadn't shut it off, but there was nothing on the monitor other than the home screen. "It's how he got his nickname. After Huck Finn who was entertaining as hell but not one to stick to the unvarnished truth."

"You're wrong this time, Boongy. As Alexis keeps pointing out, Serena is a seasoned operative of what, twenty years? I think the fact that she showed *any* emotion at all qualifies for freaking out."

Isiah looked at Alexis as he reached for the mouse. He wanted to open the browser and see if he could discover what Serena had been looking at, but not without her say-so. Alexis stood in the middle of the room, a thoughtful expression on her face.

"There is some truth to that. But it's also possible she could have discovered her favorite band was playing in town and taken off. Her reaction could have been a genuine reaction of surprise or concern or it could have been a normal human reaction to something interesting. She may be an operative, but she *is* human, too," Alexis pointed out.

"True," Huck conceded. "But if it were just a human reaction, then why bolt without saying anything to me?"

"Why don't we try to figure out what she was looking at before she left and then we can determine if it has any meaning," Isiah interjected, pulling up his browser.

He pulled out a chair and sat as Alexis joined him. Looking over his shoulder, she asked, "Do you think you can find it or do you think we need to call Eric and Yael?"

"Give me ten minutes and if we can't find anything obvious, we can call Yael and Eric. We may want to call Shah, too, at that point."

Alexis let out a disgruntled growl. "I'm seriously questioning the wisdom of entering into a quid pro quo agreement with Serena if she's going to rush off on her own at the drop of a hat."

"I don't doubt her instinct will always be to manage the situation on her own." Isiah pulled up the browser history as he spoke. "But the other thing I don't doubt is Shah's judgment. She wouldn't have made the deal if she didn't think Serena wouldn't come through."

Alexis pointed to a Web address that popped up on the browser history. "Oh shit, that's it," she said, dropping the prior topic as the website populated. "We need to call Shah."

He glanced down to see nothing more than a report from a famous infotainment television show. Alexis stepped away to make the call while he skimmed the article that had popped up. Some famous actor had arrived on the island the day before and was planning to stay for a week. The article recalled in detail the parties he'd thrown while on the island in the past, but there wasn't much more than that.

"We need to go," Alexis said, rejoining him at the desk.

"Okay, but go where?"

"Peter Gregson is a douche of the nth degree." Alexis pointed to the picture of the actor on the screen. "Believe me, I know. He's around my age and my parents made sure to pretty much know everything about all the kids I might encounter after, well you know." Her gaze skittered to Huck who was watching them.

"Gregson's dad was a sexist misogynist and his son doesn't fall far from the tree," she continued. "My guess is he's having a party tonight and Serena thinks there might be trafficked women there. Maybe even connected to the ring we encountered in Honduras since we're relatively close."

"Okay," he said, because that did make sense. "But where are we going?" he repeated.

Alexis paused and appeared to study him and Huck before she spoke. "Where's your closet? We need to find you both something to wear. We're going to a party."

* * *

"That's the room you want to gain entry to," a voice from behind Isiah said. Since he didn't want to be at Peter Gregson's party at all, he was pretty sure he didn't want to be in the private room the guy was referring to.

Isiah scanned the crowd. Huck had bailed on joining them as a guest and opted to stay outside and act as their driver. And Alexis, the one person he knew at the party, was across the room talking to someone he'd wager was a model, if her height and waif-like figure were anything to go by. With little else to look at, his attention traveled back to the door the guy behind him had mentioned.

No, he didn't want entry into that room. Unfortunately, that room was probably exactly where he needed to go. It was the only door he could see that didn't open up to the outdoors and if Peter Gregson was trafficking women into his parties, he'd sure as shit be keeping them behind closed doors.

"Actually, once they get to that room, they're so drugged up, it's not that interesting. If you want something to catch your eye, the real action is in the basement, under the garage," the man continued.

Despite knowing Alexis and he were there to investigate the possibility of trafficking, he swiveled around to tell the guy to fuck off. And froze.

Slowly, Isiah extended his hand. "We've met before but I don't recall your name.". Standing in front of him was The Gentleman. The only resemblance to Serena was in the eyes. The rest of her—well him—had undergone a chameleon-like change. When she'd first shown up in his office, he'd seen hints of her masculine-like features. Now, with whatever she'd done, there was no way anyone would mistake her for, well, a *her*.

"Sam, Sam Barron."

"That's right." Isiah shook his hand. "If I were interested in what's going on in the basement, how would I obtain an invite?"

"Sam." Alexis sidled up beside Isiah then brushed a kiss on Sam/Serena's cheek. How she'd learned his name, Isiah hadn't a clue. "I do hope you don't plan to go back on the promise you made to me. I don't handle disappointment very well."

"I'd never disappoint a lady," Sam/Serena said, picking up Alexis's hand and bringing it to her lips.

"Yes, I'd heard that about you," Alexis replied with a hint of a sly grin. Sam's eyes glinted, but he didn't smile. "Now, what's this I hear you telling my man?" As Alexis spoke, she slipped her arm through Isiah's and leaned into him. "You're not suggesting he have a little fun without me, are you?"

Isiah was glad he wasn't required for this conversation. The combination sex kitten/undercover agent Alexis had morphed into was disconcerting and while he'd done his fair share of improvisation, usually it included explosives and grenade launchers, not champagne and verbal subterfuge.

"Alexis, darling, you know I'd never suggest such a thing. Loyalty is something precious, isn't it? All I was telling him was that for those who do venture into that room, they are getting secondhand goods. The real fun is taking place in the basement. Under the garage. Not that he'd be interested."

If Alexis hadn't been pressed into his side, he never would have noticed the slight stiffening of her body. Sam/Serena's language was all part of the act, but he, too, found himself struggling not to react to the use of the phrase "secondhand goods" being applied to anyone, let alone women who had likely been brought to the party against their will to be little more than sex slaves.

"The basement? That's an interesting choice. But then again, it has access to the boathouse and boat launch, doesn't it? So easy-in, easy-out, I suppose," Alexis said. The last words were meant to sound flippant to anyone listening, but Isiah knew two things. First, she'd all but choked on those words—her fingers had dug into his arm as she'd spoken them and he'd caught a subtle, but unmistakable hitch in her voice. And second, both of them wore earpieces. Alexis's team could hear her, but so could members of the Tildas Island police force and SWAT team that had joined forces with them for the raid that would take place as soon as they located the women Gregson had brought in. Which, with Alexis's information, could mean at any moment.

"Well, as interesting as this is, Isiah, babe, I think it's time for us to go? I rarely come to these kinds of things and now I remember why. There's so much more fun to be had away from the crowds. Wouldn't you agree, Sam?" As Alexis spoke, she slipped her hand into Isiah's and leaned forward to brush another kiss across Sam's cheek. Her lips moved as she lingered for a moment, but between the low timbre of her voice and the music, he had no idea what she said.

A few minutes later, they were outside the massive mansion Gregson had rented for the week, and were climbing into the backseat of Yael's Range Rover with Huck behind the wheel. But they didn't go very far.

A mile down the road, they pulled onto a dirt road that led

to a public beach—it was closed for the night, but Shah and the local SWAT had commandeered it for their purposes as it sat less than a quarter-mile—as the crow flies—from the Gregson place.

Without much modesty, both he and Alexis changed in the back seat of the car into more practical tactical gear. It was awkward and cramped, but he'd been in worse places before and judging by the way Alexis moved, she had, too.

When they opened the door and climbed out—now wearing all black clothing and carrying Kevlar vests—he had another moment of cognitive dissonance. Twice in a week he was running an op, something he'd thought he'd left behind years ago. His instincts and training were coming back, and the gun in his hand felt like an old friend, but still...

"The paperwork is complete, Clarke," Shah said as she approached them. She'd worked some magic and he was now an official consultant with the FBI. He didn't want to ask too many questions, he just hoped it wouldn't become a regular thing. He *liked* tending to his bar.

"Are we ready?" Alexis asked, sliding a weapon into her thigh holster.

"Nearly," Beni answered as she and the rest of the team gathered around. The realization that not only was he running an op but that he was doing it as a part of a team he'd never trained with, settled a little uneasily on his shoulders, but he pushed it aside. The women who were being held inside the mansion were more important.

"We'll take the zodiac boats directly into the boathouse," Beni said. "The SWAT team will lead and once they've secured the area, we'll follow behind. They'll contain their actions to the basement to the extent they can, so that when we arrive, we can take the lead on the upstairs raid which is where we think we'll find most of the men participating in, well—"

"Rape," Isiah said.

Alexis's sharp gaze landed on him and Beni studied him closely.

"Just calling a spade a spade," he said.

"No one's saying it's not rape. I think we can all agree it's that and more," Beni responded. He didn't think they thought it was anything less, but he also knew that by calling it what it was, he'd humanized the situation. And not that being human was a bad thing, but sometimes, before ops, it was easier to disassociate and think of the people involved as objects—perpetrators, victims, suspects, casualties—than it was to think of them as human.

But other than crimes against kids, there was very little Isiah liked less than crimes against women. And he didn't need Alexis's psychology Ph.D. to know why—his mother had never been trafficked, but she sure as shit had been treated as nothing more than a piece of property for his father to use and abuse as he saw fit.

"Right," Jake interjected. "So once the basement is secure, we'll move into the upper part of the house. Everyone has seen the plans and knows their role?"

Everyone nodded and murmured their assent. A call came from the water, presumably the leader of the tactical team, and a boat engine started.

"Let's roll," Damian said, leading the team toward the water.

"Alexis, Isiah, a minute?" Shah waved them closer.

Isiah cast a glance in the direction of Alexis's team members, but nodded. Shah's request hadn't been a request.

"I want you both to hang back and let the others take the lead upstairs," she said, surprising them. "I've already informed the rest of the team and they've made adjustments."

"Why?" he asked, knowing Alexis couldn't question her director.

Shah shot him a look that reminded him of his mom when she was about to say "because I said so," but then she surprised him by answering. "Three reasons. Alexis is known in Peter Gregson's world but very few people know that she's FBI. I want to keep that as quiet as we can in case we need to use those connections again as we did tonight. She's also a trained psychologist and I think best positioned to deal with the women we're likely to find in the basement. And the third reason is that I don't want one of my agents left on their own, and since you're the least up to speed, you get to stay and watch her back. I trust that meets with your approval, Clarke?"

Her answer was awfully succinct. As if she'd had this planned all along but hadn't bothered to tell them until now. But he was smart enough not to argue with Sunita Shah.

"Fine," he said.

"Agent Wright?" Using Alexis's title was akin to a parent using a child's full name.

Alexis nodded. "If they've come from Honduras, language might be an issue, but we'll do our best." By silent consensus, together, they made their way to the others. Within minutes, they were zipping across the water as the SWAT team boat disappeared into Gregson's boathouse, visible across the wide bay.

Their captain maneuvered them closer but stayed out of range until the SWAT team called "clear." Isiah didn't think he was the only one who caught the strain in the man's voice as they motored straight into the boathouse.

On alert, they leaped from the boat onto the interior dock. A member of the SWAT team stood at an open door, his back to the frame, and silently waved them in.

Isiah should have been prepared, he should have at least given some serious thought to what they might find. But he hadn't. And damned if his steps didn't falter when he entered the room last, trailing behind Alexis and her team. He paused, dimly aware that Beni, Damian, Dominic, and Jake were already leading the SWAT team to the upper part of the house.

There weren't that many young women, but of the five that were there, all were blond and all looked like they'd just barely reached adulthood. Three sat huddled in a corner, gripping each other with everything they had, while two lay on the floor, one with her back against a wall and the other in the middle of the room—both looked like they'd been dumped there and hadn't moved since. Those two wore no clothes and their bodies were marked with bruises, burns, and even blood.

"Can you bring me two shock blankets from the boat? Officer?" Alexis asked the SWAT member who'd stayed behind with them.

"Hill," the man provided.

"Thank you, Officer Hill. We need the EMTs, too," she said. Her voice was steady and firm, but he could hear the strain of anger.

"And make sure they are women," Isiah added. The man nodded then stepped out to get the blankets, radioing in the call at the same time.

Alexis knelt beside the young woman lying with her back to the wall and gently brushed her hair away from her face as she murmured quiet words intended to comfort. Hill returned and handed her the blankets. In low tones, Alexis asked if one of the three young women—girls?—could help. As Alexis draped one of the blankets on the girl in front of her, one of the three from the corner scrambled forward and snatched up the second shock blanket. Quickly, she draped it over the other naked young woman before returning to the corner.

His mind was so focused on the young woman Alexis examined—on the unmistakable marks on her face given to her by some man, or men—that he didn't really hear a word she or anyone else said. Then suddenly, Alexis's head snapped up and she met his gaze as they both listened to the communications coming through their earpieces. They remained silent as Beni spoke, then he stilled, waiting for Alexis's instruction. Alexis's eyes searched his for a fleeting moment. Then she gave a little nod to no one in particular. "He's on his way," she said to her teammate.

Switching her mic off, she asked, "You good with the plan?" There was a hostage situation upstairs and Beni had requested his assistance. It never hurt to have an extra snipper-trained resource on hand.

He scanned the area, taking in the women, as well as Hill, who still stood guard at the door. "You going to be okay?"

She nodded. "Go. The EMTs will be here shortly and I need to stay here with them."

He lingered for a short moment, then he nodded and started toward the stairwell.

"I want Gregson to rot in hell for this," she said, giving voice to his thoughts.

He paused and studied her face one more time. He was pretty sure she wasn't suggesting killing the man, but even if she had, he could hardly blame her. Or maybe he didn't mind the implication so much because her words mirrored his feelings and validated his thoughts. He didn't stay to discuss the matter, though, and in seconds, he was moving up the stairs while receiving directions from Beni.

* * *

*A*lexis watched Isiah disappear up the stairs then returned her attention to the bloodied, beaten, and no doubt sexually assaulted, young woman on the floor. Her pulse was strong and Alexis knew that her physical recovery would be the easiest part.

Cataloging the injuries—at least the visible ones—Alexis once again damned Peter Gregson to hell. She'd told Isiah she wanted Gregson to pay and she did. She wouldn't be sorry if he got caught in any crossfire, but she wanted the world to see him as he really was—a kidnapper, a rapist, a bully. She wanted to see him stripped of all his privilege and entitlement and reduced to nothing—*that* would be a much better punishment.

One of the young women in the corner inched her way apart from the other two. "Can I help?" she asked. "Please," she added.

Alexis recognized the look in her eye—it was all too familiar. The need to *do* something, to have some sort of control.

Keeping her mic off so as not to distract her teammates, she nodded and gestured to the girl she'd just examined. "Can you come here and sit with her while I check the other? The paramedics will be here soon, but I want to check her myself."

The young woman scooted forward and gently picked up the unconscious girl's hand.

"What's your name?" Alexis asked.

"Cindy, I'm from Miami," she answered, her eyes never leaving her fellow captor's face. "This is Jane and that's Carrie." She pointed first to the woman whose hand she held then to the woman lying in the middle of the floor.

"Taken from the streets?" Alexis guessed as she moved toward Carrie.

"Yes. We didn't know each other before, but we all just aged out of foster care. I met a guy who seemed to like me." Cindy's voice cracked a little bit and Alexis glanced over. "Such a cliché, I know. I should have known better."

Alexis picked up her examination of Carrie again. She looked a little less physically battered than Jane, but Alexis suspected she'd been drugged. Thankfully, her breathing was deep—slow, but deep.

"No one should need to think about being trafficked. I know that's not the way of the world and I know women *do* have to think about it, but don't be too hard on yourself," Alexis said.

"Ma'am?" Hill said. "The EMTs are here."

Alexis stood as six women with two gurneys arrived. Once they started working on Jane and Carrie, she turned away to begin questioning Cindy and the other two young women who appeared physically unharmed. She was halfway across the room when chatter from her teammates froze her in place.

She'd been half listening to them as they navigated the house and the hostage situation, but there was no mistaking the tone of Beni's voice now—they'd reached the crisis point.

Alexis glanced at the stairs and debated whether or not to join her teammates, but with Beni's next words, she knew it would be too late.

"Take the shot, Clarke," she heard. Then the report of a weapon filled her earpiece. Her heart stopped and she sucked in a breath. Logically, it was Isiah who'd fired the weapon on Beni's command. But in those split seconds of silence that followed the deafening sound, all sorts of images of Isiah bleeding, injured, and even dead, flashed through her mind.

Adrenaline flooded her system, pricking at her nerves like tiny little knives. Her blood vessels expanded and she fought the urge to race upstairs. Then finally, after what felt like ages, Beni gave the all clear. In the stillness that followed, Alexis realized that her entire body was shaking. Not since being freed from her own captors all those years ago had her body responded with this level of fear. She had known Isiah was different, she'd known they had a connection, but until this moment, she hadn't recognized how primal that connection was.

"Clear," Beni said, followed closely by, "Nice shot, Clarke."

In a daze, Alexis made her way toward the edge of the room and leaned against the wall. Slowly, everything else came back into focus—Hill was standing at attention, his weapon at the ready. Cindy and her fellow captors were once again huddled in the corner. And the EMTs continued to do their work.

Seeing Cindy snapped Alexis from the thoughts swirling in her mind and brought her back to the here and now. "All clear," she told the room. "You're safe," she added, meeting Cindy's eye. Hill didn't lower his weapon, but at least everyone in the room seemed to take a collective breath and accept that they were truly, finally safe.

"How are they?" Alexis asked one of the EMTs.

The older woman shot her a look over her shoulder then jerked her head toward Carrie, who now lay on a gurney. "That one's been drugged. She's the one we're most worried about. It's going to be a hard recovery, but we're not seeing anything physically life-threatening."

Alexis nodded and stepped back to let the women finish their jobs. It had been a long night, but looking at Cindy and the two other young women with her—each of whom was being examined by the paramedics—it wasn't anywhere close to over.

Nor did she want it to be. Not until they had every bit of intel they could get their hands on to bring Peter Gregson, and whomever he worked with, down.

CHAPTER SEVENTEEN

THE CLOCK beside her bed turned over to three o'clock as Alexis walked into the room and started stripping off her clothes. They'd spent the last several hours interviewing suspects and victims, and although she was exhausted, her body hummed with energy.

She glanced toward her bedroom door. Isiah had disappeared into the guestroom as soon as they'd arrived home. Other than the debrief, he'd spoken barely five words since he'd taken the shot that brought Peter Gregson down. Isiah hadn't killed him—no, the man was currently undergoing shoulder surgery to repair a shattered joint—but even so, Alexis sensed that the fact that he'd taken up a weapon again and actually shot someone, weighed heavily on his mind.

She glanced at the decanter sitting on a table by the sliding door. Standing in her room, wearing nothing but her boy-shorts underwear and a tank top, she considered grabbing a drink and curling up on a divan outside. It would be a poor second choice for what she really wanted to do—go to Isiah—but two doubts held her back from pursuing that path. She didn't want their first time together to be a cliché, and relieving the tension the night had wrought, through a bout in the sheets was as cliché as it could get. But more importantly, she wasn't sure he wanted company. Yes, he'd made promises that morning—graphics promises—but that now felt like a lifetime ago. If he needed time to process what had happened at the party, which, judging by the fact he was now in the guestroom, he did, then she wanted to respect that and give him what he needed.

With a sigh, she opted for the balcony and divan. She had the decanter in hand when a knock sounded on her door.

Isiah didn't wait for her to answer and a second later, he was standing before her. Slowly, he took the decanter from her hand, his gaze never leaving hers, and set it back down on the table.

"This isn't stress relief. Tell me you know that." As he spoke, he brought his hand up and brushed her cheek, trailing his thumb along her lower lip.

"This has been a long time coming," she acknowledged. His pupils dilated at her words and he brought his other hand up to her waist.

"Since the first time you walked into my bar last November." Gently, he pulled her toward him.

She thought about asking him what *this* was about—she wanted to hear the words, she wanted to hear him say them out loud. But a flash of vulnerability on his face stopped her and realization set in. The night had affected him in more ways than one. It wasn't just the shooting that he was grappling with. No, it was his mom and all the times he hadn't been able to stop his father.

He was hurting and he'd come to her.

She nodded as her fingers slid up his chest to his strong jaw. "This isn't about what happened tonight. This is about us and what the future might bring. And about how I felt when I heard the shot and, in those few seconds before Beni called it clear when I wondered if it might have been you who'd been hit. I want this. Not just tonight and not just tomorrow. I want this," she repeated. "I want you."

She leaned forward and he dipped his head until their lips met. The gentleness with which they touched and explored and healed each other was more intimate than anything she had ever experienced before. There was nothing hurried or frantic in their coming together—no remnants of the adrenaline or fear or anxiety of the past several hours tainted this moment. No, as they undressed and moved to her bed, as they lay down and learned each other's bodies, as they came together slowly, gliding against each other in an ancient rhythm, there was nothing about the past. Only a promise of a future.

* * *

Josiah lay on his side, facing Alexis. She'd opened the sliding door and despite the heat and humidity, the distant sounds of the ocean created a soothing soundtrack in the darkness.

"I'm grateful you came tonight, but how are you?" Alexis asked. He didn't need clarification of her meaning. Alexis was a smart woman, she'd recognized the connections he'd made in his mind between his mother and the women they freed tonight.

Her hand was tucked under her cheek and he brushed his fingertips along her bare forearm. "I saw women used as an act of war more times than I care to remember when I was deployed. But I hadn't ever expected to see it here. Not like we did tonight. It's not that I didn't know trafficking happened, but I guess I thought that once I was out of the service, the most action I might see would be to escort a drunk from The Shack."

He paused and rolled onto his back. Alexis's hand came to rest on his chest and he covered it with his own. "I know there are plenty of capable women out there. I know I'm lying next to one now." He turned his head on the pillow to look at her. "But somehow that doesn't always matter when I see women being mistreated or heading off into dangerous situations. I know you can take care of yourself, but when I watched you suiting up, or when I saw those young women, I couldn't help but remember all the times my father went after my mother. And all the times I couldn't protect her."

"I was grateful you were there," Alexis repeated. "But I'll be honest, I was surprised you agreed to Shah's plan to come on as a consultant." She paused, and a small smile teased her lips. "I'd love to know how she managed to bring you on so quickly as a consultant, though. She's a scary woman sometimes."

He chuckled at the comment. The ways of Sunita Shah were definitely a mystery. One he wasn't sure he wanted to—or could —solve. "I don't plan on doing that again. Being an agent is your job, and while it might give me some heart palpitations when I think about what you do for a living, that's my problem, not yours. I'm happy being a small business owner. But with this, this particular situation, well, I felt we started it together and so we needed to end it together."

She sighed and twined her fingers with his before bringing his hand to her lips. "We didn't start this together. What we started was a simple trip to find a potentially compromised CIA asset and warn him—her—that someone in the agency was selling her identity. The whole trafficking thing is something we kind of fell into."

She was right, of course. But even so, he couldn't bring himself to regret his involvement. It hadn't been easy. He hadn't expected to ever see the things he'd seen earlier that night in his civilian life, and he'd certainly never expected to pull the trigger on a human ever again. But even so, he didn't regret it. There were eight young women who were no longer victims of trafficking because of what the team had done tonight—the five women in the basement and three they'd found upstairs. He hoped they'd get the help they'd need to recover, but at least they now had the opportunity. And even though he didn't think Peter Gregson was the head of the ring, Isiah fully anticipated that once they started digging into his finances and movements, the ring would soon unravel.

"Speaking of Serena, did you talk to her—or him—tonight?"

Alexis shook her head. "She was planning to ghost once the SWAT team showed up. I think I might have caught a glimpse of her peeking into the basement, but I haven't seen her since. I know she contacted Angela Rosen yesterday. Hopefully, it doesn't take too long to reel her in."

"How much do you know about how the CIA works? Did she have any idea how long it will take?"

"How much does anyone really know about the CIA?" Alexis said, sarcasm heavy in her tone. "Serena's plan sounded like it might take at least a few days, if not weeks, but who the hell knows?"

* * *

*A*s it turned out, they didn't have to wait weeks or even days because at eight o'clock the next morning, Alexis's phone rang and Yael and Eric were sitting in her kitchen with one CIA operative.

Alexis and Isiah jumped into separate showers—too tempting otherwise—and were downstairs within twenty minutes. The scene they walked into wasn't quite as cozy as Alexis had relayed to him, and while Eric and Serena were at the table, Yael was standing ten feet away, leaning against the wall with a gun in her hand. It wasn't pointed at anyone, but Isiah didn't doubt that former Mossad agent was at the ready.

"Serena met up with Eric on his way to the house this morning," Yael said, answering the unasked question as to how Serena had ended up at Alexis's kitchen table. "He called me rather than bring her here. She and I had a little chat about respecting people's privacy, before I agreed to let her in."

Alexis's gaze went from Yael to Serena where it lingered. Then she let out a small, resigned sigh. "Nice to see you, Serena," Alexis said as she walked over to the coffee maker. "Coffee? Espresso? Latte?" she asked Isiah.

"Coffee is fine," he answered. She punched a few buttons and in seconds, the sound of coffee beans being ground filled the room.

"So what are you doing here, Serena?" Alexis asked, leaning against the counter.

"Enjoying the coffee and the company," she said with a grin.

Alexis cocked a brow. "Don't be annoying. I've had four hours of sleep and no coffee. If Yael doesn't shoot you, I might."

Serena let out what could only be called a guffaw—a quiet one, but a guffaw nonetheless. "As if."

"What, are you, fifteen now?" Alexis shot back as she grabbed the cup of coffee that magically appeared from her machine. He'd never been into fancy coffee makers—drip was fine with him—but the speed with which Alexis was handing him a steaming mug had him rethinking his approach.

"What's going on?" Isiah asked, deciding that since he'd had at least one sip of his morning pick-me-up, he was probably in a better headspace than Alexis.

"Rosen bought it hook, line, and sinker, and she's flying to Puerto Rico today to meet me."

The mug Alexis held hit the counter with a thud loud enough that Isiah flinched, then checked to see if it had broken.

"You were concerned about appearing to trust her too quickly. You changed tactic." Alexis turned back to make her own drink.

"It unfolded like I thought it would. My message was passed on to her and she reached out directly. Expressed her condolences over Culpepper's death, yada, yada, yada. She asked me to report into Langley so that I could update her on my movements and prepare to transition to a new handler. Her request was so over the top considering I haven't been into HQ for more than six years and Culpepper and I only had contact every few months, that it was easy to counter with something that sounded a lot more conservative but is, in reality, just as outrageous. If she were anywhere near Culpepper's caliber, she would have recognized my suggestion to meet in person in Puerto Rico as suspicious. But as she's not of his caliber and my request to meet one-on-one seemed like a compromise, she took it as a win."

Alexis sipped her coffee and stared at the agent for a moment before speaking. "I get what you're saying, but it's too many machinations for how little sleep I've had recently."

"And yet, you're still able to use the word 'machinations' in a sentence," Serena pointed out.

Alexis didn't bother responding. "Okay, so you go to PR today to meet with Rosen, then what?"

Serena's gaze bounced between everyone in the room, then landed on Alexis. "Not 'me,' darling. We go to PR."

CHAPTER EIGHTEEN

NINETY MINUTES after Serena had interrupted what Alexis had hoped would be a leisurely morning, she, Beni, Dominic, Damian, and Serena were boarding a small charter plane for the twenty-eight minute flight to San Juan, Puerto Rico, leaving Jake behind to continue their research. While much of PR was still feeling—and living with—the impacts of the hurricanes from several years before, as well as the recent earthquakes, downtown San Juan still bustled with tourists and the bars still poured drinks. It was as good a place as any to meet a traitor.

After landing, Dominic and Damian headed straight to the main airport terminal in order to follow Angela Rosen, while she, Beni, and Serena headed to the hotel Shah had booked for them. They had the room for the night, but unless something went awry, the three planned to head back to Tildas as soon as Serena's meeting was over. Dominic and Damian would stay and trail Rosen.

"So, are you presenting as a man or a woman tonight?" Beni asked as she lay crosswise on one of the beds, thumbing through the hotel information magazine.

"She expects The Gentleman, so that's who she'll get," Serena answered.

"So, going out on a limb here," Beni said, rolling to her side. "You're not going to give her your real identity?"

Serena shrugged and took a sip of the beer she'd grabbed from the minibar. "I have dozens of identities that are disposable, and despite what I said about leaving the investigation in your hands, I am a little curious who will end up paying for it. So, to answer your question, no, it won't be my real identity, but it will be one I've used before."

Listening to Serena, Alexis was glad it wasn't her life. Sure, being an FBI agent wasn't always a walk in the park, but at least she had an identity of her own.

Part of which included excellent taste in clothing.

With a devious grin, Alexis pushed away from the wall she'd been leaning against and looked down at Beni. "Well, since The Gentleman is making an appearance tonight, I think it only fair that he has the escorts someone like Rosen would expect. We need to do a little shopping. The boutique in the hotel should meet our needs."

Serena snorted as she took another sip, and Beni groaned as she flopped onto her back. "Are you really going to make me shop?"

Alexis flashed her teeth. "Benita Ricci, turn yourself over to me and you won't know what hit you."

"That's what I'm afraid of," she muttered, even as she dutifully rose to her feet and slipped her flip flops on. At least she'd had a pedicure recently.

"Your fairy godmother awaits," Alexis said, sweeping by Serena on their way to the door. She'd been waiting months for an opportunity to take Beni shopping. Alexis didn't often flaunt her wealth and she didn't intend to flaunt it now, but she did intend to make good use of it.

"You know how I feel about fucking fairytales, Lex," she grumbled.

Serena's laugh followed them out the door and Alexis was still smiling when they stepped into the boutique five minutes later.

* * *

*A*lexis's silvery dress shimmered in the light cast by the street lights as she, Beni, and Serena—dressed as a man—walked to the bar where Serena's meeting with Rosen would occur. With a hem that hit mid-thigh and a back that draped practically to the top of her tail bone, the dress was fairly comfortable as far as club-appropriate attire went. On the other side of Serena, Beni wore a green dress that Alexis had insisted on. The color suited her friend's skin tone and highlighted her green-gold eyes. Not to mention that the sharp "V" on both the front and back of the dress, showcased Beni's body perfectly. Their clothing was, perhaps, a little fancier than the evening called for, but with Serena dressed in a suit and tie, the three presented the exact image they intended.

Stepping into the bar ten minutes before the scheduled meeting time, they scanned the room. According to Dominic and Damian, Rosen had arrived and gone straight to her hotel. She was currently running five minutes behind which gave the three of them time to make an entrance and find a table. Or tables as the case may be. Alexis and Beni took a seat at a half-moon shaped booth toward the back while Serena picked a place at the bar. Looking all the world as if she/he could be one of James Bond's colleagues, Serena ordered a drink then gestured toward her and Beni. The waiter glanced over then nodded, presumably taking a drink order for the two of them as well.

The restaurant and bar were already filling up, and though

Serena wore a wire so that the entire team could hear her conversation, Alexis felt a measure of comfort that her position would allow her to keep the two in sight. Based on everything they knew, Rosen only intended to sell Serena's identity—and killing or harming her would seriously interfere with that—but trusting entirely in logic didn't seem wise.

The waiter, a good looking man in his mid-twenties with a dimple, brought their drinks over then left the fruity concoctions with a wink. Alexis made a face.

"He was cute," Beni said, taking a sip of something in a martini glass that was the color of the Caribbean.

Alexis's glanced at the man as he crossed back to the bar. He did look good in jeans but he did nothing for her. "He's like twelve and my displeasure wasn't at him, but at this drink. Isn't Serena supposed to just know random shit? How on earth could she think I'd like this?" As she spoke she raised her glass. The liquid inside was a creamy white color and it was blended with crushed ice. For god's sake, it even had a pineapple on the rim and an umbrella.

"It's called a Pina Colada and he isn't twelve. He is definitely of legal age," Beni shot back.

Alexis opted not to respond and instead, she eyed the drink before taking a small sip. The sweetness of it made her mouth pucker and she quickly set it down. "God, that's disgusting. Maybe I can wave him over and order something potable." She scanned the room for the waiter.

"Oh, I'm sure you could wave him over. Any time you want," Beni said. Alexis switched her attention from the bar to Beni.

Alexis narrowed her eye at her friend. "Not interested."

"Why's that?"

Alexis reminded herself that she liked having friends. She did. Most of the time. "You know why."

Beni leaned back in her chair and took a sip of her electric blue drink. It reminded Alexis of a melted popsicle.

"I don't know why. Care to elaborate?"

She caught the waiter's attention and he crossed the floor toward her with a smile.

"I'm sure this is a lovely drink." She waved to the thing sitting in front of her. "But it's not my style. Can you bring me—"

"Let me guess," he cut her off. "A shot of whiskey or a beer?"

Beni's snort of laughter wasn't as muffled as it should have been and Alexis shot her a quelling look. Bartenders sometimes had a preternatural sense about people, but his assessment was too accurate.

"A martini. Dirty. Very dirty."

His smile deepened. "Your wish is my command. And by the way, the gentleman at the bar said you wouldn't like this. But he said he wanted to see your reaction."

Alexis glanced over to Serena who winked at her and raised her/his glass. "And I suppose he told you I preferred whiskey?" Alexis asked.

The waiter shook his head. "Nope, that was all me. But a dirty martini fits, too."

Before Alexis could respond, the man walked away. She glanced back at Beni, who waggled her eyebrows and grinned.

"Isiah and I are a thing. There, does that make you happy?" Alexis asked on a long exhale. She was *not* used to discussing her love life. Not that she ever had much of one. Or someone to talk with about it.

"Extremely," Beni said, sitting back in her seat. "So, like how much of a thing? Like Damian and Charlotte level of a thing or something else?"

Beni didn't back down from the warning glare Alexis fixed on her. No, instead she smiled. But it wasn't until Beni waggled her eyebrows again that Alexis accepted she didn't stand a chance. "Fine," she huffed. "If you must know—"

"Oh, I must. He's a fine specimen of a man."

"He is and if that was intended to get a rise out of me, it won't work. I know both of you well enough to know that fidelity matters to him and loyalty matters to you."

"Well, that's not much fun," Beni said, conceding defeat in her attempt to rile Alexis. "Actually, it's still kind of fun," she continued. "You're right in that I'm nothing but happy for you, but as your closest girlfriend—"

"You are not my closest girlfriend," Alexis interjected.

"Yes, I am," Beni stated, her tone more factual than Alexis would have liked because in truth, there probably wasn't any other woman Alexis trusted more both as a colleague and a friend. Well, Beni and Charlotte.

"And so as your closest girlfriend, I'm nothing but thrilled for you so long as he knocks your socks off in bed—or wherever—and has you screaming his name every night. I already know he treats you well outside of the bedroom—or, again, wherever."

Alexis blinked. Beni and her other teammates had always been more open and graphic in their conversations than she, and they'd always, in their way, respected the boundaries she'd put up around that topic. But things had changed.

And with that thought, it hit her how much things *had* changed. Not just her relationship with Isiah, but everything. Over the past several months, she'd spent more time with her teammates than she had with any of her other colleagues in the prior years, *put together*. She'd invited them over, introduced them to Yael and Eric, and she'd told them about her abduction, as well as her work with the local shelters on Tildas. And while the former was certainly a more dramatic tale than her work with the dogs, it was something that had happened *to* her, something she'd had no say in. Whereas her fostering and volunteering was a choice she'd made and a reflection of *her*.

Things *had* changed. And she liked it.

"Believe it or not, last night was the first night we slept

together—and yes, that's a euphemism for what happened," she responded. If things had changed, she was going to embrace it and so, in for a penny, in for a pound.

Surprise flashed in Beni's eyes and Alexis continued. "He's amazing. In more ways than one, he's amazing. And while I'm glad we're here figuring out what the hell is going on with Angela Rosen, I will admit that I was loath to get out of bed this morning. If we had not been interrupted, I would have been a very happy woman. An orgasm or three is always a nice way to start the day. But it would have been nice to just spend the day with him, too."

Alexis experienced a little thrill of satisfaction at Beni's wide-eyed reaction. Her mouth didn't drop open, but it was very near. Alexis almost regretted that Angela Rosen showed up at that moment and halted whatever response Beni might have offered.

"Angela," Serena purred through their earpieces. The tenor of her voice was husky in the growing clatter of the popular bar.

"I wish I knew that trick," Beni said, instantly all business and the prior topic of their conversation little more than a memory.

"You mean that thing she does with her voice? To give it that male, bedroom-ish quality?"

Beni nodded as Angela Rosen spoke.

"You have me at a disadvantage," the woman said. "I don't know your name."

Serena chuckled. "You can call me Al."

The waiter dropped her martini off and he probably thought her smile at Serena's joke was for him, but whatever.

"Let me buy you a drink and we can sit somewhere quieter," Serena said. Angela ordered a glass of white wine and the two moved to a small bar height table directly in Alexis's line of sight.

Beni shot her a questioning look, and Alexis nodded, letting her colleague know she could see everything.

"The powers that be aren't happy that you didn't come back to the States," Rosen said, once they were seated on the tall stools.

"Puerto Rico is the States," Serena said, casually taking a drink and letting her gaze drift around the room. To most, the pair would seem like a disinterested man in conversation with a woman who, in her slacks, silk blouse, and low heels, looked dreadfully out of place. But Alexis suspected Serena was scanning the area to see if Angela had any cohorts in the vicinity. Damian and Dominic had followed Rosen from the airport and they hadn't seen anyone with her, but that didn't mean she might not have local contacts.

"Culpepper died two weeks ago in a car accident," Rosen said.

"As you say," Serena acknowledged.

Rosen hesitated at the reaction then bullied on. "As you know, the operatives assigned to Culpepper were confidential between him and the computers at Langley that did the assigning."

Alexis had heard rumors of an algorithm that linked handlers and operatives such that no one person was ever in possession of all the information, but she'd never known if it was true or a figment of someone's overactive—and paranoid—imagination. She supposed that was one interesting thing to come of the night, at least now she had the answer to that question.

Angela continued when Serena said nothing. "There is a protocol in place for situations such as this. When a handler dies," she clarified. "It involves four senior members of the leadership team and a complex series of verifications. But the thing is, when we accessed Culpepper's files, yours wasn't in there."

Serena didn't respond for a moment and she looked more bored than anything. "Not really my problem is it?"

Angela took a large sip of her wine then set her glass down. "There were two women and two men in his files. One of those men died a month before Culpepper did and the other has been located. As I said, you weren't in his files."

Serena shrugged then twisted her head to follow an attractive woman who passed by. "Like I said, that doesn't seem like my problem." Her attention lingered in the direction the woman had gone.

"There was some talk you weren't actually one of ours."

Serena chuckled at that. "A double agent? How very <u>Tinker, Tailor, Soldier, Spy</u> of you all," she said, referencing the famous John Le Carre spy book and movie.

"The actionable intelligence you've given us leads me to believe you aren't, but I need your file number to assuage my colleagues." The file number Rosen referred to would be the original file created by the agency when Serena had been a recruit—the one that would contain her real identity.

Serena let out a long exhale. "Who will be my new handler?"

Angela cocked her head, but Alexis didn't miss the gleam of triumph in the woman's expression—what she sought was so very close to being handed over. "You know I can't tell you that. Once I have your file number, I'll submit it to the matching system, and whatever algorithm resides in those computers will match you with a handler. Culpepper always referred to you as The Gentleman. So long as your new handler doesn't use the same moniker and applies the appropriate protocols to mask your identity when reporting your intelligence back to the commission, I won't even know who you were assigned to."

Rosen spun a good tale. It was almost convincing. But they all knew she had no intention of submitting the number to the system that would match Serena with a new handler.

Alexis watched Serena's disinterested gaze lazily sweep the room. "Any chance you'll be my handler?"

Angela pursed her lips. "Unlikely, no. Especially not after this trip."

Serena straightened, then rose from her chair. "Good, because Culpepper never liked you," she said, before tossing a small slip of paper on the table. "Now, if you'll excuse me. I so rarely get a night in a city such as this. I have friends to attend to."

Alexis sipped her drink as Serena approached them. Without a word, she and Beni slid from their seats when she approached. Draping an arm around each of their waists, Serena guided them from the bar. Alexis shivered as the spy's cool fingers brushed against the bare skin of her lower back, just above the drape of her dress. To all and sundry, they would look like a well-heeled man with two willing women at his side.

Alexis hoped Angela Rosen was as gullible.

CHAPTER NINETEEN

THE THREE WOMEN considered stopping by another, higher-end bar—something that, if Angela was following them, would align with her opinions of The Gentleman. But when Dominic and Damian confirmed that Rosen had headed straight back to her hotel, so did Beni, Serena, and Alexis. Within the hour, the three were dressed in their regular clothes and on a flight back to Tildas Island—leaving Dominic and Damian to tail Rosen. Dominic had also been able to slip into Rosen's room while she'd been out and had planted a bug, so the team felt pretty comfortable in having her covered.

Alexis texted Isiah before they boarded the flight and, to her surprise, he was at the airport waiting for them when they touched down. As soon as Alexis was within reach, he tugged her into his arms and lowered his head, kissing her thoroughly.

Until someone cleared their throat.

"You interrupted us this morning, so I have little sympathy—or patience—for you, Serena." Isiah held Alexis's gaze as he spoke.

"Sorry, you know, just a little treason we needed to clear up," Serena said, clearly not sorry. "Didn't mean to get in the way of whatever you had planned. The thoughts of which might keep me up at night, by the way. You're a very attractive couple."

Isiah stepped away and flashed the spy a killer grin. "The *thoughts* don't hold a candle to the real thing."

"Aaannnd on that note," Beni interjected, stopping the conversation from going any further. "Are you giving me a ride home, or do I need to call a cab?" she asked Isiah.

Isiah bowed and gestured toward the Range Rover Yael must have lent him. "Your carriage awaits, Madam."

Isiah dropped Beni off in town first, then they made their way to Center Road and toward the point where The Shack, which was closed for the night, was located. Five minutes after dropping Serena off, Alexis and Isiah pulled into her drive.

He pulled around the "U" shaped drive and stopped the car in front of the door. The outdoor lights were on, but the rest of the house was dark and when Isiah switched the engine off, they sat in the silence.

"Everything go okay tonight?" he asked, picking up her hand. She rolled her head against the back of her seat and looked at him. She took a moment to drink in his dark eyes, his arresting features, and more to the point, his genuine interest. And concern.

She smiled and brought his hand to her lips where she brushed a kiss across it. "Actually, it went perfectly. Serena did what she needed to do, and now we wait and watch what Rosen does with the information. I know Rosen is our primary focus, but I'm curious who the buyer is. The way something like this could unfold is fascinating."

Isiah chuckled. "Says Dr. Wright, doctor of psychology." Then his eyes softened as he looked at her and added, "Only you would decide to get a Ph.D. while working full-time. And I wouldn't be at all surprised if you did it without ever mentioning it to anyone. Yael told me," he added.

Alexis laughed then made to get out the car. "I wasn't saving babies. Don't get me wrong, getting my Ph.D. was a shit-ton of work, but all I did was take a bunch of classes, do a bunch of research, and write a long-ass paper. I didn't have anything else in my life other than work, so time wasn't an issue and, as you know, money certainly wasn't an issue either, so what I did was hardly noteworthy."

Isiah, having rounded the car, joined her. Taking her bag from her hand, he set it on the ground and looped his arms around her. "Life isn't relative, you know. You can still be proud of what you've done even if your financial situation in life has made a lot of things easier for you than for others. It doesn't define you."

She opened her mouth to protest, but he cut her off. "I know full well that you had every advantage—*have* every advantage. But you should never forget that you suffered a trauma—a big one—and you *chose* to heal, you chose to take control of your life and then to go on and do something with it that might, someday, help another child or person. The kidnapping wasn't your fault, but what you've done with your life since is most definitely your responsibility and something you should feel proud of."

Alexis felt Isiah's gaze fixed on her even as she stared down at the place where their bodies rested against each other. The word "pride" didn't sit easy with her. It felt boastful and, to an extent, empty. But he was right. There were any number of ways she could have gone once she'd been rescued and returned to her family. She *had* chosen her path. And not just that, she'd chosen one that she felt good about. She *liked* what she did, liked knowing that she was helping, contributing to society. So maybe "pride" wasn't the best word, but she did have a right to feel pleased with her choices, to feel good about them and the contentment they brought her.

She sighed and brought her arms up to drape over his shoulders. "I am happy with my life. I like what I do and I like knowing that in some small part, maybe I'm helping. And I like it on Tildas Island. This island, my team, the dogs...meeting you, I feel like suddenly pieces of my life are clicking together and, at least for now, it all makes sense. That I'm where I'm supposed to be, with the people I'm supposed to be with, and doing what I'm supposed to be doing. It feels good."

It was a big admission for her, what she'd said about meeting him. After all, she and Isiah hadn't spoken more than a few words to each other prior to two weeks ago. But she wasn't a coward and there *was* something special between them. It had started with the persistent awareness that arced between them, and in such a short time, had grown to more. It had grown to trust, to respect, and to genuine *like*. The word wasn't as flashy or as profound as "love" but to Alexis, it implied a choice—something a person actively did—and because of that, liking someone was a deeply meaningful experience for her.

And she liked the man standing in front of her. She admired his quiet strength, appreciated his quick mind, and, as weird as it sounded, even to herself, she adored his easy acceptance of her dogs and especially his patience—and connection to—Red. Howdy loved everyone, so winning her approval wasn't too difficult, but Red was another story. Yes, there was definitely something special about a man who could win Red over.

And speaking of dogs, whatever Isiah was going to say in response to her admission was cut off when Howdy started barking on the other side of the door. The automatic locks on the car had kicked in while she and Isiah had been talking, and the distinctive beep-beep must have caught Howdy's attention. And once Howdy was going, Allie and George were not far behind.

Isiah laughed, "Do we need to go in before their barking raises any alarms?"

Alexis shook her head and laughed as she stepped out of Isiah's arms. "It won't set off any alarms," she said as she opened the front door and three furry bodies came barreling out in a whirl of tails and wiggles. "But the security team might wonder why I haven't reset it."

He followed her into the house, herding the dogs inside. "I think we've had enough interruptions in the past two days. Let's get the beasties in, then close the door on the world for at least twelve hours."

Once the door was shut, Alexis turned around to see Isiah kneeling and nose to nose with Red. She held her breath, genuinely unsure what Red would do. They didn't think Red had any violent tendencies and had never seen any indication of that, but they knew so little about her that Alexis wasn't certain how the dog would react to such a pointed meeting. Slowly, Isiah raised his hands and started rubbing Red behind her ears. Alexis smiled when Red submitted and closed her eyes. But then they popped back open and held Isiah's in a steady stare. A small, little doggy smile lit up Red's face, just before she leaned forward, touched her nose against Isiah's, and gave him a big ol' wet lick on his lips.

To his credit, Isiah didn't jump back. No, if there was ever any doubt that Isiah Clarke was a keeper, it vanished in that moment; in that moment when he laughed, wiped his mouth with his hand, then laid a kiss on Red, right on the soft fur between her eyes.

CHAPTER TWENTY

ALEXIS WALKED into the FBI office in Havensted ten minutes before her scheduled meeting. Jake sat at his desk and Beni was leaning against the other side, a mug of coffee in her hand.

"Someone looks like they had a good night," Jake said with a grin.

"And a good morning," Beni added.

Alexis considered ignoring them, as she would have done five months ago. But now that she'd acknowledged that things had changed, she was all for embracing it. "I did thank you very much. An excellent night. And morning. And shower."

Jake groaned and Beni grinned over her mug.

"Like how excellent?" Beni asked.

"How's Howdy?" Jake interjected. "And George and Allie. And Red, of course. Though Red's so distant, it might be hard to know how she's doing. But still, you live with her so you can probably tell how she's doing."

Beni and Alexis stared at Jake.

"What?" he asked.

"You have the most puerile mind of all of us and now that we finally have Alexis talking something other than work, you want to talk about *dogs?*" Beni said.

Jake cleared his throat and dropped his eyes as he started to shuffle some of the files on his desk. When neither Beni nor Alexis ceased staring at him, he caved.

"Fine," he said, tossing up his hands. "Despite how it might seem, I don't want to know the details of your sex lives. Or Damian's or Dominic's for that matter. I mean, don't get me wrong. I'm glad you're getting some and it's good, but beyond that, beyond knowing you guys are treating each other right—in every way—I don't want to know the details."

Alexis met Beni's gaze. Beni was hiding a smirk behind her mug. "Who would have thought our little Jakey would turn out to be such a prude?"

Alexis let out an indelicate snort.

"I'm not a prude. I just don't think people should kiss and tell," he said over their laughter.

"As glad as I am to see so much team bonding, Damian just called in. We have a few things to talk about." All three agents spun at the sound of their director's voice, Jake's chair scraping against the floor as he rose. Shah stood in the doorway of her office, her expression serious, but her eyes held a hint of amusement. Without delay, the three filed into the office.

"Rosen booked a flight to Tildas Island this afternoon. She'll be staying at Hemmeleigh tonight and leaving tomorrow night," Shah said as soon as Jake closed the door behind them. "Dominic is on the same flight as Rosen and Damian hopped on an earlier charter."

"Do we know why?" Beni asked.

Shah motioned for everyone to sit, but Alexis remained standing, leaning against the back wall of the office. "She's meeting someone and before you ask, no, we don't know who, not yet. What we do know is that despite our intel indicating she's planning something during the Summit, which might lead us to believe this trip to Tildas makes sense from a recon perspective, she didn't, in fact, book the resort until yesterday," Shah finished.

"So it wasn't planned. Perhaps it was buyer's choice," Jake surmised.

Shah inclined her head. "Likely, yes. If Calloway is the connection between the buyer of Serena's identity, and he's also involved with Rosen and whatever is being planned during the Summit, it's possible that he manipulated the buyer into suggesting Hemmeleigh as a way to get Rosen to the island."

Alexis's mind whirled. Everything in her was telling her that the choice of Hemmeleigh was more than just for the convenience of the buyer, though how it tied to the Summit, which was still eleven months away, she didn't know. And judging by the look on her teammates' faces, they felt the same way.

"But to what means?" Alexis asked. "Why would it be important for Rosen to visit Hemmeleigh now? And for only a day."

Shah shook her head. "We don't know, but we need to find out."

"So what's the plan?" Jake asked.

"We'll have Beni and Dominic keep watch at the resort," she started. "We know which room she's booked in to and have blocked out the room beside it to use as our base. Our technology is good enough that we should be able to listen to her conversations through the wall rather than alerting the staff to our interest by asking for entrance to the room in order to place a bug. I'd like to get a warrant to tap her phone, but I'm weighing that against the repercussions of filing such a request on a ranking CIA employee." Shah sat back in her chair and let out a long exhale. "She's already booked her return flight to DC for tomorrow night, so if something is going to happen, it's going to happen fast."

"We just don't know if anything is going to happen," Beni said, verbalizing all their thoughts.

Shah gave a curt nod of acknowledgment. "Go check-in and get set up, Beni. Dominic can make his way over when he arrives. Alexis, I want you to pick Damian up when his charter lands then head back here to the office so we can plan additional surveillance. Once we have a plan, we'll head to Damian's as he's given us permission to use his house as a base since it's so close. Jake, you head to the airport and tail Rosen. We know she's booked at Hemmeleigh, but we don't know if she's planning on heading straight there."

"And Serena? Do we tell her?" Alexis asked.

Shah's phone rang and she held up a finger to hold off Alexis's question as she answered. A flicker of disappointment flashed across her face before she ended the call, telling whoever it was that she'd plan accordingly.

Shah tapped her phone against her desktop as she stared at the wall opposite from where she sat. Neither Alexis nor her teammates spoke. After several seconds passed, Shah's eyes refocused and landed on Alexis's.

"Change of plan. Dominic ended up seated across the aisle from Rosen. We can't have him showing up at the resort now. She may not think anything of it, but that's a chance I don't want to take. If Isiah is still willing to act as a consultant, I want you and him to take the place of Beni and Dominic."

* * *

*I*siah handed Alexis a headset as she set up the last of the listening devices. Their cottage at the resort shared a wall with the one Rosen had checked into, and the devices, placed along that wall, would allow them to listen in on anything that happened in that room.

"She's stepping outside," Alexis said, her head tilted to the side as she held part of the headset to her ear. Her hair now fell in waves to a few inches below her shoulder and was highlighted with a soft gold. She'd undergone the style change earlier that day, concerned that if Rosen had seen her in San Juan, even from just the back, her longer braids would have made her more recognizable if they happened to run in to the woman at Hemmeleigh. The new style, with its gentle curls and wispy bangs drew attention to Alexis's eyes and he hoped Rosen hadn't gotten a look at anything other than her back because it would be hard to forget eyes like Alexis's.

"You want me to go check out the view?" he asked. Both cottages had ocean views, but he wouldn't be able to see Rosen's patio unless he stepped off theirs and moved toward the water.

Alexis nodded as she fiddled with a dial on the small monitoring device, then she picked up her phone and started to text. Figuring that she'd tell him anything he needed to know, he opened the sliding glass door and stepped out into the late evening. The summer solstice had just passed and this time of year, the temperatures at night were generally less than five degrees cooler than the days. So while the color of the sky was lighting with brilliant pinks and oranges as the sun began to drift down the western horizon, the temperatures still hovered in the mid-eighties with about the same amount of humidity. Isiah glanced at a couple wading about in the sheltered bay. People came to the islands in the summer because it was less expensive than in the winter, but god was it beastly.

Walking toward the beach, which lay less than twenty feet from their patio, the fresh-cut grass was sharp against his bare feet, tickling him between his toes, reminding him of all the times he and his sister used to walk barefoot around their island home. When he reached the edge where the grass met the sand, he paused and looked out at the ocean long enough to appear to be appreciating the view. Then he turned his head as if he were eyeing the sprawling hotel, but behind his sunglasses, he kept his attention on Rosen.

She stood on her patio, looking out at the ocean. She had no phone or computer, and standing there in a pair of long pants and a sleeveless shirt, her blond hair pulled into a ponytail off her neck, she looked infinitely lonely.

It was possible that she was plotting world domination, and he wasn't going to forget that she intended to sell out Serena, but still, she seemed...sad?

Her head tilted toward her room as his phone vibrated in his pocket. Rosen walked back inside as he read a text from Alexis telling him to come back as Rosen had just received a call. With long, measured strides, he returned to their room, slipped inside, and reached for the headset Alexis held out to him.

"No, we'll meet at the Canary. It's the beachside café not far from the main dock." Rosen paused for a few seconds, then spoke again. "Eight fifteen," she said, then disconnected the call. A few seconds later, the sounds of Rosen shuffling around the bathroom, followed by the shower turning on, filtered through their comms units.

"Looks like we're going for a drink tonight," Isiah said.

Alexis glanced at the clock on the bedside table. "I'll let the team know. Unless whoever she is meeting is coming by boat, there's only one path to get to the café. It goes by the boutique and we can hang out there until this person arrives, then follow him or her into the café."

"Do you think we'll be able to identify who it might be?"

Alexis nodded. "Unless he or she is with someone else, there aren't a lot of single people who come to the resort; it's mostly couples and families. It's possible we'll get it wrong, but worst case scenario, we'll still end up at the café."

He nodded. "Need me to do anything?"

She smiled, "You mind listening for a little bit? I want to give the team a call. They can watch the water from Damian's house; it sits up there." She pointed to a high bluff at the far end of the sweeping bay. "Coming by boat would draw more attention so I don't think that will happen, but it doesn't hurt to be cautious."

"Of course." Then, as the sound of the toilet flushing filled his ear, he made a face. "I'd forgotten how voyeuristic this all is," he said, snagging Alexis as she walked by.

He brushed his lips across hers. Her arms came around his neck and their kiss deepened. As her fingers played at the back of his neck, that urgent, almost panicked sense of need, of possession, swept through him again.

Fighting his instinct to give in to the desire, he gentled the kiss, then drew back. He still had an arm around her waist, and her hands were now resting on his chest.

"This resort is probably more what you're used to. But I have a friend with an overwater bungalow in a protected lagoon in the British Virgin Islands. Maybe next time you have a few days off we could head over there. No phones, no interruptions. Yael can stay at the hotel on the other side of the island," he added, making Alexis smile.

"Just us?"

"And the dogs if you like."

She laughed at that. "For a few days, I think I like the idea of just us."

"Excellent." He dropped another kiss on her lips. "Now, go call your teammates because Rosen just stepped out of the shower."

CHAPTER TWENTY-ONE

"I KNOW HIM," Isiah said.

Alexis switched her attention from the man who'd just walked by the resort boutique to Isiah. His lips were tilted into a frown.

"Not one of your favorites?" she asked, as they both started toward the door. Two families and one couple had walked by in the ten minutes they'd been inside the store. The man they'd seen pass was the first single person.

"His name is Philip Mariston. He's British by birth, was in the army for a while, but now works a charter business out of St. John. He's been into The Shack a time or two, usually with a woman from one of his charters that 'wants to go where locals go,'" he said, using air quotes.

Alexis pulled out her phone and sent his name to her team as she and Isiah approached the café. When they arrived, Mariston had his back to them, but she could see Rosen's face clearly. The woman did not look happy that her buyer—if that's what Mariston was—was ten minutes late.

"Table?" the hostess asked.

"Yes, could we have that one in the back, please?" Alexis

asked, pointing to one that would let her keep an eye on the couple, but also keep Isiah's back to the man who might recognize him. "We like the privacy," she added with a smile when the hostess's gaze went to the empty tables scattered around the café that had much better views.

"Oh, of course," she said with a smile. Then grabbing two menus, she led them toward a table. Isiah's hand fell to Alexis's lower back as they navigated through the restaurant. His body stayed close, looking like any other couple enjoying a night out.

"I'll have a sidecar, please," Alexis said as soon as they were seated.

The hostess didn't hesitate to take her drink order and turned to Isiah.

"A beer, please. Whatever you have on tap is fine."

"I'll let the bartender know, and your waiter will be right over with those," she said then made her way to the bar.

Rosen had ordered a drink before her contact had arrived so when the waiter set Mariston's drink on the table, she also set a plate in front of Rosen. It was a small thing but at least that meant she wasn't planning on leaving in the next few minutes and Alexis would have a chance to observe the pair.

Her phone buzzed on the table and she glanced down; a message from Damian. Jake was already in position to follow Mariston when he left the resort, leaving her and Isiah to stay focused on Rosen.

"What are they doing?" Isiah asked.

She didn't stop the laugh that escaped at his tone. He definitely didn't like being forced to stay out of sight. He glared at her, then tried to turn his head subtly enough to see them, under the guise of checking out the restaurant. But he couldn't quite get to that point without turning his whole body. Instead, he accepted defeat and looked at her expectantly.

"They aren't doing much of anything." She raised her phone and snapped a few pictures. Both Rosen and Mariston were in profile so the photos wouldn't be the best, but they'd be better than nothing.

"Rosen is eating, but they aren't talking much. A couple of words here and there," she reported. "Mariston looks bored, genuinely bored. Not the affected kind of boredom of someone new to the game. Rosen looks like she's choking down her food."

"Funny how treason tastes," Isiah said, drawing a smile from her.

A few more bites, a couple of more words, then Rosen slid a slip of paper across the table. Quickly, Alexis raised her phone and started the video as Mariston reached for the sheaf, read it, then folded it and slid it into his breast pocket. The angle was perfect, once they enhanced the video, it would be clear exactly what Rosen had just done.

"I suspect our little meeting has come to an end," Alexis said, taking another sip of her drink. Sure enough, two minutes later, Mariston rose, nodded to Rosen, and walked away. "I give it another ten minutes before she heads back to her room."

Isiah caught the waiter's attention and made the universal sign for the check. Rosen hadn't asked for hers yet, but she and Isiah wanted to be ready to leave whenever she did.

They didn't have to wait long. For such a big thing that they'd witnessed, the evening ended rather suddenly. Twenty minutes after signing their bill, Alexis and Isiah were back in their room, listening to Angela Rosen climb into bed. And it wasn't yet nine o'clock.

* * *

*A*t just after eight the next morning, Isiah laid a hand on Alexis's shoulder. They'd taken turns listening in on their neighbor throughout the night, but until now, nothing interesting had occurred. No calls, nothing.

"Hmm," Alexis rolled over, swiping her bangs from her eyes.

"Rosen has a visitor," He tapped the device in his ear. And if his hearing served him right, Rosen's visitor was none other than Philip Mariston.

Alexis blinked at him, then in a flash, she had a device tucked into her ear as she texted a message to her teammates.

"Rachel March?" Mariston said. "What the hell kind of game are you playing?"

"I don't know what you're talking about," Rosen replied. "Who's Rachel March?"

"Rachel March is also known as Amira Khan. It's *her* identity you gave me. And I can assure you, my buyer was not amused," Mariston answered.

Alexis shot Isiah a look. "Does it concern you that whoever is buying the information was able to hack into the CIA network fast enough to locate the file number Rosen gave him?"

"He either has someone who can hack in that fast or someone on the inside," Isiah said. Both options raised the same question—who did the buyer know that was capable of accessing the information, but not finding it on their own? But that question would need to remain unanswered at the moment as they had more immediate concerns.

"*Her* identity?" Rosen parroted on the other side of the wall.

"Yes, *her* identity. Not only did you give me the wrong asset, because my buyer knows the person who killed his sister was a man, but you gave me the name of an agent that died two months before my client's sister. So I'll repeat the question, what kind of game are you playing?"

Alexis started typing another text into her phone. "This isn't going to end well."

Isiah's eyebrow shot up and he almost laughed. Her comment was an understatement of epic proportions.

"He gave me that file number," Rosen said.

"And it was a man you met?" Mariston asked.

"Of course it was," Rosen answered, her voice exasperated, but also tinged with a hint of panic and undertones of confusion. "I know your client wants The Gentleman, and I assure you, that's who I met."

"Then he didn't give you the right file number and he's played you."

Isiah glanced at Alexis. She wasn't even trying to hide the grin that Serena's ploy elicited.

"There was some talk that he wasn't really one of ours. It's possible that's true and, as you say, he played us," Rosen said.

"Or he was on to you and played you," Mariston replied.

Silence filled the room, then Rosen spoke again. "I suppose it's a possibility. So what now?" Rosen asked. "I assume your client wants the money back?"

Mariston chuckled. "If only it were that easy."

"It is. I can have it wired back to the account it was sent from right now." The panic in Rosen's voice wasn't so subtle now and a glance at Alexis told him she heard it, too.

"Sorry," Mariston said, "It isn't. It's time for you and me to take a little boat ride."

"Boat ride?" Angela repeated.

"Pack your bags," Mariston ordered.

"I don't need to pack them, I never unpacked them," Rosen replied, sounding confused. "But why do you need me to go with you? I can just have the money wired back."

Mariston never replied, but Rosen uttered a surprised, "What the hell?" which was followed by an ominous silence.

"We need to get over there," Isiah said. "He's going to kill her if he hasn't already."

"He hasn't killed her and we need to get to that boat," Alexis corrected, moving toward the sliding glass door. Opening it, she took a few steps outside then quickly reentered the room. "There's a speed boat at the dock. That has to be his."

"Alexis, we need to stop this now," Isiah insisted.

She paused in her search for something. "Yes, it's more than likely that he's going to kill her, but not until after he gets her to where he's been told to take her. You heard him. He's been instructed to bring her to his client. She's safe for now, but if we go barging in there? You can't tell me that you think he's unarmed."

"And letting him take her away, or worse, getting on the boat ourselves, is the only way to save her? You can't believe that?" he countered.

"I can and I do. If we go into the room now, I have no doubt he'll kill her right away. But if we let him get out onto the dock, he won't want to do anything to call attention to himself. If we can keep him outside and off the boat, or, worst-case scenario, allow him on the boat but manage to get on ourselves, we have a chance. We have a chance of saving her *and* finding out who this client is and what, if any, connection the buyer might have to Calloway. Calloway's name has been connected to criminal activity twice this year and I'm pretty sure this isn't the last we'll hear of him. We need to learn everything we can about him and that includes who his network is." Alexis's voice was strong and filled with conviction.

Isiah studied her, his heart beating a rapid—and distracting —rhythm. Finally, he sighed. He didn't like it. But she was right. "Grab whatever you can that you think we might need. I want to keep listening as long as possible." She started gathering a few items as he spoke—a small gun she tucked into a holster under her peasant blouse, a knife she slid into a sheath that lay against her hip under her shorts. Once she was kitted up, she started handing him a small armory, even as he continued to listen.

"We need to go now," Alexis said.

"To the boat?" he asked, reluctant to leave before they knew as much of Mariston's intentions as they could.

Alexis nodded. Then, without leaving him a chance to protest, she started out the door.

* * *

*A*lexis knew she owed Isiah an explanation, and she planned to give him one, but they needed to hurry. Once he closed the door behind them, she took his hand and walked as fast as she could, without appearing hurried, toward the boat dock.

"Whether or not we end up on the boat with Mariston, my team will be on the water themselves, so we'll have him covered."

"Is it worth it, Alexis?" Isiah asked. He was speaking about the risks they were taking, not just to obtain intel, but to save Rosen. And it was a legitimate question.

"Probably not," she answered honestly. "But I can't not try, not when it comes to Rosen. I have no sympathy for her, but I can't let anyone get killed or tortured if I can stop it."

He was silent as they navigated their way along the grass, avoiding the beach and the early sunbathing guests. When the dock was less than twenty feet away, he sighed.

"You're right. We can't. But even so. Her life is not worth yours. She took the same oaths you did, she's not an innocent bystander. Promise me that you will *not* trade your life for hers."

Intellectually, she knew his request wasn't unreasonable—yes, it was an emotional plea, but it was also a logical one. Of the two agents sworn to protect the United States and its people, only one of them had betrayed that oath and it wasn't Alexis. But when the chips were down, she didn't know if her instinct would allow someone else to die when she could stop it, even at the cost of her own life. Her training, which had started long before she'd joined the FBI, might kick in and she'd be diving in front of that bullet before there was any conscious thought about what she was doing.

"I have no intention of doing that." Because at least that

much was true. "But let's do our best to not get into that situation at all. And if you could, please just play along."

"Play along with—"

"Oh my god!" Alexis exclaimed loudly, dragging him out on the dock toward the waiting boat. "Is that a Ducati Cigarette boat?"

The man at the wheel startled at her exclamation and jerked his attention from the resort to them. His eyes swept up and down her body, then he nodded.

"Oh," she said, pulling Isiah to her side and hugging his arm tight against her as she 'admired' the boat. "This is the boat I was telling you about, Baby." She sounded so un-Alexis-like that it took him a second—and a little pinch on his side—to catch on.

"The one that you just got that you're so excited about?"

She bobbed her head. "They're pretty hard to get and ours is a newer model, of course, but this one's not bad. How do you like it? How's it handle on the ocean?" she asked the pilot.

His eyes darted behind them but she hadn't heard or felt anyone step onto the dock, so Mariston wasn't close yet.

"It's good. On days like this. We don't take it out when there's any weather to speak of." The man's accent was pure Southern. South Georgia if she had to guess.

"It is a perfect day isn't it?" Alexis said. "Do you charter her? I'd love to take her over to Jost Van Dyke," she continued without waiting for an answer. "Our boat was just delivered to our house on St. Barts, but our captain has been on the mainland visiting his family so we haven't been able to try her out."

She was babbling to pass the time and to keep Isiah from having to talk. She had a very specific image she wanted to portray and it wouldn't do to have Isiah butting in to make her sound like anything other than a spoiled princess.

"Uh, yeah, sometimes," the man said as a small vibration shook the dock under her feet and a board squeaked behind her.

"Do you have a card or something? I'm not here for very long, but if we have the time I'd love to take her for a ride," she said.

"Sorry, she's not available."

Alexis spun toward the voice behind him, 'gasping' in surprise. "Oh, you startled me. Is she yours? Is *she* okay?" she asked. The first question was about the boat but with her second question, she pointed to Angela Rosen who walked limply beside Mariston. Clearly, Mariston had drugged her, but with what, Alexis couldn't tell. The agent's body seemed able—if a little lethargic—but her eyes were completely vacant.

"Clarke. What are you doing here?" Mariston asked, ignoring her question and turning to Isiah.

"Uh." He let his gaze drift down, then slowly he looked back up and nodded toward Alexis. "This is Zoe. We met at The Shack last night."

Alexis flashed a big smile at Mariston.

Like his colleague, Mariston's eyes raked over her before turning back to Isiah. "You didn't strike me as the type." The type to go home with a woman from his bar was the unspoken end of that sentence.

Isiah shrugged and grinned. "Seriously, who wouldn't be?" He emphasized his answer with a jerk of his head toward her as if to question why any man wouldn't have done the same. It took everything in Alexis to not roll her eyes.

"So you don't charter?" she asked again, pressing against Isiah so hard she was pretty sure the side of her breast was going to have a permanent indent from his arm.

"We don't and if you don't mind, we need to get going." Mariston moved to pass them.

"But your friend said you chartered," she whined.

"He lied," Mariston said, as he handed Rosen over to his colleague who helped her into the boat. Alexis had to work hard to keep from staring at the agent. She had no idea what kind of drug Mariston could have given her that more or less left her physically capable but almost entirely mentally incapacitated.

"Baby," she whined to Isiah.

She was grateful that the look Isiah flashed her could just as easily passed for one of a slightly annoyed but indulgent boyfriend when, in reality, what was probably going through his head was more along the lines of "what the hell are you thinking?"

She plastered on a fake smile, went onto her toes, and kissed him. "Please."

He sighed. "Mariston, any chance you can take Zoe out? If not today, then some other day? Some other day in the next day or two because after that, she flies home to Los Angeles," he added after another pinch in his side.

"Sorry, I don't have time for this," Mariston said as he started to step into the boat.

Isiah stepped away from her and grabbed Mariston's arm. "Seriously, can you do a dude a favor and take her out?"

"You need to let go of me, Clarke. Trust me on this one."

Isiah's eyes narrowed on Mariston and Alexis knew this was the make it or break it point. They could back away and let him go or they could finagle a way on to the boat themselves.

Rather than step away, Isiah asked, "Something going on, Mariston?" Apparently Isiah had fully embraced her plan to stick close to Mariston and they were going for door number two.

"Nothing you need to worry about," he answered.

Isiah didn't let go of his arm. A beat passed, then two. "I'm not so sure. Who's that woman? She seems kind of out of it."

Mariston let out a deep sigh. "Let it go."

"Oh, now I really can't. We both served, man. You know I can't walk away if I think someone needs to be protected and by the looks of it—and your sketchy attitude—that woman needs my protection."

Alexis moved away from Isiah, not far, but far enough that if either he or she needed to draw a weapon, they wouldn't be in each other's way. She also positioned herself closer to the boat in case she needed to jump in—she hoped it wouldn't come to that, but it was always good to have options.

"Remember, you made me do this. I have a timetable I need to stick to and don't have time for this," Mariston said before he withdrew a small pistol with a silencer on it from his pocket.

Alexis didn't have to fake her startled inhale. She'd counted on him being armed. But it was the silencer that threw her.

"Whoa." Isiah held his hands up, palms out. "I didn't mean anything, just, well, Zoe and I will be going."

"You know I can't do that now." And to his credit, Mariston did sound disappointed. "Your girlfriend comes with me."

"Like hell, she does," Isiah said.

"Look, Clarke. I can shoot you and her and be in that boat and on my way before your bodies hit the ground. I don't want to kill either one of you—it will draw too much attention to me to have you die here, but I will if you don't leave me any choice."

"How can you think I'll just let you take her?"

"Because if you don't, you'll both die."

"Take me, then," Isiah said.

Mariston chuckled. "No way in hell am I going to get on a boat with you. But if I take your little socialite girlfriend and you don't send anyone after me, I promise you can pick her up in two hours on Jost Van Dyke."

"In what shape?" Alexis asked, cutting off whatever Isiah was about to say.

"Zoe," Isiah admonished.

Mariston inclined his head. "It's a fair question. I promise you'll be dropped off on Jost unharmed, other than any discomfort you might feel from the boat ride. I take it you can swim?"

She nodded.

"Good, because there are no docks on Jost."

"I know," she snapped back.

"Zoe," Isiah said.

She hated the look on Isiah's face, hated knowing what she was doing to him, but she had faith in her team, and in Yael, who, for good or bad, would always know where she was.

"I'll be okay," she said, holding his gaze.

"You can't think you'll get away with this?" Isiah said to Mariston.

Mariston shrugged. "By the time you pick little Zoe up, I'll be long gone. You're welcome to try and find me, of course, but it will be a waste of time. Let her go quietly now and we can all forget this ever happened."

"Isiah?" Alexis drew his attention back to her. "Tell Yael. She'll know what to do." She'd told him in Honduras that Yael had ways of tracking her, she hoped he remembered now.

"I don't like it." His fists clenched at his sides. She didn't much like it either, but it was the choice she had if she wanted to be able to live with her conscience.

She took a deep breath and thought of her team. She thought of Yael and of that day, all those years ago when she'd been rescued by the kidnap and ransom team. But today wasn't anything like that day. She was no longer that child, she had more people who had her back than ever before, and they were better prepared.

"I've been here before," she reminded him quietly. "I'll be fine."

And before he could protest any further, she stepped into the boat.

CHAPTER TWENTY-TWO

THINKING OF DAMIAN AND CHARLOTTE, Alexis eyed the low railing of the boat as she took the seat Mariston directed her to. Less than five months ago, Nik Balraj had tied her friends to the metal railing that ran atop the side of his boat and taken them as part of a plot to blow them up.

Back then, the team hadn't been prepared for Balraj's boat abduction, but they'd learned their lesson. Now they had an FBI boat as well as a network of people whose boats they could leverage depending on which marina they needed to depart from.

Grateful that Mariston didn't seem inclined to tie her up, Alexis turned her attention to the retreating shore. Isiah still stood on the dock watching, but judging by the way he moved, he was already on the phone to either Yael or her teammates.

Between Isiah's motivation, Yael's ability to track her, and her teammate's skills, Alexis wasn't sure how things would go down, but she was confident she'd be fine.

Hopefully.

Mariston eyed her as his accomplice opened the throttle when they left the bay. He stood like a man at ease on a boat, feet apart, leaning casually against the back of the passenger seat, his gun still in his right hand. She supposed it wasn't quite as important to tie her and Rosen up when Mariston could keep an eye on them while someone else navigated. That, and it might have drawn attention to him—or taken too much of his time—had he done so while at the dock.

"Your boyfriend's not going to give me any trouble, is he?" Mariston asked.

Alexis stared for a moment, then she looked away and shrugged. "We just met. He's not my boyfriend, but he is a good guy. I don't know him well enough to know what he might do, but he might do something."

"You better hope that that something is just show up on Jost in two hours to pick you up."

She darted a look at Mariston. "Believe me, I am."

He studied her for another moment, then looked to Rosen. Alexis took the opportunity to wiggle her phone out of her back pocket, and, under the guise of tugging her shorts down a little bit, she slipped it under the seat cushion. She didn't want Mariston to notice she had the device and take it away from her.

She weighed the idea of engaging with him, of asking him about Rosen, but in the end, she opted for silence. She already knew what Rosen had done and what Mariston had planned for her. Alexis just wanted to know who his buyer was, and that was information he wasn't likely to share.

Both she and Mariston looked up as a boat swung by them a hundred yards away. Mariston straightened, but when it continued toward Hemmeleigh, some of the tension left his body and he returned his gaze to the open ocean. Alexis almost smiled. He had no idea that that boat contained a world of hurt for him. She recognized both it and the people in it—Jake and Beni were on their way to pick up Isiah. She didn't know where Damian and Dominic were or what their part of the plan was, but she wouldn't be at all surprised if they showed up in a helicopter.

The thought of them hanging from a chopper made her smile.

Which drew Mariston's attention. He didn't say anything, just narrowed his eyes at her. In response, she raised her face to the sun and let her eyelids drift almost closed.

"Did you know your boyfriend is a former SEAL?" Mariston asked. She lowered her head and looked at him, surprised that he was the one striking up a conversation.

She shook her head. "I knew he was in the service, but not a SEAL." She had no interest in letting Mariston in on how well she and Isiah knew each other. "Is that why you didn't want to take him on the boat? How do you know him?" She already knew the answer to the second question, and she could guess the answer to the first.

Mariston shrugged, much as she had done earlier, as his gaze swept across the open water. It was a beautiful day and there were several boats out. "Yeah, seemed like a better idea to take you than him. I really don't want to kill anyone if I don't have to, and he seemed the sort to try and get all heroic and shit. I've been into his bar a few times. I don't know him well, but I know him enough."

"So, you live on Tildas?" She didn't think she'd get any useful information talking with him, but she may as well pass the time.

"Sometimes. I make my way around the Caribbean, depending on the charters I have."

She'd thought he ran his own charter business, based on what Isiah had said, but it sounded like he was more likely crew, which gave him the freedom to move around and pick up work wherever he wanted.

"What's up with her?" Alexis asked with a jerk of her head toward Rosen. The agent sat clutching the railing on the opposite side of the boat, her face turned to the wind.

"She stole from someone I've done some work with. He wanted to talk to her so I'm bringing her to him." Mariston's answer was surprisingly straightforward, if not quite the full story.

"He's not going to hurt her, is he? I mean, can't he just turn her in?"

Mariston almost chuckled at that. "I don't know what he's going to do with her, but no, the kind of theft we're talking about isn't one you can bring the cops into."

He was watching her closely as he spoke and so she responded as he'd expect. She widened her eyes, darted them to Rosen, then to his gun, and mouthed a silent "O".

Alexis held her tongue for what she thought was the appropriate amount of time for Mariston to think her horror had shifted to curiosity. "So is she drugged or something? Or just, you know, slow?" She'd seen the effects of Rohypnol, and whatever Rosen had been given seemed to have a touch of the same effects—at least on her mind. But it had a completely different effect on the body. Unlike Rohypnol, Rosen seemed in full, though maybe slightly sluggish, control of her body.

"Or something," Mariston side-stepping her question. Alexis let her attention stay with Rosen as the psychologist in her sorted through the options. Maybe some kind of Rohypnol-like drug mixed with a barbiturate. Whatever it was, she didn't like the effect it was having on Rosen. Again, not that she had much sympathy for the woman, but if the drug was out on the streets and available, it wasn't hard to conjure up a hundred uses of it that weren't good.

Mariston suddenly jerked straight, startling Alexis. His attention focused over her shoulder. "I should have fucking known."

She didn't have to turn to know what had caught his attention, but it would be expected of her and so she did. Sure enough, a couple hundred yards away was the boat carrying

Jake, Beni, and now, presumably, Isiah as well, although she couldn't see him from where she sat.

"I really wish he hadn't done that," Mariston said. When Alexis turned back around, his eyes were narrowed on her.

She was pretty sure that until this point, he'd only been contemplating killing her. But now the choice had been taken from him. In some ways, she questioned her teammates' decision to make their presence known, but she also recognized that at this moment, they might have different information than she had.

"What are you going to do?" she asked. She had her weapon, but his was already drawn, and there was no way she could get to hers before he got a shot off.

"I need to slow your boyfriend down. I don't want to kill you, and I'll try not to, but hell, we're in a boat so all I can do is my best. So that's what I'm going to do."

As Mariston raised his arm, Alexis rose with him. She didn't have much time to analyze the situation, although, in the back of her mind, she recognized that hitting the water at the speed they were going could also kill her. Even so, she'd rather hit the water uninjured than with a bullet in her. And so she did the only thing she could think of, she bent her knees and launched herself over the low railing.

Just as a powerful punch hit her in the stomach, taking her under.

CHAPTER TWENTY-THREE

NEVER IN ISIAH'S life had his stomach pitched like it did when Alexis hit the water. He hadn't heard the shot—thanks to the silencer—but he'd recognized the motion the Mariston had made and that had been enough.

"Faster, Jake." Isiah strained forward as if he could add speed to the boat by willing it.

Jake and Beni were talking about something, but he ignored them, focusing only on the water. He also tried to ignore all the voices in his head telling him how unlikely it would be to survive a shot at close range or a tumble into the ocean at the speed Mariston and his accomplice had been traveling. Instead, he focused on scanning the water's surface, looking for any sign of Alexis's head bobbing up.

"Come on, Alexis," he pleaded quietly. Or at least he thought he'd been quiet, but when Beni's hand curled over his shoulder, he realized he must have spoken loud enough to be heard over the roar of the motors.

"There!" Jake said, pointing, even as he made a subtle adjustment to their direction. Isiah's gaze tracked Jake's finger and he squinted against the glare as he tried to spot what Jake had seen.

There was nothing but the blue of the Caribbean stretching out before him. "Where?" he demanded, shouting over the engines.

Jake didn't say anything, but he throttled back their speed ever so slightly and pointed again.

And then Isiah saw it. Alexis's head and the top of her shoulders hovering above the waterline. He wasn't too macho to admit that the phrase "sick with relief" suddenly made a lot of sense. The only thing that kept him from completely losing it was the fact she wasn't yet back in his arms.

"Pull up slow, McMullen." The command was a logical one, but twenty feet away from Alexis, streaks of ruddy red-brown started to cloud the normally clear blue water, and Isiah couldn't get to her fast enough.

"Jake," he managed to choke out.

"I see it, Clarke."

Yes, they all saw it. Blood. Blood in the water. And it was everywhere.

"Alexis!" Isiah called as Jake inched closer. "Are you hurt?" he demanded. As he spoke, he scanned both Alexis and the area around her, looking for any sign that she needed him in the water. They weren't far, but Jake could still get them closer to where she treaded water faster than if he swam to her.

"I'm okay," she called back, her breath sounding labored. "The blood's not mine."

That's when he noticed Alexis wasn't alone. He'd seen Angela Rosen go over the edge with Alexis, but hadn't given her much thought. He didn't care if she lived or died, but judging by the way Alexis was holding Rosen in a lifeguard-hold, she cared.

"She's been shot," Alexis said when they were close enough to hear. Alexis's hair was plastered to her face and she used her free hand—the one not holding Rosen above water—to swipe it out of the way. It did little good when a small swell washed over her, leaving her sputtering and her hair back where it had been.

"She came out of nowhere," Alexis said as they pulled up beside her, and Jake held the boat steady in a subtle combination of forward and reversals of the engines.

Blood pooled in the water around the two women and without a thought, Isiah stripped his shirt off and dived in. Jake may have been raised on the water, but as a former SEAL, he was no slouch.

"Throw the preserver," he yelled to Beni as he reached for Rosen. "You okay?" he asked Alexis as he relieved her of Rosen's dead weight.

"I'll be bruised and sore tomorrow from the fall," Alexis managed to say as they bobbed up and down—even on a smooth day there were always a few small waves and swells on the open ocean. "But I'm okay. She jumped in front of the bullet. I didn't even know that she was aware of what was going on. I *still* don't know, but she did. She took the hit and sent us both over the edge."

"Up," he ordered with a jerk of his head toward the boat when Beni tossed the preserver to Alexis then lowered a short, metal ladder. There was no back deck on a boat built for speed so getting Rosen up wasn't going to be a gentle endeavor, but he wanted Alexis on the boat first. He wanted to be sure she was okay, and then he'd carry the unconscious Rosen up the ladder himself. He had no idea if she was alive or dead—there was a lot of blood, but water had a tendency to spread so it was possible there was less than appeared. Still, he did give a thought to sharks as he watched Alexis climbed the five rungs and step into the boat. They didn't have Great Whites in the Caribbean, but they did have a few aggressive ones he'd rather not encounter.

"What can we do?" Alexis asked, leaning over the railing. Her shirt was plastered to her body and if he wasn't mistaken, she had some seaweed in her hair. But seeing her looking down on him, unharmed, was one of the most beautiful sights he'd ever seen. And no doubt she'd kick his ass if she knew that's what was going through his mind at this particular moment.

"Just stay back. And maybe see if there's a medic kit on the boat. If she's alive, she's going to need care."

As he spoke, he maneuvered Rosen into a fireman's hold—not the best for someone who'd been shot, but it was the easiest way to carry her—and quickly climbed the ladder.

Easing Rosen down onto the deck, he could see where the bullet had struck her, or maybe where it had exited. To the left of her belly button was a small round hole in her blood-soaked shirt.

"There's a pulse," Beni said. "But we need to get her to care quickly." As she spoke, she began striping Rosen of her clothes, tearing them indiscriminately so as to get a better look at the wound.

"The boat ride is going to be rough on her," Isiah said, handing Beni the shirt he'd taken off before diving in. She folded it and pressed it against the wound.

"What boat is that?" Alexis asked.

Isiah looked up to see what Alexis was pointing at. It was a large, grey, military-looking boat about a half-mile away. There weren't any big bases in the region, but both the US and the British had a navy presence in the area.

Jake consulted an instrument on the panel before answering. "Navy research vessel," he called out.

That was something Isiah was very familiar with. "They'll have a medical berth on board. Maybe even a doctor. Jake, call it in and confirm. If they do, ask for permission to board and give them our status."

Leaving Jake to do his thing, Isiah turned back to Beni as Alexis handed her a towel she'd dug up from somewhere. "Is there anything we can do?" he asked.

Beni folded the towel and placed it over his shirt as she shook her head. "No, she likely needs surgery, and she definitely needs blood. All we can do is what we're doing until we get somewhere with medical facilities."

"We've been granted permission," Jake said then, without warning, he gunned the engines and they headed toward the navy vessel. The ride was a little bumpy, but blessedly short and less than ten minutes later, they were pulling into the on ship berth—the captain of the boat having opened the gate for them so they could pull directly into the hull.

Crew swarmed them as Jake killed the engines. Three helped tie them off and four jumped aboard with a stretcher.

"I should have known it was you all. Really, we have to stop meeting this way," came a voice from a catwalk above them. Isiah looked up as Beni worked with the four navy crew to get Rosen on the stretcher. A woman leaned over the railing, her curly hair falling in front of her face. She wore shorts and her long, very bare, legs, stood out in stark contrast to the navy uniforms around them.

"Sugar, I told you once and I'll tell you again, I'll meet you anywhere, any time," Jake called back.

"Almost dead CIA agent, McMullen," Alexis muttered, as the four crew lifted the stretcher and maneuvered Rosen off the boat. A doctor rushed onto the deck and he and Beni immediately put their heads together as they followed the crewmen to the medical berth.

"You say that now McMullen, but you were saying something altogether different at Lola's three months ago," the mystery woman said. Jake opened his mouth, no doubt to defend himself, but she spoke over him. "Hey, Alexis. I'd ask how you're doing, but you're soaking wet and cold enough that I can see your nipples from here. And since you also arrived with a half-dead woman, I'm guessing you're not doing so hot. Here." She unzipped her sweatshirt and tossed it down.

"Nia, good to see you," Alexis said, donning the sweatshirt. It rarely got cold enough in the Caribbean for a sweatshirt, but no doubt parts of the ship were air-conditioned. "This is Isiah Clarke, by the way. Isiah, that's Doctor Nia Lewis, she's the head of the Marine Research Center, though what she's doing on a Navy boat I have no idea."

Nia waggled her eyebrows and jerked her head toward the group of mostly male crewmen still loitering around. "Not doing as much as I'd hoped."

"She's basically a brilliant doctor but the social equivalent of Jake. It's kind of scary how alike they are," Alexis said to him as a crew member helped her from the boat.

"You need a wingman?" Jake called up. "You and me, we could hit the canteen together. You know, stir some shit up."

Nia chuckled, then started heading toward the stairs that would lead her down to them. "I've been on this boat for six weeks and have more or less stirred as much as I can, but maybe I'll take you up on that when we're back on shore. I hear Lola's has a new cocktail."

"Jesus, I'm never going to live that down, am I?" Jake asked, stepping up behind him and Alexis. Going from thinking he'd lost Alexis to listening to pre-pubescent chatter, was giving Isiah a headache.

Doctor Lewis stopped at the bottom of the stairs as they approached. When he, Alexis, and Jake stood before her, she looked closely at each of them. She might be joking around with Jake, but the concern in her hazel eyes was very real.

"No, you're not ever going to live it down. Not as long as I'm around to tell the tale," she said, tipping her head to brush a kiss on his cheek. She gave Alexis a quick hug then reached out to shake his hand.

"It's nice to meet you, Isiah Clarke. Now, why don't I take you all to the captain and you can tell him everything he thinks he needs to know."

"You can take us to the captain," Alexis said. "But we have some calls we need to make before we answer any questions.

The man who shot Agent Rosen and tried to kill me is still out there. And I suspect my boss is going to want to stop him."

* * *

*a*lexis climbed the stairs behind Jake and Nia, Isiah following. They were halfway up when something brushed her hand. Glancing down, Isiah held his phone out.

"You need to call Yael. Or text. Or let her know you're okay somehow."

She hadn't given Yael much thought since she'd gone overboard and she appreciated his reminder that there were a few people who would be worried about her. Taking the unlocked phone, she dashed off a quick text to Yael then handed the phone back to Isiah just as Jake's buzzed in his pocket.

Pulling it out, Jake answered as they hit the upper deck and started toward the captain's bridge. "Alexis is fine. Rosen's been shot." He swiveled and mouthed "Shah," to her as he listened to whatever their director was saying.

If Alexis hadn't been watching so closely, she would have missed the slight tensing of Jake's shoulders and the way his free hand jerked into a loose fist. "Yeah, we're thirty seconds from the captain's bridge, we'll dial into the comms as soon as we're there."

He hung up and, with a nudge, urged Nia to walk faster. Nia glanced back and whatever she must have seen on Jake's face was enough to get her to all but jog the last twenty feet.

"You left your phone on the boat," Jake said, over his shoulder as they followed Nia. "Damian and Dominic are airborne and following the signal. Shah sent the channel, we can listen in."

They entered the captain's bridge—the command center—as Jake finished talking and without taking a breath, he told the captain what they needed. Fifteen seconds later, a crew member had dialed in and the sounds of a helicopter filled the room.

"We've got our eyes on him," came Damian's voice. Alexis didn't bother to hide the small smile that flitted on her lips— looks like Damian and Dominic got their helicopter ride after all.

"We're passing into British air space now," came a woman's voice that Alexis didn't recognize and who she assumed must be the pilot.

"We've been cleared. Continue as ordered," Shah responded.

For a few minutes, no one spoke and nothing but the sound of the helicopter and the wind filled the room. Then Dominic spoke. "They appear to be heading toward a private island south of Cooper Island."

"Evanston, identify the island" the captain ordered.

"On it, sir," the crew member responded. Alexis glanced over to see a young man pulling up a map. It would be interesting to know who the island belonged to and what, if any, ties they had to Mariston, but for now, her most pressing concern was the safety of Damian and Dominic.

"There's a large house," Damian reported. "And what looks like a boathouse. I don't see any way other than by boat to get off the island, so if he goes to ground, we'll have him cornered. Any chance we can get some assistance from our colonizing neighbors?"

"Let's keep the political commentary to a minimum, Rodriguez," Shah said. "I'm calling it in—"

But the rest of Shah's statement was lost as the sound of an explosion rocketed over the radio.

CHAPTER TWENTY-FOUR

"RODRIGUEZ! BUREL!" Shah barked, the strain in her voice coming through loud and clear. Jake looked over and met Alexis's gaze. Alexis had never met anyone in her life who could flip from charming and goofy to deadly serious as quickly as Jake, and as their eyes stayed locked, she all but felt the intensity pouring off him. He was *not* going to lose two teammates today. It was a ridiculous thought—sitting where they were, there was literally nothing she or Jake could do about what might be happening to Damian and Dominic. But if his force of will alone *could* accomplish the feat, could protect their teammates, then they'd be as safe as the day was long.

Suddenly, Damian's voice crackled across the comms speaker. "Holy fuck. What the hell was that?"

Alexis let out a long, controlled breath. If Damian was talking—and asking a question—then he, and the others, were likely okay.

"After almost getting blown up with Charlotte in February, I would think you'd be able to recognize a bomb when one goes off," came Dominic's smart ass reply. "I mean, I know you probably didn't get much action as a Ranger—"

"Fuck off, Burel. You okay, Shorty?" Damian asked.

"Caught me a little by surprise, but we're all in one piece," the pilot answered.

"I need a status report, boys," Shah demanded, and Alexis had the errant thought that Sunita Shah was probably the only person who could get away with calling Dominic and Damian "boys."

"The boat entered the boathouse and as soon as it was inside, the entire building blew," Damian reported.

"Any chance Mariston survived?"

"Not a chance," came Damian and Dominic's simultaneous reply.

"Care to elaborate?" Shah asked.

"Uh, not really, but we'll take some pictures. Right now, I think I see his leg floating in the debris," Damian answered.

That was an image Alexis did *not* need to elaborate on.

"Right," Shah said. "Take some images, document the scene the best you can, then get back to Tildas. I'll call my colleagues in the BVI, they'll probably want to take over and frankly, with Mariston gone, I won't mind if they do."

"Roger that," Dominic confirmed.

"You think the owner of the island is involved?" Isiah said quiet enough that only she could hear.

She lifted a shoulder. "Hard to say at this point, but we'll look into it. At least we still have Rosen," she added. Hopefully.

"What did I miss?" Beni said from the door to the bridge.

Alexis, Isiah, and Jake all looked up at the sound of her voice.

"Looks like someone died. Or maybe I shouldn't joke about that. No one died, right?"

"Just Mariston and the pilot of the boat," Jake said. "Dominic and Damian are fine."

Beni let out an audible exhale. "Well, unfortunately, so did Rosen."

Alexis shouldn't have been surprised—Rosen had taken a

bullet to the stomach from close range. But even so, disappointment at losing the investigative lead—if not the life—rolled through her. "Damn," she muttered.

"We did everything we could, but she'd lost too much blood, and there was too much internal damage. But yes, I agree with your assessment, Lex."

"Anyone else find it interesting that Mariston, who was supposed to be bringing Rosen with him, was killed in a bomb?" Jake asked.

"Fucking, Nik Balraj," Beni muttered. The four of them had all gathered in a tight circle. Alexis knew the navel crew was watching them, but they kept their voices down.

"For such a punky looking guy, he's caused a lot of damage," Jake said. It was true, Balraj did not look like your typical gun-for-hire. He was five foot six, probably weighed no more than a hundred twenty pounds, and was missing a few teeth.

"We don't know it was him," Alexis said. Beni and Jake both shot her a look. She rolled her eyes. "Well *someone* had to at least *say* that. I didn't have to *mean* it."

"With Rosen gone, are we shit out of luck in terms of finding out her—or Balraj's—connection to the Summit?" Isiah asked. "I know it's not my job and believe me, I plan to give up this 'consulting' gig," he said, making air quotes, "as soon as we dock on Tildas. But I don't like the idea of an explosives expert for hire wandering around the Virgin Islands."

"You're not alone in that," Alexis said, then she smiled. "We'll look into the owner of the island and see if there is a connection to Calloway. But when it comes to both Rosen and Balraj, we haven't lost everything. We still have an ace up our sleeve. An ace by the name of Serena. Or The Gentleman, if you prefer."

CHAPTER TWENTY-FIVE

ALEXIS LOOKED up as Dominic let out what could only be called a war cry. Charlotte was on top of Damian's shoulders, and Nia was on Dominic's and the four were playing Chicken in Alexis's pool. A game made much more interesting by the addition of George, Allie, and Howdy, who wiggled and swam between the pairs in full on doggy bliss.

Her gaze drifted to Beni, who was standing at the table that held all the food for their impromptu potluck. She had a glass of juice in her hand and looked to be contemplating which dessert to select. Alexis smiled when she slid one of each onto her plate.

"I don't know what you do to these wings…" Jake said to Isiah before taking another bite of one of many wings loaded onto his plate. When he finished chewing, he skewered Alexis with a look. "I cannot believe you kept a gem like The Shack a secret from all of us for so long."

Alexis shook her head at Jake as she reached for Isiah's hand. "You can read, McMullen. There are reviews and even blogs written about it. Including one particular blog that specifically covers those wings."

"There is?" Isiah turned toward her, surprised.

There was more than one, but Alexis knew he wasn't too into reading reviews of his restaurant. Or even caring too much about social media in general. He just liked running a bar that served good food and good drink to good people. Well, to mostly good people—Mariston *had* been a patron, but that was something no one mentioned.

"There is," she confirmed. "It's very complimentary. You should tell your mom." After all, it was his mom's recipe. He smiled back at her.

It had been two days since they'd returned to Tildas. Rosen's body had been sent back to her family for burial and the details of what had happened that day were kept intentionally fuzzy in the official reports. No one on their team, including Shah, was interested in painting Rosen a hero for saving Alexis, but neither did they want to divulge her true reason for being in the Caribbean in the first place. Rosen hadn't been working alone and the fewer people who knew that *they* knew about her activities, the easier it would be to keep investigating them.

Thank god they had Serena on their side, now. Not that she hadn't ever not been on their side, but she and Shah had agreed to stick to the original deal—Shah would provide Serena with any information they came across regarding the trafficking ring and in exchange, Serena would continue to feed any intel to the team that she learned about either Rosen or Calloway.

But that still left the question of Nik Balraj and his tie—if any—to the Summit.

As if answering a summons, Alexis's new phone vibrated with an incoming message. Unlocking the device, she read the short note sent from an address she didn't know and would probably never see again.

"FYI, had a little chat with Nik yesterday. Three weeks ago, he was sent an email asking if he could supply certain items to someone on Tildas Island next May. He didn't like that someone he didn't know had contacted him, so he looked into it and found that the date

was during the Summit. He said that after his last encounter on Tildas Island, he had no interest in being anywhere near there, especially not when security would be tightest. He never responded to the email. When a follow up was sent three days later, he deleted his account and is now, (except for our conversation), pretending he never saw either email in the first place. Maybe he isn't as dumb as I thought."

At the bottom of the message was an email address, presumably the one that sent the original message to Balraj. It wasn't a lot to go on, but at least it appeared that they wouldn't have to worry about their favorite explosives expert during the Summit. That was something, wasn't it?

"Good news?" Isiah asked, leaning over and dropping a kiss on her shoulder. Red lay on the couch on his other side, her head resting on his lap. She opened an eye at his movement then snuggled back down when his free hand came to rest on her neck.

She held the screen up for him to read.

"I'll send this to Shah and start digging into the email address," she said, once he'd finished.

"Tomorrow," Isiah gestured to their guests with a subtle motion of his head.

"Fine," she said on a mock sigh, then laughed as Red rolled over with a grunt of pleasure. "You know, Howdy was going to be my first foster fail, but now I'm thinking it might be Red. I think she's pretty bonded to you."

"Wouldn't that make her *my* foster fail?" Isiah pointed out, his eyes alight with mischief, but she knew he was fully grasping what she was saying.

Alexis tried to look serious as they discussed this serious subject, though she couldn't help but be lighthearted. She knew where she and Isiah were headed—as a couple, as partners—and it felt more right than she ever thought it would.

"You and Red are a bonded pair. Since I have no intention of letting you go, that means she comes, too. Luckily, I have the room."

The smile that had been playing on Isiah's lips widened. "You're not letting me go?"

"Nope." She shook her head. "Definitely not."

"I like the sound of that," he said, then he leaned over and covered her lips with his. In the background, Alexis could hear Jake complaining about the PDA, but she ignored him.

When Isiah ended the kiss, he only pulled back far enough to look into her eyes. "What do you think about putting both our names on Red's adoption papers?"

THE END

Did you enjoy Alexis' and Isiah's story?
Are you curious about book number 3 'A TOUCH OF LIGHT and DARK' featuring Nia & Jake's story? Keep reading for a sneak peek!

Did you know that we first meet Damian & charlotte in my award-winning Windsor Series? They make their first appearance in book 2, THESE SORROWS WE SEE. If you're interested in the Windsor series, check them out HERE.

A TOUCH OF LIGHT AND DARK

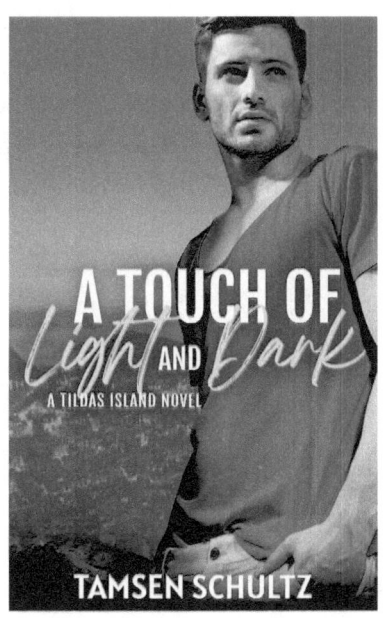

When Power Goes to the Highest Bidder

Dr. Nia Lewis is as comfortable dancing the night away as she is in the quiet underwater world she's been appointed to protect as the head of the Caribbean Marine Research Center. But when her team discovers a group of fish behaving in a way they've never seen, and there's a subsequent break-in at her lab, she knows that whatever is going on is something bigger than what she, or her center, can handle.

FBI Agent Jake McMullen doesn't mind working with Dr. Lewis—not one bit. After all, she's one of his closest friends and, despite some pesky little flutters of attraction, there's no one he'd rather spend his time with. And if the assignment also means spending time underwater? Well, the former pro-surfer couldn't think of a better gig. That is, until they discover a body resting on the ocean floor, designer drugs cropping up at island hotspots, and tourists committing inexplicable crimes.

What should have been a straightforward investigation uncovers a threat to the islands neither Jake nor Nia would have ever foreseen—especially when the name of an old nemesis is linked to it all. And with not one, but two hurricanes headed directly for them, the only question is, can they keep the islands they love from being a pawn in a powerful conspiracy?

If you're drawn to beauty edged with darkness, you'll want to dive right into this exhilarating mystery.

PART I
A TOUCH OF LIGHT
AND DARK

CHAPTER ONE

Dr. Nia Lewis pulled into a parking spot at the Caribbean Marine Research Center and turned off her car. As it always did, the sign that proclaimed the spot "Reserved for Dr. Lewis," gave her a little thrill. Against all odds, not only had she obtained her Ph.D. in marine biology ten years ago, but she now headed the biggest marine research center in the Caribbean. It wasn't the best in the world, but it was the best in the Caribbean. And she loved every minute of it.

Well, except for maybe this specific minute.

She glanced down at her skirt and heels and considered leaving. She was due to meet her friends, Jake McMullen and Dominic Burel, in downtown Havensted, the main town on Tildas Island, in fifteen minutes. There was no *real* reason she needed to be at the lab. The samples she'd started running earlier that day on a couple of fish she'd collected the day before could wait until tomorrow.

She wrapped her fingers around the key and clicked the ignition over once. The radio blared from the speakers, and the air conditioning blasted, blowing her curly hair away from her face. But with her fingers on the key, one click away from starting her engine, Nia hesitated.

"Fuck," she muttered, turning the key back toward her and yanking it from the ignition. It wasn't as if Jake and Dominic couldn't entertain themselves without her. In fact, those two could entertain themselves inside of a bucket; waiting for her at the beachside bar of one of the island's trendier hotels would be no hardship. It would be better to just take ten minutes now and check on her damn samples than it would be to wonder about them all night.

Throwing her door open and sliding from her seat, the October heat and humidity hit her like a wall, and she sucked in a deep breath. She'd been raised in the Caribbean—on Tildas Island itself—and so with two more deep breaths of the ocean scented air, her body more or less adjusted. But, no joke, living in the tropics wasn't for sissies.

Adjusting her skirt, Nia made her way from her parking spot to the main entrance of the research center. Using her pass card and a code, she let herself in, pausing just inside the door to let the cool, air-conditioned air caress her skin. The motion-sensing lights flickered on, and though normally a receptionist would be there to greet employees and direct visitors to the visitor center, at nine o'clock on a Saturday night, the building was empty.

Crossing the reception area, she pushed through a door marked "employees only" and proceeded down a long hall. Bypassing several of the main labs, Nia walked to the back of the building and toward a side lab—*her* side lab. It was a small room that was hers and hers alone. A place where she tinkered, tested, and theorized. A place where she discovered, failed, succeeded, and created. She'd recently published her fourth paper based on findings she'd reached in that room. It was no secret that it was her favorite place in the large complex.

As she walked the hallways, her thoughts settled and

centered on the samples that had brought her back to the lab. The tests she planned to run the next day would probably show nothing—at least she hoped so—but even so, how she'd even come to have the samples was a bit of a strange story and one that baffled her.

Making the last turn, she pushed through a fire door and let her mind drift back to Friday afternoon to when she and a few colleagues had been running checks on a small, coral nursery north of Tildas Island. A school of fish had been leisurely circling her and her colleagues when one of the fish had literally swum into her. It hadn't been the first time she'd been booped by a fish, but usually when that kind of contact happened it was in the middle of a frenzy.

Surprised by the gentle, but strong, bump, she'd turned to see what had hit her hip only to find a parrotfish hovering at her side. It had paused, seeming to contemplate what to do about the obstacle in front of it, then after a beat, it had tried to swim through her again. The behavior had been so odd that Nia had stopped what she'd been doing to watch.

And that's when the second fish had entered the picture. It hadn't swum into her like the first one, but it had hovered right in front of her belly, as if confused about how to get around her.

After she'd spotted four more fish acting in the same unusual manner, she'd called them to the attention of the two research assistants diving with her. Perplexed by the conduct, they'd ended up collecting four of the six for testing. There were lots of bacteria and viruses that fish could get that would alter their behavior, but she'd never heard of anything that resulted in what she'd witnessed. Her curiosity as a biologist had been piqued, but so had her responsibility to the people—and marine life—of the Caribbean. If something was negatively affecting the ocean and the animals that lived in it, she had a duty to investigate.

And so here she was. At her lab. On a Saturday night.

Rounding the corner just before her destination, Nia slowed her steps. The motion-sensing lights in her lab, visible through the small window in the door, were already on. She paused, confused as to why that might be. Her lab was locked, and while a couple of the research assistants had keys, none of them had mentioned coming in tonight.

Then again, neither had she. Her decision had been a spur of the moment thing, driven by her curiosity and lack of patience. It was possible one of the RAs had done the same.

But if they had, they would have let her know. Everyone who worked at The Center knew that no one was allowed in her lab without her approval, and there was no way anyone would go against that edict and risk getting fired.

No, something felt, well, *off*.

Looking at the door, and the little window into her space, Nia quickly ran through the options in her head. She could either enter the lab, and hope that whoever was in there was friendly, or she could pull back and call security.

She nearly snorted at that last thought. The Center had security—of course it did—but it was *island* security. The men and women who made up that department were good people, but on an island with very little crime—other than petty crime targeting tourists—their response times were sometimes a little on the slow side. Or a lot on the slow side. Like if she called them now, she might never make it to meet Jake and Dominic because she'd be waiting so long.

But while calling security didn't seem like the most efficient option, charging into her lab didn't seem like such a hot idea either. At least not without a little more information.

Eyeing the small window in the door, Nia made a decision. Reminding herself of the low crime rates, and reasoning that it was probably an RA who'd forgotten to tell her they'd be in, she inched her way closer to the door, keeping her back to the wall.

Her logic was sound, but that didn't keep her heart from

racing or her palms from sweating as she paused in the corner where the door met the wall. Leaning forward, she strained to listen. Surely if an RA were in there, she'd hear the usual lab noises?

Her ear was practically plastered to the door when a jarring crash of breaking glass erupted from the other side. On instinct, she jumped back, pressing her body against the wall. That was most definitely *not* the sound of one of the RAs.

Reaching into her pocket, she palmed her phone. If someone had broken into her lab, the island police were a better bet than The Center security. It took her two tries to unlock the device, and in that time, whoever was on the other side of the door started moving a table and its legs rumbled and screeched against the industrial flooring.

"This is 9-1-1, what's your emergency?" the dispatcher answered.

"This is Dr. Nia Lewis of the Marine Research Center. I think someone has broken into my lab," she whispered loudly, hoping the responder would be able to hear her.

"Are you safe, Dr. Lewis?"

Was she? Probably not. But when the sound of her spectrometer being moved across the counter—a sound she was all too familiar with—filtered through the door, she knew she wasn't going to go anywhere. That was an expensive piece of machinery and damned if she was going to stand by and let someone send it crashing to the floor like they'd done earlier with what she assumed had been one of the holding tanks.

"Dr. Lewis? Are you safe?" the responder repeated.

"For now, yes. I'm also pissed," she said. "They are still here, and it sounds like they are destroying my lab."

"You need to leave the building, Dr. Lewis. As quickly and as safely as possible," the responder directed. "Can you do that?"

Oh yes, she could do that. But she wasn't going to. Not yet, anyway. Her life wasn't worth the spectrometer, but it went against everything inside her to stand by and let something happen to that machine. Perhaps she could create a diversion and scare the person away?

Stepping toward the window, she peeked her head above the frame, all the while cursing biology for not designing people's eyes to be in a location that would allow them to see without having to expose a large part of the head—honestly, evolution could have learned a thing or two from some fish.

The man, and it was a man, had his back to her, and appeared to be contemplating one of the three mini-fridges she kept on the counter. Dressed in jeans and a black t-shirt, he didn't look very tall, but he was built like a tank and definitely not someone she'd want to encounter in a dark ally. He jammed a hand on his hip and ran the other through his shaggy blond hair. There was nothing special about the small appliance he stared at, and Nia wondered what it was that drew his attention.

"Dr. Lewis?"

So fixated on the man in her lab, Nia startled at the sound of the responder's voice.

"Sorry, I'm here," she whispered, shifting so that her back was against the door and her face was no longer in the window.

"The police are on their way. Are you safe?"

That question was getting a little old. "For now, yes," she said. The man had no idea she was there, so until he learned otherwise, she was safe.

"Good. You should hear the sirens shortly. Can you stay on the line with me until they arrive?"

"Yes," Nia answered.

She itched to look back inside her lab again, and as the hours —okay, seconds—stretched, the itch became a twitch. She fought the urge to do something, even if that "something" was just to tap her foot, and forced herself to stillness.

She could hear the responder typing away on her computer, maybe starting the paperwork for the call already. But that was all she heard. Nia frowned. Considering there was a man in her lab who had, until he'd stopped to contemplate the mini-fridge, been moving around, shouldn't she be hearing something else? Or was he still staring at it?

The distant sound of a siren permeated the walls of The Center, and for the first time in what felt like ages, some of the tension left Nia's body. She hadn't heard any more destruction, and the police would soon be there—she didn't know what state her lab would be in once she got a look, but at least it sounded like her spectrometer was going to be safe.

Right?

Taking courage from the imminent arrival of Tildas Island's finest, Nia rolled to her side to peer into the lab one more time. As she did, two things struck her simultaneously. First, she should have remembered that if she could hear the sirens so could the man in her lab. Second, there was no way out of her lab other than through the door she now stood in front of.

The man's face popped up on the other side of the window, and Nia screamed. Which led to a third thing striking her—the actual door. It flew open, catching her first in the head then the rest of her body. She went flying across the hall and hit the opposite wall, her head snapping back against the hard concrete. The man didn't bother to pause as he fled, and Nia slumped to the ground as his figure—looking fuzzy in her current state—retreated. The last thing she remembered thinking before closing her eyes and drifting off, was to wonder whether or not her spectrometer okay.

CHAPTER TWO

"I NEED to get into my lab," Nia insisted as a paramedic flashed a light in her right eye.

"Can't. Cops are in there," the paramedic said, moving the light to the other eye.

"But how will they know if anything is missing if I'm not in there?"

The paramedic sat back on her heels. Nia had refused to lie down on a gurney so she was still sitting on the floor with her back pressed to the wall, not far from where she'd first fallen. It reminded her of high school when she and her friends would take shelter from the random rainstorms and congregate in the halls. Only back then, she never had a headache like the one she sported now.

"Not my job," the paramedic said as she reached into her bag. "I'm not Agatha Christie." No, according to her uniform, her name was P. Jobard.

Nia narrowed her eyes at the woman. "Aren't you supposed to be sympathetic or, at the very least, soothing?"

P. Jobard looked unimpressed as she rolled Nia's head to the side to get a better look at the ginormous goose egg forming where she'd hit her head against the wall.

"What can I say," Jobard said. "You got the B-team tonight."

At a loss for how to respond to that, Nia tried to get a better look inside her lab. The police had left the door open, and she could see two of them talking while a third looked to be dusting for prints. Not long after she'd come to, Nia had given one of the officers, Detective Anika Anderson, a brief statement. But she had no idea what Detective Anderson could be discussing so intently with her colleague when they had such little information to go on. Maybe they were talking about their fantasy football teams?

Nia's grumbling complaint was cut off when a phone vibrated to her right. Looking over, she saw her device just out of arm's reach. P. Jobard didn't look like she was interested in helping a woman out.

"Hand me that phone and you won't hear another word from me," Nia said, not above a little bribery. Or was it blackmail?

The paramedic let out a huff, but she also reached for the phone and handed it to Nia. Shit, there were five texts and two calls from Jake. She was supposed to have met him and Dominic an hour ago, and she was never late. As an FBI agent, Jake wasn't too prone to freaking out, but this was definitely his version of that.

"*Sorry,*" she typed. "*Problem at the lab. Won't make it tonight.*"

She'd barely hit send when the "read" notification popped up along with the little bubbles indicating Jake was typing.

"*What kind of problem?*"

Nia considered not answering the question, but not only would Jake not let her drop it, if she were honest with herself, the fact that he cared—and the fact that she truly *believed* he cared about her—was something special that she wasn't willing to cast aside. She could count on two hands the number of people who ever expressed any genuine interest in her well-being, and Jake was always first on that list. The other six were Jake's teammates and their significant others.

Her life was definitely weird when the people she considered her closest friends were the five members of the elite—and temporary—FBI task force assigned to the island in preparation for The Summit of World Leaders scheduled for the following May. Then again, maybe the fact that they were temporary was the reason she'd clicked with them eight months ago when she'd fished Agent Damian Rodriguez, and his now-fiancée Charlotte, out of the water after their boat had exploded.

And wasn't that a sobering thought.

"Hello???" Her phone vibrated in her hand.

"There was a break-in. My lab is trashed," she typed.

"You okay?"

"A little banged up, but fine. Just waiting to get into the lab and talk with the police."

"We'll be right there."

"You don't need to come. I'm fine," she said.

"We don't need to, but we're coming anyway. Let the local law enforcement know."

Jake's last text didn't require an answer and so she slipped the phone into her pocket. She considered calling her parents to assure them she was okay, but the thought didn't go any further than that. She'd only be setting herself up for disappointment if she did. Her family didn't fall into that small group of people who cared about her well-being. At all.

"We done here, yet?" Nia asked P. Jobard.

"Yeah, we're done," Jobard answered, rising from her squat. "Ice the goose egg on the back of your head. The cut on your forehead doesn't need stitches, but I put a butterfly bandage on it to hold it together. Be sure to change it every day. It's possible you have a mild concussion, but since your eyes are responding and you're clearly alert, I'm not going to require you to visit the hospital. If possible, you should stay with someone tonight to keep an eye on you." As she'd delivered her diagnosis, she'd packed her bag, and by the time she was done, P. Jobard stood over Nia looking down at her.

"You got someone to stay with tonight?" Jobard asked.

Nia raised an eyebrow at the woman. *Now* she was solicitous?? "I got it covered," Nia lied.

The paramedic eyed her, then nodded. "I'm out, boys and girls," she called to the men, and woman, in blue. "She's all yours," she added when the officers turned her way.

Nia let out a sigh, followed by a much less genteel grunt as she dragged her ass off the floor and stood. "Looks like I'm all yours," she said. "Now, can we figure out what, if anything, is missing from my lab?"

* * *

"Tell me again what you know," Dominic demanded as they navigated the streets of Havensted toward the Marine Center.

Jake scowled out the passenger window, startling the person stopped at the red light next to them. He eased the tense expression and winked at the white-haired woman who smiled back as she accelerated away. But he didn't feel like smiling. No, his mind was going all sorts of places it shouldn't, and his whole body was coiled tighter than a cobra since Nia had sent her text.

How hurt was she? Why hadn't she called him? She was one of his best friends and they saw each other three or four times a week, wouldn't that alone warrant a call? Not to mention the fact that he was an FBI agent. But had she been so hurt that she couldn't have reached out to him before she had?

His stomach churned at the thought.

"Jakey, you okay over there?" Burel asked.

No. "Yeah, why?"

"You made a weird sound."

"I'm worried about Nia," he said, amazed his voice sounded somewhat normal.

"I'm sure she's fine," Burel said with an annoying level of confidence.

Jake reined in his anxiety. The truth was, he wasn't quite sure *why* he was so anxious. Nia was obviously well enough to be texting, and her texts hadn't sounded like she was scared. But still...

"Tell me what you know," Dominic repeated, bringing Jake's thoughts back to facts. What few they had, anyway.

"This isn't an interrogation, Burel. I'm not going to have any more, or different, information than the first time you asked me. Or the second," Jake said. He'd told Dominic what little he knew as they'd left the beachside bar. It had been a condition of getting Dominic to leave at all as he'd been a bit wrapped up with a woman visiting the island from Estonia.

"If you want to go back, I can drive myself and you can get a cab home. Or whatever," Jake added. Jake had a bit of a reputation when it came to driving and he rarely ever drove—and almost never drove anyone else's car—and so they'd taken Dominic's car to the bar.

"It's Nia," was all that Dominic said.

Jake's thoughts and emotions might be all over the place, but Dominic's simple statement brought some calm to the storm. When the chips were down, Jake could always count on his colleagues to be all in. And when those chips involved someone that one or all of them cared about, there was never a doubt or question about what would be done. Because they would all do whatever it took.

And there was no doubt that they all cared about Nia. She'd helped them out on more than one occasion, but even more than that, she'd become their friend—and one of Jake's closest friends. Maybe that explained why he was teetering on the edge of a panic attack at the thought of her being hurt? If something happened to Nia, the whole team would feel it. Yes, maybe that explained this weird turmoil he was experiencing—he was carrying the weight of what it would do to his friends if she were hurt. Logical or not, Jake grounded himself in that belief as they parked the car at The Center—he was taking one for the team, and he'd pull on his big boy boxers and deal with it. Surely Dominic was feeling the same as he was, but he was just doing a better job of hiding it.

When they finally walked into the lab, Jake's attention zeroed in on Nia, who was deep in conversation with two police officers. At the sight of her standing on her own, clearly alert, he took what was probably his first deep breath since receiving her text. Letting some of the tension ease from his body, his gaze swept over her. Her sun-streaked hair fell just above her shoulders and she wore a black tank top with thin straps. With her back to them, he took in the familiar expanse of tanned skin—skin that took on a rich golden hue thanks to her Danish ancestors—and the smattering of freckles across her shoulders. Her skirt landed just below the middle of her thighs, and although it was loose enough to dance in, it was still tight enough to show off her curves. And yes, Nia was his friend, but he'd have to be dead not to notice her mile-long legs or curves.

"Doc," he called out. The three turned, Nia wincing at the movement. "You need to take care of that concussion," he added with a smile.

"It's a potentially mild concussion," she shot back. "And how did you hear that?"

"We ran into the paramedic on our way in. Dominic flashed his badge and that smile, you know the one." Jake gestured to Dominic, who complied and graced them with his trademark smile. Both officers blinked, but Nia was unfazed.

"Right. Of course he did," Nia said as they stopped beside

her. She'd known them long enough to know exactly what kind of things that smile could get Dominic.

"So, what happened here?" Jake asked. Nia hadn't been exaggerating when she'd said the lab had been trashed. Papers were strewn around the room, two of the mini-fridges had been emptied, and fish guts—or whatever Nia was looking into—and shattered glass were scattered all over the floor. Three empty tanks remained on the counter that ran along the back wall of the room, but one had clearly been tipped and the contents had tumbled to the ground. Filter equipment, sand, and glass lay in a heap, and a large puddle of water reflected the fluorescent lights of the ceiling.

"This is a local investigation, Agent," the male officer said.

Jake lifted his eyes from the scene to Nia. She shrugged. "Jake, Dominic, this is Detective Anderson," she said, gesturing to the female. "And this is Officer Schuyler. Officers, these are Agents Jake McMullen and Dominic Burel."

Since neither of the police held a hand out, Jake went back to perusing the scene. "You okay?" he asked Nia, taking in the violence of the room. She'd said she'd been a little banged up, but with Nia, that could mean anything from a scraped knee to missing an arm. Clearly, it wasn't the latter, but he could see a butterfly bandage on her forehead that he was pretty sure wasn't a fashion accessory.

"I got hit in the forehead by the door when the guy was fleeing," she said. "I got thrown against the wall and hit my head."

"You saw him?" Jake asked. There was a lot in her statement that made him uneasy—not only had she *been there* when the break-in occurred, but she'd seen the man, too. On the one hand, she might be able to identify him. On the other, that meant he could probably identify her, too.

Nia started to nod, then abruptly stopped and took a deep breath. Her eyes were tight and she was a little pale—which, considering her perpetually suntanned complexion, spoke more about how she felt than she would ever vocalize.

"Again," Officer Schuyler said. "This is a local investigation."

"He had blond, shaggy hair, brown eyes, and one of those noses that looks a little pig-like—kind of round on the tip with big nostrils. You know the kind I'm talking about?" she said, ignoring the cop. When Jake nodded she continued. "Other than that, I'd guess he was maybe five foot seven? Not tall, but built like a brick shit house."

"Anything taken?" Dominic asked, making his way to the side of the room to get a better look at the remains of the aquarium.

"I'm going to have to ask you both to leave," Officer Schuyler said, straightening his shoulders and adjusting his belt.

"Oh give it up, Ronnie," Detective Anderson said. "She's not saying anything to them now that she wouldn't tell them later. She's had a bash on the head and her workspace violated. Cut her some slack and let her tell us everything at one time."

Ronnie opened his mouth to object, but the women silenced him with the most cutting glare Jake had ever seen. Impressed, Jake turned to see if Dominic had caught it. Dom had his eyes back on the wreckage, but he was grinning.

"Thank you, Detective Anderson," Nia said.

"Yes, thank you," Jake said. "And we're not here to interfere, but Doc is a friend."

Anderson flashed Nia a supportive smile, but the look she shot him told him he better watch his step.

"So, anything missing?" Dominic repeated the question.

Nia's gaze swept the room. Her brow furrowed and she frowned. "I haven't been able to go through the papers, but he did a hard reset on my spectrometer and took off with two fish."

"Hard reset?" Anderson asked.

Nia nodded, her attention going to the large machine in the back corner of the lab. "I think he wanted to trash it, but it's really heavy and I don't think he could tip it over. But the hard reset erases the stored memory."

"So, you lost data?" Anderson asked.

Nia shook her head. "No, it backs up to a cloud drive. If it didn't do that, I would have lost some data, but as it is, it's really nothing more than an inconvenience as we'll have to recalibrate it. But that's the extent of the damage. At least that I can tell right now."

"And the fish?" Jake asked.

Nia shrugged. "Two parrotfish we brought in yesterday."

"He took two parrotfish?" Officer Schuyler asked, deciding to do his job and join the conversation.

"I'm guessing those aren't fancy expensive fish?" Dominic asked.

Detective Anderson shook her head. "You dive off the dock out there," she said, gesturing with her head in the general direction of The Center's small, private marina. "You'll probably see a dozen of them. Why did you have parrotfish?"

Jake walked over to join Dominic as Nia answered. "We were out checking on some coral beds yesterday, and they were swimming around us acting a little unusual. I brought two to my lab because I wanted to check their health, make sure there's not something going on that could threaten the marine life. It was actually some samples from their skin that I was coming to check on tonight. I wanted to make sure my RA finished the prep work so I could run the tests tomorrow."

"These the samples?" Jake asked, pointing to the remains of several glass test tubes and their stoppers scattered around the floor.

"Yep, that's them," Nia said, staring at the mess.

"But nothing else was taken?" Officer Schuyler asked.

Nia shook her head. "Like I said, I haven't had a chance to go through the paperwork, but from what I can see, that's it."

"Can you think of any reason someone would want those

fish?" Anderson asked. Jake had grown up in Hawaii and knew exactly how prevalent parrotfish were in tropical waters, and he was as confused as the cop as to why someone would break into a lab and walk away with nothing but the pair.

Again, Nia shook her head. "I honestly can't."

Jake eyed her. She glanced at him, then quickly looked away. He slid his gaze to Dominic, who raised a brow in question, but when Jake gave a small shake of his head, Dom went back to his examination of the lab. Whatever it was that Nia wasn't saying, they'd get it from her later.

"Looks like he broke in through the side door down this hallway," came a voice from behind Jake. He turned to see a third officer, this one clearly more junior than the other two since he looked no more than twenty.

"Don't you have an alarm?" Schuyler asked.

Nia stared at Schuyler for a beat as if trying to determine if the question was a serious one. She turned her back on the officer and made a face at Jake as she answered. "Of course we do. But it didn't go off, or I would have received an alert. We also have surveillance cameras in the reception and visitor areas and at the main door between the public and private areas of The Center. There's also one by Perry," she added.

"Perry?" Jake asked.

"The fridge that holds the few controlled substances we keep at The Center," Nia answered. "It's not a regular fridge. It's heavy and specially insulated and has a couple of different locking mechanisms. It wasn't broken into, though. We checked before you got here."

"But Perry?"

"The Fridge," Dominic said. Jake turned to his colleague for more of an explanation. "William 'the Fridge' Perry, the football player."

"Ah," Jake said. He'd heard the name before, but as he'd never been much of a football fan—living most of his life on a surfboard before joining the FBI—he hadn't made the connection.

"If the power goes out, there's a few seconds before the generator kicks in," Nia said. "In that time, the doors remain locked, but the alarm is disabled. It's a gap we're aware of but can't really fix. I don't know if there was a power outage earlier this evening, but that's the only reason I can think of as to why the alarm wouldn't have gone off."

"We'll have an electrician out tomorrow to see if we can figure that out," Detective Anderson said. "There wasn't a general outage in this area, but it's possible there was something more targeted."

Nia looked around her lab. "And by 'targeted,' you mean just The Center." It was a statement, not a question. The potential seriousness of the situation was slowly sinking in, but rather than letting fear take hold, Jake could see Nia's mind trying to make sense of it, trying to solve the problem. This lab— The Center—was her life, and he didn't doubt that eventually, the implications of it being violated would hit her. But for now, she appeared to be focusing on the question of "why" like the excellent scientist she was.

"Dr. Lewis, I think we're done here for the night," Detective Anderson said. "We collected lots of prints and will start to run them tomorrow. Since you're a federally funded entity, we have the prints of the folks who work here and we'll eliminate those, but we'd appreciate it if you could come in and maybe look through some photos to see if you recognize the man who was here tonight."

Nia nodded but her attention was still on the mess that used to be her tidy lab.

"We'll also get an electrician out tomorrow to check the alarm," Officer Schuyler said. "Do you have a ride home?"

"Yes, she does," Jake answered.

At the same time, Nia said, "I can drive myself. I'm fine."

"Of course you're fine," Jake countered. "But your head got a little shaken up tonight and you shouldn't be driving."

"So I should ride with *you*? It seems like I'm taking a bigger chance with that than driving on my own," she said.

He grinned. "Fair point, but I promise, I can drive like a normal person when I want to."

Nia looked at him skeptically, then her gaze switched to Dominic, who lifted a shoulder. "He picked Charlotte up from the airport this week."

"Damian asked *him* to do that?" Nia asked, pointing to Jake and clearly surprised.

"Upon pain of death if either Charlotte or the car was damaged, but yeah, he did," Dominic answered. Nia's attention lingered on Dominic, and he shook his head, answering the question in her eyes. "I could take you home in my car, but then he'd be driving yours back to your house unsupervised, and I'd advise against that. You're hurt, I don't generally trust him behind the wheel, but I do trust him with you."

Nia seemed to consider that answer, then finally, she let out a long sigh. "Fine," she said. Jake thought he should probably be offended at her reticence, but he was just glad she was going to let him make sure she got home safely. Besides, his reputation with cars was a carefully cultivated one, and he could hardly blame her or Dominic for thinking of him exactly what he wanted them to think when it came to his driving skills. The truth was, he was a damn good driver. He just hated it—give him a surfboard in a storm and he was a happy camper but ask him to drive ten miles and he wanted to pull his hair out.

With some reluctance, Nia handed her keys over and twenty minutes later, Jake pulled her car into her driveway. She lived in a small bungalow in a newer development that was a mix of locals and a few snowbirds that couldn't afford something on the beach.

"Thanks for the ride," she said, opening her door.

Jake ignored her and exited the car. "I have the keys, it's not worth arguing with me," he said as he jangled them in his hand.

He could see the calculation in her eye—could she grab them if she lunged fast enough? She couldn't, not even on a good day. And wearing heels and sporting a mild concussion, she had no chance. He grinned when annoyed acceptance settled on her face.

"You're such an asshole," she said, walking by him toward her front door.

The epithet rolled right off him. His teammates called him that every day. Usually more than once. As far as he was concerned, it was a term of endearment.

"You want any water or anything?" Nia offered after he closed and locked the door behind them. "Not quite the night I had planned, but hey, I'm alive, so no real complaints." She walked into the kitchen as she spoke and reached for a glass on the drying rack beside the sink.

"Nah, I'm good," he said, leaning against the tile counter. "The good news is that if you still plan to get up at six, I only need to wake you up once in the middle of the night since the paramedic said not to let you sleep more than four hours at a time."

Nia's eyes slid to the clock on her microwave as she filled her glass. It was eleven o'clock.

"How do you know I wake up at six?" she asked after taking a sip of her water.

Jake shrugged. "Remember that night of Carnival when you were out with Dominic and me? You said you had to leave because you wanted at least two hours of sleep before having to get up and go to work the next day. It was three-thirty in the morning, so accommodating the time it would have taken you to get home and adding two hours to that, gives me a six o'clock rising time."

She stared at him. For a weirdly long time. Then she turned and started to walk toward her bedroom.

"That's too much math for me right now. I have a concussion," she said as she walked away.

"It's only a potential mild concussion," Jake called back, parroting her earlier words.

She didn't bother turning around, but he did like the one-finger salute she threw him over her shoulder before disappearing into her room and shutting the door on him.

* * *

*N*ia winced as her bedroom door shut behind her a little more forcefully than necessary. Kicking off her shoes, she wandered into her bathroom, thinking a shower and some ibuprofen might be in order for the night.

She didn't worry about Jake settling himself in. He'd spent enough time at her place to make himself comfortable in the guestroom. In fact, it was practically his room. Not that he stayed over that often, but he was the only person who'd ever used that room.

She popped two pills, then she stripped out of her clothes, letting them fall to the floor. As she did, the events of the night started to catch up with her. She hadn't given it much thought at the time, but the realization of how close she'd come to someone who was clearly comfortable with violence—even if just against property—shook her. She shivered as memories of the night filtered through her mind like a series of snapshots. She wasn't sure if she'd ever forget the wild look in the man's eyes when his face appeared in the window.

Turning on the water, she stepped under the spray, hoping the warmth would soothe her. She forced herself to stop thinking about the man and his crazy eyes and instead started to mull over the question of why. Why would someone break into her lab? The Center itself had a few controlled substances and some very expensive equipment, but he hadn't been after any of that.

The water streamed over her body, and she let those thoughts percolate as she gently washed her hair and body. She had more questions than answers, but at least the process occupied her mind and kept her from dwelling on the man who could have done much more harm to both her and her equipment.

After shutting off the water, she dried off in the shower, then stepped out. As she hung her towel, her gaze caught on her phone sitting on the counter. Should she call her mom? Jackie Lewis wasn't likely to care one way or the other if Nia had been hurt, and she certainly wouldn't care about the damage to the lab.

Nia stared at the phone for a beat, then raised her eyes and looked at herself in the mirror. Her gaze lingered on the butterfly bandage that had survived the shower, and as her attention focused on the edge of the cut visible along the top edge of the bandage, she could feel the rumblings of a pity party starting to happen. Her lab had been broken into, she'd missed a night out with Dominic and Jake, and the only reason she was contemplating calling her mom was because if Jackie found out about the incident from anyone else, it would be yet one more thing Nia had failed to do for the woman who'd gone to the trouble of birthing her.

With a sigh, Nia picked up the phone and dashed off a quick text as she walked into her bedroom. Jackie wouldn't care enough to reply, but even so, Nia deliberately turned the sound off and set the device face down on her bedside table. She didn't need to be confronted with her mother's neglect tonight. Not when she was feeling so raw and the idea of a pity party was feeling more and more attractive by the second.

Pulling a tank top and a pair of boxers from her drawers,

Nia slipped into her go-to pajamas then slid between her sheets. In the next room, Jake's bed creaked, and a pang of longing lanced through her. What she wouldn't give to crawl in next to Jake and have him hold her. There was no doubt in her mind that he'd keep the looming pity party at bay. But even more than that, having someone like Jake—someone kind and capable and endearing—care for her might be enough to remind her that, despite her family's opinions otherwise, she was *worthy*. Worthy of friendship, worthy of care, worthy of love.

But even though the draw to go to him was strong and she knew he'd welcome her—and welcome her platonically—it was a line she wasn't sure she wanted to cross.

Rolling over and hugging an extra pillow to her chest, she thought back to those first few times the two of them had gone out. Jake was a good looking man—tall, well built, with sun-streaked brown hair, slate blue eyes, and a face that looked like every girls' fantasy of the perfect surfer. The spark of attraction she'd felt toward him would have surprised exactly no one, least of all her.

There had been a few moments when she'd thought she'd caught a hint that her interest was reciprocated. But then it became clear that friendship was all he had in mind, and she'd decided that having Jake's friendship was more important than maybe giving something more a go—especially when the *something more* would only have to end once Jake left the island. They'd been more or less inseparable—or as inseparable as their jobs would let them—since she'd committed to the friendship-path, and she didn't regret a moment of time they spent together.

She let out a sigh and closed her eyes, willing herself to forget about the comfort Jake might offer and fall asleep. The pills still hadn't taken effect yet and her head throbbed, but she did her best to ignore the pain. Unfortunately, she didn't have the strength to ignore both the pain and the memories of the past few hours, and within a few minutes, her body started to tremble. Not big shakes, but little ones, little ones that were big enough to remind her that maybe she wasn't as strong as she thought she was.

Jake's bed creaked again, and her mind flitted back to what Dominic had said to her that night. He trusted Jake with her.

And so did she. He had come as soon as she'd told him what had happened, he'd driven her home, he'd insisted on staying to make sure her concussion wasn't a problem. The crazy thing was, none of his actions surprised her. It was what Jake did and who he was. He cared for those in his life as easily as he breathed.

Letting out a long breath, she swung her legs over the side of the bed and rose. She wasn't sure if what she was doing was the right thing, but if ever there was a night she needed, or wanted, someone to tell her everything would be okay, tonight was it.

She left her room and walked down the short hallway. Pausing before his door, she hesitated, then knocked gently.

"Come in, Doc," he said.

Quietly, she opened the door just enough to see him lying on his side, facing her. She stared at him for a moment, a moment of indecision.

"Need a hug?" he asked.

She did, she desperately did. She managed a nod.

"Come here, sugar," he said, flipping back the covers. "I'll keep the demons at bay."

CHAPTER THREE

THOUGH JAKE WAS NOWHERE in sight, a fresh pot of coffee sat in the machine when Nia woke the next morning.

She'd curled into his side all night, and he'd rubbed her head and kept the shakes away until she'd drifted into a deep sleep. As promised, he'd also managed to wake her up once, around three in the morning. He'd given her someone to lean on when she needed it, and she was grateful, more than grateful, for the gift.

But at the moment, if she were honest with herself, she was also feeling a little selfish—she would have liked to see him before he'd left. She had an interesting—and probably not very fun—day ahead of her and she could have used the laughter he brought into her life. He also had that disheveled sexy look going for him in the mornings, and it always perked her up. They may be just friends, but she wasn't blind. And seeing him in her kitchen, in his boxers with a cup of coffee, wouldn't have been a bad way to start her day.

That said, waking up to a fresh pot of coffee wasn't a bad alternative. She poured a cup then went to the fridge to pull out some yogurt for breakfast only to find a note taped to the door.

"Meet at The Shack at four this afternoon," Jake had written, referring to a bar on the southeast side of the island. Owned by Isiah Clarke, the significant other of another agent, Alexis Wright, The Shack had become the de facto gathering spot for the five members of the FBI special task force.

She stared at the note, not because the substance was anything special or surprising, but because she really had no clue where he'd found the tape. She couldn't remember the last time she'd ever used any, so had no earthly idea where it might have been or how long it would have taken Jake to find it. But he'd probably gleefully gone through all her kitchen drawers as he searched. She smiled at the thought. Leave it to Jake to not take the easy way and text.

After eating a light breakfast and finishing her coffee, Nia headed into the lab. Early on a Sunday morning, no one was in to greet or distract her when she arrived, and she got straight to work, sweeping up the glass, plastic, sand, and gravel. By the time the floors and counters were clean, a couple of the research assistants and her associate director had stopped by. Each of them had come in to check on their own projects, but once they'd heard what had happened, they had all offered their help. The intermittent interruptions had been a welcome break —especially once she'd started sorting through the hundreds of papers that had been tossed from her files and scattered around the room, like some kind of bizarre ticker-tape parade.

By three in the afternoon, exhaustion had kicked in, and as she slid the last sheet of paper into a hanging file, she contemplated texting Jake to tell him she'd meet them another time. As she considered her options, her fingers drummed on the metal cabinet—the cabinet that once again held everything it should since, oddly, nothing had been missing. It was too early to go home—if she did, she'd end up grabbing a quick meal and a glass of wine, and would no doubt fall asleep much too early to have a good night's sleep. She didn't relish the idea of being questioned by her FBI friends—because she knew that was the primary reason Jake wanted her to stop by—but it beat sitting around the house. Especially if she could get Isiah to make her some chicken wings. No one made wings like Isiah Clarke.

Decision made, she locked up her lab then made her way to her car, planning a quick stop at the liquor store before heading out to The Shack. It seemed weird to bring alcohol to a bar, but both Isiah and Alexis enjoyed a good whiskey, and if Isiah was going to host her after hours, then he deserved a host-gift.

Forty minutes later, she walked into the bar, bottle in hand. The Shack sat up on a hill, and the outdoor veranda had, in her opinion, some of the best views on the island. It was also far enough from the hustle and bustle of Havensted that very few tourists made their way to the watering hole. Not that that was a problem on a Sunday afternoon when the bar was closed, but during the week, it made for a nice change of pace when she wanted a beautiful place to relax and enjoy a drink and good food without the crowds.

"Just in time, Nia," Isiah said as she joined him at the bar.

"In time for what, is the question," she replied, handing the bottle over.

Isiah glanced at the label. "You didn't have to bring that, but I'm certainly not going to turn down a bottle of Oban," he said, as he placed the bottle on a low shelf. "As to your question, just in time for the food. They're all outside with a big plate of wings, and I was about to bring out some mini-rotis—pork and potato, today. Go ahead and join everyone, and I'll bring you a drink when I bring the rest of the food. You should make them wait until you've had at least one before they start the inquisition."

Nia smiled. Isiah was a retired Navy SEAL who'd taken to bar-ownership like a fish to water and was one of the most chill people she'd ever met. "Make it a double and I should be good," she said, pointing to a local rum.

"On the rocks?"

"Of course," she said.

"You got it."

When Isiah disappeared into the kitchen, Nia joined the group on the wide verandah. With tall ceilings, fans, and screens to keep the bugs out, it wasn't hard to figure out why the large, circular table that sat on one end of the space was a favorite.

She'd just finished greeting everyone and assuring them she was fine when Isiah returned with the food and her drink. Grabbing an open seat between Jake and Dominic, she gave Isiah a heartfelt "thank you" as she relieved him of the glass then raised it to her lips. There was nothing quite like the way a cold rum turned to liquid heat as it traveled down her throat.

The food provided a distraction—at least for a few minutes —as everyone passed around small plates and started to pile wings and rotis on them. She'd been looking forward to eating, but as she watched her friends descend on the food, the reason for her being there crept back into her mind and she found she didn't have much of an appetite. During the day, she'd been able to push aside *really* thinking about how violated she felt—it was easy to focus on cleaning and re-ordering her lab and answering questions from her colleagues. But here, with Jake and all the others, she had no illusions about what was coming, and she almost wondered if reliving it would be worse than living it.

"Eat," Jake said, setting a plate in front of her that held a couple of wings and a small roti. "If for no other reason than to absorb that rum you're drinking since I doubt you've eaten much else today."

She started to protest, but then realized he was right. She'd had a bag of chips and some trail mix from the vending machine in the kitchen at The Center, but nothing more than that since her breakfast.

"Eating isn't normally a problem for me," she muttered,

picking up the roti. "But you're right, I do need some sustenance."

"There's nothing normal about what happened last night," Jake said. The matter-of-fact tone of his voice reassured her that he wasn't coddling her, just stating a fact. Which was good because she didn't want to be coddled. At least she didn't think she did. She'd never really *been* coddled, so maybe she did want it?

"Whatever you're thinking right now, turn it off," Alexis said. Nia blinked and looked at the agent. "Whatever it was," Alexis continued, "we can talk about it if you want to, but first, you need to eat."

Nia glanced down and she still held the roti in her hand. She hadn't taken a single bite. "Right," she said, then bit into it. The flavor of spiced potatoes and pork exploded in her mouth, and suddenly, she was ravenous.

Fifteen minutes later, the table looked like a swarm of locusts had descended, done their best, then moved on. Nearly empty plates were scattered across the surface holding various pieces of evidence of the feast they'd devoured—a remnant of wings here, a few fallen potatoes there. Yes, the food had just been finger food, but it had been plentiful and, of course, delicious.

Nia sat back and took a sip of her drink. Lowering her hand, she let the bottom of the glass rest on the arm of the chair. "Okay," she said. "Lay it on me. I don't know how much more I can tell you than what I told the police last night—which I'm sure Dominic and Jake have relayed to you all—but ask away."

Damian, who sat on the far side of the table with his fiancée, Charlotte, glanced at Beni. Of course, the first question would come from one of those two. In truth, the five members of the task force were all peers and they had a director to whom they all reported. But between them—Damian, Beni, Dominic, Jake, and Alexis—Beni and Damian seemed to take up the role of team leader more often than not.

"Why don't you tell us what you saw?" Beni said, leaning back in her own chair and taking a sip of her beer.

As succinctly and as quickly as possible, Nia recounted everything she'd heard and seen during the short time she'd been in the building with the perpetrator. When she was done, Damian asked if anything had been taken at the same time that Alexis asked if she'd been to the police yet to look through the mug shot books. She answered Alexis's question in the negative, saying that they'd asked her to come by when the main office opened on Monday, then turned to Damian.

"Just the two parrotfish," she said.

"Parrotfish?" Isiah asked.

"Yes, parrotfish," Jake said. "But there was something hinky about them wasn't there, Doc? Something you didn't tell the police?"

She glanced at Jake, not all that surprised that he'd noticed her omission the night before. She wasn't sure why she hadn't mentioned anything to the police. She didn't have anything to hide, but absconding with two parrotfish had seemed so absurd that she didn't think it could be anything more than a joke.

Jake gave her a small nod of encouragement, and she turned back to the table. She didn't think the theft was meaningful, but she took a few minutes to tell them the origin of the fish and why she'd had them in her office in the first place.

"You said you brought in four, but you only had two in your lab. Where are the other two?" Jake asked.

"In one of the shared research labs," Nia answered. "I took two for testing and we wanted the other two for observation. And yes, before you ask, they are both still there and acting completely normal. We were going to release them today, but I decided to hold them and we'll run some blood tests on them tomorrow. I can compare it to the samples I took from the fish in my lab. As long as neither sample shows something that might have a broader detrimental effect on the eco-system, then I'm not that concerned. As I said last night, I have no idea why that man would have taken the two from my lab."

"If it's not something like a bacteria or virus—something that would have a broader impact—what might make the fish behave the way they did?" Alexis asked.

Nia thought for a moment before answering. "It would be uncommon, but the most likely culprit would be something they ate. Honestly, though, it was almost like they were on drugs or something. Their bodies were functioning, but their brains seemed to be shut off. A bacteria, and maybe even a virus, could do that. But if it's not either of those, I'd have to do more research."

Sitting beside Alexis, Isiah stirred. His gaze traveled around the group then landed on Alexis.

"What are you thinking?" Alexis asked softly.

Isiah hesitated, then answered. "She's using almost the exact same words you used to describe Angela Rosen," he said. "The body is functioning, but the mind is somewhere else entirely."

Nia's attention shot to Alexis. Nia knew about Angela Rosen —a CIA agent who'd been shot while she and Alexis had tried to escape a kidnapper—but only because Nia had been on the Navy research boat where Rosen had been brought for emergency care immediately after the shooting. As the case was mostly classified, that was the extent of her knowledge, and until now, she'd had no idea that something other than a bullet wound had been wrong with Rosen.

"Would drugs cause the same reaction in fish as in humans?" Beni asked.

Nia nodded. "Some drugs, yes. The dosage would need to be different to account for size, of course, but it's possible."

"Who else could have known that you had these oddly behaving fish in your lab?" Damian asked.

Nia started to answer that no one other than she, and the researchers with her that day, knew, but then she paused. Because that wasn't entirely true. "A couple of us went to The Taphouse after we finished for the day. We were talking about the fish and how crazy they were behaving. We were laughing about it because we'd never seen anything like it before. Of course, we all knew it could potentially be bad news—like I said, we were, *we are*, most concerned about a bacteria or a virus— but we were all still laughing about it. You know what that place is like," she said, turning to Jake. The Taphouse wasn't a place any of the others would likely go—Damian and Alexis tended to stick closer to home with their partners, while Beni preferred the nightlife in Havensted and Dominic preferred places less, well, gritty. And The Taphouse was nothing if not gritty.

"It's possible any number of people could have overheard you," Jake said, finishing her thought. Nia nodded.

"But who, and what are the odds that it would be someone who would know something about why the fish were acting the way they were?" Beni asked.

Nia shrugged, but it was Jake who answered. "If those fish got into something they shouldn't have—"

"Like maybe finding a stash of drugs somewhere," Dominic interjected.

Jake nodded. "It wouldn't surprise me in the least to find out that someone in The Taphouse would know something about it."

"I've heard of drugs being left at ocean drop spots—tied to buoys or weighted down and dropped near a reef—for dealers to pick up a later, but I haven't heard of it happening *here*," Alexis said.

"It's only a matter of time before a good idea spreads," Dominic interjected with a wry grin.

"When were you at The Taphouse?" Jake asked, pinning her with his dark blue eyes.

Nia lifted a shoulder. "After the dive and closing up The Center. Maybe eight o'clock."

"So chances are that if it was a drug drop gone wrong, whatever is left of the drugs has probably been picked up already since it's been, what, nearly forty-eight hours since you collected the fish?" Beni asked, clearly pondering whether a search of the area was warranted.

"That's certainly enough time to go collect something if there was anything there to collect," Nia said.

"I hear doubt in your voice," Jake said, sliding his unfinished drink over. She glanced at her glass to find it empty. She hadn't remembered finishing it, but she set the tumbler down on the table and shook her head at Jake's offer. A double rum wasn't enough to get her tipsy, but she had to drive home and any more alcohol might do the trick.

"It just sounds far-fetched," she said. "Not the drugs being dropped in the ocean for later pick-up. That actually sounds reasonable, maybe even brilliant. But the fact that maybe some of those drugs leaked and somehow some fish ingested them, and then we happened to come along and see them acting high as kites. And then, not just all that, but that someone who might be involved in the initial drug drop—or perhaps pick-up—overheard us talking about it in a bar? It's possible, I suppose. The scientist in me has to admit that it's a possibility. But the statistician in me also has to acknowledge that the odds aren't good for that chain of events."

Jake shot her a look that made her feel like she'd taken away his favorite toy. He liked adventure, and nothing piqued his interest quite like a good dose of intrigue. But what he was thinking might have happened had a less than 5% chance of being possible, and she wasn't going to pretend otherwise.

"Did you find anything in the blood samples that you took from the fish that went missing?" Jake asked.

Nia's gaze bounced around the table before landing on Jake.

She felt a little chagrinned at the answer she had to offer, but she didn't shy away. "I didn't even look."

Jake wasn't the only FBI agent at the table to frown at her, and yes, now that she'd mentioned it, it did seem odd that the results of the blood samples—the only evidence she still had in her possession of the two missing fish—hadn't been the first thing she'd looked at that morning. But she was a scientist, not law enforcement, and although she wanted to understand why her lab had been targeted, her primary goal for the day had been to get it back up and running before The Center opened to the public on Monday and she got pulled into other tasks.

"I'll look first thing in the morning," she said, avoiding everyone's gaze. She didn't have anything to feel guilty about, and yet somehow, she felt…inadequate. As if she'd failed them.

"Look, it's late and I didn't get much sleep last night," she said, rising from her seat. Everyone but Charlotte and Beni rose as well, startling her with the sudden movement and the cacophony of chair legs scraping against the floor.

As sure as she knew her own name, she knew they were planning something. Something—whatever it was—that she wasn't ready to participate in because it would likely involve her being asked a gazillion more questions, or would require that she consider things—like the man she'd only caught a glimpse of—more than she wanted to.

"I'll give you a call if I find anything tomorrow in the tests," Nia said, stepping away from the table. "Isiah, as always, the food was amazing. Thank you."

He nodded to her and, beside him, Alexis started to speak, but Isiah slid his hand into hers and squeezed. Alexis hesitated, then slipped from Isiah's hold and gave Nia a hug. "Take care of yourself tonight and get a good night's sleep. Call if you need anything," she said.

Nia assured Alexis she would, and as she spoke, Charlotte stood as well and rounded the table. "I have the day off tomorrow. Call me if you want to grab lunch," she said, as she wrapped her arms around Nia and gave her a hug, too. That seemed to shift the focus of the moment and it was another ten minutes and five more hugs before she made it to her car.

As she navigated her way back to the west side of the island, she pondered the strange truth that she was more at home with those five FBI agents and their significant others than with her own family.

CHAPTER FOUR

"I SHOULD HAVE ASKED her where they picked up those fish," Jake said to Beni as he leaned back in his chair. The two of them, and Dominic, were occupying their desks at the FBI office on the north side of Havensted on Monday morning while Damian and Alexis were conducting a security training at Hemmeleigh Resort where The Summit of World Leaders would be held in seven months.

"You're bored and it's been a while since you've been out on the water, so you're looking for an excuse to go diving," Dominic said. "You know you don't do well when you don't get out on the water, so why don't you go? It's slow here today. Take your gear and head out. If you want to feel productive, go diving around Hemmeleigh and see what kind of underwater threats we need to consider for The Summit."

Everything Dominic said was true, but Jake's recent lack of dive time was not the root of his agitation. No, an early morning call from his father—a man Jake would like nothing more than to be estranged from—took those honors. Well, that and still worrying about Nia. Something had happened in that beautiful, complex brain of hers just before she'd left The Shack and despite going over that part of the conversation at least a dozen times in his head, he couldn't, for the life of him, figure out what had put that pensive look on her face.

He switched his attention to Beni. He wasn't sure what he was looking for from her, but maybe something other than "go for a dive," because as much as he wouldn't mind being in the water, he was definitely not in the right headspace for it at the moment.

"I'll give you ten seconds to remember that you shouldn't even bother looking to me for sympathy," Beni said without looking up from the file she was going through.

Her response was curt, but it did the job and made him laugh, pulling him away from his own thoughts. It was so *Beni.* "Beni" and "sympathy" didn't go in the same sentence.

"I'm being whiny, aren't I?" he said.

"No more than usual," Beni answered.

He glanced at Dominic, who shrugged. "I'd say 'annoying' more than 'whiny,' but 'whiny' works, too."

Jake let out a long exhale and craned his head to get a glimpse of the peek-a-boo view of the ocean they had from their office. Fuck, maybe he did need to get out on the water—maybe not for a dive, but maybe a swim? He'd practically grown up in the ocean and it was definitely in his blood. There was nothing, absolutely nothing, like straddling a surfboard and catching the first glimpse of a beautiful wave—the possibilities were endless and the world was wide open.

Of course, he couldn't surf. Not anymore. Even if the Caribbean had the right waves, the knee injury that had taken him off the pro-tour more than ten years ago had also, more or less, forced him off a board altogether.

A familiar darkness started to cut into his psyche as memories of Hawaii, and the career that had ended so abruptly, began pushing their way into his mind. If he let them take hold, what would happen next wasn't a place he wanted to go—not mentally, not physically.

"I gotta go," he said, rising from his seat, his chair scraping against the wood floor. Both Beni and Dominic looked up, but he ignored them. "I have my cell. Call if anything comes up." And with that, he left. He'd catch hell from Dominic later, although Beni would probably let it slide—she was as badass as badasses came, but was also selective about which battles she picked and those she walked away from, and anything having to do with *feelings*, which he was clearly having at this moment, tended to fall into the camp of things she let slide.

He made his way down to his jeep parked in the building's garage and he was pulling out of his spot when a call came in. He considered ignoring it and heading toward the warehouse he rented on the northwest side of Havensted, but he'd told Dom and Beni to call if anything came up. It would be pretty shitty of him not to answer if it was one of them. Besides, he'd only left because he'd needed a distraction—whether it was the warehouse or work, either would do.

But when his cell phone connected to his Bluetooth, his heart stuttered. Pulling to a stop in the middle of an aisle, he hit the answer button.

"What's going on, sugar," he said, keeping his voice casual.

"I don't know, Jake," Nia said, the fact that she hadn't responded to his use of the nickname she—only sometimes—hated, told him how serious her call was.

"Talk to me," he said, putting the car back into gear and exiting the garage in the direction of The Center.

"I ran the tests on the two fish we still have and compared those results to the results I had on the two that were stolen..."

"And?" he prompted.

"They all ingested some drug—the same drug. It was mostly out of the systems of the two fish we still have, but the markers are all the same. But the thing is," she hesitated, and he could all but see her, standing in her lab, staring at the two sets of results.

"The thing is?" he pressed.

"It's like nothing I've ever seen before, Jake," she said, her voice clear and strong. "It's a synthetic drug, for sure. But it's not presenting as any drug we know."

* * *

*J*ake stood behind Nia, looking over her shoulder at the two test results. He could see what she'd been referring to in terms of the similar markers on each of the four fish—and two were definitely higher in concentration than the other two.

"Walk me through what these are," he said, pointing to the little spikes in the graph.

"That's a barbiturate," she said, pointing to one. "But that's a benzodiazepine," she said, pointing to another. "Benzodiazepines largely replaced barbiturates, except in a few cases, so it's unusual to see them in the same sample. But where it gets weirder is here," she said, pointing to two other spikes. "The first is a version of amphetamine, though it's not pure. The second is scopolamine, also knowns as Devil's Breath and the only naturally occurring drug in the sample."

"What would this kind of drug cocktail do?" he asked, mostly to himself, as he stared at the sheets. He wasn't a chemist or even a scientist of any sort, and so the pages wouldn't reveal any more to him than Nia had shared, but still, he studied the peaks and valleys and numbers and chemical markers.

"In a person, I don't know," Nia said. "But I told you how the fish were acting...like their bodies were fully functional but their minds were blank."

Jake considered the implications of that and it didn't give him the warm fuzzies. He thought back to what Isiah had reminded them all of the night before—that Alexis had described the deceased CIA agent Angela Rosen in much the same way—and it didn't take a genius to figure out that someone, somewhere in the Caribbean, appeared to be experimenting with designing drugs.

If it didn't impact Tildas Island and the upcoming Summit, it technically wasn't in the jurisdiction of the task force to look into. But even if the drugs weren't circulating on the island, the drug trade wasn't comprised of upstanding, law-abiding citizens and it *was* the team's job to make sure *those* people didn't pose a threat to the security of the upcoming event.

"Can you show me where you found the fish? Or tell me, if you can't get away right now?" he asked.

Nia set the pages down and turned around to face him. "You want to go look *now?*"

He nodded. Her hazel eyes studied him. True, he might be looking for an excuse to get out on the water, but he also truly did want to see if there was any evidence of a drop point. He didn't expect to find any drugs or a smoking gun or anything like that. But if he could find some evidence as to *how* the drugs were dropped and how the spots were marked, that would be more information than they had before.

"Jake, what's going on?" Nia asked.

He shifted and let his gaze drift to the papers until Nia placed her hands on his cheeks and forced his attention back to her. "Something is bugging you and it's not just that," she said, jerking her head toward the results. "Talk to me. I'll take you to where we found the fish, but I need to know what's going on in that mind of yours before we go, if for no other reason than for our safety when we get in the water."

He tried to pull away at the suggestion that he would *ever* put them in danger, but she didn't let him. In fact, she slid her hands higher and pinched his earlobes between her fingers. "Don't even think of blowing this off," she said.

"That hurts, Doc. I didn't know you were into pain," he tried to joke.

Nia's eyes narrowed. "You have no idea what I'm into, sugar," she shot back. "But I can tell you what I'm *not* into and that's two things. The first is a friend who dodges a simple question, and the second is a dive buddy with something else on his mind. Talk to me, or we don't go."

He considered pulling the FBI card and making it a formal request. He really considered it. But then his eyes locked on hers. Nia was a tall woman and in the heels she wore, the top of her head came up to his eye level. She was inches away from him, her face slightly turned up, refusing to let him back away.

Over the months he'd known her, he'd seen the scientist-Nia, the friend-Nia, and the fun-loving-partying-Nia, but he'd never seen *this* Nia. This Nia that wasn't letting him back away from taking a step toward something more—not *more* in a romantic sense, but *more* in the friendship sense.

Jake was a man who lived his life on the surface, letting the wind—or whim—take him wherever he felt like going at the moment. But as her eyes stayed locked on his, refusing to give him any quarter, a physical change started to pulse and course through him. There were reasons he'd chosen to live his life the way he had, but with her steady hands on his face and her unrelenting presence, he started to feel grounded. And like parts of a complicated lock clicking into place, Nia suddenly made him feel safe.

Slowly, the anxiety that had been building in his system since earlier that morning ebbed away, leaving behind something calmer and clearer.

"We can talk about it in the car," he said, all teasing gone from his voice.

Again, her eyes searched his. "Promise?"

He nodded and slowly, she released her hold on his ears and

slid her hands from his face. She didn't pull them away altogether, though, and her palms landed on his chest.

When her gaze drifted to somewhere behind him and her finger started tapping a disjointed beat against his shirt, he knew she was making plans—determining which boat to take, what equipment was needed, the tides, the dive times, and all those things an experienced diver, and responsible head of the Marine Center, would take into consideration. Nia might be the life of the party when they hit the bars, but she didn't become the head of the largest research center in the Caribbean because she could dance the night away. She was damn good at her job and it was a thing of beauty to watch her do it.

Finally, she stepped away. "We'll take the smaller boat. The water is smooth today so it should handle fine and it's easier with just the two of us."

He felt the loss of the connection as she turned toward her computer. "Before you shut your computer down, can you send those results to Beni?" he asked, managing to remember at least some of his professional duties in the midst of what felt a little like a crisis of identity.

She said nothing, but the clack of the keys told him she was doing as asked. A few minutes later, she powered down, unplugged the device, and slid it into a bag. "The boat is gassed and ready to go. My equipment is in our equipment room, along with fresh tanks. Do you want to grab your own or see if we have something that works for you? We keep extras for when other researchers and scientists visit."

He reached for her bag and slung it over his shoulder. "If you have something that you think will work for me, let's go with that since mine is at home and it will add an hour to the day if we have to head over and get it before we leave."

Nia crossed her arms and let her gaze drift over him. It wasn't a sexual perusal, not in the least. Yet, something about it made him wonder what it would be like if it were.

Startled at the thought, he stepped back, putting another few feet between them. His head was definitely messing with him today. He might be able to handle the foray into a deeper friendship, but anything more than that? Uh huh, no way. A deeper friendship was one thing; sex was another. In a perfect world—in the world of Alexis and Isiah, and Charlotte and Damian—the two co-existed. But they didn't in his. Not because he didn't believe that friendship and sex could go together, but because together, that would be *way* more emotion than he could handle. Was he a coward about that? Yes, without question. But he needed his carefully curated life in order to keep from falling down the emotional and mental rabbit hole that he often teetered on the edge of.

"Yes, we'll have something that works for you," Nia said, oblivious to the emotional danger he'd just sidestepped.

"Great, let's go," he said, turning toward the exit.

Nia came up beside him and slipped an arm through his. It didn't mean anything—she'd done it a million times since they'd first started hanging out. But the part of his brain that had just put the words "Nia" and "sex" in the same sentence wondered if it *could* mean anything. And if it *could*, did he want it to? Did Nia?

She bumped her hip against his as they walked—a particular talent of hers—and he turned his head toward her. She was smiling up at him. It was a nice smile, a friendly one. Not one that made him think she'd been thinking the same things he had.

Especially not when the smile shifted into a grin.

"And just because it's only a short drive to the equipment warehouse and dock, don't think you're going to get away with not telling me what's bothering you," she said.

Nope, she was most definitely *not* thinking the same things he was.

* * *

*W*hat had possessed her to grab Jake's face and force him to talk to her, Nia hadn't a clue. Well, scratch that, she did. The errant thought she'd had the night before about him and the team being more like family to her than her actual family hadn't turned out to be so errant. No, it had festered—no, not festered, that made it sound like a disease—but it had fermented overnight and turned into something completely different than the original toss-away thought.

And then Jake had walked into her lab, strung tighter than a bowline in a storm, and suddenly, *he* mattered. Not just as a going-out buddy or someone she had a ton of fun with—which she did—but as someone who *meant something* to her. Of course he always had, but something had shifted inside her when his eyes had met hers. When his eyes had met hers, and she'd seen a flash of pain there. It hadn't lingered and she hadn't a clue what had put it there, but it was clear that Jake was in pain—not physically, but mentally—and she was no more willing to walk away from it than she would be if he'd broken his arm. He meant too much to her.

"So talk to me," she said, leading Jake to the path that ran from The Center to the marina rather than to her car. It took the same amount of time to walk as to drive and so she'd made the executive decision not to coop Jake up in her car for the ten minutes it would take them to get to the dock.

"I was worried about you," Jake said. "You can't think that breaking into The Center was just about the two fish. Nobody is that weird. I've just been waiting for the other shoe to drop and it was making me antsy. Now the other shoe has dropped."

"That's sweet, and I appreciate the concern, but maybe you can do me the favor of not treating me like an idiot and tell me what's really bothering you," she said.

Jake stopped in the middle of the path. She didn't bother to stop and wait for him. She was the master of evasive answers when it came to things that were, well, uncomfortable, and she'd known a half-truth would come out of his mouth the moment he'd inhaled before speaking his first word.

"That was what was going on," he insisted when he caught up with her.

"I'm sure it was," she said as they paused at an intersection and let a safari taxi pass by. "But it wasn't the only thing. Talk to me about that other thing."

They crossed the street and started down the winding walkway toward the water. The smell of the ocean whispered around them, mingling with the scents of the lush foliage that lined the path. Jake was quiet for a long time, but he'd eventually answer—if for no other reason than to ensure he'd be able to join her on the boat for the dive. Of all the members of the task force, Jake would most appreciate how uncompromising she'd be about their safety.

Finally, when the top of the warehouse came into sight, Jake slowed his steps and stopped. This time she stopped with him.

"I got a call from my father this morning," he said. "That's not a way I like to start my day."

Nia searched her memory for anything Jake might have mentioned about his family but quickly realized that, like her, he hadn't ever mentioned a thing. She stared at him, waiting for him to elaborate.

"My family," he hesitated. "We're not close. Not like normal families. Or maybe not like families *should* be." He looked down at her as if expecting her to acknowledge that she understood what he was talking about.

"My family lives here on the island," she said. "Has for generations. There are a lot of us. But I don't see them very often. Or talk to them much. And when I do, I usually end up regretting it. They aren't bad people, but they are bad family. At least to me."

Jake's eyes searched hers. Her heart rate kicked up and a flush that had nothing to do with the temperatures warmed her cheeks. Suddenly, she understood what a difficult task she'd laid at Jake's feet. If his family was anywhere near as messed up as hers, maybe she would have been better off letting that sleeping dog lie.

But then again, she hadn't really had a choice. Not if she wanted to be sure his head was in the game when they both went into the water.

Jake gave a rueful chuckle and started walking again. "Well, my family is bad family *and* bad people. They are sketchy as shit, and it's a fairly regular occurrence for them to call me and ask me to do some favors for them. In fact, that's the only reason they ever call me."

Wow, she wasn't entirely sure what that meant, but she had a pretty good idea what kind of favors someone sketchy could ask of a well-respected and well-positioned FBI agent. "How big is your family?"

"My mom died when I was young," he said as they rounded the bend and the bay came into view. "My dad owns a few luxury resorts on a couple of different Hawaiian islands, and my older brother helps run them. My younger brother has decided to not even bother with using the family businesses as a smoke-screen for their criminal activity and has gone straight for a leadership position in a particularly nasty group that he refers to as businessmen but that I, and my fellow FBI colleagues, and any reasonable person, would refer to as the mafia."

She couldn't help it, it was grossly inappropriate, but she laughed. Jake pulled her to a halt at the side of the parking lot and glared down at her. Which, of course, made her laugh even more.

He crossed his arms and watched. Finally, she pulled herself together and reached for his arms, wrapping her hands around his bare skin.

"I'm sorry," she said. "I'm really sorry about your mom, Jake. That must have been so difficult. But, I just...well, I know this isn't the point, but honestly, how the hell did you get into the FBI?" she asked lightly, fighting another smile. "I mean, what kind of screening did you have to go through? Did you have to turn in a contact to prove your loyalty? Or maybe set someone up? Not that I'm not glad you are an agent and not that I doubt your loyalty in the least, but seriously, how did that happen?"

She kept hold of his arms, his skin warm under her fingers. His muscles twitched then finally, after what seemed like minutes, but was probably only ten seconds, a hint of a grin teased Jake's lips. Seconds later, it was a full-blown smile.

"It was an interesting process," he conceded with a chuckle. "And no, I didn't have to turn anyone in my family in or set them up. Other than that, I can't tell you what more was involved."

"Or you'll have to kill me?" she teased as she let her hands slide away and they resumed their walk across the parking lot.

"Something like that," Jake answered.

They walked in silence until they reached the equipment warehouse door. She spoke as she plugged in the code, "I probably shouldn't have laughed, Jake. It can't be easy for you. But you're one of the best people I know and it's fucked up that that's the kind of family you come from. Although now that I know, I'm even more impressed with you and the way you've chosen to live your life. What did your dad want from you this morning?"

He looked away from her and toward the bay as he answered. "I like that you laughed, sugar. It reminded me of the good things in my life—like friends who can make fun of me and my fucked up family and not hold them against me. I can get...distracted by my family, and sometimes, if I think about them too much, things start to feel, well, dark, and I start to wonder if I'll ever be free of them. Your laughter made that darkness go away."

She reached out and took his hand in both of hers though she remained silent, knowing he had more to say.

His fingers curled around hers as he spoke. "This morning, he asked if I knew anything about Samuel Haines, a young, recently elected state legislator."

Her family was messed up, but she was suddenly glad they had next to no contact. How her family spoke to her was nothing compared to how Jake's seemed to treat him.

"I'm sorry," she said.

His gaze flickered down to her and one side of lips tipped up in a wry grin. "Yeah, me too." He paused, then reached up with his free hand and brushed a curl that had blown into her face behind her ear. "I'm good now," he said. "Really, I am."

She studied his face and knew he was speaking the truth. She wasn't much into new age stuff, but the coiled energy he'd carried into her lab less than an hour ago was gone, and in its place was the steady, focused Jake she knew well. He wasn't quite as lighthearted as she was used to, but she believed him when he'd said he was good. He'd be better, eventually. But for now, he was good.

She smiled up at him. "Then let's go see if we can find any more stoned fish."

CHAPTER FIVE

"So, where are we going exactly?" Jake asked as they motored out of the bay and headed west. It hadn't taken long to gather gear and tanks—they'd even found a spare pair of clean board shorts for him to change into—and now that he was relaxing in the passenger chair beside Nia, he realized she still hadn't told him where they were headed.

"A small bay on the north side of Lovango Island," she said, raising her voice over the sound of the wind and the engines.

It would take a little over an hour to get to Lovango—a small island to the northeast of St. Thomas. It was privately owned now, but back in the colonial times, it housed nothing but brothels—brothels the sailors would visit before ending their journeys a mile further to the west in the commercial harbor of Charlotte Amalie on St. Thomas. The name—a riff on "love and go"—always made his inner thirteen-year-old grin.

Nia glanced over and rolled her eyes at him. "Seriously. You and Dominic. All I have to do to make you laugh is mention Lovango Island."

And laugh he did, because, well…they might have just stumbled upon a potentially terrifying new drug, but for now, it was a beautiful day, he was on a boat, and he was about to go diving with Nia. Sometimes it was pretty damn easy to look at the silver lining.

He sat back, turned his face to the sun, and left Nia to pilot the vessel. Once they rounded the west side of Tildas Island, it was more or less a straight shot north to Lovango, and it wouldn't be until they hit the waters around St. Thomas that they'd have to slow for the shoals and reefs. Until then, he'd keep an eye out for flying fish and dolphins and just enjoy the ride.

When they entered the channel between St. Thomas and St. John, Nia throttled back to a less breakneck speed. As she steered them toward Lovango, he rose and started checking the equipment. By the time they reached a small bay on the north side of the private island, he had their vests hooked up to tanks and the tanks hooked up to the dive computers they'd each carry.

"We'll tie up there," Nia said, pointing to the only floating buoy. Years ago, in order to stop people from dropping anchor and destroying coral, the government had set up several free mooring balls pretty much everywhere a boater would want to tie up. As an island-boy, Jake appreciated the concern for the natural habitat, but it did still sometimes surprise him to find them off private islands.

Using the long pole-hook, he snagged the loop at the top of the buoy, pulled it up, and tied the boat to it before dropping it back in the water. When he turned around, Nia was stripping out of her shorts, revealing the sleek one-piece bathing suit she'd changed into. He'd seen her in tank tops and, hell, he'd even seen her in more revealing suits. But there was something about the way her lithe body moved with comfort and confidence as she prepared to dive. A strange sense that he could watch her for days move around the way she was washed over him.

"Here," she said, tossing him a rash guard shirt and, thankfully, breaking his train of thought. While there'd been a time or two when they'd first started spending time together that he thought he'd recognized something more than friendship between them, he'd ruthlessly pushed that awareness into the dark recesses of his brain—she hadn't seemed to return the interest and, more to the point, he hadn't wanted to jeopardize their friendship. So why brief little hints of attraction teased at him now, he couldn't say. Nor could he say what he thought about them.

He yanked off his cotton t-shirt and raised his face to the sun, taking a moment to absorb the feel of its rays on his bare skin before pulling on the thin shirt he'd wear under his dive vest. Some people hated the heat, but he had never been one of them. Sure, there were days it was uncomfortable. But there was nothing like the first kiss of sun on your skin. Especially if it was followed by a chance to be in the ocean.

He opened his eyes to find Nia staring at him, her gaze roaming over his body, unaware that he watched. Her attention trailed up his chest then to his face. For a microsecond, when her eyes met his, he could have sworn he saw a question in them. The same question he'd asked himself at her lab—what if there *was* more between them? But then she blinked and gave him a wry smile.

"What? Do I have a glob of zinc on my nose or something?" he asked, pulling the long-sleeved rash guard over his head and glossing over that split second of awareness.

Nia chuckled and shook her head as she donned her own shirt. "You know you don't. I'm glad I know you well enough to be well acquainted with your flaws and quirks—*and* annoying habits—otherwise, you might render me speechless. You are a fine specimen of a man, Jake McMullen," she said, waving at his body.

"You like this, do you?" he said, dramatically gesturing to his chest, as he flashed her a Cheshire Cat grin. "It is a fine specimen, I agree. You know the worst part? I don't even really work at it."

Nia shook her head and laughed as she tossed him a mask, that brief moment behind them. "Come on, Captain America," she said. "Gear up. We have some fish—or maybe drugs—to find. The day is full of possibilities."

Despite their teasing, neither took safety for granted, and they spent a few minutes checking and rechecking the gear, before lifting their vests onto their shoulders and securing them across their bodies.

"So once we're in, where to?" he asked. They'd stay close, within ten feet of each other, but Jake liked to have an idea of the direction.

"A reef is starting to take hold there," Nia said, pointing to a spot forty feet to the east. "It's naturally occurring, but because it's new, we wanted to set some beds up here to see how our coral does against what's happening on its own. Our bed is there," she said, moving her finger to point a little further to the east another twenty feet or so. "This is an unusual area," she continued as she tightened a strap around her waist. "There is a large rock formation twenty feet down. It more or less follows the curve of the island and it's about ten feet wide. After that, there's a drop off to sixty feet. The coral—both the natural and ours—is growing on the ledge on the eastern end of the rock."

As he made a final adjustment to his vest, Jake perused the waterscape, picturing in his mind's eye Nia's description. When he was ready, he turned to his friend. "Lead the way?"

In response, Nia flashed a brilliant smile then rolled overboard. Thirty seconds later, he was beside her. Then, with one last adjustment of their masks, they sank under the surface.

* * *

*T*here was very little Nia loved more than being underwater. The noise—actual and philosophical—of the world dimmed, and nothing but nature and wonder surrounded her. She'd heard it said that scientists knew more about space than what lay beneath the ocean's surface and if it were true, she was okay with that because it meant fewer people invading her underwater sanctuary.

Twenty feet down, she reached the rock formation and, with a glance back, she assured herself Jake was with her. They'd dived together several times and she wasn't worried about his competence, but if they were diving using the buddy system, they needed to stick to the protocols. He gave her the okay sign, and she started following the ledge of the rock, letting the gentle current rock against her body.

A small school of black and yellow angelfish darted in front of her and a barracuda glided through the water below them. There wasn't a lot of food near the rocks and so not many fish, but as the coral began to grow, more fish would come, and with more fish, more coral would grow.

The new coral came into view—a few small specimens of fused staghorn and finger corals. Continuing past the fledgling beds, she led Jake to the coral nursery The Center had installed a year ago. They weren't there to check on the babies, but Nia couldn't stop herself, and she let her eyes drift over each of the tiny specimens. Some looked to be doing better than others, but overall, she was pleased with their growth.

She turned to ask Jake what he'd like to do next, but as she started to gesture, a yellow-tailed snapper bumped into her. Just like the parrotfish had a few days earlier.

She and Jake both stilled—as much as the water would let them—and after a moment, two more snapper came swimming up the rock drop off toward them. Both paused two feet away. She glanced at Jake. He was watching the two animals who appeared to be watching him. After a beat, he reached out and touched one on the nose. It bounced back an inch but didn't scuttle away.

He shot her a look that, even through his mask, she could read—he was as confused as she'd been when she'd had her first experience.

She glanced around but saw no signs of anything where a drug shipment could be left or tied to for later pick-up. And it would have to be tied to something to keep it from drifting on the currents. She considered whether the nursery—with its piping and wiring—could be used, but quickly dismissed the idea. It was simply too lightweight. If anything heavy had been anchored to it, the entire structure would pull away with even the gentlest of currents.

Jake reached out to get her attention, then gestured down. She supposed it was as good a plan as any. She couldn't see anything around where they were and down the rock wall was where the snapper had come from. She nodded and took the lead.

Slowly, they descended, following the wall. As they got closer to the bottom, the smooth, flat rock gave way to large boulders. Enough light still filtered in from the surface to create shadows in the crevices, but it was much dimmer at sixty-two feet than it had been at twenty.

Letting Jake take the lead, they began to make their way along the boulders, peeking into holes and gaps as they progressed. Jake slowed to get a look inside a particularly big gap and Nia paused to consider the area while he searched.

Taking in the somewhat bleak "landscaping" and solid rocks around them, she supposed it could be a good place to set up a drug drop. There was very little of interest here to recreational divers and it would be easy to anchor something into the heavy rocks. She glanced over her shoulder to check on Jake, and when she saw his legs poking out from behind a boulder, she turned her attention back to her surroundings.

Suddenly, a flash of silver reflected through the water about thirty feet away. The marine biologist in her refused to look away—identifying fish was as natural to her as checking for cars when she crossed the street. Another flash greeted her, then another. She frowned. There weren't a lot of food sources near where they were, so seeing more than a fish or two here and there was unusual. But sure enough, as her eyes adjusted to looking at where she'd seen the flash, she could see shadowy forms of several small fish hovering over the same area.

Which could only mean one thing—there must be a food source.

She got Jake's attention and pointed to where she wanted to go. He nodded and gestured for her to lead the way. She'd never balked at leading a dive, but the unusual gathering of fish was definitely giving her second thoughts. It was possible there was some animal that had died and was providing a feast, but somehow she couldn't bring herself to believe that.

She hesitated. This was one of those times where she could ignore her intuition and forge ahead, or she could acknowledge what she was feeling and ask Jake—as law enforcement—to take the lead. If nothing was there, she'd look foolish. But if there were...

With a metaphorical sigh—because actual sighs were hard when breathing through a regulator—she gestured Jake ahead. She'd rather look foolish than risk unexpectedly coming across something she wasn't prepared for.

His blue eyes searched hers from behind his mask, then he nodded and swam ahead, the movement of his fins causing a current of water to rush over her skin. As soon as he passed, she swung out away from the wall and came up on his left side, letting him stay a few feet ahead of her.

As they approached, the swarm of fish became clearer. What

had been little more than darting shadows coalesced into distinct fish—angelfish, parrotfish, jacks, and snapper. They formed a loose ball spreading about twenty feet across, but all circling the same area.

Jake looked over his shoulder and motioned for her to stay back, clearly having picked up on the strangeness of the sight. Ignoring him, she closed the gap between them to a couple of feet. She might be okay with him taking the lead, but she wasn't okay letting him venture close to the unknown without her.

Obviously not under the influence like the others she and Jake had seen, several of the fish scattered as they approached. As they fled, the rapid movement of so many fins caused the fine sand on the ocean floor to kick up and obscure their view. In response, Jake slowed, signaling her to do the same. Together they hovered in the cloudy water accompanied by only the sounds of their regulators.

Slowly, the sand began to settle. The seconds ticked by and with each passing one, Nia's anxiety ratcheted higher. She was starting to think she needed to give herself a stern talking to about the uselessness of thinking the worst when the worst—or close to it—took shape before her eyes.

ALSO BY TAMSEN SCHULTZ

2) Six

3) Devil

4) Nora

www.ingramcontent.com/pod-product-compliance
Lightning Source LLC
Chambersburg PA
CBHW020933260626
47169CB00006B/1694